A career in the construction industry took Richard V. Frankland abroad to Zambia and Jordan before he returned to England to work with a Japanese trading house in London administering civil and industrial engineering projects. Moving back to near his birthplace along the south coast with his wife and two daughters, he read for a Masters degree in Maritime Studies and now operates a talks business under the title of 'The History Teller'.

His thriller-writing career started after he saw two very sinister-looking characters at Heathrow. *Batsu* is the sequel to *A Cast of Hawks*, which was published in 2010. Apart from writing, his other interests are sailing and watercolour painting.

BATSU

Also by the Author

A Cast of Hawks, *Vanguard Press*, 2010
ISBN: 978 184386 607 7

Richard V. Frankland

BATSU

Vanguard Press

VANGUARD PAPERBACK

A CIP catalogue record for this title is
available from the British Library.

ISBN 978 184386 859 0

*Vanguard Press is an imprint of
Pegasus Elliot MacKenzie Publishers Ltd.*

www.pegasuspublishers.com

First Published in 2012

**Vanguard Press
Sheraton House Castle Park
Cambridge England**

Printed & Bound in Great Britain

Acknowledgements

My grateful thanks to those whose knowledge has done so much to shape this book starts with my wife Sandra. Her careful sanity check of the plot, together with grammar and spelling advice has been invaluable. I must also thank again Lucy Tanner, of HM Coastguard, for her clear explanation of Coastguard/Police liaison. My thanks also go my publishing team who have done so much in accepting the raw manuscript and turning it into a book. I could not complete this page without thanking photographer David Plumb for his patience and skill in obtaining the brilliant cover image for this paperback edition.

To my wife Sandra and daughter Caroline without whom this work would have been the poorer.

Chapter 1

"Get up!" barked the warder, begrudging the order that would start the process of releasing the prisoner he most wanted to crush into obedience.

Yoshi Hamaura awoke with a start and glared at the warder. "Why?"

"You do not question order, you obey, *shitabataraki*," Warder Onishi replied in a low threatening voice, his face inches away from the prisoner's, raising his baton threateningly.

Hamaura sneered back, goading the warder into striking him.

Warder Onishi reluctantly moved back, lowering the baton. Slowly but just fast enough to avoid further conflict, Hamaura got to his feet.

"Step out of your cell," Onishi ordered. "Now!" he shouted, as Hamaura hesitated.

"Where are you taking me?"

"Somewhere, where you will be of no more trouble to me," came the sour reply. "Put your hands behind your back."

Hamaura complied and felt a twinge of fear as the handcuffs were put around his wrists and snapped closed. Warder Onishi's reply had a strong hint of more severe confinement about it. Hamaura was not someone who could accept isolation; he needed the company of others. He was aware that other prisoners, disturbed by the noise, were peering at him from the small windows by their cell doors. "What time is it?" he asked.

"Walk," ordered Onishi, prodding Hamaura in the back with his baton, intentionally ignoring the question.

The Red Brigade terrorist had been a thorn in Warder Onishi's side ever since he had arrived in the prison. During his entire stay he had not once earned any privileges and had shown only disobedience and contempt to the officialdom at the prison, always the nail that stuck up never to be hammered down. Japan prided itself on its rehabilitation programmes for its prison population, based on strict rules and discipline; Warder Onishi had never before been completely thwarted in his task. He was still trying to comprehend the order given to him fifteen minutes ago, requiring him to prepare this hate-filled inhuman specimen in front of him for release.

In the reception area by the holding cells Hamaura was ordered to take a shower and given a battery razor to shave with. He was then issued with his civilian clothes and placed in a cell and given breakfast. At 0400 hours his shoes and trouser belt were returned to him and, in a daze of incomprehension, he was marched, between two prison officers, out of the north entrance of Tokyo's Katsushika Prison main building and down the long drive to the gatehouse, where he was given his personal items - his wristwatch, comb, wallet and twenty thousand yen. He looked at the nice clean banknotes with surprise; he had arrived in prison penniless.

"We were ordered to give such sum. If it ensures that you are out of my sight so much the better," said Onishi.

He was led out to the side gate where he found his cousin and co-conspirator, Teiji Kimura, standing between two prison officers. Neither man spoke, both unable to comprehend fully that they were to be released. Then Warder Onishi stepped from the gatehouse and strode across to them.

"Your freedom has been granted at the request of the American Government, but I am confident that we will meet again as neither of you are capable of living peacefully and obeying the law," Onishi said before nodding to the officer with the gate keys. "Let this low-life back on the streets."

Outside the gate the two men looked at each other, both apparently helpless to act.

"We are free Teiji-kun, free. I never thought this day would come so soon," said Hamaura excitedly.

His cousin stared back at him and looked almost on the point of crying, then appeared to take hold of his emotions. "Yes, but now we owe someone a vast debt," Kimura replied.

"Oh, I am so pleased to see you cousin. How did they treat you in there?"

"Where are we?" asked Kimura, not willing to answer his cousin's question. "I have never been to this part of Tokyo until I was brought here in the prison van."

Hamaura turned back to the gate to ask for assistance in finding a taxi or train station but the guards had already retreated back to the gatehouse.

It was then that a taxi turned into the approach road and drove towards them. Stopping alongside them the driver wound down the window and asked. "*Anata-no Hamaura-san to Kimura-san des-ka?*"

"*Hi, so desu,*" Kimura confirmed, relieved that some friends were aware of their release.

Without another word the driver, using a lever by his driver's seat, opened the rear doors and as soon as they got in, used the lever again, to close the doors and drove off. The route he took snaked through back streets scarcely wide enough for the vehicle, instructed as to the route via the mobile phone he held to his ear. All the time the driver was glancing in his rear-view mirror to see if any vehicle was following, reporting to the person giving him directions.

Hamaura looked at his watch, then checked it against the taxi's dashboard clock, both showed the time as being 4.45 a.m. Ten minutes later the taxi stopped at a crossroads and the driver opened the doors. After paying him, the two men got out, and the taxi drove away. Moments later a white van sped towards them, stopped, and the side door was slid back.

"Get in!" a voice ordered. "Get into this crate and close the lid, quickly!"

As soon as the lid was closed they could feel the van accelerate away at speed and both men were thrown back and into a third person crouched in the crate. Suddenly the darkness was illuminated by the man's torch.

"My name is Iwaki. I am in charge of your release plan."

Hamaura and Kimura identified themselves and bowed a formal greeting as best they could in the cramped space.

“This crate is lined to prevent signal from any tracking device they may have planted on you,” explained Iwaki. “We must make sure they have no way to trace you.”

Adjusting his position he reached into a bag and withdrew a short black plastic wand and flicked a switch on its handle. Instantly a high-pitched bleeping was heard, that caused them all to cover their ears. Iwaki hurriedly adjusted the sensitivity dial until only a faint noise could be heard. It took only a few minutes to find that transmitters had been planted into both of the men’s wristwatches.

“I thought they may have planted them in your arms or legs. They obviously had only short time to prepare,” Iwaki said. “We can get out of this now; leave your wristwatches in this crate.”

Climbing out of the crate whilst the van sped along was not easy, but after a struggle all three were out and the crate lid closed again.

Looking forward, Kimura could see they were driving along one of Tokyo’s elevated expressways. Traffic was light at this time of day and mainly consisted of heavy lorries.

“What is behind us?” asked Iwaki.

“Fish market truck, with trailer I think,” replied the driver.

“Hamaura-san, reach round behind crate and quickly open rear doors, then get out of way,” Iwaki ordered.

Holding onto the side ribcage framing of the van with his left hand, Hamaura reached round the crate and grasping the internal door handle turned it and pushed outwards. The rear doors swung open and, as he pulled his arm out of the way, Iwaki, pushing with his feet, propelled the crate out and into the path of the truck to be smashed to pieces as the lorry’s front bumper struck it.

On seeing the doors open the truck driver sounded the horn and started to change lanes but was too slow to avoid the crate, which, on impact with the vehicle’s nearside front wheel, punctured the tyre, causing the driver to lose control. Instantly the vehicle started a series of wild swerves that ended with the truck and trailer jack-knifing before straightening again in a broadside skid and overturning.

In the van, now stopped whilst the rear doors were closed again, Hamaura laughed and cheered at the sight of the smoking vehicle, which completely blocked the expressway. He was very impressed by the spontaneous and spectacular actions of Iwaki, but unaware of the effort and frantic planning that had secured his safe release.

Only four days earlier Iwaki had been in North Korea when he had heard from his Tokyo housemaid of the strong possibility of the pair's release. The message had been a real surprise and had created a problem as to how to get back in time to make the necessary arrangements to ensure the men's long-term freedom.

His hastily prepared plan to use these revengeful Red Brigade activists to play a part in countering Western cyber espionage was good enough to convince North Korean senior commanders of the importance of his return home. Seen from the Koreans' point of view, they could assist by using some of their agents in Britain, but ensure that the blame for the attack was firmly with the Red Brigade, thus reducing the political backlash that would undoubtedly follow. Already considerable pressure was being placed upon their long-term allies, the Chinese, to bring North Korea into line with Western capitalist demands; they did not want such pressure to increase. Added to this, was the possibility of exposing the traitors who were assisting the British and Americans, and to destroy their lines of communication.

The Sang-O class submarine, diverted from patrol of the southern territorial waters, had taken him on board just off the North Korean coast near Sijungho Lake. Going below he had yet again been appalled by the stench. How grateful he had been that it would be only 60 hours cooped up in the 34-metre tube of heat and noise. How the fifteen crewmembers survived, weeks at a time, in those conditions he could never understand. He had rowed the last mile in an inflatable dinghy, landing on the shores of Japan using the shelter of a rock arch and hidden cove near the village of Suizu. There a loyal member of his group had met him by car and brought him back to Tokyo where he had worked without rest to make the necessary arrangements.

* * *

A week later a gum-chewing prostitute tottered on ridiculously high heels down a sun-baked side street in the Shinjuku area of Tokyo. It was strange for her to be going home in the early evening but today had been unusual. Her Yakuza pimp, a local boss in the Japanese mafia, had ordered her to a third-floor room over a pachinko parlour some two hours ago. There, she and another prostitute were told to take care of two men. The men had surprised Kishi Oda, as they were not the high-ranking Yakuza bosses that she normally serviced. In fact, she was sure they were not Yakuza at all, or come to that, like anyone who Kazuo Yamaguchi would normally tell her to bed with. She laughed to herself as she remembered their haste, as if they had not been with a woman for years, but job done, she had been told to go home.

Cars were parked all down her side of the street and she idly glanced at each one as she strolled along. Then she noticed a man, apparently asleep, in a car further on, his head resting against the door pillar. It was a good quality car and, she thought, a good chance of earning a quick fifty thousand Yen without Yamaguchi taking his cut. Glancing around to check that no police were about, she approached the car, pleased to see that its side windows were wound down. Adjusting the collar of her blouse to ensure a good view of her cleavage, she bent down and, putting on her best smile, looked in at the man, only to recoil in shock at the sight. He had been garrotted and the weapon used, still around his neck, was tied behind the headrest, stopping his head from dropping forward. She went to scream, but no sound came out, nausea welled up inside her and she turned away, only to turn back in surprise at the sound of a police radio from inside the car. Panic-stricken she turned away again, anxious to escape into the alleyway that led, through a maze of small alleys, to the rear of the pachinko parlour she had just left. Twenty tottering steps into the darkened alley she tripped and was sent sprawling over the body of a second man. Scrambling to her feet, her eyes now adjusting to the gloom, she saw that he too had been garrotted. She promptly threw up, her vomit cascading down the alley wall and into the rainwater gulley. Hurriedly she opened her handbag and pulled out some paper tissues. A condom packet, caught up in the wad of tissues, was flicked unnoticed across the alley. Quickly, she wiped her mouth, threw the tissues away, and then shaking uncontrollably, tottered the rest of the way to the pachinko parlour, letting herself in by the back door.

"What is this?" demanded Yamaguchi, as Kishi Oda stumbled blindly into him at the foot of the back staircase.

"Two men dead, one in alley, other in car where street crosses alley, both police I think."

Dead bodies near to one of his parlours were for Yamaguchi bad news, even if they were respectable businessmen with heart attacks. Two dead policemen could spell disaster. Thinking quickly he got six of his *shatei* or 'young brothers' to find the bodies and hide them. In fifteen minutes they had reported back that the bodies had been dealt with, but the car radio message had informed that more police were on their way, and there was much blood on the driver's seat and in the alley.

"Where did you put the bodies?" Yamaguchi asked.

"In hotel waste bin, Boss. We poured washing detergent over them to hide any scent from dogs."

"You have done well. I will remember."

Yamaguchi thought again for a few seconds then said, "Shibata-kun take Kishi-chan to Madam Toda." Yamaguchi used the familiar '*kun*' and '*chan*' for these younger members of his organisation in preference to the more formal 'san'. "When she is cleaned up, take her home. I will call on her later."

"Hi! Hi!" responded a young *shatei* wearing a snakeskin suit, dark glasses and sporting an Elvis Presley hairstyle. He bowed deeply to Yamaguchi and left with Kishi as soon as another of the 'young brothers' had checked along the alley to make sure all was still clear then, within minutes the pachinko parlour was empty, except for the customers at the ground floor slot machines and the clerks.

Later as his black Pontiac limousine swept along the west side of the Imperial Garden Lake, Yamaguchi sat morosely in the back cursing his stupidity. How could he have been such a fool, to accept such high payment to entertain such low-class men? He had been told that they were prison officials, but now it was obvious they were escaped prisoners who were being tailed by the police. What Yamaguchi would learn later was that the men were none other than Yoshi Hamaura and Teiji Kimura, foot soldiers of Red Brigade faction leader, Tadashi Murata.

*　　　*　　　*

Oblivious to Yamaguchi's guilty introspection, Hamaura and Kimura were now sat, eating and laughing with each other, in a first-floor room of a house in Yokohama. Sitting with them was Rikuto Iwaki, their guardian, and assassin of the two policemen. A movement of the sliding screen accessing their small room silenced them instantly and had Iwaki pointing a pistol in the direction of the opening. The not so pretty face of Emiko appeared from the darkness beyond and the three men relaxed. Her name meant grace with beauty, sadly a misnomer, that Iwaki cruelly teased her with in front of others. It was only fear that kept her working as his housekeeper. Following the old traditions, she waited silently for one of the men to speak to her.

Iwaki, obviously well aware of her presence, took some small pleasure in making her wait before finally turning towards her again and grunting, "Yes?"

"Please excuse me, message from a Dr Higashi in America," she said, on her knees, bowing her head to the floor and then proffering with both hands some sheets of paper.

Iwaki replied with a grunt, taking the sheets from her hand. Instantly Emiko left, closing the screen behind her. Iwaki read the message, then read it again, growling as he did so. The others in the room became concerned.

"Higashi say your sister dead, shot by FBI or CIA, he not know which. Young Yamada also killed and an Arab named Madadhah, who you would not know about."

"How?" asked Hamaura. "Who killed Fumiko? Does he know name?"

Iwaki held up his hand as a request to wait until he had read the message again.

"Higashi understands that their yacht was intercepted by navy launch with FBI and CIA agents on board, gunfight took place," he said, still holding his hand up for quiet. "Higashi thinks maybe Englishman, Vaughan, may have survived Atlantic and informed how attack was to be made."

Iwaki had received from Hamaura's sister, full details of the terminal damage to their yacht, and the hijacking of Vaughan's boat to complete the voyage from England to America. In her letter, written from Higashi's clinic two weeks before, she had suggested that Vaughan might have escaped, rather than fallen overboard and drowned. Iwaki explained all this to the two men seated with him.

"American news is full of the defeat of Murata-san's plan. The only success has been your release from prison. They all paid heavy price for your freedom. I can tell you now that Murata-san was captured by British police and is in prison awaiting trial, together with young Yukiko Nagano. They were betrayed by her English boyfriend, at least that is what Ishihara-san, in London, informs."

Iwaki reached forward, picked up his cup of sake and sipped at the warm rice wine. His companions sat looking down shaking their heads dejectedly.

"This is too much bad news you tell to us Iwaki-san," said Hamaura looking up, his jaw twitching with emotion. "I will take retribution on person responsible for the death of my sister."

"Do you not think you have first a debt to repay to Murata-san?" Iwaki asked, with a hint of annoyance in his voice.

"Of course, I spoke without good thought, please ignore my stupidity," replied Hamaura, bowing. "First we must make plan to free Murata-san then *batsu*, we must plan *batsu*," he emphasised the Japanese word for retribution by performing a karate-style chopping motion with his right hand.

"What form will your plan for Murata-san's freedom take?" Iwaki asked impassively. He did not wish to reveal his own plans before he had given Hamaura chance to calm himself, and offer his own thoughts to the problem of rescuing Murata.

"Please allow me a few minutes to consider more clearly."

Iwaki bowed an acknowledgement. When Hamaura's sister, Fumiko, had contacted him, to inform him of the demands that would be made to the Americans concerning her brother and cousin, he had little belief in them being met. However, once the 'Kinoko Kumo' attacks on the American power network had commenced, he had heard, from his contacts inside the prison, that arrangements were being considered in case America requested the release of these two young soldiers of the true Red Brigade. It was now just over a week since he had so secretively returned from North Korea to make the arrangements for them to be met outside the prison. At the time he had tried to get a message to Fumiko to include Murata and Nagano in the release demand but maybe it had failed to arrive, as there had been no response. Whether the power of American diplomacy would have been enough to force the British government to comply he did not know. Now, however, the task would have to be completed in a different way.

The release of Hamaura and Kimura from prison had triggered the cat and mouse game to throw the police off their trail. The tracking devices, planted in both men's wristwatches, had been dealt with but even then the police manhunt was becoming a serious nuisance. Iwaki had then had the idea of diverting the police's attention away from the remnants of Murata's faction and pinning the harbouring of wanted criminals onto the Yakuza or, as the police preferred to call them, *boryokuden*, 'violent ones'. Iwaki knew of Yamaguchi's greed and it had been a simple thing to arrange for the 'happy hour' that had ended with two policemen dead and Yamaguchi suspected of involvement. Originally Iwaki had intended just to make an anonymous phone call to the police, to inform them of the location where the two men had been 'entertained'. He knew that these two men would leave more than enough forensic evidence to confirm their time spent above the pachinko parlour. It would not take the police long to learn who owned the place. Waiting for Hamaura and Kimura across the street from the alley, he had seen the two detectives arrive in their car. Knowing that his two charges would soon be returning along the alley, Iwaki knew that he must act. Had both officers got out of the car, he would have been forced to shoot them but as only one left to investigate along the alley the solution was much better. Guns are noisy, lengths of fine wire aren't.

Approaching the car had been straightforward and the execution was carried out simply and silently. He had then entered the alley to find that the other detective was holding Hamaura and Kimura at gunpoint. The fool had not heard him coming, or positioned himself to guard against attack from behind and was just raising his radio to his mouth when Iwaki struck. The phone call Iwaki made from the Shinjyuku metro station payphones afterwards had the backup police swarming into the pachinko parlour as soon as they arrived at the scene.

Iwaki was older than his companions and with age had come a particularly acute cunning. His nickname was 'Yurei', meaning ghost, appearing, like some phantom, only to disappear the next moment, never drawing attention to his movements. He was also a good observer of people, quickly learning their strengths and weaknesses. He was not very superstitious, unlike Hamaura who, like many Japanese, followed the old beliefs. During the last few days, as he had moved the two men from one safe house to another, he had noticed Hamaura going to great lengths to help a spider in the morning, that he would be happy to kill in the evening; following an ancient Japanese belief that spiders found in the morning were a sign of good luck.

Iwaki's observations brought him to the conclusion that, by using the right approach, Hamaura at least could be easily manipulated. Kimura, however, was a very different man and much more difficult to read; in the days since his release, he had spoken very little. Iwaki had learnt that the two men had been kept apart from one another whilst in prison. Hamaura had been put with burglars and fraudsters, whilst his cousin had the company of those confined for manslaughter and other crimes of violence. During his incarceration, Kimura had apparently suffered being raped, an act that had inspired in him a vehement homophobia.

"We must leave Japan," Kimura said suddenly.

"Ah so," said Iwaki. "Where you think to go?"

"Canada, then Iceland and from there to England," came the confident reply.

The other two stared at him in surprise. "How you think we do that?" demanded Hamaura.

"Fishing boat to remote spot on Canadian coast. Drive, as tourist, to east coast. Your sister had contact there. French Canadian, I remember."

The other two men nodded thoughtfully.

*   *   *

"It is essential that none of you make any statement to anyone concerning your involvement in the 'Kinoko Kumo' attack," said Commander Campbell.

"Kinoko Kumo?" questioned Sarah Vaughan looking confused.

"It apparently means 'Mushroom Cloud' in Japanese, and was Murata's code word for their attack," informed Campbell. "The most likely people to comment are of course your children who, innocently I am sure, will be totally unaware of the implications of telling their story."

"Sarah has gone to great lengths to explain to the girls what the dangers are," replied Ian. "Commander, is there any way we can obtain complete anonymity? We would even be agreeable to relocation," he continued, and glanced to his right at Sarah, seeking her confirmation but got no reaction.

"That is not so easy to achieve. You see, under our law the accused has the right to face his accusers in court at his trial."

"Surely it would be if there is sufficient evidence, other than mine. Forensic for example," said Sarah, her chin stuck out aggressively.

"We are in the process of testing the forensic evidence through the CPS, er, Crown Prosecution Service, at the moment," said Campbell. "Though there is enough to link Murata with the coach luggage compartment, whether he and Nagano were in there on the day of your escape cannot be proved. We do have a match linking him with the death of Mr Drummond, in whose lorry he travelled to London. Sadly however, as we have still not found the weapon he used to kill Julian Makepeace, your evidence would be of great value, especially as we do not have very good forensic evidence to link him with your kidnapping."

"What about PC Forge?" asked Sarah, her voice now carrying a tone of desperation. "He saw Murata and witnessed him firing his gun into the hedge trying to kill me!"

"He was too far away to give a positive identification. If a defence counsel pushed hard, Forge would not be able to satisfy a jury," replied Campbell. "If the CPS accepts the strength of the forensic information gathered from yours and your daughters' clothing, we shall request that the prosecuting counsel refrains from calling you as a witness. We cannot however, at this time, impose that constraint upon a defence counsel."

The meeting had been a long one, held only the day after Ian Vaughan's return from Washington, in a safe house occupied by Sarah and the girls since her release from hospital. Commander Campbell of the Counter Terrorist Command had been questioning Vaughan about his kidnapping and forced transatlantic sail in the company of two Red Brigade faction terrorists. Sarah and their daughters had been held hostage to Ian's co-operation, by the gang's leader, in an old farmhouse near Chichester. She had sat in astonishment, as she learnt for the first time of the treatment and torture to which her husband had been subjected. As his story neared its end she was shocked to learn that her husband had actually shot and killed two of the gang and killed a third by smashing his skull with the yacht's emergency tiller. The fact that he had also correctly identified the gang's target was something that she knew he was intelligent enough to work out, but the killings somehow frightened her. She looked at him yet again, and realised that something about him had changed. She had sensed the change as he had descended the steps at the airport. His eyes, once laughing and friendly, now held dark secrets and his movements were tense. The weeks they had been separated had imposed a distance, normally gained by years of being apart. Suddenly she realised that she was looking at him as if he were a stranger.

An hour later DS Weaver was packing up the recording equipment, sealing the tape cases and placing them all into a padded black case. "I think that's the lot, sir. Do you want me to send the typed statements back to Mr and Mrs Vaughan for checking?"

"Of course, Sergeant. I do not want any slip-ups with this, it is far too important," replied Campbell, giving the man a baleful glare. DS Weaver was the unit's Japanese expert and, though very competent in that sphere, lacked a lot in terms of following precise police procedures.

"I've made tea and sandwiches," said Sarah Vaughan as she put her head around the living room door. "Everything is laid out in the garden. May I call your driver to join us?"

Campbell instinctively looked at his wristwatch. "That's very kind of you, but we can't stay long I'm afraid; meetings in London you understand."

"Your driver?" Sarah asked again.

"Oh, er yes, that would be fine."

On the way out to the garden DS Weaver mused on the prospect of the lovely WPC Tucker joining them for afternoon tea on the lawn. Would Campbell have allowed the invitation to be extended had it been PC Wheatley driving them, he wondered, before concluding that it would be most unlikely.

As the three men sat themselves on the cushioned wicker chairs set around a teak garden table the two women appeared, walking down the side path. To the men's surprise the ladies had their arms around each other and were laughing happily.

"I take it that you know each other," said Campbell. "Of course, Tucker, you took the girls to the hospital on the day they all escaped from the farmhouse."

"Oh, we have met several times since then," said Sarah. "Caroline has been a great source of comfort to the girls and me."

Ian Vaughan raised his eyebrows in surprise.

"Caroline came down on her off-duty days and was wonderful playing with the girls and helping me get my mind round what had happened," said Sarah, giving Caroline a hug.

Campbell, who had stood up as the ladies approached, pulled a chair out to let Sarah sit down near to the teapot. He hesitated a second, his old world manners in conflict with his position of authority rendering him unable to instantly repeat the courtesy to WPC Tucker.

Ian Vaughan, recognising the dilemma, moved the chair to his left and said, "Sit here in the shade."

WPC Caroline Tucker smiled at him and sat down.

"So you are the Caroline the girls mentioned to me yesterday," Ian said returning her smile. "You definitely have a fan club there."

"It was a pleasure to come and see them, really. They are so lovely and had been through so much, you must be very proud of them."

"Yes I am. In fact I'm amazed at how well they seem to have coped, especially with Sarah having spent so long in hospital. When I was in the States, I was just so relieved that they were all safe; caught up in the drama of the search I failed to consider the psychological impact of what they had been through, especially Sarah. I'm so grateful to you being around to help. Do you live locally?"

"No, I have a small flat in London but it doesn't take long by train."

Ian was stunned by her comment. "Good heavens, you went to all that trouble?"

"I assure you it was no trouble, in fact I thoroughly enjoyed myself," Caroline said, before looking meaningfully across at Sarah and pointing to the house.

"Of course Caroline, you know where everything is," said Sarah. "I won't pour your tea until you get back."

Ian was aware of DS Weaver staring at Caroline Tucker's shapely form as she walked back across the lawn and through the French doors of the house. He leaned across and in a low voice said, "Down boy, you're on duty remember."

Weaver flushed slightly and grinned.

Campbell had put on his sunglasses and was using their screen to study Sarah Vaughan as she set out the sandwich plates and poured the tea. She looked quite serene now but at times during their interview her reactions had been unsettled and extreme. He recalled the discussion with Mrs Fitzgerald, his secretary and WPC Tucker, just prior to the visit.

"Excuse me, Commander, before you leave could we have a few private words with you?" Mrs Fitzgerald had asked.

In his office both women had accepted a seat, then Mrs Fitzgerald had started to explain their fears with regard to the mental state of Sarah Vaughan and their fears for the impact upon the case against Murata. "Caroline, I'm sorry, WPC Tucker, came to me a few days ago," she had said, "and explained some concerns with regard to Sarah Vaughan. Again this morning she repeated these worries and we felt you should know before today's interviews." The two women had exchanged glances then WPC Tucker had said. "You see, sir, I have been talking to her a bit about her ordeal and have come to the conclusion that she has been seriously affected by it. The fear induced by Murata, during her time at the farmhouse, has left a deep psychological scar and I am sure she will never be able to face Murata again without breaking down completely."

Campbell had wrongly assumed that Tucker's only conversations with Sarah Vaughan had taken place soon after her arrival in hospital, when they had been setting up her protection arrangements. Now it was clear they had actually become friends.

"What would have made her trauma worse, would have been the miscarriage, sir," Mrs Fitzgerald had added. "To go through that prolonged period of imprisonment, constantly being threatened, then the awful mental agonies of losing an unborn child would be terrible. I read the hospital report and learnt that possibly the exertion during the escape coinciding with a miscarriage caused such internal injury that she will be unable to bear any more children and believe me, sir, I know, only too well, how devastating that feels." He had been shocked by their comments and cursed himself for sending the hospital report along to Jackson without reading it himself. His assisting chief inspector was a brilliant detective but as hard as nails; Jackson would not have picked up the emotional significance of the miscarriage. The other thing that had touched him was the implied revelation from his secretary. He knew she was childless and had assumed that it was a career choice, but now it was apparent that it was not.

As Caroline Tucker returned to the garden there was the sound of the telephone ringing in the house and a few minutes later the

Vaughans' protection officer stepped out into the garden and called, "Mr Vaughan it's for you, from the States."

Ian leapt to his feet and ran inside.

Picking up the receiver he said, "Ian Vaughan, who is it calling please?"

There was a pause, then, "Hi buddy, this is Brumen, you got a minute?"

The deep voice of the FBI agent who had been assigned to look after Ian during the hunt for the terrorists in the Washington area made Ian smile.

"Of course I have. How are you and how's the arm? How did you get hold of me here?"

"Some guy at Scotland Yard called Jackson had the call transferred. I'm fine, the arm still aches like hell and I can't sleep on that side but hey that's not what I called you about. You sittin' down, cos I got some rocky news for you."

"Yes, let me have it," Ian replied with a sigh. "What's happened?"

"I shouldn't be telling you this but I think you deserve to know as soon as possible."

"What do I need to know?"

"Shortly after the threat message, received on the morning of the shoot-out, one of the President's aides, a woman called Marcia Caswell, contacted the Japanese Prime Minister, Mr Kato, and demanded that Japan comply with the terrorists' demands for the release of Yoshi Hamaura and his cousin Teiji Kimura."

"Don't tell me they complied," said Ian, a tone of dejection in his voice.

"Poor old Kato does not appear to have been given much choice, as it appears this arrogant bitch claimed to be talking on behalf of the President who, she said, was 'not available' at the time due to the extreme nature of the threat."

"Whatever possessed her to do that?" asked Ian incredulously.

"She's one of these 'I know best' characters. She was about when I was on the President Protection Team just after he was elected. I was only a stand-in for a week. Anyways every time our team leader got a safe route organised she would come along and insist on changes."

"This though, is a lot more than altering a walk-through or a car journey."

"Yeah, I know. Some time ago there was a rumour that it was she who was actually the President," Brumen said with a chuckle.

"What will happen to her? I mean this is a major diplomatic incident."

"God only knows, but I gotta go, I see Metcalfe headin' my way an' I gotta play my fuzzy memory routine. Just you keep your wits about you and stay safe, eh?"

"Thanks pal for the heads up on this. What's all this about a fuzzy memory?"

"Oh nothin'. The Japanese are trying to round the two up again, so maybe things won't turn out bad after all. Stay in touch man."

The phone went dead leaving Ian sitting staring blankly across the hall.

"Who was that on the phone?" It was Sarah, standing just inside the French doors.

"Oh, just Brumen from the States, checking that I had arrived home in one piece. Really I think he is bored sitting around in hospital."

"Oh," Sarah replied. "Our guests are about to leave. You'd better come and say your goodbyes."

At the gate, under the ever-watchful eyes of the police protection officer, Ian and Sarah waved as the black Jaguar swept away down the lane to disappear in the shadows of Snellings Copse.

"I'd better get the girls from the summerhouse, it's past their teatime," Sarah said, turning away without looking at Ian.

"Wait a bit, tell me what's wrong?" he asked. "You've been on edge ever since I arrived back."

"That's because this whole thing is your fault," she said, turning to face him. "If you had just let them sort themselves out we would have been alright and we would have had a son by now. Oh yes, if the pregnancy had gone full term we would have had a son!" she shouted at him. "Ian Vaughan, the yachtsman's Good Samaritan, just had to go and help and look what happened! The girls have been mentally scarred for life! I died; yes died, did you hear that, I died!" She was screaming at him now. "You'd be a widower if it wasn't for the paramedics!" Tears were streaming down her face, her voice breaking with emotion.

Ian took a step forward wanting to put his arms around her and comfort her but she backed away, her arms out, holding him at bay.

"I wake up every night seeing that burn scar across Murata's face and feel that he's in the same room again, spitting his contemptuous threats against the girls and me."

Ian, shaken by the verbal assault she had made, was unable to find any words.

"Don't even try to justify what you have done to this family," and with that she turned and fled towards the summerhouse.

Ian made to follow her but realising his presence would only make matters worse he returned to the back garden. After a few minutes had passed he started to gather the tea things together in an effort to find some normality. Having loaded and set the dishwasher he returned to the garden and walked to the end. As he stood staring out across the fields beyond, he thought through his actions that fateful morning at Bosham. Hailing them, to warn of the submerged spit was natural, as was the assistance to pull their yacht off when it had stuck hard. Even the damage assessment and advice was acceptable, but now, in that cold, clear, twenty-twenty vision of hindsight, why had he not left it up to them to get alongside the quay? Why had he escorted them and, once there, why had he gone to offer more advice? Sarah was right, he should have left them once they were back on their buoy, and sailed off.

The thing was, he hadn't left them to it and, as a result, his lovely wife had suffered the tragedy of a miscarriage and she and their daughters forced to endure the ordeal of being held hostage. At that moment a feeling of utter loneliness and dejection swept over him, forcing him down to the ground, to sit with his head on his knees and his eyes shut. For a few moments he wondered whether the gang, faced with the problem of a damaged boat, would have been able to continue the attack, which was now being called the most serious that the United States had faced. Remembering the cold, callous and calculating way in which both Fumiko Hamaura and Yunis Madadhah had carried the attack through, he had no doubt that his actions had not changed that outcome.

Now he had the additional fear of Hamaura's brother and cousin being released. What would Sarah make of that, he wondered? He silently thanked Campbell and his team for keeping the information to themselves and not giving Sarah further cause to blame him. He was sure that they already had the information.

"Are you going to sit there all night?" The curtly spoken words cut through Ian's depressing thoughts. He looked up and was surprised to see that it was almost dark.

"The girls are in bed and probably asleep by now," Sarah continued.

"What happens now?" he asked, his voice was flat, reflecting the emptiness and hurt he felt inside.

"I've been thinking about separation." Ian gasped at her statement. "To be honest, I am finding it increasingly difficult to come to terms with all this," she replied. "Mummy was horrified when I told her how you got us involved."

The shock of her statement regarding their future left him dumbstruck.

"Now I learn that you actually killed three people," Sarah went on, tears returning to her eyes. "I feel as if I have never known you."

"Wait, surely you can't be serious," Ian replied, "I am so, so sorry about what happened, but how was I to know who they were and what they were capable of? They appeared to be ordinary people like us, just going sailing, and who just ran into a bit of trouble. It all happened so quickly, I didn't see it coming."

"And that bit of trouble, as you call it, has led us to this situation where the girls and I are still trying to recover from our horrific ordeals and you changed from family man to killer!"

"Killer! Weren't you listening when I was explaining it to Campbell! Didn't you understand the situation I was in when the shooting started? Didn't you understand how many lives were at stake if they had succeeded? You make me sound like I'm some common murderer!"

"I'm not talking about it anymore," she said, turning and running back into the house.

At the French doors she turned and said loudly, "Look in the writing desk before you go to bed and work out how to pay all the bills that are there."

At two o'clock the following morning, Ian climbed the stairs, now worried as well as depressed. During the months since his redundancy they had not had any income at all, except for a small amount of redundancy money. The bank statements revealed that almost all of their meagre savings had been used up, and settling the bills that awaited payment would put them seriously in the red. How could he persuade a bank manager to advance a loan when he did not even have a job? In the few moments he had been free to think of their future, since his escape from the yacht, his thoughts had always been directed to finding a small business that he could take over and build up. Now in the full glare of this financial and marital crisis, would he have to remain content with being an employee?

At their bedroom door he tried the handle, only to find that Sarah had locked him out. There was a note taped to the door, 'Bed made up in spare room'. He thought back to the previous night, the night of his return. He had been so exhausted that he had crashed into bed to fall asleep almost instantly and, when he had woken that morning, it was to see that he had slept alone, her pillow undisturbed. Looking round, he saw the WPC member of the protection team standing quietly at the top of the stairs and, turning away, heavy at heart, he crossed the landing to the spare bedroom.

On the other side of the bedroom door Sarah lay wide awake. She had heard Ian's footsteps and the tentative turn of the door handle. She held her breath until she heard the sound of him moving away in the direction of the spare bedroom. Again she went over the events of the day in her mind. Every time she got to the warning from Commander Campbell about disclosure to anyone of the kidnapping, her stomach shrank with the feeling of guilt. That afternoon, covertly, from her mobile phone, she had called Rebecca and been almost hysterical when swearing her to total secrecy. Rebecca, whom she had known since her school days, had been her obvious confidante and was the one who had pointed out the danger Ian had placed them in. Though Caroline Tucker had been wonderful with the girls and had tried to help her in suggesting counselling, it was Rebecca she trusted. The imprisonment and miscarriage had been awful and so hard to put behind her, but the man directly responsible for that had been arrested and would be punished. The person equally to blame, but who would not be punished was Ian, with his thoughtlessness in going to extremes to help total strangers. Yes, Rebecca was right, she should never forgive him that.

"You're too doe-eyed over Ian," Rebecca had said that afternoon. "If Jerry had put me in danger like that I would have left him on the spot."

After weeks of this style of comment from Rebecca it was no longer in Sarah's mind to make any excuses for Ian. Thinking back, Rebecca had been against her marrying Ian when their engagement had been announced some eight years ago. He had been a relative newcomer to their group and not linked, like the others, through school, college or university. Sarah had met him when she and some of the group had taken part in a sailing challenge. Ian had been the skipper of their charter yacht and had appeared to Sarah as something of a strong, silent, handsome hero type. The weekend had proved fun and exciting; thanks to her new hero, their team had won and she was smitten. When on the following day he had phoned to invite her out, she had been over the moon with excitement. On that first date, she learnt that he was actually an engineer and the sailing event was just to help out his friends who owned the boats. A year later and they were getting married. Had Rebecca been right all along, had she been rushed into marriage? Now with two daughters, an out-of-work husband she felt she no longer knew, a mortgage and what appeared to her to be a mountain of other debts, she pondered the question.

Ian looked up from the application form he was studying as Sarah came into the kitchen; he and the girls were sat at the kitchen table eating breakfast.

"You didn't sleep either?" he asked, observing the dark shadows round her eyes.

"No," she replied, and then smiling at the girls said, "Has Daddy got you breakfast? That's nice. I wonder whether he will do the same for me."

Ian got to his feet and moved over to the worktop. "Tea or coffee?"

"I think it'd better be coffee."

"Do you want some of this porridge, I made too much for the girls and I?"

"Yes, that would be fine."

"I'll put some toast on as well."

"Not for me, the porridge will be enough."

"I've just been reading through this Criminal Injuries Compensation Form; that was very bright of you, I would not have thought of seeking help like that."

"According to the lady I'm dealing with, the process takes a long time," said Sarah, sounding thoroughly exhausted. "It will mean us getting assistance from elsewhere to tide us over. You will have to get a job, Ian, and give up this search for a business of your own."

"I've hardly had time to do any search, have I?" retorted Ian sharply, his own tiredness sapping his normal patience. "No sooner had I started the search than the Murata thing happened."

Louise and Clare had stopped eating and were looking nervously at their parents.

"How can we afford to buy… oh I'm not going to even discuss it," said Sarah, getting up, placing the half-finished bowl of porridge on the worktop and pouring some more coffee.

"We do need to… no, this probably isn't the best time," he replied, seeing the girls' expressions of fear at their heated conversation.

Chapter 2

Chief Superintendent Ishii of the Special Assault Team drummed his fingers on his desk as he impatiently waited for his opposite number, in the Tokyo Metropolitan Police, to come out of a meeting to take his call. CS Ishii held a unique position within the Tokyo SAT. Two years before he had been called to secret meetings with Prime Minister Kato, the Minister for Defence and two military intelligence civil servants. The result of these meetings was the formation of a small unit of highly trained officers, drawn from the Japanese defence forces and the police.

"*Mushi, mushi*, Hino speaking," a voice said at the other end of the phone.

"*Ah dommo, dommo*, Hino-san, Ishii of Special Assault Team here. I am calling about murder of your two detectives in Shinjuku area."

"Ah, you have information; we are trying to discover which *boryokuden* is involved in this," said Hino, using the Japanese police force preferred name for the criminal organisation, the Yakuza.

"We believe it is not the Yakuza who responsible," replied Ishii. "We are certain this is work of the Murata faction of Red Brigade. Phone tip-off mentioned names of Hamaura and Kimura I understand."

"Ah so, that is very interesting. How you come to conclusion of Red Brigade when it was on Yakuza territory?"

"It would be most unique for Murata group to trust Yakuza with such important thing as the safety of two special members of their faction. As you know Yoshi Hamaura is brother of Fumiko Hamaura, who was recently killed by FBI/CIA agents in America. He is very dangerous member of group; we were lucky to catch him before he could complete Shinkansen attack."

"Murata faction finished. He is in prison in Britain and will surely be sent to America for trial," replied Hino.

"Except for Hamaura's sister, Murata faction was weak before, but now these two are on the loose their strike ability has increased greatly. Young Kimura is very clever; we never really broke him down in questioning. Had both not been arrested together he would have walked free."

"It is my great regret that we did not find their mangled bodies under that fish market truck," said Hino. "Anyhow you did not contact me to hear of my wishes. What is it that you want?"

"We are certain this has international terrorism implications and, as you know, this department is linked with FBI, British SAS and CTC. So, with your acceptance, we would like to work alongside your investigation team and assist them."

"Ah, thank you for offer. I will give it some consideration and get back to you. Please excuse, I must return to meeting. Thank you again for offer."

After their polite goodbyes, Ishii put down the phone, smiling to himself. Normally when an offer is met by the response that it will be 'given some consideration' it meant that the offer had been politely rejected. This time, however, he was confident that Hino-san would shortly be calling back with his acceptance; Ishii's earlier call to the Superintendent Supervisor had ensured that.

It was no surprise therefore, that Chief Superintendent Ishii was greeted one hour later, at the crime scene, by two of his officers, Lieutenant Commander Umeko Morohashi and Inspector Masato Ariyoshi. Inspector Ariyoshi had just returned from a tour of duty on the Imperial Protection Team, where he had received high praise for his work. The Lieutenant Commander was new to the team and something of an experiment. She came with the highest credentials from the Japanese Maritime Defence Force. Her background was naval intelligence but her record also showed her to be a competent officer at sea, serving time aboard coastal patrol vessels countering the threat of North Korean terrorist infiltration. The secondment had been Ishii's brainchild and part of his plan to develop the SAT into a role closer to that of the British MI5/MI6 model. Taking them to one side, away from the Metropolitan Team, Ishii said, "This is most important case and could lead to Special Assault Team becoming a truly international force. Murata faction, as you know, have attacked United States. They are Japanese and we are responsible for tracking them down and ensuring they are kept locked up forever."

"What are your instructions, sir?" asked Morohashi.

"I believe the two detectives were either led here, or trapped here, in order they could be murdered and blame placed upon members of Yakuza," Ishii said, quietly. "Find out what you can. Share any evidence with Metropolitan Team; I do not want any complaints about us withholding information. You understand?" Both officers nodded their understanding.

After Ishii had left, Ariyoshi walked over to the Metropolitan Team and asked if the local precinct officers were available. A sergeant stepped forward and introduced himself as being one of those who patrol the area.

"What is this road like on normal day?" Ariyoshi asked. "Do many people walk up and down it?"

"No, this road very quiet, but always many cars parked here early morning. Many big company offices in that direction," he informed, pointing in the opposite direction to the alley. "We never had trouble here before. Two years ago, street girl working here for few nights, she was arrested, that is all."

"Thank you," Ariyoshi said. Nodding his head in the direction of the alley he walked to where the blood had stained the stone paving; Morohashi followed behind.

"The first body was in squad car and second body here," he said looking about him. "Now according to Met guys, they received a radio call from detective Kubota to say they thought they spotted Hamaura and Kimura rushing from a van, into this alley, and that DS Watanabe was going to check it out."

"When he got this far he was killed?" questioned Morohashi.

"No, I was told that after ten minutes they reported back in, saying they had found nothing, but would stay in the area for a while to check," he said, bending down to study the wall and side gulley a few paces further along.

"Somebody moved the body neatly; there is no trail of blood to indicate direction," said Morohashi. "Well organised I would say."

"The Met say they had another radio call about an hour later, this time from Watanabe to say DC Kubota had seen something and was going to investigate," Ariyoshi said, almost to himself. "When precinct ask if they required backup, there was no response. I would guess they kept trying, then after maybe ten minutes or so sent a team just in case."

"It would take backup some time to get here, say twenty, maybe even thirty minutes; so plenty of time for whoever to move the bodies," said Morohashi.

"Yes, that is so. What I am trying to work out is, whether person who was sick just there, came across the body of Kubota. If so, why did they not report it?" he paused thinking. "Maybe they did, but not to us."

"Yes! You are right, she did," said Morohashi, using two ballpoint pens to pick up Oda's discarded tissue. Ariyoshi stepped closer to inspect what she had found. "The woman must have used this to wipe her mouth. You can see the lipstick and traces of her vomit. Here, hold this," she said, transferring the pens holding the tissue to Ariyoshi.

Crouching again, she reached into her handbag and took out a pair of tweezers. Carefully she picked up an unopened condom packet. Looking at each other, both raised their eyebrows in understanding.

Making their way back to the Metropolitan officers, they requested sample bags and handed over the two items.

"Where did you find these?" questioned the DI in charge.

"I marked the spots with sticks number 47and 48. They are just beyond the bloodstain, on the right-hand side, opposite the vomit in the gully," Morohashi said.

"You are?" he asked.

"A member of the Special Assault Team."

"I meant your name."

She took her badge from a pocket and held it up. "That is all you need to know."

He turned and looked questioningly at Ariyoshi. "And you?"

Ariyoshi nodded, holding up his own badge.

The DI gave a grunt of disapproval and was about to walk away when Ariyoshi asked, "Have you let any of the pachinko parlour customers go?"

"No, we have only just started to question them."

"Good, we would like to ask if any of them saw a woman or women walk out of the back room of the parlour, maybe prostitutes."

The DI frowned.

"If you look at tissue we have just handed in, you will see traces of vomit and lipstick and only small distance away was unused condom."

The DI nodded in understanding. "Yes, I will get team to ask that question."

* * *

Three days later the investigation was no further forward. Yamaguchi had been brought in for questioning, but that had been a waste of time. His lawyers swiftly obtained his release. The two prostitutes, seen by only three of the forty or so customers, led to four different identifications, one of whom was in hospital, two serving prison sentences and the last having moved to Nagasaki a year ago. While the police were working hard to solve the crime and bring those responsible to justice, Kishi Oda was enjoying a free holiday in the mountain town of Takayama, courtesy of Yamaguchi.

It was the smell that revealed the location of the bodies when the bin was collected from the rear of the hotel that afternoon. In itself the discovery did not reveal much more to the Metropolitan Police other than the method of execution; to Lieutenant Commander Umeko Morohashi of the SAT it meant a great deal. Since being assigned to the case she had spent all her time away from the murder scene researching information known about the Murata faction of the Red Brigade. Very few of the group had been identified, namely Murata himself, Fumiko Hamaura and her brother Yoshi and Teiji Kimura. The rest were shadowy characters that were known to exist but so far had not been clearly identified.

Recent estimates put the number at thirty, of which eight could be considered main players. The group had, to all intents and purposes, been inactive in Japan for the last five years, and rumours abounded of a faction war over direction and control of the organisation. It was the bodies resulting from this war that intrigued her; the garrotte had been used on several occasions, indicating that one or more members of a group preferred this weapon. According to the SAT intelligence reports, both sides in the faction war had suffered heavy loses and it was thought that Murata had fled Japan some two to three years ago. The recent attack on the United States, launched from Britain, proved the intelligence report to be accurate. At her initial briefing she had been informed of the White House staff's demand for the release of the two terrorists and, based on the evidence so far, it was very likely that the police hunt to recapture them had got too close, resulting in the killings. The question was, what would they do now?

"The DNA results have come through from the lab," Ariyoshi said, interrupting her thoughts. "They confirm that Hamaura and Kimura enjoyed themselves on that makeshift bed above the parlour. The lab also say that the tissues and condom have identical DNA traces that confirm they were in the possession of the same person. It also matches some DNA on the bed. That I think proves the prostitution connection."

"It proves also that Ishii-san was correct in his assessment," Morohashi replied. "That treat was organised by Murata supporters to direct police hunt towards the Yakuza. Nice try, very clever."

"The anonymous phone call was a good touch, it guaranteed that the Met police would be searching the parlour before anyone could dispose of that evidence."

They were about to go off duty when they were called into the Chief Superintendent's office to review progress.

"Morohashi-san, what are your thoughts about their next move?" asked Ishii.

"Well, sir, I think that the killing of those two detectives means that Hamaura and Kimura must either go into deep hiding, here in Japan, or leave the country."

Ishii nodded. "Murata appears to have very strong traditional ideas about honour and loyalty," she continued. "From what I have gleaned, reading the intelligence files, anyone who has wavered in their support has met an untimely end."

"What is your point?"

"My point, sir, is that such 'loyalty' will inspire Hamaura and Kimura to attempt to free their leader."

Ishii smiled and nodded again. "Well done, you have read my thoughts exactly."

"The elections in Britain will probably delay any request by the United States for Murata's extradition," said Ariyoshi.

"Yes, you are probably correct," responded Ishii. "I will check with the American Embassy to see if any request has been made. We will meet again tomorrow. Bring a suitcase, packed ready for overseas assignments."

* * *

"You must understand Mr Vaughan that we cannot make up back payments of benefit unless we know, and can confirm, what you have been doing in the intervening period since you last attended here," explained Mrs Marshall at the Social Security Office.

"Look, will you just make a phone call to this senior police officer?"

"His explanation better be good, because you cannot claim benefit for time spent in custody unless we have full court details," she said, looking at the police officer stood by the department's doorway.

"I wasn't in police custody," replied Ian, becoming more than a little frustrated that he was unable to explain in full. "Please, if you just give that officer a call."

Reluctantly Angela Marshall lifted her phone and put in the number Ian had given to her. "Chief Inspector Jackson?" she asked in a haughty voice as the call was answered. The name confirmed, she continued by explaining the reason for her call in a tired, almost exasperated tone.

The change in her facial expression indicated that Chief Inspector Jackson's response was sharp and to the point. A fairly short conversation followed, during which she wrote down two reference numbers and circled them. "Oh, right, yes I understand Inspector, thank you for your time."

The volume of Chief Inspector Jackson's parting comment, emanating from the receiver, left Ian in no doubt that he had been very annoyed to be contacted on this issue. Ian was puzzled, until he watched her scroll down the screen on her computer and saw, in bold lettering, 'Witness Protection Reference' and alongside it the two numbers she had written down on the pad.

"I'm sorry, it appears that you should have been receiving payments throughout the period. There has obviously been a glitch in the system somewhere. Leave it with me, I will ensure that payment to your bank account is made today."

Trying hard to control his temper, Ian thanked her and, with his protection officer, left.

* * *

In the Counter Terrorist Command Section at New Scotland Yard, Mrs Fitzgerald interrupted Commander Campbell's briefing from Inspector Deacon regarding an incident and arrest at Heathrow. "I have the Prime Minister on the phone sir."

"I'll wait outside sir," Deacon said and stood to leave.

"Thank you Deacon," replied Campbell, reaching to pick up the handset. "Campbell here."

"Ah, Commander, Geoffrey Talbot here. I thought you should know straight away that I have, with great reluctance I must add, accepted the resignation of the Home Secretary, Oliver Makepeace."

"Thank you for letting me know personally, Prime Minister."

"It appears that his son was in some way mixed up with this Murata bunch and even encouraged their use of the family holiday home near Chichester."

"The gang, of which Julian Makepeace was a member, actually held a family hostage there, Prime Minister," informed Campbell.

During the term of this government, Campbell had little cause to celebrate their presence. The statute book had almost doubled in size with the introduction of knee-jerk legislation, brought in to grab press headlines and give the impression that the measures would improve the people's lot. Now, to his great annoyance, Campbell knew that the Prime Minister was about to ask him a favour.

"I'm not sure that it is certain he was actually a member, Commander."

"Oh, we are absolutely sure, Prime Minister."

"Does that have to be trumpeted around at this time?"

"It will undoubtedly be mentioned in court, in a few days' time, when Murata is brought before an initial hearing."

"Ah, is that so," Talbot said, sadly. "Does that evidence have to be heard at that time?"

"Yes, Prime Minister, it does."

"Mmm. When is the date for the hearing?"

"Next Tuesday, Prime Minister."

"Oh. Well, thank you for telling me all this, Commander. I may get back to you later, goodbye."

"Goodbye, Prime Minister," said Campbell, replacing the receiver, smiling broadly.

Almost immediately the intercom on his desk buzzed again.

"Excuse me Commander, but I now have Chief Superintendent Ishii of the Japanese Special Assault Team on the line from Tokyo," informed Mrs Fitzgerald.

Surprised at this communication, Campbell thought for a moment or two before reaching for the telephone. "Good evening Chief Superintendent. What can I do for you?"

"Ah, good morning Commander Campbell. Am I correct in that you are the officer in charge of the Murata case?"

"Yes, Chief Superintendent, you are. How can I help you?"

"It is more about how we can help you, sir. Over the last year I have been working, under the instructions of Prime Minister Kato, to build a special team of experts in antiterrorism. You are obviously aware of the release of Miss Hamaura's brother and cousin?"

“I am,” replied Campbell, now taking a lot more interest in the conversation.

“Good. What you may not know of is they discovered the electronic tracers that were placed in the two criminals’ wristwatches, and destroyed them.”

“No, that news had not reached us,” said Campbell closing his eyes in despair. “Can I assume that you no longer know of their whereabouts?”

“That is correct Commander, I am so sorry,” Ishii said, annoyed that his team had not been made responsible for tracking the men after their release. “A few days ago the two were seen in the Shinjuku area of Tokyo by two Metropolitan officers. Sadly the officers were murdered before backup could reach the area and the two terrorists got away.”

“Do you think they are still in the Tokyo area?”

“No, we believe that they have either left, or will shortly be leaving, our country. There is no logical reason for them to enter the United States, but there are reasons for them to travel to Britain. They have a debt to repay to Murata and we believe they will make every effort to fulfil that debt.”

“We have already circulated their details to our ports and airports but, as you know, it is difficult to be sure they would be picked up,” said Campbell.

“Quite so, Commander, that is why I am proposing to send two of my best officers to assist you. I believe there will be an attempt to free Murata.”

“Our security surrounding Murata is very tight, Chief Superintendent. I’m not sure that your men could contribute much more.”

“Our people have spent much time in studying the attack methods of this group, Commander; in Japan they were very successful in obtaining, by forceful means, the release of gang members held in prison. My team have become expert in pre-empting and countering these methods.”

“Chief Superintendent, let me discuss this proposal with some of my colleagues and I will get back to you.”

After taking contact details, Campbell called in Chief Inspector Jackson.

"Casting back in my memory, the Japanese government has caved to blackmail demands quite often. The Japanese Red Brigade normally took hostages in another country and left the rest of it to diplomats to sort out," said Jackson. "If they did anything like that here, with our present government, they would probably get away with it."

"Quite so," agreed Campbell. "That is why I am considering Chief Superintendent Ishii's offer. If his people can help us with the response, should an attack be made, then the chances of it succeeding could be reduced. In any event, they should have a better grasp as to how this group thinks and acts."

"I'd run it past Weaver, sir. He knows some of their people, I gather."

"He's down with the Vaughans, checking statements. I'll give him a call a little later when I have discussed terms with CS Ishii."

*   *   *

On arrival back at the safe house Ian Vaughan was disappointed to see a strange car in the drive. Once indoors he could hear a muffled conversation taking place in the dining room and entering he saw Sarah and DS Weaver hunched over a pile of papers. They both looked up.

"DS Weaver has brought the statements down for us to check," said Sarah. "I have nearly finished checking my bit. I'm sure the sergeant would like a drink of some sort."

Ian looked at Weaver. "Tea or coffee perhaps?"

"Tea would be great, thanks."

Returning with the tea tray, some minutes later, he found Sarah making her goodbyes. "Won't stop for tea, I'm joining the girls for a swim in the pool."

"Oh, right, I will see you later then," said Ian, saddened that he could not impart his good news regarding the benefit payments.

As the door closed DS Weaver looked across the table at Ian, noting the darkness around the eyes and his general depressed demeanour. "Your wife seems to be struggling to recover from her ordeal," he said. "Something or someone is preventing her from moving on."

Ian lifted his head and looking at the young officer the other side of the table, saw in his expression grave concern.

"At the moment I think it is me that is the problem," he said dejectedly. "She blames me for getting us involved with the gang. If I had just left them alone, once we had pulled their yacht off the spit at Bosham, she would have been fine, we would have had a son and that bastard Murata wouldn't have traumatised the girls. Maybe they would not even have made it across the Atlantic."

"What makes you say that?" asked Weaver incredulously. "Maybe they would have lost a couple of days while the yacht was repaired and replacement crew found, but that would not have stopped the attack, believe me."

"No?" said Ian, unconvinced. "Not according to my wife and mother-in-law," he added bitterly.

"Let me assure you, as one who has studied the Japanese and in particular their terrorist groups, they would have completed that attack. The only reason that you were taken along was that the yacht you were on had no auto-helm or GPS system."

Ian looked back across the table, the numbness in his brain lifting slightly. "Really?"

"Yes, really," replied Weaver. "The coastguard officer, Phil Saints, was very certain that your survival was purely down to that. Had your boat been fitted with all the gizmos that were on theirs, you and your family would have been killed."

Ian felt a cold chill run over him.

"You were also able to raise the alarm and, as I understand it from your statement, were able to tell the Yanks how the attack would be made. Damn it, you even ID'd them. Think what would have happened had you not been there. Christ, it makes me feel sick to think about it."

"A hell of a lot of people died as a result of those power cuts when the whole of Baltimore and those other places were completely blacked out," Ian replied.

“Millions more would have died if they had succeeded in destroying that nuclear power station.”

“I suppose so, thanks, I really needed that. Things have been rather difficult since I got back from the States. I’m finding it hard to get some perspective on things at the moment.”

The checking of the statement took quite a time, especially as Ian felt that some corrections were necessary. He hoped that Sarah would come back in time for DS Weaver to repeat his earlier analysis. It would sound a lot better coming from him.

Signing the last page Ian asked, “What happens next?”

“Well, they have been charged and the CPS has confirmed that they will be proceeding with a prosecution, so we now wait for the date of the initial hearing.”

“Do you think the States will demand Murata’s extradition?”

“Funny you should ask about that, we were only discussing it yesterday,” DS Weaver replied. “Not too sure what the Home Secretary has powers to do in the run-up to an election.”

A jazzy beeping had Weaver reaching into his jacket for his mobile. “Excuse me, I’d better take this, it’s the Commander.”

Putting the phone to his ear he said, “Yes sir?” then listened to what seemed a long set of instructions. “They’re pretty sure of the danger then, sir. May I ask who it was in Tokyo you were speaking to?” There was a pause whilst Commander Campbell explained. “If that comes from Chief Superintendent Ishii, it will be absolutely kosher, sir. He is one of the brightest brains over there and is putting together a very elite squad.” Campbell was obviously issuing further instructions and DS Weaver quickly pulled out his notepad and started writing furiously.

“Immediate action then, sir. I’ll get straight onto it. When will you be arriving, sir?”

Slipping the phone into his pocket again DS Weaver turned and looked at Ian. “It sounds as if the White House has dropped you in it. Some high-powered member of the President’s staff managed to order the release of Hamaura’s brother and cousin; the Special Assault Team in Tokyo believe that they may well be on their way over here.”

Ian did not react.

"This isn't exactly news to you, is it?"

"No, FBI agent Brumen, phoned me. That was the call I took yesterday when we were all out in the garden. I didn't say anything to anyone, as I didn't want to alarm Sarah any further. I assumed you people already knew anyway and I was hoping that the police in Japan would catch up with them straightaway."

"We knew about the release alright, but I'm afraid that the chances of them being picked up again are remote. The police did all they could, you know, plant electronic tracers on them etc. but they discovered and destroyed them quite spectacularly shortly after they left the prison." Weaver paused, wondering whether to explain more. "This is for your ears only."

Ian nodded. "Go on."

"The Commander said that even though the tracers were dealt with, the Tokyo police were still able to close in. Tragically two detectives got too close, and there was no backup. It appears that they were murdered and, in the resultant flurry of police activity, the two terrorists were spirited away. It is believed that they are now out of the country."

"Oh good God," Ian said despairingly. "Does Campbell really think they are heading this way?"

"Yeah, he does and so do I," said Weaver, looking very grim. "Murata's gang are classic samurai thinking, but evil intent. They will undoubtedly try to free Murata, their loyalty is absolute."

"Why would that necessarily involve me and my family?" Ian asked.

"They may want to avenge the death of Fumiko Hamaura."

Ian looked away, his eyes appeared to be concentrating on an object far away at the bottom of the garden, but he did not see it. All he could see was the flash and smoke from the gun he had held that day, and the woman's head jerk back as the bullet smashed through her forehead and ripped off the back of her skull. How could he stop this nightmare? What was Sarah's reaction going to be when she was told? Surely this would drive an even larger wedge between them. Ian now knew that his wife could not take anymore and that this news would probably destroy any hopes he had of reconciliation between them.

The slam of a door brought Ian's mind back to the present. His ears told him that Sarah had returned alone.

"You still here, Sergeant?" she said rhetorically. "Would you mind taking a stroll around the garden? I need to have a few private words with my husband."

"Yes, of course," Weaver replied, feeling and looking rather embarrassed. "Just give me a shout when you're ready, as I have some things to explain to you both."

Sarah watched him walk across the lawn as she closed the French doors. "I left the girls playing in the summerhouse."

"That's good, look, things have happened in Japan, which means some changes," Ian said.

"Quite, I've decided that the girls and I are going to accept an offer made by Jerry and Rebecca and move to Derbyshire for a time, until you get yourself sorted out with a sensible job and this whole Murata thing is out of the way. I can't stay here as a virtual prisoner anymore and, as it is obvious the girls and I can't go home, I intend to take them to Derbyshire, where nobody knows us. Also Ian, I am not going into the witness box to face that awful man, I don't care what he has done, I just can't face him again."

"What the hell are you talking about? The chances are you won't have to face him," Ian said, flabbergasted by her statement. "You have been talking to Rebecca?"

"Yes. I've been all alone here and had to talk to someone I could trust, and Rebecca is my closest friend."

"Where is this coming from Sarah? Is it you speaking or your friend Rebecca and that creep of a husband of hers?"

"Jerry is not a creep, he's a decent man who has made a very generous offer of help," she snapped back. "And no, it is not Rebecca speaking, I have been giving this a great deal of thought."

"Our separation may not be possible," Ian replied, and told her of the release of Hamaura's relatives and the possibility of their arrival in England. Predictably she accused him of further endangering their daughters and herself. The near hysterical outburst lasted a full five minutes ending with Sarah in floods of tears and Ian losing his temper and making the mistake of telling her to 'Get a grip'.

Commander Campbell arrived to find Ian sitting morosely in the lounge glaring out of the window and Sarah locked in their bedroom, packing.

DS Weaver had briefed Campbell on the events that had led to this sad situation. "I couldn't do anything," he had said helplessly. "They were going at it hammer and tongs. He seemed to be talking sense, but Mrs V had lost it altogether. I tried to point out to her that the gang would probably have succeeded in killing millions of Americans, had it not been for her husband; but that doesn't alter what happened to her and the two girls I suppose."

"Um, thank you Sergeant. Go up to her room and ask her to come down will you," requested Campbell.

When Sarah Vaughan entered the room, her appearance shocked Campbell. She was very pale, with dark shadows around her eyes. She gave the impression of being utterly broken.

Campbell invited her to sit, then pulled up a chair for himself and immediately explained the release of Yoshi Hamaura and his cousin. Sarah's only response was to shrug.

"I understand from DS Weaver that you no longer wish to assist us with the prosecution of Murata and Nagano, Mrs Vaughan."

Sarah turned her tear-stained face away from him. "I cannot face that man again. Ever!"

"I also understand that you wish to separate from your husband, for the foreseeable future."

"Yes, I am going to stay in a friend's house in Derbyshire, with the girls. When this is all over then..." her voice trailed away and she sat silently staring at the fireplace.

"Do your friends know the reason for your separation?" Campbell asked.

"Yes," she replied hesitantly. "After I came out of hospital, I had to talk to someone about it, and I have known Rebecca since we were at school together."

"How did you make contact?"

"By mobile phone," she replied, feeling very guilty at breaking the rules that had been explained to her regarding contact with anyone other than the safe house team.

"Did you disclose the address here?"

"No, I just explained that we were in hiding. I told them not to tell anyone else."

"You now appreciate the danger their knowledge could place you in?"

"I am confident that they will not say anything," she replied haughtily, giving Campbell a scornful glare. "Rebecca and Jerry are good friends of mine."

Campbell sat silently for a time contemplating his next move. The last thing he wanted was for Mrs Vaughan to be uncooperative and also to be so far away from London. He needed her to be somewhere at hand, to receive psychological treatment. His assessment was that she was having some form of breakdown; with help, she may be persuaded to assist at the trial by giving evidence.

"In view of their knowledge and the potential danger to yourself and your daughters that now exists, I feel it necessary to have you moved immediately to another 'safe house' we have in Surrey," Campbell said. He risked overemphasizing their danger in order to get Sarah Vaughan into a place where she could receive help.

Sarah went to protest but Campbell got in before her.

"We believe that the men, recently released from prison in Japan, pose a significant threat. We also believe that first they will try to assist Murata to escape, and may well consider you and your daughters to be ideal hostages to achieve that. If that fails we consider it possible that they would kill you."

"That is ridiculous," said Sarah. "This is not a Hollywood movie. Men don't go around kidnapping and killing innocent people."

"It didn't stop Murata and his gang before, did it?" interjected DS Weaver. "I have spent the last five years studying the Japanese terrorist organisations and this group is by far the most lethal. They would not think twice about killing you, or anyone who threatens the life or freedom of their leader."

Sarah shivered; the harsh way that DS Weaver had phrased his comment brought the reality forcibly home to her.

"When do we have to leave?" she asked dejectedly.

"I will arrange for cars and a shadowing escort to be here in approximately one hour from now," Campbell said.

Without another word Sarah left the room and was heard running upstairs. The men sat in an uneasy silence.

"Before we leave we must relieve your wife of her mobile phone," said Campbell, "and Sergeant I want a full report on why the phone was left in her possession."

"Right sir, I will get onto it straightaway," replied Weaver, looking more than a little nervous.

Leaving the two CTC officers, Ian stepped out onto the lawn and slowly strolled across to the swimming pool. He was struggling to understand his wife's behaviour. The Sarah he had known before that fateful day in Bosham Creek was warm, loving and, above all, calm. Then, after she had escaped, there had been his call from the States ending in the bitterness of her goodbye: 'Go find the bastards and kill them'. It was so out of character and had shocked him at the time by its severity and hatred. He had hoped and prayed that after the thwarting of the attack and deaths of the four terrorists, she may have drawn a line and moved on. As he had greeted her at the foot of the air bridge steps, he had sensed immediately that she was still full of hatred, but he had not recognised that the hatred included him. He recalled DS Weaver explaining to her how the plot would have succeeded, had it not been for her escape and his own actions but she did not want to listen to reason.

Unable to resolve anything, Ian returned to the lounge and sat staring out of the window.

After a quarter of an hour the door opened and Sarah walked in carrying a suitcase. "I've packed my case and two for the girls. Your two sailing kit bags are in the spare bedroom. You'll have to use those."

"Okay," Ian said. "I won't be long."

As Ian zipped up the second of the two bags there was a ring at the doorbell and he could hear the voice of WPC Tucker as she greeted Sarah. He was pleased to know that it would be Tucker who was taking them; she seemed to help Sarah somehow.

The isolation of the safe house made the move away more discreet as there were no neighbours to witness their leaving.

Finally the convoy of three cars got underway with two uniformed officers in the lead car, followed by WPC Tucker driving the Vaughan family, then DS Weaver, with another armed plain-clothed officer, bringing up the rear.

Sarah, on Ian's insistence, sat in the front alongside Tucker and the two were soon chatting away calmly. Ian, on the other hand, was still trying to understand exactly what had happened to the woman he loved. Why had she changed so much and why was she so unforgiving of an act he had done in all innocence?

"Are you alright, Daddy?" asked Clare, sensing but not understanding his feelings.

"Yes," he said, ruffling her hair. "I'm fine. How about you, are you looking forward to this new adventure?"

Her bright blue eyes looked up at him. "Not really Daddy, I'm a bit frightened."

"There's nothing to worry about. It will be like going on another holiday."

To take their minds off the immediate future, he got out a drawing pad from his small bag and started playing picture games with the girls. As usual on long car journeys, within half an hour, both of them had fallen asleep.

It was dark as they approached the new safe house. Ian noted the lead car's radio message to the police protection team at the house, warning them of their imminent arrival. The convoy turned off a suburban road of expensive houses into a wooded lane. Clearing the trees their car slowed and turned into a private cul-de-sac, leaving the other two cars behind. In the headlights Ian noticed two men standing either side of a gateway in a high brick wall. One man signalled and Tucker accelerated up the road, in through the gateway and up the drive towards a large Edwardian house. As the car swept through an archway into a well-lit courtyard, Ian took in their new surroundings. On two sides was the high brick wall and on the other two sides was the house and, so Ian thought, an old stable block above and to the right of the archway they had passed through.

The little voice of Louise asked, "Are we there yet?" Her eyes, bleary with sleep, looking around her as she stretched and yawned.

"Yes, we have just pulled up, Tinkerbell."

"Where are we?" she asked.

"I don't know," he said, smiling down at her. "I think it is somewhere in South East London."

"Oh," was all she said, before pulling on the door handle.

"It won't open, Daddy," she said indignantly.

"I have to come round and let you out," said WPC Tucker as she turned and smiled at Louise.

"Can Daddy get out as well?"

"I would think so."

As they assembled at the rear of the car, the door to the house opened and a plump lady in a pink floral dress and white pinafore hurried down the steps and across the courtyard to greet them.

"Good evening Mr and Mrs Vaughan, hello girls, I'm Ruby Finch, but you call me Poppy," she said, shaking hands with them all.

The warmth of the welcome seemed strange when compared to the cool atmosphere of the journey there. WPC Tucker had tried to get the conversation to include Ian, for whom she felt sorry, but on each occasion Sarah had cut him out. Now, as she watched them enter the safe house, she wondered how long he would be able to tolerate his wife's hostility.

Inside the house, Poppy noted with sadness the request for separate bedrooms made by Sarah Vaughan. The young girls, though nervous of their new surroundings, soon warmed to Poppy, as did Ian, but by contrast his wife was almost rude in her behaviour. Poppy's e-mail report to Commander Campbell, later that evening, recommended that a psychological assessment be started immediately.

* * *

In the secure block at Bellmarsh Prison, Tadashi Murata was alone in his cell, completing his second Tai Chi session of the day. Relaxing, he turned and sat on his bunk and went through the events of the day. The police questioning had stopped some weeks back, however his 'lawyer', Jirou Ishihara alias Takumi Ishihara, had been a regular visitor. Jirou and Takumi were, in fact, related and Jirou bore a quite remarkable resemblance to his uncle, the much respected Takumi Ishihara, who had died of stomach cancer two months previously. Jirou's grief-stricken aunt had so far failed to inform the Japanese Law Society of the death of her husband, a fact known to Rikuto Iwaki; therefore when checks were made, Jirou Ishihara, using the name of his uncle, was given clearance to visit Murata and act as his legal advisor. The Ishihara family in the Akita area had disowned Jirou soon after his marriage. His young wife's extreme views, and his obvious agreement with her, soured any relationship, and left the rest of the family no choice but to distance themselves from the couple.

The confidentiality of Ishihara's meetings with him meant that Murata was fully aware of the success of the attack on the east coast power network and the resultant release of Fumiko Hamaura's brother and cousin. The information had come from Dr Higashi in the United States. The answer that eluded him was why Fumiko had triggered the 'punishment' phase of the attack. He had ordered that the nuclear power station should only be attacked if the ransom and prisoner release demands had not been met. She knew that the demands had been met and therefore the 'punishment' phase was not necessary. Had she, instead, turned and run from her pursuers, maybe she would still be alive to carry on as his successor. He felt the loss as if she had been his daughter. How strange, he thought, that such emotion could be held for someone so full of hate towards the world.

According to Ishihara, Dr Higashi was obtaining the confidential report of the CIA/FBI operation that foiled Fumiko's final strike. Murata was surprised that Higashi would go to such lengths. He had misjudged him, as he had Ishihara here in London; both men were proving to be of great value.

Chapter 3

She stood at the passenger meeting point in Heathrow's Terminal 3. It was just after 1610 hours and she was feeling strangely nervous. Her orders were to meet a Lieutenant Commander Umeko Morohashi of the Japanese Defence Force. Curious eyes studied her WRNS uniform with its smart hat sat neatly upon her flaming red hair and her lieutenant's gold epaulettes on the shoulders of her white uniform shirt. The reduced Irish Republican Army threat allowed the wearing of military uniform off base, a sight not seen for many years.

Glancing at the flight information monitor, she noted that the JAL 401 flight from Tokyo's Narita Airport had landed two minutes in front of schedule. Walking into the coffee bar, alongside the passenger exit doors, she ordered a cappuccino and went and sat on a high stool overlooking the doors, looking at the multicultural scene passing in front of her. Twenty minutes later she noted the monitor showed 'Baggage In Hall'. Finishing her coffee she picked up the 'Idiot Board' and walked round to where the pre-booked taxi drivers and company chauffeurs were standing. Holding up the name board she was instantly aware of why it was called an 'Idiot Board'; yes, she felt a right idiot.

Now amongst the throng surrounding the arrival area, she became taken up with the greetings of loved ones and friends. Apart from the self-important businessmen, striding out as if the world depended upon their timely arrival, the other passengers exited the doors anxiously searching for a familiar face, to have their expression transformed to joy on mutual recognition. So taken up with the scene being played out around her, she missed the arrival of the smartly uniformed figure, until the officer was standing directly in front of her. Snapping to attention, she saluted and was relieved to observe an equally disciplined response coinciding with a gentle warm smile from a beautiful oriental face.

"My name is Umeko Morohashi." Penny Heathcote noted that her new acquaintance did not mention her rank.

"Penny Heathcote," she replied. "Welcome to the UK."

"Thank you. Have I kept you waiting long?"

"Oh no. It was just right and allowed me time to grab a coffee."

They smiled at each other, and then Morohashi raised a questioning eyebrow.

"Oh, we go this way; I have my car parked in the multi-storey," Penny said, feeling slightly embarrassed at not immediately handling the meeting arrangement.

"Are you okay pushing that trolley or would you like me to takeover?" Penny added as an afterthought.

"I am fine, thank you," replied Morohashi, as she led the way to the lifts. London had been her frequent haunt during her student days and subsequent leave periods. She loved the great English women authors: Jane Austen, Charlotte Brontë, as well as the more modern, Daphne du Maurier and Agatha Christie. During her last visit she had travelled to Brontë country, then across to the Lake District where she discovered Beatrix Potter. What joy *The Tale of Squirrel Nutkin* had brought to her young niece.

Penny Heathcote, now walking slightly behind, felt like the spare bridesmaid who had missed the rehearsal.

At the pay point she was horrified by the parking charge levied. "My God, I only wanted to rent the space, not buy the freehold."

Umeko Morohashi smiled; she had taken an immediate liking to her greeter, with the amazing red hair, bright blue eyes, freckled face and warm happy smile.

The Mini Cooper's tyres squealed on the concrete surface of the spiralled exit ramp. At the barrier Penny reached up and inserted the parking ticket into the machine and moments later the barrier lifted. Leaving the shelter of the building, Penny switched the wipers on to clear away the drizzle falling from a leaden sky and pointed the car towards the tunnel leading to the M4 and central London.

"I hope you don't mind, the Commander has requested that you stay at my place until the situation becomes clearer and a proper plan is established."

"Are you sure?" replied Umeko. "A hotel would have been fine for me. I feel I am putting you to a lot of trouble."

"The Commander did not want your presence to draw any attention. He thought that staying in a hotel and travelling to Scotland Yard would tie you to the Hamaura and Kimura release." Now she was talking business, Penny felt more relaxed and in control. "Our uniforms should not have linked us to antiterrorist work as you came through at the airport. You never know who is watching; from here on it will be plain clothes. You will be working out of a satellite office that poses as a small publisher. It even produces some books. The Commander is writing his memoirs." Glancing at her passenger, Penny gave a big wink and smiled.

"What is he like?" asked Umeko.

"A good boss to work for, does not micro manage but keeps you informed of his thinking." Penny checked the rear-view mirror and steered the car into the right-hand lane to follow the signs for Chelsea. "His team is very varied, with academics, information analysts and a wide range of other experts. I've worked for him since joining the Naval Intelligence section of MI5 and was very sorry when his desk was moved to New Scotland Yard. By far the largest group under his control is a section of the CTC police."

"My boss, Chief Superintendent Ishii, is very much the same in the way he runs his department. By the way he mentioned a DC Weaver."

"Oh yes. I don't know him very well. I think he is a DS now and is referred to as the section's Japanese expert," replied Penny. "You will probably meet him tomorrow with the Commander."

"Ah, that is good. Ishii has sent a bottle of 'sake' for him."

Penny glanced at Umeko, giving her a surprised look.

"Oh, it is Japanese custom. Ishii-san liked him a lot when he visited."

"Your English is very good, where did you learn it?"

"My parents were very insistent that I should learn to speak it well and spent a lot of money ensuring that I did. The schools I attended were very strong on English language and literature. I even had lessons with a lovely English lady who lived near to us. She had married a Japanese man who was an artist." She looked sad. "They were both killed in the 1995 Kobe earthquake."

"How very sad," Penny said. "I lost my fiancé, three years ago. He was killed by a mudslide in Peru. The term 'natural disaster' seems so cold and heartless. It never appears to address the sense of loss, shock and heartache, felt by those who have lost friends and loved ones somehow."

Umeko reached across and patted Penny gently on the shoulder.

Turning sharply left just before the Thames Embankment, Penny, with practised skill, squeezed the Mini into what looked like an impossibly small gap in the row of parked cars outside an Edwardian apartment block. Heaving Morohashi's suitcase out of the car's boot she staggered with it to the building's pillared entrance and tapped in a code. Holding the door open with her foot she dragged the suitcase in, then held the door for Morohashi who was carrying her hand luggage. In the lift Penny pressed the button for the top floor. The flat itself enjoyed an oblique view of the Thames from the lounge. "This actually belongs to my parents but they spend most of their time now either at the villa near Rome or the family home in Gloucestershire." This was said without a trace of snobbery or boastfulness; Penny's family were "old" money. "Your bedroom is through here," she said, leading Umeko along a short corridor. The room was a good size with a double bed and a large wardrobe. In the corner was a pink hand basin with a mirror and glass shelf over it. The view from the window looked over a side street to the rear of the building.

*　　　*　　　*

Whilst Umeko Morohashi was settling into her London posting, Ariyoshi had arrived in Washington and was finding his way around the Westin Washington Hotel. Entering the restaurant, he found a table by the wall from which he could observe the doorway. He was halfway through his ham, eggs and hash browns when he noticed a tall, slightly built man talking with the headwaiter. After a few moments the two headed in his direction.

"Mr Ari Yoshi?"

"Hi! I am Ariyoshi," he replied, standing with both arms down at his sides and giving a small polite bow.

The reception surprised Metcalf who had held out his right hand, expecting a handshake. Suddenly Ariyoshi produced a business card and offered it to Metcalf, who was now rather flustered and embarrassed, especially as he realised that he had left his own cards back in his desk.

"Hi there – er – thanks – my name is Metcalf. I was headin' the team that took out Hamaura and Maddadhah," he said, showing a sense of great pride. "We're holdin' an internal inquiry today. Maybe you'd like to listen in?"

"Ah, thank you," responded Ariyoshi. "That would be most interesting." He paused then said, "Maybe tomorrow I can start to contact major Japanese companies here in your country."

Metcalf looked confused but said nothing.

"When do inquiry start?" asked Ariyoshi.

Metcalf looked at his watch, "I booked a meetin' room from 9.30, so we had better hurry as I want to just clear some points before we start."

The point clearing he had in mind was to ensure the writing out of any part played by Ian Vaughan. Metcalf's major problem was that the one surviving agent from the marine search could be singing from a different hymn sheet, and that would not do his own career any good at all. When visiting Brumen in hospital he had emphasised the need to keep this an FBI/CIA victory, but he wasn't that confident that the message had got through. He was still confused as to how Vaughan had got onto the launch, and then turn up, by some miracle, on the beach near the terrorists' transmitter. Brumen, however, had been no help at all in clearing up that confusion.

On the way into the FBI's Washington headquarters, Metcalf boasted to Ariyoshi how his direction had led the team to trace and finally corner the trio led by Fumiko Hamaura.

"I suspected all along that there had to be another more powerful transmitting device used to trigger the power cuts. Finally, of course, it was just such a device that was used to damage the APWR station at Mission Creek. Damn shame the marines couldn'a get at it in time."

It was a very impressed Ariyoshi who accompanied Metcalf through the corridors towards the meeting room. Everywhere there appeared to be activity, with queues forming at photocopy machines. Turning right, down a wide corridor, Metcalf stopped and entered an office on his left.

"Hey Iris, what's all the hullabaloo about?"

Iris Chambers looked up from her computer. "Today's inquiry of course. We tried to contact you over the weekend but you didn't pick up."

"I was upstate visiting the wife's parents," he replied, wondering why the mobile phone he always carried had missed the calls. "It's only an internal debrief damn it, who in hell's name ordered this?"

"The President, sir," Iris replied.

Metcalf swallowed hard. "The President!"

"On Friday evening, but you've no need to worry, I've issued copies of your report to the panel. They will probably call you around 10.30."

"Where's Agent Brumen?" Metcalf demanded to know.

Iris looked up, shocked by his tone. "I honestly don't know; he's been at home since he came out of hospital."

"Well they can't have an inquiry without Brumen. His information would be vital to the outcome."

"The inquiry has been organised by the Director's office, maybe you should check with them."

Metcalf turned on his heels and, without further comment headed at a fast walk to the elevators, a rapidly rising sense of panic causing his stomach to churn. A puzzled Ariyoshi, following on behind, was getting the feeling that all was not well. The Director's suite, on the seventh floor, was deserted except for a junior clerk.

"I guess they are all in the Conference Suite down on level four," she replied in answer to Metcalf's angry question.

Back in the elevator Metcalf appeared to be totally unaware of Ariyoshi, who for his part, thought that silence was probably the best policy. His host appeared to be very distracted by the events.

At the entrance to the Conference Suite, many senior ranking military personnel were gathered amongst the dark-suited FBI and CIA officials. As Metcalf approached, an attractive and smartly dressed middle-aged lady intercepted him.

"Excuse me Agent Metcalf, but as you are a witness you should be waiting in either the anteroom, or maybe you would prefer to be at your desk. We will call you in good time to discuss your report."

"What is all this about? My team has not been fully debriefed. You cannot possibly have an inquiry with the scant information we currently hold."

"President Huckle is anxious to have this whole drama investigated as soon as possible. I understand that the report you sent to Director Johnson has already been circulated," replied Sheena Primlow, inwardly delighted by Metcalf's discomfort.

"Excuse me," said Ariyoshi, who had been standing patiently to one side. "Maybe it better I return to hotel?"

"You are?" asked Primlow.

"I am Inspector Ariyoshi of the Tokyo Section of the Japanese Special Assault Team."

"Ah, Ariyoshi-san, I have been trying to find you. We were expecting you here yesterday. Please follow me and I will direct you to your seat." Starting to guide Ariyoshi through the crowd, she looked back over her shoulder and said to Metcalf, "We shall call you ten minutes in advance of your giving evidence."

Metcalf, mouthing a protest, could only watch as Primlow and Ariyoshi disappeared from view.

As she left the conference room Sheena Primlow had a smile of satisfaction on her face; for years she had suspected that Arnold Benton Metcalf had achieved his exalted status by stealing the credit due to others. This operation, however, had terrorised the nation, leaving the population feeling as vulnerable as they had after the 9/11 attack. If Metcalf thought that he could unfairly steal all the credit, he was very mistaken.

Metcalf was summoned after the panel had heard, by satellite link, Commander Campbell's statement from London, concerning the forced commandeering of the Vaughans' yacht, leading to the conclusion that some form of attack was soon likely to take place in the USA. That had led neatly to Metcalf's report and his assignment of Brumen and Capello to the case.

Throughout his evidence Metcalf tried to play down his report, constantly stating the initial nature of the document, which he had hoped to improve as other more detailed information became available. As he left the inquiry he passed Brumen in the corridor.

"I hope you remember my instructions regarding FBI/CIA involvement," Metcalf said, almost menacingly.

"Oh sure, I remember alright," replied Brumen.

Brumen had been brought directly from his home to the building in an official car; the shattered bone in his right arm prevented him from driving. On his approach to the conference suite he was directed to wait in a side office whilst Ian Vaughan's debriefing interview video was played to the panel.

When he finally entered the suite, Brumen was directed to a desk on its own in the centre facing the inquiry panel. The preliminaries over, the chairman of the panel spoke.

"Agent Brumen, you are the only survivor of the FBI/CIA team involved in the marine search for the terrorists?"

"Sadly yes, sir," replied Brumen.

George Hammond Braddock looked down at his notes before continuing. "Tell us, whose astute idea it was to search for this group on the waters of the Chesapeake?"

"Ian Vaughan's, sir."

"Really? When was this?"

"On the day he reported to the Morehead City Police Department," said Brumen.

"Before the recommendation from Agent Metcalf?"

"As far as I am aware, Agent Metcalf did not support the idea of a waterborne search."

A ripple of comments flowed around the room.

"There appears to be some confusion here," said Braddock.

"It may speed up proceedin's if I went through the sequence of events that involved CIA Agent Capello, myself and FBI Agent Agnes Gleeson."

Braddock looked to both sides, seeking approval from the panel members.

"I think we all agree to that, Agent Brumen. Please proceed."

It was three o'clock in the afternoon when Brumen started his statement and, except for the overnight recess, he continued uninterrupted through to the following midday.

His statement was followed by the detailed report concerning the weapons that were fired and forensic reports on the bodies recovered. The only other survivor from the launch crew, Leading Seaman Abbott, reinforced Brumen's account of the search and gunfight. During his description of his rescue from the burning wheelhouse by Ian Vaughan, Abbott became quite emotional.

Marine Lieutenant Travis and bomb disposal officer Captain Fraser Fawkes Jnr finished the military and FBI/CIA field staff evidence. At this point the panel switched to interviewing members of the power station staff who had been involved with the maintenance and commissioning work undertaken by TN Nuclear. Following this, the staff that remained on duty at the power station, during the desperate but successful emergency shut down, were called and gave what information they could. The only two men involved in the emergency shutdown who were not called, were the Chief Engineer, Steffan Etchells and TN Nuclear's Commissioning Foreman, Harry Burton. They were still in hospital receiving treatment for severe radiation exposure. Finally the FBI/CIA executive were questioned as to their actions and input to the operation.

On day six Metcalf was asked to return to the inquiry. As he entered the room Ariyoshi hardly recognised him as the same man that had picked him up from his hotel the day after he had arrived. Pale and gaunt, Metcalf sat himself at the witness desk, head bowed, shuffling his notes nervously.

"Agent Metcalf, since your testimony last week, this panel has heard from many witnesses, including Agent Brumen, Mr Ian Vaughan, Leading Seaman Abbott, Lieutenant Travis and Captain Fraser Fawkes Jnr. Though their statements appear to be corroborative, your version of events appears out of step; in fact I would go as far as to say it is totally misleading," said George

Hammond Braddock, before peering at Metcalf over the top of his spectacles. "Can you offer any reason as to why your evidence is so different?"

"As I repeatedly stated at my previous appearance here, I had not completed my internal enquiries and therefore had made one or two assumptions based on the very limited information I had available," replied Metcalf, now sweating profusely.

"Director Mitchells, you have two questions to ask of Agent Metcalf, I believe," Braddock said, craning his head round to look in the direction of a bald hard-faced man seated on the extreme right of the panel.

"I have indeed Mr Chairman." The man paused for a moment or two, fixing Metcalf with a hostile stare. "Agent Metcalf, can you explain to us why you claim to have ordered the marine search when Agent Brumen insists that he and agent Capello of the CIA had to go to a higher authority to achieve this?"

"Mr Chairman, this was a highly unusual situation; I could not immediately justify the enormous expense, based on the word of a lone sailor offering some vague suggestion of a terrorist threat," said Metcalf. "My initial assessment was that, should a terrorist group come to these shores in a small sailing craft, it would be unlikely that they could pursue an effective attack from such a vessel."

"So you were not, as you claimed earlier, the initiator of the marine search."

"Probably not, no," mumbled Metcalf.

"Speak up man. Yes or no?" snapped Mitchells.

"No," replied Metcalf, this time loud enough for all to hear.

"My second question relates to a statement made by Captain Fraser Fawkes in which he said that Mr Vaughan, in a mobile phone conversation with you, strongly recommended that the reactor at Mission Creek be put on emergency shutdown."

Metcalf went to speak, but Mitchells held up his hand.

"Agent Metcalf, there is no record of you passing this, seemingly sound advice, to your superiors, who were overseein' the whole of this operation."

"Mr Vaughan is a sailor, not an expert in the control systems of nuclear power stations. I therefore contacted the Chief Engineer at Mission Creek, who advised me that sabotage, of the nature suggested by Mr Vaughan, was highly improbable. He did say that, in view of my contact, he would instigate tests to prove that they had full control of the reactor," replied Metcalf, his jaw stuck out belligerently.

"You obviously do not read the briefing reports of your field operatives, Agent Metcalf. Had you done so, you would have learnt from Agent Brumen's report, submitted, I see, the day after Mr Vaughan landed at Morehead City, that the man is an experienced engineer and project manager," retorted Mitchells angrily. "Mr Vaughan, in fact, only sails as a pastime."

Muttering, in the body of the room, required the chairman to use his gavel, to bring the inquiry to order.

"I would go further and suggest that, had you respected your field agents, you would have also taken Mr Vaughan's advice seriously and passed it on to superiors. As a result, your failure has cost lives and the immeasurable cost of a nuclear power station; all of which could have been saved had you followed the correct procedure and reported to your superiors."

Metcalf flushed in annoyance. "I would put it to the panel that I acted correctly in seeking the advice and guidance of an expert. At that stage of the operation it would have been a serious overreaction to order the shutdown of such an important utility."

"I would put it to you, Agent Metcalf, that such a decision was not yours to take, but that of your superiors!" shouted Mitchells.

Metcalf stared back, stony-faced, obviously not in agreement with the criticism.

"May I clarify some timings?" asked a slim, tanned, uniformed member of the panel, directly to the left of the chairman.

"Certainly Admiral Sheldon," replied the chairman.

"I have been looking at phone records covering conversations held using Captain Fraser Fawkes' mobile. At 1606 hours on the day of the final attack, Captain Fraser Fawkes contacted Lieutenant Petter at headquarters and requested Petter to locate you, Agent Metcalf. According to Lieutenant Petter's telephone log he contacted your secretary, er, Iris Chambers, at 1612 hours and was put through to you in a meeting at 1615 hours." Sheldon looked across at Metcalf with a puzzled expression on his face.

"Bearing in mind the urgency of the message conveyed to you, by Lieutenant Petter, can you explain why you delayed contacting Captain Fraser Fawkes until 1631 hours?"

The room was hushed, everyone's eyes upon Metcalf.

"I – er – there was only a short delay between me responding to the call and then taking action by contacting Chief Engineer Etchells at the power station."

The expression on Sheldon's face turned from puzzlement to anger. "Your phone records show that there was a further fifteen minute delay between you finishing the conversation with the Captain and Mr Vaughan and you dialling the number to the power station. Ignoring station telephone operator delays, this still totals thirty-one minutes' delay, directly attributable to you."

Metcalf looked down dejectedly and shrugged.

"Who were the other people in that all important meeting with you?"

"Incident Director Johnson and Senior Agents Inglemann and Delmano," replied Metcalf.

"In fact the very people you should have passed Mr Vaughan's comments and advice to," said Sheldon. "Which leads me to my final comment. Agent Metcalf, this panel has heard expert testimony that the Mission Creek emergency shutdown procedure takes only five minutes. Yes, five minutes to initiate irreversibly."

Metcalf's expression was blank. He was now realising that he was going to be the scapegoat and that his career was over, but there was more to come.

"Mr Leverson," said Chairman Braddock. "I understand you have questions for Agent Metcalf."

"Thank you Mr Chairman. Agent Metcalf, we have learnt from Agent Brumen's statement to this panel, that just prior to the commencement of the waterborne search, permission was granted by your superiors for Mr Vaughan to take an active part. Can you explain to this panel the grounds on which you chose to rescind that decision?"

"After consideration I believed that my agents had sufficient information with which to identify the terrorists, and that Mr Vaughan would have been placed at undue risk. Had the terrorists been captured, his evidence and ability to identify them would have been crucial."

"Agent Metcalf, our agencies were well aware of the group's identities. Had they been captured, corroboration of who they were would have been simple," Leverson paused, and then said, "You appreciate that it was Mr Vaughan, whose suggested direction of the search, led to the tracking down of the terrorists."

Metcalf shrugged again but said nothing.

"That fact is obviously lost on you I see."

"General Forbes, do you wish to ask anything?" asked Braddock.

"Agent Metcalf, in your report you clearly state that your team were responsible for the shootin' of the terrorists, both afloat and at their beach hideout."

A cold chill settled over Metcalf's stomach. Now he knew that Brumen had set him up by withholding information concerning the gun battle between the navy launch and the terrorists' yacht on the Potomac. "I assumed that as no weapon was fired by either sailor or soldier on that day, the deaths of the terrorists must have been the result of fire from my field operatives."

"This inquiry is not interested in your assumptions, Agent Metcalf, especially as they have been misleading and have caused a great deal of confusion," said the General, glaring over his glasses.

Metcalf appeared to shrink, then sitting up straight said, "I apologise to the panel, but lacking any opportunity to adequately debrief my only surviving field agent present on the day, I felt that my conclusion was the only one possible. The weapons fired were all FBI issue; had I been allowed time to conduct a proper team debriefing and assessment, I am sure these issues would have been clearer."

"Why then did you personally issue your report to Incident Director Johnson before such enquiries had been made?"

Metcalf appeared to crumple again.

Not receiving an answer to his question, the General continued, "According to the lab report on the guns fired, there were only two weapons used. The first was a .38 calibre issued to Agent Brumen but, on the day, held by Agent Gleeson. This weapon accounted for the death of the terrorist Yunis Madadhah. The other weapon was a Magnum .44 that, records show, was issued to Agent Gleeson but fired by Mr Vaughan. This weapon accounted for the death of Fumiko Hamaura and a young woman at present unidentified, but believed to be a member of the gang, and the wounding of Hiroshi Yamada." The General looked up at Metcalf. "The autopsy conducted on Yamada confirms that he actually died from a hard blow to the left temple, which ended the desperate struggle on board the yacht between this Yamada and Mr Vaughan."

Metcalf just stared ahead, his face expressionless, his brain unable to take in anymore.

Tossing his notes onto the panel bench, General Forbes lent back in his seat, then with no small hint of sarcasm said, "This inquiry has no record of Mr Vaughan becoming an employee of either the FBI or CIA and him being assigned to your section."

Then the chairman, Braddock, spoke. "Mr Metcalf –" Metcalf's head jerked up to face the chairman, it was the title 'mister' that had penetrated his consciousness, "– earlier today I received the sad news that Chief Engineer Frank Etchells died in the early hours of this morning. His death, from radiation poisoning, was a direct result of the exposure he endured during his courageous efforts to regain control of the reactor area at Mission Creek. His efforts, combined with those of TN Nuclear's engineer Harry Burton, avoided a nuclear meltdown. I know that everyone present here today will appreciate the apocalyptic proportions that such a catastrophe would have caused."

Metcalf buried his head in his hands. The room went completely silent, no coughing, chair creaking or foot shuffling, not a sound, until, after several seconds had passed, the chairman signalled to two security staff to come forward and escort Metcalfe from the room. As the doors closed behind them, the chairman announced that the inquiry would go into recess whilst the panel prepared their report on the findings.

Two versions of the report were issued. The first, and more widely circulated, was a sanitised version removing all references to Ian Vaughan at his personal request. Ian desperately wanted to protect his family from press intrusion into their lives. The second and more detailed report was issued under restriction, the number of copies being limited to only the highest rank of the services involved, plus one copy to the President's office. All were marked 'Secret and Confidential'.

On the day copies of the more detailed report were issued, female staff on the second floor of the White House found themselves inconvenienced by the 'Out of Order' sign on their washroom door. Tests of the door handle proved that it had been locked. Had they gained access they would have discovered the dispatch clerk, Abel McPherson, hard at work. However no one questioned why, they just accepted the inconvenience and went down a level to use the facilities there. Digital photography is a wonderful thing, permitting detailed pictures to be taken in light conditions that a conventional film camera could not attempt. The 427-page report took nearly two hours to photograph. Two hours work for $1,000 was, Abel thought, a generous reward, especially as the man had promised a special bonus. Putting the package back into the 'Security Cleared' pouch, he slid it under his overalls. He then removed the memory card from the camera, lifted the bucket, mop and plunger, unlocked the washroom door and, removing the sign, walked down the corridor to the men's washroom. Entering the cubicle furthest away from the main downpipe, he undid the access plate for the drain rod, wiped his fingerprints off the digital camera and slipped it into the pipe. Using the plunger he gave the camera a sharp shove, sending it slithering along the drain, hoping that subsequent toilet flushes would take it away from the building altogether. After replacing the plate he took off the overalls, leaving them, together with the mop, bucket and plunger in the janitor's room along the corridor. McPherson then hurriedly made his way to the President's Chief of Staff's office, where he left the package with a secretary. On his return to the Post Room Glenda Armitage bawled him out for wasting time talking.

"I was not talkin'. Last night I was eatin' in de chilli house two blocks down from my place. I won't be eatin' dere again," he replied, holding his stomach. "I'm sorry but I gotta get home, I feel real bad."

"Just you clock out now, Abel. Why is it every time we're busy, you find some excuse eh?"

Abel McPherson gave her a hurt look, then turned and, picking up his lunch box, made a moaning sound and rushed off in the direction of the nearest washroom.

Watching him disappear along the corridor, Glenda Armitage shook her head. "I just don't know why they employed him, he hasn't done a decent day's work since he's been here."

In the washroom cubicle, McPherson opened his lunch box and taped the camera memory card to the inside of the sandwich wrapping, placed the metal teaspoon between it and the plastic yoghurt pot and closed the lid. After clocking out he had to pass security. Sweating, he put the lunch box on the X-ray conveyor and stepped through the security arch. As his box emerged, a security guard reached forward, opened the lid and looked inside. Seeing the spoon he closed the box again and handed it to McPherson. Fifteen minutes later Abel McPherson was strolling through Lafayette Park; his route took him past a bench on which an oriental man was seated, reading *The Wall Street Journal*. Sitting down near to the man, Abel McPherson placed his lunch box on the bench between them. The oriental man responded by placing an identical lunch box next to it. Folding the paper, the man picked up McPherson's box and opened the lid. Removing the sandwich, he unwrapped it, nodded, put it back in the box and closed the lid.

Reaching down, Abel picked up the other box and opened it. On top was also a sandwich, which he removed to reveal ten crisp 100-dollar notes on top of a clear plastic bag of what looked like flour.

"Hey is dis de bonus I think it is?" asked Abel, with a wide smile on his face.

The oriental man nodded, then standing, walked away, to be swallowed up in the lunchtime crowd enjoying the sunshine.

Following the strict instructions he had received by phone, Abel picked up the sandwich and ate it before completing his journey home.

*   *   *

Leroy Bones was sprawled naked across the bed they shared as Abel came into the room. "Hey wot you doin' dis time o' day?"

Kicking two empty beer cans under the bed, Abel tossed the lunch box to his gay lover. "Look in dare man. I felt de need for a long, long weekend."

Leroy opened the box and gave a low whistle. "How much is dare man?"

"Five hundred dollars," he said, having stashed the other five hundred behind the gas meter. "Look at de bag underneath."

Putting the money to one side, Leroy opened the plastic bag, took a pinch of the white powder inside and sniffed it in deeply. "Wow man, dis is some good shit."

Across town Dr Higashi, sitting in the back seat of his car, put the memory card into his camera and connected that to his laptop computer. He was impressed; the despatch clerk had done well. Higashi read a few, randomly selected, pages of the document and, satisfied that sufficient information was included for Hamaura and Murata, he carefully disconnected the link and requested his wife to drive them back to the clinic. As they left the city, heading south, Higashi mused on the events of the last few weeks. How sad it was that, after all his hard work, Fumiko Hamaura should die on the day she had left his care. Then had come the demand from her brother and Murata for information. At least now he was out of Murata's debt. No more nervous weeks treating and hiding criminals. Higashi contentedly closed his eyes. Yes, even the Abel McPherson contact would be secured. No way would he survive the weekend. Yes, that, for Abel, was going to be a trip too far.

*   *   *

At New Scotland Yard, Campbell's secretary, Mrs Fitzgerald, was transferring a call to his office.

"Excuse me Commander, I have the American Ambassador on the phone for you."

With a sigh Campbell lifted the receiver. "Campbell here."

"This is James Beaumont, Commander, look, may I call you Alec? I feel that our work together on the Murata affair has earned a greater friendship than the diplomatically formal."

"Yes, of course you may," replied Campbell, feeling somewhat uneasy and out of his normal comfort zone.

"You had better call me James; Jackie gets a little annoyed when my old college friends call me Jim," said Beaumont, laughing. "Anyway Alec, I am phoning to give you my personal invitation to a dinner, here at the Embassy, for all of those closely connected to the Murata affair. Now that includes you and a partner plus Jackson and his wife and, of course, Mr Saints and his wife."

Campbell was on the point of explaining that he would not be bringing a partner, when a thought occurred to him.

"That is very kind of you, er, James. When is it and what time etc.?" asked Campbell.

"On the twenty seventh, in the evening at seven o'clock; formal dress, as I have an important announcement to make. The President wants me to use the occasion to highlight the need for this level of international intelligence exchange on terrorist activity," Beaumont said with a note of pride in his voice. There was a pause, and then he said, "Alec, I was hoping that Mr and Mrs Vaughan would join the party, but we have been unable to make contact with them."

"Are we on a secure line, er, James?"

"Oh, yes."

"Good. You see due to the release, in Tokyo, of Fumiko Hamaura's brother and her cousin, Kimura, we have thought it best to get the Vaughan family into a safe location."

"You really believe that they are in danger?" asked Beaumont.

"Yes. Our understanding of the two who were released is that they will probably make their way here and try to obtain the release of Murata. Should they arrive here it is possible that they will seek out the Vaughans, either as hostages, or purely to avenge the death of Hamaura's sister."

"I see." There was a pause. "This is a very sad business Alec. What that family has been through so far, and still it appears not to be over," Beaumont's tone reflected his regret. "Maybe sometime in the future I will be able to meet them and express my personal thanks."

"I would hope so, James. There is no doubt that they have all been very brave."

The formal invitations arrived the next day by courier and Campbell had strolled down to Jackson's office to check that he would attend. On his way back WPC Tucker passed him in the corridor. "Um, er, Caroline?" he called after her. Caroline Tucker stopped and slowly turned around to face him.

"Me sir?"

"Yes, I was wondering whether you had anything planned for Friday the twenty seventh, in the evening?"

Tucker took out her i-pad and studied her calendar entries.

"No sir, I don't think so, but it will be PC Wheatley's shift sir, I could ask him to switch, if you require."

"No, it's not that; I've been invited to attend a formal dinner at the American Embassy, in connection with the Murata case, and wondered if you would be able to come along as my partner," he said, feeling somewhat shy and more than a little nervous. "I thought, as you were part of the team." His voice faded away as he realised the stupidity of adding the last comment. It wasn't anything to do with her being in the team, it was because he liked her and somehow felt better when he was near her.

Her pale blue eyes looked away from him. "I regret my wardrobe doesn't run to formal embassy functions sir," she replied, by way of a decline to the invitation.

Campbell was about to offer to buy any dress she desired when Mrs Fitzgerald appeared at his side. "I have the head of the CPS on the phone, sir. He said it was very urgent."

"I'll come straight away," he replied, before looking back at Caroline Tucker and saying, "Excuse me, I must attend to this."

"Of course, sir."

On the way back to his office he tried to understand why he had issued the invitation. He had been to many functions since his wife died, always on his own; why did he choose this occasion to take a partner?

In his office he picked up the phone. “Campbell here.”

“Duncan Gabriel, Commander, I’ve just had the PM on the phone, telling me that the States are issuing an extradition order on Murata. Have you heard anything about it?”

“No, Sir Duncan, I haven’t.”

“He has said that we should not proceed with the prosecution of this Murata character as the extradition may well make the process a waste of time.”

“Are you suggesting that their legal process take precedence over ours, Sir Duncan?”

“No, most certainly not,” replied Sir Duncan with an offended tone. “And besides the order would have to include a guarantee that Murata would not be executed, even if their sentence is the death penalty.”

“Then I suggest that we proceed on Tuesday as planned. The diplomatic issue concerning the extradition is something that both the current Home Secretary and Shadow Home Secretary must agree on during this run-up to an election. Frankly I cannot see Charlotte Brightwell going along with it, without at least testing it through the press, and that will take time.” Campbell knew that frequently politicians would release such information and wait for press and public response before making a decision such as this; especially at a time when votes at the ballot box could switch sides over such an issue.

“Good thinking Commander. I shall contact her straight away and sound the waters.”

As Campbell put down the phone he smiled with satisfaction. It was always nice to thwart politicians when they were trying to circumvent the law purely to protect their party’s reputation.

*　　　　*　　　　*

"Come on through to the kitchen dear, the Commander is just finishing his breakfast," said Mrs Craven as she answered the front door of Campbell's home the following morning.

WPC Tucker had never been invited into the kitchen before. "Tea dear?" Mrs Craven asked. WPC Tucker nodded.

"Thank you, that would be nice."

"The Commander was very disappointed that you felt you couldn't go as his partner to this embassy thing," said Mrs Craven in a motherly sort of way. "He was so annoyed with himself for not considering the short notice to get a dress and that sort of thing," she continued diplomatically.

"It wasn't that Mrs Craven. At the moment I just can't afford evening dresses," Tucker replied. "Also he only asked me as he wanted me to feel part of the team when, well, I'm not really, I just act as one of his drivers."

"You know, I don't think the team thing was anything to do with it," replied Mrs Craven, as she placed a cup of tea on the table in front of Tucker. "In all the years I've known him after his wife died, I've never known of him inviting another lady to a function, and he gets to quite a few in a year."

Mrs Craven's comment made Caroline feel strange. It wasn't fear or even nervous excitement; for the first time she started to think of her boss, Alec Campbell, in a more personal way.

"I'll just take this toast through to the Commander. Pour yourself another cuppa if you need one," and with that, Mrs Craven left the kitchen.

Caroline sipped her tea and thought yet again about the polite, highly intelligent and yes, mildly good-looking man she worked for. In the months during which she had been attached to the section, she had grown to like him, yes, but had never considered any contact outside of work. She thought hard about why she was even considering a personal friendship with such a senior figure, before silently admonishing herself. Of course she could consider it, she was well educated and came from a good middle-class family, it was not as though, socially, they were poles apart. She then suddenly recalled, without understanding why, the moment she had learnt of the death of Yunis Madadhah, the man responsible for the death of Colin and the boys. That instant even now seemed strange. She had felt as if she had lost something, or was it that she had let go of something? Whichever it was, maybe now was the time to move on. The man who had killed her wonderful husband and lovely sons was dead. Was there any real reason for her to continue pushing to become a full member of the Antiterrorist Branch? Was there any reason for her to continue a career in the police?

"My daughter... oh, sorry dear, did I make you jump?" Mrs Craven's return had caught Caroline by surprise and made her spill a few drops of tea onto the floor. "It's alright dear, I'll clean that up in a jiffy. Now, as I was saying, my daughter manages one of these boutiques and she's always offering to sell at cost price to me. If you like, I'll have a word with her."

Caroline went to make a polite refusal when the door opened and the Commander walked in.

"Ah, here you are. I see that you have been admitted to the inner sanctum. Only the very privileged get such an opportunity," said Campbell with a broad grin.

"Don't you take any notice dear," retorted Mrs Craven. "And remember what I said, Annette would be only too pleased to help."

As they waited at traffic lights before crossing Westminster Bridge, Campbell broke the silence that had existed since they had driven away from his house. "Annette, er, Mrs Craven's daughter, runs a boutique, I believe."

"I believe she does, sir," replied Tucker, wondering what her answer would be to the next question. She quickly looked into the rear-view mirror and saw Campbell staring out of the side window, smiling.

"May I hope that you are reconsidering my invitation?"

"It is a possibility," she replied, trying hard not to smile. Then, noting that the traffic lights were changing in their favour, she accelerated the car across the line towards the bridge.

* * *

Mrs Fitzgerald was waiting for Campbell by the lifts. "The United States have formally issued an extradition order for Murata, sir."

"You came down here just to tell me that?"

"I wanted you to know as soon as possible. The Prime Minister's office have been on the phone three times already this morning."

"It is a matter for the CPS and Home Secretary to sort out," said Campbell. "The next time they phone, I want you to tell them that, and to tell them I am not able to get involved."

"I fear that we will be pestered with this until they get their way, sir," said Mrs Fitzgerald.

"No we won't," said Campbell. "I want you to cancel all of my appointments for today. I am going to take a day's leave. If they ask, I've gone fishing."

"But, sir."

"When did I last take a day's leave?"

"Between Christmas and New Year," she replied promptly. "But won't they be annoyed if you take a day out when this event has occurred?"

"Yes," replied Campbell, smiling broadly. "They most surely will."

As anticipated, the Shadow Home Secretary rejected the notion of complying with the American request immediately, supporting Sir Duncan Gabriel's stance that British justice must be seen to be done as a priority. The press were informed immediately.

The government put a heavy emphasis on the severity of the terrorist group's crimes in America and the need to show solidarity in the fight against terrorism. The opposition predictably offered the counter argument. They claimed that extradition should only be considered after a trial and sentencing had taken place in Britain. A trial would ensure that, in the unlikely case of Murata being acquitted by an American court, his arrest and immediate return to a British jail would be assured.

As Campbell strolled along the towpath by the River Thames above Marlow, broadcasters and other news pundits were having a field day discussing the legal and moral points of both arguments.

One thing was guaranteed however: the initial hearing would go ahead as planned. On Campbell's return home, late that evening, a harassed Mrs Craven greeted him at the front door.

"Where have you been? Every man and his cousin have been phoning, even the PM."

"Good evening, Mrs Craven. Am I to understand that you have had a busy day?" replied Campbell, with a mischievous grin.

"I most certainly have! It's all very well you standing there, smiling, but I didn't find it very funny. Anyway where have you been? Why all this panic to speak to you? The only thing on the news has been this extradition thing."

"You recall me mentioning that Oliver Makepeace's son was involved in this chap Murata's gang?"

"Yes, I do. You didn't seem too surprised at the time."

"I wasn't, anyway, details regarding his association with the gang are likely to come out during the initial hearing of Murata's case. That was the real cause of the resignation of Oliver Makepeace, from the post of Home Secretary. The Prime Minister is anxious to keep the details under wraps until after the election, to avoid further embarrassment to the Government at a crucial vote-catching time," Campbell explained, confident in his housekeeper's complete discretion.

"Well really, fancy them trying to cover that up. They won't be getting my vote next time, that's for sure. Have you had an evening meal yet?"

Chapter 4

Hamaura and Iwaki found crossing the Pacific hard with only Kimura unaffected by the trawler's motion. The remote beach landing was not without incident, as the two seasickness sufferers clung to the sides of the semi-inflatable ship's tender. A stiff onshore breeze was blowing, driving large clouds across the sky, and obscuring the full moon. A deckhand from the deep-sea trawler directed the craft towards the surf, which was breaking some way out before racing up the sands. Suddenly he cut the throttle and turned the craft round, swivelling as he did so to keep his eye on some object on the beach.

"There is someone there," he said with a note of alarm.

Hamaura strained to look past him, but could see nothing.

Kimura reached into his bag and produced a small pair of binoculars, flicked the lens caps off and focused on the beach. "Ah," he said, chuckling. "We have very honourable greeter to meet us."

"Who?" Hamaura demanded to know. "There was no mention someone meeting us," he continued, with a note of deep suspicion.

"Grizzly bears make up their own minds who they greet. We will have to wait for a time or move into next bay."

For ten minutes they rode the waves waiting for the bear to lose interest and go back into the forest behind the beach. Eventually the animal sauntered south along the sand and, climbing some rocks on the point, disappeared from view.

The deckhand got the tender as close in as he could, but that still left the trio to wade, in chest-deep breaking surf, to dry land, holding their belongings above their heads.

As Hamaura dumped his bag on the dry sand above the tide line, he turned and looked back, scanning the ocean. The small craft had been swallowed up in the dark troughs between the waves; only a vague dark form of the trawler was visible.

"This way," growled Iwaki, heading towards the north-east corner of the beach, a gun in his hand. The others followed obediently each looking from side to side fearing the surprise return of the bear. At the tree line they found a track leading away from the beach and followed it; after half a mile or so, they came to a large clearing. Iwaki switched on a torch and started to inspect the ground. *"Ah, domo domo,"* he said, as he carefully followed faint tracks leading to a bush between two large trees.

"Come, help pull this undergrowth out of way," he ordered.

The sharp prickly leaves of the holly tree, combined with the thorny bramble stems made the task painful and time consuming in the dark. Eventually they cleared enough to expose a camouflage net, the removal of which revealed a Jeep, not new, but in good shape.

Iwaki searched under the rear kerbside wheel arch and triumphantly held up a small canvas bag. Opening the drawstring neck of the bag he tipped the contents onto the Jeep's bonnet. In the torchlight they could see two sets of ignition keys and three badges, naming them as employees of Takashima Exploration (Canada) Inc. Iwaki handed out the badges.

In the Jeep they found safety shoes and suitably logo'd warm jackets and hard hats.

"We wait until mid morning before we leave," said Iwaki. "Leaving now could draw attention if there is anyone nearby."

The sun was well above the horizon by the time that Kimura turned the key in the Jeep's ignition and powered the vehicle the two miles up the track to what passed as a road. They were heading east, across Vancouver Island to Port Hardy and its airport; the almost deserted roads an extraordinary experience compared with what they were used to in Japan. Near Port Hardy they checked in at the Airport Inn.

Kimura and Hamaura shared a room, leaving Iwaki gratefully on his own. He needed time to think and to plan. Would Murata accept his terms for support? Shared leadership and differing objectives had been the cause of Murata's current situation. Would he, like Iwaki, agree to the involvement of North Korean interests? Iwaki believed fervently that political objective transcended national border. Could he persuade Murata to support his call to unite South East Asia and Japan to achieve the objective of casting out royalist and capitalist ideals and bring equality to all men?

At breakfast, two Korean men joined them, both dressed as Takashima Exploration employees. Iwaki surprised his companions by speaking fluently to the new arrivals in their own language. Breakfast over they checked out, but waited in reception. Within minutes a man entered wearing a uniform bomber jacket with a gold wing above the left breast pocket. Looking around he approached the group.

"Itoh-san?" he asked.

Iwaki sprang to his feet. "I am Itoh," he lied. "You are Aidan Robertson?"

"Yeah, pleased to meet you. If you are ready, I have filed a flight plan so we should be able to take off straight away after loadin'. There are still just three of you comin'?" Robertson asked.

"Yes, just these two and myself. The others are our local staff, just delivering seismology equipment for us."

"That's good cos we are on the limits of payload to flight distances," said Robertson, feeling a little anxious about the task ahead. "Say, why is it you are hiring me to cross Canada, when it woulda' been a lot cheaper and much quicker to go one hop scheduled flight?"

Speed was not the essence, Iwaki wanted low security, and if possible, anonymity.

"Ah, you see my company want me to report on several prospective centres for our future exploration work. Hotels, offices to let, that type of thing."

"Oh sure, I get it, you're the reconnaissance team."

"That is correct."

"Well I know several of these towns so if you need any help just give a shout."

"Thank you, but I have clear instruction from Head Office."

At the airport, security was minimal, as Iwaki had expected, and their cargo was loaded, after weighing, without any problem. Taking the Koreans to one side, Iwaki produced a white canvas bag containing $30,000 from his rucksack and handed it to the senior man. “It is all there as agreed, plus a small bonus, you have done well.”

Iwaki and his two companions ran across the airfield apron, holding their jacket hoods in place against the wind and rain. Boarding the plane all three were surprised to see a pretty and shapely stewardess waiting just inside the door to greet them. Robertson Air wanted to make a good impression, in the hope of further well paid work.

Cargo secured and passengers buckled into their seats, the Dash 6 engines were started and clearance for take-off requested. As the aircraft taxied towards the northernmost point of the runway configuration, Iwaki noticed the lustful expression on Hamaura’s face as he eyed the stewardess. “Hamaura-san. If you make one move towards that lady or treat her in any way disrespectfully, I will kill you. Do you understand?”

This had been said in Japanese, Iwaki looking straight at Hamaura with a big smile on his face.

Reluctantly Hamaura tore his eyes away from the enchanting Elsbeth Hamilton. *“Hi wakarimasu.”* (I understand.)

“We must appear to be worthy of a respectable company. Any bad behaviour could destroy our cover,” continued Iwaki. “You will remember that, until this is over and your debt repaid.”

* * *

In London Jirou Ishihara studied the report in amazement. Murata must have some very bad *Kami* (spirit) following him for this man Vaughan to cross his path. Idly he wondered what Fumiko’s brother would do. Ishihara knew that he was often reckless and totally out of control. The Ghost will have a hard task to keep him in check.

His meeting the following day with Murata was interesting, in that the man seemed to respect Vaughan’s interference and actions, as if he had been a worthy contestant in a sumo wrestling contest. In truth, Murata did not hold a grudge, recognising that anyone had the right to fight back when his or her family were threatened. Any anger he reserved for Fumiko Hamaura and Yunis Madadhah, who appeared to have allowed Vaughan to make his incredible escape.

"Why did she do it?" Murata growled.

"Why did she do what?" asked Ishihara.

"When all our demands were met; why did she trigger punishment phase."

Ishihara shook his head. "I do not know, but such action has put you in bad situation. The Americans will want to exact the ultimate punishment."

"Maybe she wanted to show herself as leader," Murata said, not appearing to have heard the other man's comment.

"Prosecution lawyer say they are expecting extradition application any day now. In fact he does not know why they have delayed so long."

"Nothing will happen before court hearing takes place here," said Murata confidently. "English government have called election, no quick decision will be made by them during such time."

The two men sat in silence, each contemplating the future, which for Murata it was at least jail, for Ishihara the uncertainty of exposure and the consequences of that. Again he looked at his notes on English legal procedure.

"When we first met, Murata-san, you intended to plead not guilty. Are you sure you wish to change that plea?" Ishihara asked.

"Of course, here I am only charged with double murder and kidnapping. In America they will charge me with terrorism and probably multiple murder," Murata replied. "Here I will go to prison, there I will probably be shamed by execution."

"I have sent petition to British Home Secretary, claiming that you were not involved in attack in America, and if brought to trial there you would not receive fair hearing."

Murata nodded his approval. "With Hamaura, Yamada and Madadhah all dead there would be no one to counter such statement."

"The Ghost has a plan," confided Ishihara. "I do not know detail. All I know is that it relies on him arriving here before your extradition."

Murata nodded. The Ghost, he thought, what would be his price? Which side was he really on? Always questions, questions, never honest answers; how he hated this war between the two factions. Neither he nor that ideologically vacant Yamamoto knew whom they could really trust. He had been sure of Fumiko Hamaura, but now he had grave doubts as to her loyalty and intentions. Not for the first time did Murata sense paranoia twisting his thoughts.

As Ishihara left Belmarsh Prison, he was also considering trust and loyalty. Would Yamamoto, the banker, accept him back into his circle, or would he be cast out like the others who had taken Murata-san's side in the faction infighting? Their fate had not been pleasant; most had met an untimely end or been betrayed and imprisoned. These thoughts troubled him throughout the day until he made a conscious and definite decision, to wait for the Ghost.

* * *

Much earlier that same morning, Penny Heathcote was reaching down two fine china mugs from the top kitchen cupboard. "Indian or green?" she asked.

"Oh, green please."

"It only comes with echinacea."

"Pardon?"

"It is a flowering herb added to the green tea for good health. It is said to raise the activity of the blood's T-cells which fight infections such as colds and flu."

"Oh is that so?" said Morohashi. "Please, I will try."

"I only bother with a cup of tea in the flat of a morning. On the way to the office I invariably stop at Tom's Kitchen. Great breakfasts there," said Penny. "Saves coming home to a lot of washing up."

Umeko Morohashi smiled. "That is fine, when do we have to leave?"

"In ten minutes, if that is okay."

"Mm, yes, I will go and dress."

Penny watched fascinated as her guest rose and gracefully left the kitchen, leaving the gentle swishing sound of silk briefly hanging in the air.

They stepped out into a beautiful day with clear blue skies and the streets washed clean by the overnight rain. They walked the half-mile to Tom's Kitchen, stopping occasionally to look in shop windows. Umeko tried the full English breakfast, but in spite of the delicious flavours and excellent standard of cooking, found the quantity too much and left a quarter of it on her plate. The meal having taken longer than Penny had planned meant them hurrying through the side streets to DELCO Publishing plc.

"Good morning Lorna."

"Hello," came a dull reply from the young lady behind the reception desk.

"We have a new member of staff, would you go through the normal induction with her?" Penny asked, before turning to Umeko, and, without waiting for Lorna's response, said, "Lorna will run through the usual checks, just to make sure you are who you say you are. Nothing personal, everyone has to go through this."

During the next two hours, Umeko Morohashi and Lorna filled in forms, took retina scans, finger and palm prints, all of which crosschecked with secure route information from Tokyo.

Umeko could not help comparing her two new colleagues. Penny, diminutive with a bright and bubbly persona was in complete contrast to Lorna who was tall and slender, with a pale face and languid eyes. She held her head on one side, as if she lacked the strength to keep it upright. In response to questions she would give a shrug that made her arms flail about her, seemingly uncontrolled. Her voice was well modulated and her language erudite but, unsettlingly, she appeared to be totally humourless.

During the course of the session Lorna had dealt with two visitors. Each had been met with the same disinterested, dull greeting, which ensured their swift departure.

Umeko Morohashi smiled to herself. Yes, she could not think of anyone more suitable to be the DELCO Publishing plc's receptionist. No budding author would wish to entrust their precious manuscript into the hands of a company with such a dull and negative front office presence.

*　　　　*　　　　*

"In view of the events that led up to the arrest of Murata, we are very concerned for the safety of Sarah Vaughan and her two daughters," explained Commander Campbell to Morohashi over a working lunch with the DELCO team.

"Really Commander, why would you believe them to be in danger now?"

DS Weaver, sitting opposite her, looked up with interest.

"Sarah Vaughan in particular would be a devastating witness against any denial Murata may be considering," replied Campbell.

Morohashi was beginning to like this man. He was approachable and keen to listen to his team, to whom he was polite, not bullying. Underlying this was a sharp brain and steely resolve, together with firm discipline that kept his team on their toes. Yes, Penny was right, he was a good boss.

"I understand that the family have been moved to another 'safe house'," said Morohashi.

"Yes, we thought that, with the possibility of Hamaura's brother and cousin slipping into this country, we should do what we could to protect them."

"That is very interesting," she replied. "As you know we have been tracking this group for some years, but they have always managed to stay one step in front of us. However, in the course of that time we have learnt a lot about how they react under certain conditions. Our experience with this group suggests that, in the case of the Kinoko-Kumo attack, the Vaughans were just in the wrong place at the wrong time. Killing or kidnapping Mrs Vaughan, or their daughters, would not be looked upon by Hamaura's brother as either a useful way to free Murata, or a way to exert leverage on the British government." Morohashi hesitated for a moment.

"Commander, something I failed to mention earlier, is that it is quite probable this group will take a senior member of a large Japanese company hostage, here in England, as an attempt to secure the release of Murata. My instructions from Chief Superintendent Ishii are to make contact with such companies and offer warning and advice."

"Do you need any assistance in doing that?" he asked.

"I was thinking this morning that if I posed as DELCO company representative doing sales push, I could hold confidential meeting with the companies concerned, to alert their own security staff, while still remaining undercover."

"What an excellent idea, Lieutenant Commander," said Campbell. "We can issue you with business cards and some brochures, in order to support your cover. We do actually publish some selected technical works from here."

There was a silence between the two for a few minutes, as they ate, then Campbell asked, "What about Ian Vaughan? Would you consider him to be in danger? You only mentioned his wife and daughters earlier."

"Not initially. If Hamaura enters the United Kingdom, his first action will be to free Murata. Hamaura and Kimura have a great debt to repay."

"That would come before taking revenge on Ian Vaughan for the death of his sister?"

"Oh definitely yes. Murata's release would be a matter of honour," Morohashi replied. "Also, would he know that Mr Vaughan was the man who killed his sister?"

"We are not prepared to take the risk that he doesn't," replied Campbell. "Long experience has taught us that any prison has its own information network. I sometimes wish that mine was as good."

"If that is the case they will try to free Murata, then I am sure that Hamaura will search out Mr Vaughan and kill him."

Everyone in earshot stopped eating and turned to stare at her. The shock effect her statement had upon the audience around her was emphasised by her matter-of-fact delivery. Penny Heathcote visibly shuddered.

"You seem very confident of that, Lieutenant Commander," said DS Weaver.

"Yoshi Hamaura has a reputation for holding grudges. He is also a risk taker, which is how he was caught last time. Like his sister he has psychopathic tendencies, though we suspect that he does not have her intelligence," Morohashi said, her facial expression grave.

As the lunch things were being cleared away, Campbell approached Morohashi again. "Are you happy with the accommodation arrangements made for you?" he asked.

"Oh yes, I am very comfortable, and Penny has made me most welcome. Thank you for asking."

"Excellent, I will keep you informed of any intelligence we receive, and I trust that you will keep me advised of anything you hear from Tokyo."

"Of course, Commander."

"As you are probably aware, Lieutenant Heathcote is one of our intelligence analysts, therefore if this goes live, and fieldwork is required, I will probably team you with DS Weaver."

Morohashi nodded in understanding.

"Commander is it possible for me to observe the Japanese lawyer who is supporting or rather defending Murata?"

"Yes of course, but may I ask why?"

"I am afraid that we have some doubts."

"His credentials appeared to be in order, according to our Foreign Office. He will undoubtedly be in court on Monday, for the start of the initial hearing process," said Campbell, his face now showing concern in response to her remark. "I do not advise you attending there, but we can arrange for you to have a good look at him as he enters and exits the building.

"Sergeant Weaver!" called Campbell, interrupting a joke Weaver was relaying to Penny Heathcote in the far corner of the room. "You will be observing the initial hearing on Monday, when Murata is brought up in front of the bench?"

"Yes, sir."

"We will need you to be mic'd up, so that you can alert WPC Tucker and Lieutenant Commander Morohashi when Murata's lawyer is leaving the building."

"Right sir," responded Weaver. "Do you know at what time the case is being called?"

Campbell gave him a withering glare. "May I suggest that you look up the court lists for Monday, Sergeant."

Weaver blushed. "Oh yes, of course. Er, sorry."

Morohashi spent the next two hours on the secure line to Washington, learning of the FBI internal enquiry. Piecing together the information received from Campbell during the morning and Ariyoshi's account of the Stateside operation, she became more fearful for Ian Vaughan.

Leaving the office at six o'clock that evening alongside Penny, Morohashi was quiet.

"You seem a little worried, can I help?" asked Penny.

"Oh no, it is nothing," Umeko replied. "What are we doing this evening?" she asked to cover her concern.

"Lorna is coming round later with some Chinese takeaway. Hope you like it."

"You are friends with Lorna?"

"Oh yes, she's immense fun."

"Really?"

"You will see."

Umeko finally crawled into bed around two in the morning, unable to remember a time when she had laughed so much. The plain dull, humourless girl from reception revealed herself to be a witty, lively and thoroughly charming companion. Her sides aching from so much laughing, Umeko could only wonder at the clever daytime act, faultlessly performed by Lorna.

* * *

The nearly three thousand mile journey took them six days to complete; landing at Leth Bridge, Brandon, Hurst, La Tuque and Charlottetown before the final leg across to Newfoundland's Deer Park Airport. At all but Charlottetown, the three would check into the nearest hotel to the airport, then take a taxi into the town centre, ostensibly to conduct their survey. Twice it provided Hamaura with the opportunity to relieve his frustration, in the company of a street girl, much to Iwaki's displeasure. He did not want anyone remembering their passing through.

The constant drone of the aircraft's engine over the six long days numbed the brain and they were all glad when the journey was over. Few had paid them much attention when on the ground; only at Brandon were any questions asked, but the presentation of false passports and a fake drilling licence got them through.

Iwaki's Korean friends had arranged for a hired pick-up truck to be waiting for them at the airport, and after loading the cargo onto the truck, and tipping Aidan Robertson, the three drove off in the direction of St John's.

The grey skies and torrential rain did a lot to mar their impression of Newfoundland. The drive along a seemingly never-ending view of birch and pine forest or slate-grey waters of the lakes, quickly became boring. It was a surprise therefore when they came to settlements of neat, well-decorated, clapperboard houses, in plain but tidy surroundings.

It was very late when they pulled up outside a rundown looking property, its peeling paint and broken house number board telling a story of neglect. Iwaki got out of the truck and stretched, then flailed his arms and ran on the spot, in an effort to wake himself up. A thin strip of light showed through the gap in the storm shutters that masked the window to the right of the front door. Iwaki knocked, his knuckles sending a small shower of paint flakes to the doorstep.

"Is that you Charlie? Where were you last night? Too drunk to come home I suppose and lost your keys. You'd better be sober or you be sleepin' out there tonight, you hear!"

"Just let me in," replied Iwaki, mimicking a Canadian accent.

To his surprise the door opened to reveal a blonde in her late thirties, dressed in a grubby pink housecoat and black slippers. Her shock at seeing Iwaki delayed her reaction to slam the door shut, allowing him the two seconds required to step into the house, clamp his hand over her mouth, and pin her against the wall.

"You be quiet and sensible, and you will not get hurt. Understand? I want to know where Charles Raymonde is. I have a job for him."

Judging from her eyes that she would co-operate, Iwaki slowly removed his hand.

"I ain't seen him for two days. The bastard has probably got so drunk they slung him in jail again," Brigitte said with some feeling. "Who are you, and what do you want him for?"

"Let us sit down. We will wait for him to return."

"You can't stay here."

"Oh really," Kimura said. "Are you going to stop us?"

Brigitte's eyes flared with hostility but she said nothing.

Iwaki, with unexpected gentleness, guided her across the room and indicated for her to sit in an armchair. "Take the truck and park it round the back, out of sight. Then bring in our kit," he said to the other two.

"What are you gonna do to me?" Brigitte said nervously.

"Nothing," Iwaki replied. "We are just going to wait for your Charlie."

Something in his tone made her shiver.

"He ain't done nothing to hurt you," she said, desperately trying to make some sense of what was going on. "Has he?" she added fearfully.

"We just want him to take us out fishing."

"Well you're goin' about it a bit strange."

The previous evening Brigitte had gone round to Paul le Garde and his brother Matthew's apartment, and begged them to find Charles. The two brothers had been his regular crew since he had gone out on his own and bought *Le Martinpêcheur*, a deep-sea beam trawler. Her pleadings had both men roaming the downtown area of St John's in search of their skipper. It was three o'clock in the morning when Matthew spotted Charles swaying dangerously on the waterside of the steel harbour edge curbing and relieving himself into the waters below. The brothers had taken him back to their apartment and spent four hours forcing black coffee into him and walking him round the streets to sober him up. They knew that Brigitte was close to walking out on the man, who they were sure could not live without her there to help him through the 'black dog days' of depression. The halibut fishing had been good for the last three seasons, and the odd delivery job that the brothers didn't talk about, meant that the trawler was all but paid for. On the face of it, Charles Raymonde should have been the happiest man in the world, and his many friends were baffled as to the cause of these periodic dark moods.

It was eight o'clock when Raymonde thanked his crew and started the walk up the street to his home.

"Gone on a bender again eh?" shouted a woman from her front step two doors down from his house. "Brigitte will walk out on you soon, you mark my words. She's too good for you."

Raymonde ignored her. To his certain knowledge her husband was about to ditch her for a bar girl from The Cotton Club. Climbing the steps to the porch, he went through his pockets in search of his keys. Turning the key in the lock and, pushing the door open, stepped inside.

Three things took him by surprise. The first was that Brigitte was sat in the armchair, when she would normally have been at work. Second, was the sight of a wiry oriental man sat on the coffee table looking coldly but calmly at him, and third was the feel of a gun barrel being pressed into the back of his neck just below the skull.

The wiry oriental stood and took a step towards him. "I am a friend of Fumiko Hamaura," he said.

Behind him Brigitte gave a sharp intake of breath as she recognised the name of the female terrorist, shot whilst attempting an attack in the States.

Raymonde did not react. He had also recognised the name, but had hoped that the recent news of her death would be the last he would ever hear of her.

At a nod from the wiry little man, the gun was removed from his neck.

"You take us to rendezvous south of Iceland. We pay."

"I'm not in that business anymore, Monsieur," Raymonde replied.

The blow to the back of his right leg had Raymonde collapsing to the floor before the kick into his side had him double up in pain.

Brigitte screamed, stopping almost immediately as Iwaki turned on her with his hand raised.

"That was wrong answer," Kimura said to Raymonde, as he stepped back from him towards the door. "Try again."

"Such a journey is impossible without a full crew," said Raymonde.

"Fumiko told me that your crew co-operated well when price was right," Kimura said. "Job is simple. You and your crew take us to place, then you can all make more money by fishing on the way back."

"Oh God Charlie, what have you bin doin'?" Brigitte sobbed, from the corner of the room.

"Oh shit, I just did a couple of delivery jobs and asked no questions. Lots of the boats have done work like that. Fishin' ain't all easy you know," he said, clutching his side and getting to his knees.

He went to stand but his right leg couldn't take his weight and he fell onto the sofa that was along the front wall.

"We are waiting," said Kimura.

"When?"

"You and I go collect your crew and we make ready with provisions and fuel," said Iwaki. "We leave at four o'clock tomorrow morning."

Turning to Brigitte he said, "You will enjoy an ocean cruise as well."

"I can't just not turn up for work. They'll be phonin' soon to find out where I am."

"You will explain you have dying relative, and you must go to them. If you don't maybe some relative of yours may need to come here."

"Do what 'e says Brigitte. They won't let you stay 'ere believe me 'oney. Not alive anyways," said a dejected-looking Raymonde.

As if on cue the telephone in the passageway let out a series of electronic beeps.

Iwaki reached down, and taking Brigitte's hand gently pulled her from the chair. "You will make this an honest request. Do not mention a relative whose funeral you have been to before."

Brigitte, trembling with fear, nodded.

When she returned, followed by Iwaki, she was in tears.

"What happened 'oney?" Raymonde asked with alarm and concern.

"That slime ball Anders was on, an' said that they were thinking of cutting back on staff, an' I shouldna bother comin' back."

"That's cos you kneed him in the nuts that time. I guessed 'e would be gunnin' for you sooner or later," said Raymonde, limping over to her and putting an arm around her shoulder. "Don't worry 'oney, you're best out of that workhouse they're runnin'. Ain't no one likes working there, especially with Anders gropin' their butts."

"There ain't no other place around that employs girls like me without no qualifications," she sobbed.

"Hey, you go an' get dressed an' put your make-up on, you'll feel better."

"What have you got us into Charlie?"

"It'll be okay 'oney, I promise, it'll be fine."

With tears running down her cheeks she pulled away from him and headed down the passageway to the bedroom.

Iwaki gave a jerk of his head towards Kimura who immediately followed her and waited with his ear to the bedroom door to ensure that she made no attempt to escape.

When she returned Iwaki looked at Raymonde. "We go now," then he turned on Hamaura, who had been looking at Brigitte, and said in Japanese, "You make one move towards her and it will be your last. She is good woman who you will treat with highest respect." The sentence though starting softly rose in a crescendo with the last phrase shouted.

"I ain't leavin' 'er 'ere if there is goin' to be a problem for 'er," said Raymonde, glaring at Iwaki.

"There will not be any problem," Iwaki replied confidently.

"There better not be."

"We go now," said Iwaki. "We use your truck."

They returned late in the evening to find the others sat eating a meal.

"I left yours in the oven, Charlie, it should be okay."

*   *   *

"All rise!" commanded the Old Bailey court usher.

All conversation stopped as everyone in the courtroom stood, eyes focused upon the door to the judges' chambers. The judge entered and, with a bow, matched by both legal teams, took his seat on the leather-cushioned chair under the Royal Coat of Arms. Jirou Ishihara was trying very hard to stop shaking and appear calm and confident. Nothing had prepared him for the scene that surrounded him. The wigs and gowns worn with such confidence and, yes arrogance, by the prosecution team and court officials, he found to be incredibly intimidating. This, backed with the knowledge that his understanding of the law could be easily written in large characters on a grain of rice, only served to increase his apprehension.

The pageantry had started with the arrival of the clerk of the court and the harassed-looking usher, both wigged and gowned. The logger, who scurried around the court, carefully checking microphones and recording equipment, shortly followed them. Then entered the prosecution barrister, James Edward Hamilton-Courtney QC and his clerks burdened with files and legal reference books. The sealed evidence bags were brought in by two policemen and placed on the table below the clerk's and logger's bench.

The previous day the thirty-strong 'Jury in Waiting' had been assembled in the courtroom and the twelve chosen to hear the case selected by the time honoured method of shuffled cards bearing their names. As archaic as this seemed to Ishihara, witnessing the event, he could not see a fairer way of randomly selecting twelve people from the group of thirty. Each was then questioned as to their knowledge of the defendant, or any witnesses in the trial. They were also questioned as to their knowledge of the case about to be heard. As none of the twelve, four women and eight men, declared any former relationship, or knowledge, the process of swearing them in commenced. Here again the tradition seemed to Ishihara to be antiquated in the extreme, with each juror in turn taking the oath.

After the procedure of jury selection Ishihara was given a brief tour of the courts and a short lecture on the history associated with them. Arthur Hargreaves, the clerk assigned to the task, was quite proud of his knowledge. When asked by Ishihara about the severity of English eighteenth-century law, Hargreaves enthusiastically told the story of the execution nearby of two coiners in 1786. "In those days," he said, "women were not hanged like the men were. Their fate was far worse; both ladies were burnt at the stake. God knows what would have happened to someone convicted of terrorism!"

The gruesome detail provided by the clerk seemed to increase Ishihara's fear of what was to come.

Today he had arrived two hours before the trial was due to start and had briefly met with Murata in one of the holding cells beneath the building.

"Murata-san, I have not told to British your intention to plead guilty."

"Mmm!" growled Murata. "Why you delay?"

"I have not yet heard from the Ghost and extradition negotiation is moving very quickly. A full trial will extend your stay in this country and maybe give chance for the Ghost to arrange things."

"I see; can you actually conduct my defence?"

"No one has questioned my credentials."

"How long can the hearing last?"

"Maybe one, maybe two weeks."

"No. Guilty plea will still require full evidence to be heard. That will take much time, the British enjoy listening to every detail."

A few minutes before the judge had made his dramatic entrance, Ishihara, sensing rather than hearing anything from the area of the dock, turned to see Murata and little Miss Nagano being led into the armoured glass screened area, each handcuffed between two prison officers. The three had acknowledged each other with polite bows.

When everyone had resumed their seats the judge, Sir Aubrey Neville Beresford, turned his severe face to the prosecution counsel. “Mr Hamilton-Courtney, I understand that you are representing the prosecution in this case?”

Leaping to his feet, Hamilton-Courtney replied, “That is correct my lord.”

The steely gaze swept across the courtroom and settled on Ishihara. “And you sir, Mr, er, Ishihara, are representing both of the accused?”

Ishihara went to respond then realised that he had not stood. Springing to his feet, he bowed and replied, “Hi, er, yes that is correct, er, mm, my er lord.”

Sir Aubrey coolly studied the defence counsel for a few seconds. “Mr Ishihara, it is unusual for an overseas counsel to take on the task of defending an accused in a case as serious as this. My concern is for justice to be done. Are you confident that you can carry out the task before you?”

Ishihara stood again and bowed. “Yes er my lord.”

Sir Aubrey gave Ishihara a disdainful glare before saying, “Very well. Read out the charges.”

The charges, including murder, kidnapping and co-operation in the theft of a yacht, also mentioned the use of British territory for the planning, preparation and launch of a terrorist attack upon a friendly nation.

“How do your clients plead?” demanded Sir Aubrey.

Ishihara stood and turning to look at Murata, gave a questioning look. Murata stared back and just nodded. “My clients plead guilty my lord to the charges of kidnap and murder, but innocent with regard to the charges concerning terrorism.”

Under normal circumstances it would be expected that those in the public gallery would react in some way, but there was silence, the case was being held in camera with both public and press galleries empty. It had taken the government several days of legal argument to win the decision. Their case was that any trial concerning Murata would influence any hearing he may face in America. Much to Campbell’s disappointment, the Prime Minister had managed to delay the details of the scandal concerning the ex Home Secretary’s son from becoming public prior to the election.

Ishihara left the Old Bailey that evening weak, even nauseous with the sense of relief at having survived the day with only the judge raising any question as to his status and competence. Stepping out onto the wet pavement he put up his umbrella against the rain and stood looking up and down the road for a taxi.

"He is not the lawyer Takumi Ishihara," said Morohashi confidently.

"The Foreign Office were quite sure that he was who he said he was," replied DS Weaver, who had just sprinted from inside the court and leapt into the unmarked police car's rear seats.

"This man does not walk with crutches, or use a wheelchair," she replied. "The real Takumi Ishihara suffers with diabetes and has had to have his right foot amputated, according to information I received this morning."

"Oh shit," said Weaver, shaking his head. "The Commander will roast my nuts over this; having had the word from the Foreign Office I never thought to do any further checking."

Morohashi studied the photograph on her lap. "His face is remarkably similar, I can understand how the error could have occurred."

"Can you tell that to the Commander?" Weaver asked, his voice almost pleading. "I get the feeling that I'm not on his favourites list at the moment."

"I will get Tokyo to check Takumi Ishihara's home and office," she said. "Something is very strange. Murata's group must have known that this would check out."

"You think he is a member of Murata's faction?" asked Weaver.

"If not he is a sympathiser to Murata's cause."

"Excuse me interrupting," said WPC Tucker. "But why not just use the real Takumi Ishihara, why substitute?"

Morohashi paused before replying.

"My guess is that this man is in contact with Hamaura and Kimura, and is being used as the contact man."

"Of course yes, silly of me."

Morohashi glanced at Caroline Tucker, surprised. It was very unusual for a police driver to ask a question. It had been timely though, and had caused Morohashi to really consider the reason for the plant.

A taxi pulled up in front of Ishihara, and after brief instructions, he got in and the vehicle moved off.

"Shall I follow?" asked Tucker.

Morohashi turned and looked at DS Weaver.

"Yeah," he said. "Let's hope he is going home. We can then get a better idea as to what the set-up is."

"Please let me out," said Morohashi. "I will contact Tokyo. See you tomorrow."

Before Weaver could question her, she had leapt from the car and was crossing the road.

"Come on, let's go or we will lose him," ordered Weaver.

The journey was difficult for Tucker as the taxi could use the restricted road lanes, but still she managed, skilfully keeping the taxi in sight. In Portland Place the taxi stopped and Ishihara paid it off, and started walking up towards Park Crescent. Dropping Weaver off ahead of Ishihara, Tucker returned to the Yard leaving him to continue the trail on foot.

An hour later, Weaver reported in from the Kenton area of London. Soaked to the skin, he was standing opposite a mock Tudor-style semi-detached house in a quiet tree-lined road. On leaving Tucker, Weaver had followed Ishihara up Portland Place, across Park Crescent and through the small park to Regents Park underground station. There he had flashed his badge at the ticket inspector and followed his quarry onto the platform for the northbound trains. At Kenton, Ishihara got off, obviously unaware that he was being followed. Outside of the station he walked over the railway bridge and, just after passing a line of small shops, he turned right up a typical suburban street. Half a mile on he crossed the road and went up a short driveway to the house. As he approached it, a short dumpy woman opened the door and bowed him in. Weaver was now feeling conspicuous and, having learnt all he could from his observations of the house, concluded that this was now a job for the eavesdroppers.

In the days that followed in court, the various witnesses were called to give their evidence and were dismissed, under caution, as soon as they had done so. Ian Vaughan was one of the earliest to make his statement from behind a screen. He confirmed seeing Murata and Nagano, together with the rest of the gang, arrive at the boatyard and witnessing, the following day, them abducting his wife and daughters at knifepoint. Few questions were asked regarding the voyage across the Atlantic, other than those seeking confirmation of Murata's status within the gang. The exception being the rendezvous north of the Azores, when the crewmember, sent to replace Vaughan, had arrived. Suffering with seasickness and a broken arm the young man's fate had been sealed; Fumiko Hamaura had executed him on the spot. Ian's description of the incident had brought gasps from the jury.

At the request of the prosecution, the jury were taken to Bosham and shown the boatyard, moorings and quay, before being taken on to the property, owned by the then Home Secretary, that had been used to hold Sarah Vaughan and her daughters hostage. Once a charming farmhouse, it was now a burnt-out ruin thanks to Murata. Whilst there, they were guided out across the field, over which Sarah and her daughters had escaped, to view the spot where Julian Makepeace was shot and died as he climbed the fence running along the edge of the by-pass.

The plea of guilty relieved Sarah Vaughan of appearing, her written statement being read out to the court was considered sufficient and stood unquestioned by Murata's defence counsel. Murata had angrily rejected Ishihara's idea to insist she give evidence in person. During her time in captivity Murata had come to respect her. Her concern for and care of her children, coupled with the fearless demands for their release, had impressed him.

During the period of the trial, surveillance had been set up at both the front and back of the property Ishihara was renting. It had been decided not to expose him at this stage as he was probably the contact man and Campbell was desperate to gain any intelligence regarding the arrival or movement of the current fugitives. Phone tapping had started, and the listeners to the various telephone conversations were soon to discover that, whilst Ishihara's legal practice received no calls at all, his textile trading company was doing brisk business. Apart from that, all other calls were of little interest, being made by Ishihara's wife to her group of friends.

The really interesting information had come from Tokyo, where they had learnt of the death of the real Takumi Ishihara and the recent suicide of his adoring wife. More importantly, they had discovered that it had been the real Takumi Ishihara who had advised on and orchestrated the defence of Yoshi Hamaura. Though he had refused to be part of the courtroom team, he had been the man advising on the numerous legal arguments.

At the end of the Murata ten-day trial the jury took just one hour to agree a verdict of guilty to all charges. Sentencing was set for two weeks from the day. Even the outcome of the trial had been withheld from the public, both sides agreeing that publication would prejudice the American court case.

Other than Commander Campbell's small team, no one knew that Ishihara was not who he claimed to be. Likewise Ishihara had no idea that he and his house were under observation.

Unable to attend the court, Lieutenant Commander Morohashi commenced her undercover calls to the major Japanese companies with UK offices. For many it brought back memories of the 1970s when various terrorist organisations were employing hostage taking as a means to obtain their demands.

Chapter 5

Whilst the three Red Brigade members had been crossing the Pacific and Canada the Vaughans had been enduring a strained existence at the safe house. Arguing almost constantly now, Ian and Sarah Vaughan were testing the patience of almost everybody, as well as upsetting their children.

The arrival of Commander Campbell had been unexpected. Asked about the whereabouts of Ian, Poppy pointed out of the window at the forlorn figure seated on the garden bench below the tennis court. "There he is, Commander, poor soul. I hope you have brought him some good news, that wife of his is giving him a very hard time. In fact she's giving us all a hard time."

As usual, the atmosphere at breakfast had been tense with Sarah and Ian Vaughan talking only to their children, and avoiding even eye contact with each other. Poppy, who was a highly trained counsellor, had never met anyone so resistant to contact as Sarah Vaughan. Rarely would an answer be more than one word, and she would make any excuse to leave if Poppy tried to advance any conversation.

"I am not sure to be quite honest with you. I do know that his wife will be delighted," replied Campbell.

Poppy looked at him and shook her head.

The Commander stepped out onto the patio and down the steps to the lawn. The armed policeman in the corner of the garden took a careful look before returning to his vigil of the closed gates and garden walls. Campbell took his time strolling across the grass, in order to give Ian time to drag himself away from whatever deep thoughts he was having. "Good morning. May I join you?"

"More questions?" Ian replied.

"No. This time I bring some news that may relieve some of your anxiety," said Campbell. "I believe that it would be better if both you and your wife heard what I have to say, so I have asked Mrs Finch to get your wife to join us."

"Were you surprised at Murata's plea?" Ian asked.

"Oh no. The plea of guilty, he hopes, will keep him in a British prison where he will be well treated. Murata, I am afraid, is under the misapprehension that such a tactic will help him avoid extradition."

"Yes of course. If found guilty in the States, of plotting a terrorist attack, he could face the chair."

"There are definitely voices calling for it over there," replied Campbell. "We, however, would block any request for extradition unless it was guaranteed that the death penalty would not be imposed."

"Huh. Really?"

The sound of the patio doors sliding open had both men looking up. Sarah appeared and walked slowly across to them.

Campbell stood and smiled at her. "Good morning Mrs Vaughan, I trust that you are well?"

"As well as any other prisoner I suppose," she replied.

Campbell's expression changed to sadness but he said nothing, moving instead to bring a folding chair from the tennis court level and place it alongside Sarah.

"I have good news for you both. Recently we have had reason to review the status of the threat posed to you both," said Campbell smiling. "We have been joined by a Lieutenant Commander from the Japanese Special Attack Team who is undoubtedly an expert in Red Brigade tactics. She has assured us that, based on previous experience, it is very unlikely that you, Mrs Vaughan, or your daughters, would be at risk should Hamaura and Kimura show up in this country. Apparently their normal modus operandi is to kidnap a high executive of a major Japanese company, and use him as a bargaining chip."

"That may work in Japan, or some other countries, but is it likely to work here?" said Ian.

"It is doubtful whether they would appreciate that, and if they did, it would still rule out the kidnap of your wife and daughters again."

"I'll go and pack," said Sarah, standing and making to walk away.

"Just a moment please, Mrs Vaughan," said Campbell, shocked by her response. "Though you and your daughters are probably safe, your husband is not. In fact our revised assessment places him at great risk, in view of the fact that he was responsible for the death of Hamaura's sister."

"Well that settles it," said Sarah, obviously about to walk away. "The girls and I are not going to stay around and get caught in the crossfire. So I am going to pack now and return to our house."

"Sarah love, this is madness," Ian said, standing and trying to stop her from walking away. "Let's sit down and talk this over rationally."

Snatching her arm away she said, "I'm going back to the house today with the girls. Then I'm going to phone Rebecca and accept Jerry's generous offer for the three of us to live in their Derbyshire cottage."

"For Christ's sake Sarah, use your brains will you," retorted Ian. "How can anyone protect you and the girls up there?"

"Weren't you listening? We don't need it!" Sarah shouted back.

The guard again turned his attention away from perimeter surveillance.

"Keep your voice down. The windows of the house are open, the girls will hear us rowing again."

"I don't care anymore Ian, I've had enough. You may as well know that I have asked Margarette Torsen to start divorce proceedings on my behalf."

Ian's legs appeared to give way and he sat down hard on the bench. A few seconds passed with him looking at her in amazement. "That man hater, on what grounds for goodness sake?" he asked.

"Irrevocable breakdown," she shouted angrily, before turning and marching determinedly towards the house.

Throughout this quick-fire exchange of words, Campbell had stood up, shocked, embarrassed and eventually saddened as he witnessed the scene unfold. As the patio door slammed to behind

Sarah, he turned to Ian. "I am so terribly sorry. I had hoped that my news might have brought a more positive outcome."

Ian shook his head. "It's not your fault. That poisonous bitch she calls a friend is behind all this. I just pray that, away from her pernicious influence, Sarah will eventually see some sense."

"Maybe her move to Derbyshire is not all bad news. Whilst she is there we can arrange for light protection."

"That will really upset her," replied Ian. "Didn't you notice the 'prisoner' comment? Frankly that has been the main problem here. The security has been very tight and none of us has had much real privacy. I'm sorry. That sounds ungrateful, but it is what has been annoying her most."

"Don't worry, apart from the local patrolman, maybe calling by with a short welcome, she will be none the wiser that we have watchers looking over her and the girls. Just get me the address and I will set the ball rolling." Campbell thought for a moment then asked, "Does your wife have any particular personal interests like bird watching or playing bridge, you know what I mean. It would make a difference as to how we set up their protection."

"Gardening, walking, sailing. She's a good swimmer. She will enjoy the stately homes in the area, and she reads a lot."

As he was driven back to the Yard, Campbell made a note to question Caroline Tucker about Sarah Vaughan, to see whether she could add any more to the picture. The prospect of a conversation with Caroline gave him a pleasant feeling. Soon his disciplined mind took over again and he turned his thoughts to other terrorist threats. Those one could not blame on other nations; those that were founded on the racial and religious hatred within Britain's ever more complex, multi-cultural society.

In the house, Sarah was busily packing the girls' clothes as Ian appeared at the bedroom door.

"Have you given any consideration to the impact this will have on Clare and Louise?" he asked, quietly.

"Yes," she replied curtly.

Ian waited for her to expand upon this simple response, but Sarah just continued to gather up and fold clothing items and thrust them into the cases on the bed.

"When will I get to see them?"

Sarah stopped what she was doing. The question was one she had not fully considered. She knew that the girls loved Ian as he did them. Would they pine for him up in Derbyshire?

"When this whole sorry business you have got us into is over."

"You can't do that. You can't stop me from seeing my daughters."

Sarah spun round to face him, her face full of rage. "Watch me!" she shouted. "If you come near to us you will bring with you danger. Don't tell me that you won't, you know how hateful and determined these people are."

Ian looked down at the floor. She was right, if the worst happened and the two terrorists turned up in England, he could tow danger behind him. "All right. You win, but only until this nightmare is over."

Leaving her to finish packing, he went downstairs to the study and picked up the morning paper again. Turning to the 'Situations Vacant' page he read again the advertisement he had studied earlier. 'Project Supervisor, MoD establishment, facilities expansion project, West Country.' He had all of the necessary qualifications, and from previous work that his former employers had assigned him to, had some level of security clearance. Sitting down at the computer, discretely situated in the corner of the lovely oak-panelled room, he opened up 'Word' and started to type. Ten minutes later he printed off his letter, requesting an application form, addressed the envelope and then went in search of Poppy.

He eventually found her outside, giving instructions to the gardener about the pruning of a bay tree.

"Poppy, could I have a word?"

She smiled. "Of course you may."

"Is it possible to post this from here?"

"Yes, so long as you have not used this address for the reply," she answered.

"No, I have used our home address."

"Would you mind if I just read through it?" she asked.

He handed her the envelope and letter.

"This is no problem. I will put a first class stamp on it, and it will go this lunchtime."

"Also, I would like to contact the Commander. I have a plan that I would like to discuss with him."

"I will try and arrange that now," she said, smiling. "I do hope this works out for you. Being here hasn't been easy for any of you I know, but I think it has been far worse for you."

It was early evening before Poppy announced that the Commander was on the phone.

"Thank you for taking the time to get in touch, Commander. After our meeting this morning I have been giving the whole issue of Murata, Hamaura, and anyone else who wants a slice of me, some consideration."

"Yes, and what is your conclusion?" asked Campbell.

"I have formed the view that I will never be safe all the while Hamaura and his sidekick are at large. Sarah has made it abundantly clear that I represent a danger to her and the girls if I am close to them. Should those two make it undetected into the UK, she is probably right. Whilst I am holed up here Hamaura will find it nigh on impossible to get at me. Therefore he is very likely to seek out Sarah and the girls and kill them to get at me."

"I follow your logic so far. What do you suggest? Make yourself a target?"

"In a way, yes, more the bait in a trap," said Ian. "I have sent off to be considered for an MoD job in the West Country. The job title is Project Supervisor, it was in today's classified ads."

"I know you took a similar risk in the States, but then they were not aware that you were still alive. This is a very different thing, they could take you out from a distance with a sniper's rifle even," said Campbell.

"I think that this Hamaura will want to see the whites of my eyes. If he is anything like his sister, he will want to see the fear and be sure of the kill," replied Ian.

"Mm. Let me think about this for a while. I need to discuss it with others."

Sarah and the girls left the following day; the girls in tears at the news that Ian would not be joining them. Now alone, Ian walked around the grounds more like a caged lion than ever. Three days later that the application form arrived, collected from the Royal Mail sorting office near to his home and delivered to the safe house. All of their mail was handled in this way with the sorting office being unaware that the WPC was not Sarah Vaughan. Ian completed and returned the form by special delivery the same day.

* * *

The weathermen had predicted a warm weekend and for once it appeared as if their predictions would hold good. As Chief Inspector Paul Jackson alighted from the taxi outside the US Embassy in Grosvenor Square the heat of a perfect summer's evening rose up from the parched pavements. "What is it like inside Paul?" asked his wife Susan excitedly.

"All marble and marine uniforms," he said. "If you just wait a few minutes you will see for yourself."

Ambassador Beaumont and his wife, at the door to an anteroom on the first floor, greeted them. In the centre of the room stood a group of senior embassy staff talking to Coastguard Watch Manager, Phil Saints and his wife Stella. As the Jacksons joined the group Allen Kline, the legal attaché, made the introductions and asked the waiter to fetch drinks for the new arrivals. A movement at the door caused Jackson to look up. His jaw dropped as there, standing in the doorway shaking hands with Jackie Beaumont, was a very beautiful WPC Tucker.

"Close your mouth Paul, you look like a paralysed goldfish," said Susan Jackson digging him in the ribs with her elbow. His facial expression, however, didn't change as he had then recognised Alec Campbell as the man gently taking hold of Caroline Tucker's arm to guide her across the room.

"Well I'll be damned," he said.

"I'm not sure about damned, but divorce is likely if you don't stop ogling that young woman," his wife said. Stella Saints, alongside her, giggled.

Very soon the room filled with people including the British Foreign Secretary and the new Home Secretary, both with a gaggle of senior civil servants.

The five-course meal passed to the accompaniment of the normal babble of conversation. The seating placed Caroline Tucker between Allen Kline on her right and Harry Middleton. Positioned on the other side of the table, and slightly offset, Campbell would frequently look across at her admiringly as she conversed with and obviously charmed both men.

Once the dessert course was cleared, Ambassador Beaumont tapped his wine glass to attract his guests' attention. He then stood up and delivered an eloquent speech, expressing America's and his personal thanks to the British personnel involved in countering the 'Kinoko Kumo' terrorist attack. The climax of the speech was the presentation of three framed letters of appreciation on vellum and personally signed by President Huckle. As Campbell, Jackson and Saints, each received their letters in turn, the American staff stood to applaud them. Beaumont finished his speech with the assurance of closer antiterrorist intelligence co-operation from the United States. The Foreign Secretary then took the opportunity to reply, emphasising the importance the British Government, and his Party, placed upon mutual collaboration in this area.

"Did you enjoy the evening?" asked Campbell, as the privately hired chauffeur car glided out of Grosvenor Square.

"Yes, I did, very much. I was very fortunate to be seated between two very interesting and charming men," replied Caroline.

"So you won't mind accompanying me again then?"

She hesitated before replying, "I am not too sure where this is going, sir," she said holding up her hand to prevent him responding. "Until this evening, I was your police driver. When Chief Inspector Jackson came over and said it was nice to see me there, I informed him that you had felt my assistance with the code breaking merited a good meal. He laughed and I am sure I recognised a look of relief on his face."

"I wish I had never said anything about you being in the team," interrupted Campbell.

"Please let me finish, sir. You see, I do not wish to see you as a subject of idle and over-exaggerated gossip, and neither does Chief Inspector Jackson. Also, I have no wish to be gossiped about either."

Campbell sat silently for almost a minute, and then asked, "Will you come and have dinner with me, at my house tomorrow evening? Mrs Clayton is the very soul of discretion. We can consider where this is going then."

She turned her head away and stared out of the car window, her brain desperately trying to sort a million thoughts at the same time. What was going to win, her heart or her head? Whichever way she decided, she knew she would have to find another job outside of the police.

"I will say yes, but do not be surprised if I phone and cancel at the last minute."

"Watching you across the table this evening, I was made very aware of what I have been missing in my life. I hope that it will be the doorbell that rings tomorrow evening and not the telephone," Alex Campbell replied.

* * *

The voyage out into the southernmost tip of Icelandic waters had been uncomfortable for Hamaura and Iwaki. Much of their time had been spent on their bunks, despite the intake of seasickness tablets. Kimura, however, appeared to flourish in a nautical environment, earning the grudging respect of Charles Raymonde and his crew. A high pressure weather system, centred just south of them, was providing south-westerly winds and a quartering swell. The sea state meant that the trawler had an uneasy motion that did not appear to affect Kimura at all, but had rendered both Iwaki and Hamaura incapable of doing anything other than lay down. To Raymonde's relief, the following sea and pleasant weather considerably assisted their progress ensuring a timely arrival at their destination and hopefully an end to this risky voyage. The absence from the bridge and day cabin of Iwaki and Hamaura did a lot to calm Brigitte who, after three days, had agreed to prepare the meals, which did much to improve the well-being of all.

It was at ten o'clock at night that the yacht was sighted. Her masthead light sector changing from red to green as they crossed her bows. There was no radio contact, only a flashlight signal of the letters R and B replied to with the letters IIA. It was the yacht that sent across a dinghy with which to transfer the passengers and cargo.

Hamaura and Kimura took the first journey, arriving at the yacht's side to be looking down the wrong end of a sawn-off shotgun. Once on deck they were searched and their identities checked.

"Right boyos, you're clean," said the heavily bearded crewmember in a misleading soft southern Irish accent.

On returning to the trawler the boatman climbed onboard. "Where's the stuff?" he asked. "You better have brought it, otherwise your friends 'll be walkin' back."

Iwaki pointed to the crate alongside him.

"We can't be takin' that with us," the boatman said. "Jesus I don't know."

Iwaki took the lid off the crate and started to remove the seismography meters that lay at the top of the load as window dressing, should the cargo have been subject to a cursory check during their crossing of Canada. Throwing them over the side and removing two further layers of large bubble wrap he revealed ten boxes of C4 explosive.

Charles Raymonde gave a low whistle. "You can get that stuff off my boat straight away."

Iwaki gave him a sour look, before carefully removing the ten boxes from the crate.

Suddenly he rushed to the side of the boat appearing to be sick into the sea. Recovering, he padded his pockets as if searching for something. "I have left my pills by my bed," he said, weaving his way to the trawler's superstructure.

Five minutes later he returned, holding up the box of travel sickness pills. "They are not so good, but better than nothing."

The cargo transfer took five trips to complete; carrying first the explosives then boxes of grenades followed by M4A1 Carbine rifles, boxes of ammunition and attachments such as Aimpoint Target Assist and grenade launchers. Finally, two dozen M9 Beretta pistols were handed down into the dinghy, to sit in a case between Iwaki's legs as the craft bounced its way back to the yacht.

As the dinghy moved off Charles turned to his crew. "Okay guys, let's go 'ome. Hey Paul, go down and 'ave a look around the cabin they were usin'. I think 'e may 'ave left us a present."

Everyone looked nervously at Charles. "Come on get to it!" he shouted.

As the men dispersed to their duties, Charles grabbed Brigitte by the arm. "I feel the need for a quiet time with you up in the bows."

She looked at him with surprise. "Charlie if you think you're gonna make it with me in... Oh, you think he has planted somethin'?" Charles nodded. With their arms around each other the two sidled towards the bows of the trawler as she turned and headed on her new course.

In the bows, sheltered by the anchor winch housing, Charlie pulled Brigitte down out of sight. "Wait 'ere, I'm gonna check some things before we get too far away."

Running back to the wheelhouse he entered and, crossing to the chart table, pulled a black bag from below it. Opening the bag he pulled out two wraps of fifty-dollar bills.

"What do you make of those Matthew?"

Matthew le Garde felt some notes between his figures, then, removing one from the middle of the wrap held it to the light to study the watermark. "Seems okay to me Charlie. You got some doubts?"

"Yeah. I didn't like that seasick stunt back there," replied Charlie. "Somethin' don't seem right. If 'e was gonna sink us would 'e 'ave given us good money?"

"If it were me I sure wouldn't."

"Get the guys on deck, an' take the straps off the life rafts, will you Paul."

Without saying a word Paul le Garde left the wheelhouse.

As he did so Brigitte came in, pushing Charlie to one side. "Let me get at my handbag Charlie."

"I thought I told you to stay put."

"Shut up. Where's the money he gave you?"

Matthew handed her the wraps that he had been studying.

Taking what looked like a pen from her handbag, she removed its top and scribbled over some of the bank notes.

"Hey stop that. Shit that's a fifty dollar bill you're puttin' green ink all over."

"No it ain't, they're all duds," she replied glaring at Charlie. "This was gonna work out okay you said. Jesus Christ Charlie, God help the world when you tell us things might get bad."

"How do you know they're dud?"

"Old man Paston gave each of us girls who work on the counter one of these pen things. They only leave a mark on ordinary paper, not on real banknote paper. That's how I know!"

The sound of running feet announced the assembly of the crew on deck. Setting the autohelm, Charlie reached up and unclipped the EPIRB distress beacon and ushered everyone out onto the open deck. As he left the wheelhouse he was weighing in his hand the EPIRB unit.

"What is wrong Charlie?" asked Paul.

"We got a problem. Some bastard, probably the one we thought to be an okay guy, 'as taken the power cell out of this."

"Ain't no one gonna be able to find us?" Brigitte asked, her voice trembling in fear.

"'Fraid not 'oney."

* * *

On board the yacht, now out of sight of the trawler, the crew were carefully hiding the cargo in the several special compartments around the boat. The final item was the explosive. "There's two slabs of C4 missin' from this box," said Donald Cassey, standing on the foredeck, looking accusingly at Iwaki as he held the box back from the man kneeling by the forward hatch. "What else is missin?"

"That was your, how you say, insurance," Iwaki replied.

"What do you fuckin' mean, insurance? Tell me, what do I need insurance for?"

At the instant he finished speaking a bright flash lit up the sky to the north-west of them, followed by a shock to the yacht's hull and the rumble of an explosion.

Donald Cassey stared at Iwaki. "Don't tell me. You didn't trust 'em."

"I was concerned that lady may talk to the wrong people when she got home," Iwaki replied.

"Well I hope you fuckin' trust us."

The two men stood and stared at the point on the horizon. After a few minutes a glow of a fire could be discerned.

"That'll be the fuel gone up," said Cassey as he turned away and completed the stowage of the arms haul, then went below, leaving the helmsman and Iwaki on deck. For the next hour Iwaki seemed rooted like some statue barely blinking. The point on the horizon that held his gaze no longer glowed, the fire had burnt out. Finally, confident that the trawler had gone down with all hands, he went down to the chart table to discuss the landing point in Scotland where he wanted to be put ashore.

* * *

On board the trawler Charles had got everyone up into the bows as the vessel steamed westward on course for Canada.

"Why are we all up here?" asked one of the hired hands as he passed Charles the screw-topped tub of floating and rocket flares.

"When they opened up that crate of theirs, I saw boxes of C4 explosive. I think they may 'ave planted some below somewhere. If they are as good as their reputation, they would 'ave planted it down near the keel, probably in the bilges below the engine. This is probably the furthest place away from an explosion."

The man crossed himself. "You're a bastard for not tellin' us who your passengers really were." He went to take a swing at Charles, but Paul le Garde grabbed his arm.

"A fight ain't going to help you stay alive friend."

"Maybe, but I would have felt a whole lot better. If we get out of this I'm goin' to tell the world so help me."

"So will I," said Charles. "As God is my witness, if they 'ave planted anything to 'arm us, or the ship, I will call down the biggest manhunt ever known."

The hired hand sulkily turned away and joined his mate, who had been standing just aft of the anchor winch housing listening anxiously.

Half an hour had passed since they had watched Iwaki leave in the yacht's dinghy. The group were silent, each in their own thoughts. The life raft canisters had been brought forward and secured over the front of the bows, away from any direct force of an explosion, but located where they could be quickly released.

"Mercy o' God it's cold out 'ere," said Philippe, the youngest of the hired hands. "I am goin' t' get somthin' warmer to put on."

"Stay here boy, I'm sure we 'ave a problem. The engine room and accommodation area is the most likely place for those bastards to plant somthin'," said Charles.

"Well nothin's gone pop yet, eh?" said the boy getting to his feet and making his way aft.

He was just opening the door to the bridge structure when it happened. It was as though the craft had been lifted up by some invisible crane and dropped again, whilst at the same instant the air was sucked away from them. Then came the flash followed by the blast and the ear-shattering thunder of the explosion.

Matthew, who had stood to watch Philippe as he had hurried along the deck, was blown bodily back against the waist-high bow structure, his backbone snapping as his body was almost broken in two by the impact. The two men who had been sitting on the deck aft of the anchor winch housing were picked up by the blast and thrown like rag dolls clean over the bows and into the icy cold sea beyond, their bodies peppered with small pieces of steel fragment from the shattered bridge structure.

Charlie had rolled on top of Brigitte saving her from serious injury and Paul le Garde's equally quick reactions had saved himself from all but two slithers of metal that had imbedded themselves in his left leg.

Almost instantly the stricken vessel began to sink by the stern; her keel, below the engines, blown out, and the galley beneath the bridge vaporised by a second charge. It was the second charge that blew a massive hole in the accommodation structure, sending shards of metal in all directions.

Charles was the first to move, staggering to his feet and releasing the lashings on the two life rafts. Looking back he saw Brigitte screaming as she staring in horror at the body of Matthew, folded grotesquely backwards, on the rapidly sloping deck, his dead eyes and mouth wide open in terror staring sightlessly at the sky, his chest pierced through with two long strips of steel. Charles stooped and picked her up in a fireman's lift, helped by Paul. Fear gives a man superhuman strength, and it was this that enabled Charles to swing himself and Brigitte up and over the high bow bulwark to drop into the ice-cold North Atlantic, with Paul le Garde falling almost immediately beside them. Within minutes the two had got Brigitte into one of the life rafts as fuel, on the surface of the sea near to them, ignited, illuminating the last moments of *Le Martinpêcheur* as she slid beneath the waves amid gouts of air and the loud rumblings of her death throes. Charlie, now aware that the life raft was being blown towards the inferno, pushed the injured Paul up and into the raft; then holding onto the raft's ladder kicked as hard as his freezing legs would allow him, pushing it clear of the blaze. Weak from the exertion and chill, Charlie almost didn't make it, but finally, with a few feet to spare, he was able to cease his frantic efforts and concentrate on getting into the safety of the raft.

Brigitte, who had not stopped screaming from the moment the charge went off, had coiled herself into a small ball, her arms and hands over her head. It was Paul alone, impeded by his wounds, who had reached out from the raft canopy to grab the collar of Charlie's jacket, and, with all the strength he could bring to bear, haul him into the raft.

It was close to midnight two days later when the co-pilot of the delayed Icelandair flight F1589 flying from Reykjavik to Madrid stared out of the cockpit side screen at the shimmering ocean 32,000 feet below him. There was always something magical about the scene, even tonight with the new moon barely lighting the cloudless sky. Looking back at the cockpit instruments he went through the routine checks, then returned back to his contemplation of planet earth.

The flash, like the sudden shorting of two electrical wires, fixed his focus onto one tiny area of ocean. Then, after a few seconds, he could see the red glow of a distress flare.

"Geir, look down there, someone has fired off a flare."

Geir Bjornsson clambered out of the pilot's seat and, bending over the right shoulder of his co-pilot, asked, "Where am I looking?"

"Seven o'clock," answered Finnur Stefansson. "It's still quite bright."

"Got it. Let's make a circle and try to fix the position."

Neither man would know until days later that theirs was the fourth aircraft to fly over a flare launched from the life raft. Only two more rocket flares were left in the tub.

Taking the aircraft off automatic pilot, Geir Bjornsson made a short announcement to the flight deck crew and passengers. Then put the aircraft into a turn.

"Can you quickly calculate the position while I radio Reykjavik?" asked Bjornsson.

"Can't see it anymore. They don't last much more than half a minute," replied Stefasson. "Hold it, they've fired off another one, keep the turn going."

The plane had completed fifty degrees of turn before the rocket burnt out, enough for Finnur Stefansson to calculate an approximate position.

It appeared to take some time for Reykjavik to respond, but when they did the message was reassuring.

"Reykjavik we calculate that the flare is fifty-seven degrees forty-seven north by twenty-five degrees forty-eight west, do you receive, copy?"

Reykjavik, confirming the co-ordinates, assured Bjornsson that surface craft in the area would be alerted. Putting the aircraft back on course Bjornsson looked across at his co-pilot. "Switch the landing lights on and off a couple of times, will you? That should let them know that we've seen them."

Back on course, Geir Bjornsson reset the automatic and informed the cabin crew and passengers of the details concerning the short detour. Switching the microphone off he turned to his co-pilot. "That was well spotted, Finnur. I always think of the *Titanic*, when she went down. They fired off flares and no one took any notice on a ship a few miles south of their course. They thought it was a firework display. Kind of makes you a bit wary."

Within ten minutes five Icelandic trawlers were heading towards the area, and the Icelandic coastguard were refuelling a vessel to return immediately to sea to join the search.

In the life raft Paul le Garde, having launched the flare, anxiously watched the lights of the aircraft; for a minute he thought that, like the rest, they had not seen that pinpoint of red light on the surface of the vast ocean. Then the plane had altered course. Grabbing a second flare he removed the cap exposing the firing trigger, and pointing the tube upwards, but angled slightly downwind, pulled the trigger. With a loud fizz the rocket shot up into the sky to hang on its parachute 300 metres up emitting 30,000 candela of red light. To his delight the aircraft circled them, then he saw its landing lights flash and his spirits rose.

"We 'ave been seen, Charlie! We 'ave been seen mon ami!"

A shivering Charles Raymonde tried a weak smile. "That's great, did you 'ear that Brigitte, we 'ave been seen by a plane. They will radio for 'elp."

All Brigitte could do was open one eye, and nod.

After forty-eight hours in a life raft the cold saps all strength, especially if you had spent time in the water before making it into the raft. The emergency rations had helped boost their energy levels for a time, but the cold was continually eating away at their physical and mental reserve.

Four hours later when the first of the trawlers searching was approaching the area, the ICGV *Tyr* coastal patrol vessel cast off her lines in Reykjavik and was heading at twenty knots towards the area. With almost a day's sailing before she could reach the search area her captain was praying that one of the fishing boats would soon report success in their search. He knew all too well the effects of long-term exposure in a life raft.

* * *

Ian Vaughan had heard nothing about the job for more than a week, which to him was like a year. Then the home post arrived, with a request for him to attend an interview. He learnt that the previous Project Supervisor had collapsed and died of a heart attack whilst on site, and a replacement was urgently sought. By the end of the month he received confirmation that he was in the final two for selection and attended a second interview. Apparently it was his previous security clearance that won him the position and, overjoyed, he made contact with Commander Campbell.

"Just to let you know that I have got the job in the West Country."

"Really? Congratulations. You are obviously going to take it up, in spite of the risks you are taking."

"Commander, I have to finish this for good; either they get me or I expose them to arrest and this nightmare finishes. On my side, I know what they look like, whilst they won't have a clue about me. I've been thinking. Even on the day of the kidnap Murata hardly saw me, so it is unlikely that even he would recognize me, especially as I lost weight on the voyage, that I haven't put on again."

"When do you start?" asked Campbell.

"Next Monday. They need someone on site in a hurry."

"I will be sending a car for you tomorrow morning, early. It will take you to a facility we have, where you will receive some training. Be prepared to spend two days there."

Late on the Thursday evening it was a bruised but wiser Ian Vaughan who returned to the safe house to pack all of his belongings in preparation for the move to the West Country. Now more than ever he realised the risks he was taking, should his enemies show up. His lessons in unarmed combat were, he was told, little use against any opponent trained in martial arts. He had, however, impressed his instructors with his weapons' skills, particularly with a pistol. "Shoot twice in quick succession," he was told. "The nervous system allows a few seconds for them to react after the first hit. The second normally stops that. If they are terrorists make it a head shot if possible, that will stop them triggering any bomb they are carrying." The lessons of where to sit in a restaurant, and how to move around the streets fascinated as well as frightened him. It was hard to believe how vulnerable one was against a determined aggressor. "Walk quickly and know where you are going. If you stand still, make sure it is in a doorway. Stay in the crowds and keep moving, use shop windows to watch for followers. You have very good eyesight, use it to look at people from a distance..."

Then the real shock came when he was summoned to the senior instructor's office, where a tough-looking major in combats was waiting for him. "We are going to sign you on for the period of this operation, and you will be armed. I don't have to tell you how dangerous it is for someone as inexperienced as you to be let loose in public with a gun. I can only suppose that our masters know something about you that we don't."

Then followed form filling, interspersed with more disparaging comments from the major, before he was dismissed.

At his final briefing he was told that there would be watchers, but they refused to identify them.

"If you know who they are there will be eye contact that will give them away and make them a target. If you know they are close you will take your eye off the ball, you will never be able to relax out there. Do you understand?"

"Yes," he had said.

"I doubt it," had come the reply.

As he left the establishment he was given an ID card in a CTC wallet and an automatic pistol and ammunition, together with the latest photographs of Hamaura and Kimura. On impulse, he requested to call by the safe house and packed a third bag with his sailing things before taking the train. Later, as the countryside flashed by he went through the file he had been given containing instructions for emergency contact and a profile of his two potential enemies. At the back of the file he found a personal note from

Campbell, wishing him well and assuring him that watchers were in place in Derbyshire. At Paddington Station he purchased a couple of magazines for the journey before settling into a corner seat on the Plymouth train, carefully watching his fellow passengers. The journey proved to be rather fraught as his attention was taken away from his reading material every time there was a movement in the carriage. By the time the train reached Exeter, he had resorted to just glancing at the pictures. It was then that he saw it, in the 'boats for sale' section - Saltram 36 for sale, only lightly used. Getting out a pen he circled the advertisement, whilst thinking glumly how he could possibly consider such a purchase in his current financial state. Smiling to himself he thought, 'You got to have a dream.'

Leaving the train at Totnes he walked over to the bus stop and waited for the number 164 Kingsbridge bus. On the journey he looked out from the bus and could see that the harvest was in full swing. Large combine harvesters cut wide swathes through the wheat while deep trailers, pulled by tractors alongside, collected the grain spewed from the combine's side chute. At the rear of the large machine straw cascaded to the ground ready for the following balers to pick up and wrap into large round bales which shone like enormous gold coins in the hot mid afternoon sun.

The rural scene had the effect of relaxing Ian, and the heat of the day was soporific. He was dozing when at Harbertonford, the bus stopped to let three elderly ladies, weighed down with shopping, get off. The driver was about to close the doors again when a shout attracted his attention to the opposite side of the road, where two oriental men stood waiting for a gap in the oncoming traffic so that they could cross. Dirt on the windows prevented Ian from having a clear view of the men. His stomach went cold, the adrenalin rush bringing him to full wakefulness. Surreptitiously removing his pistol from its underarm holster he hid it beneath the magazine on his lap. Moments later, the two men boarded the bus, purchased tickets and started to make their way to the rear, near to Ian.

"You goin' into work already Lee?" asked a young man, as the two came up to him.

"Yeah, boss he like us early to help wi' preparation," the first Chinese man replied.

The men stopped and, selecting seats opposite the young man, entered into conversation with him. Returning the gun to its holster, Ian shook his head. Would he be doing this every time he saw someone with oriental features? What had he said to Campbell? Ah yes, I know what they look like, but they don't have a clue about me. With these thoughts, he relaxed, but promised to himself to view the photographs of the pair on a daily basis. He must never forget exactly what they looked like.

At Kingsbridge he got off the bus and made his way up the steep incline of Fore Street to the Kings Arms Hotel he had booked for the next few days. Reserving a corner table in the restaurant, he went up to his room and unpacked the few things he would need for his short stay. As he removed the file from his bag, the wad of photographs fell to the floor. Picking them up, he sat on the bed, and for the next hour studied the pictures.

Next morning, as usual, he awoke five minutes before his alarm clock was due to go off. He took his toilet bag and towel along the corridor to the general bathroom; his single room apparently did not deserve en suite facilities. He waited patiently outside the door for the current occupant to leave and, after five minutes, was about to return to his room when the door opened and his heart missed a beat. There, standing in the doorway, was a very attractive oriental woman. On the instant that she had raised her head and looked at him, he had thought her to be the ghost of Fumiko Hamaura. An instant later, he realised that this lady was very different. There was no cruelty is this lady's eyes, or hardness in the set of the mouth. This face showed intelligence, confidence and grace.

"Are you alright?" she asked. "You looked very shocked at seeing me."

"I'm sorry," Ian replied. "I was miles away in my thoughts, and didn't hear you even open the door," he lied, trying a smile to cover this lame excuse.

"Ah so," she replied. "Would you step aside please, you are standing in front of my bedroom door."

Swiftly Ian moved to his right to let her pass, aware of the sound of her silk robe and the discrete scent of her perfume. Later, when he entered the dining room, the lady was just getting up from her table to leave. He made his way across the room trying to avoid eye contact with her, still embarrassed by their earlier meeting.

After a hurried breakfast he left the hotel in search of a flat or room to rent. He wanted to be within the town, somewhere quiet but not exposed. By mid afternoon, his body and mind were becoming exhausted with the search for the ideal location. One or two places were possibilities, but not quite right. Either they were too open, or lacked alternative escape routes. Then he found it, on a notice board outside a newsagent, 'Studio Bedsit to Let'. The location was ideal, as it was in the very centre of town, amongst a warren of alleyways. Knocking at the brightly painted door he sensed that this would be just right.

The door opened and a pleasant woman in her late forties, early fifties asked, "Have you come about the studio?" as she raised an oil paint-stained hand to her face, brushing aside a lock of hair.

"Yes, is it still available?"

"It is, ever since that crook and so-called artist, Roger Pauley disappeared owing two months' rent."

"Oh, tough luck, I don't suppose the police showed much interest."

"Not a lot, no. Do you want to see the room?"

"Yes please, if it is convenient that is. By the way, my name is Ian Vaughan, I'm down in the West Country to complete an MoD project just this side of Plymouth."

"I'm Miranda Cox, pleased to meet you," she replied wiping her fingers with a turpentine-soaked rag before shaking his hand.

"Follow me," she said, turning and climbing an open tread staircase leading to the first floor.

The room took up most of the first floor area and was bright and airy. A window at the front overlooked the approach path and entrance to the alley, whilst the two windows to the rear offered a view of the backyard and a rear alleyway that Ian had discovered earlier, offered escape in two directions. On the other side of the alley were back gardens to other properties, in themselves possible routes out. The front far corner of the room was partitioned off for a shower, hand basin and toilet. Along the wall above the staircase was ranged a sink, draining board and old electric cooker. Cupboards under the front window and sink provided storage space. Other than that the room was empty.

"Don't tell me he took the furniture as well?" said Ian.

"Yes he did, not that it was worth very much."

"Would I have to furnish the room, or are you going to provide the basics?"

"I thought it would be better if the tenant brought in their own."

An hour later Ian had negotiated the rent down to a realistic level, and he set off to find a store that sold flat-pack furniture.

Whilst Ian dined that evening, at his hotel in Kingsbridge, Umeko Morohashi was waiting to meet with a team from the Japanese Defence Force at the Jury Inn Hotel in Plymouth. This group were undergoing computer software training at the MoD Defence Communications Facility (DCF), currently being expanded, at Yealmstoke Head. Further intelligence information from Tokyo indicated that, like the senior staff of major Japanese companies, these highly qualified and senior specialists could be at risk from North Korean agents, ordered to delay or prevent the 'know how' reaching Japan. When she had mentioned this to Commander Campbell he had shown great interest.

"You know that Vaughan has gone to work on one of these sites," he had said. "How confident are your people that they are a target?"

"Oh, no more than they are about any other intelligence coming out of North Korea I would think," she had replied.

It had then been decided that she should meet with the group and at the same time observe Ian Vaughan, but not introduce herself to him.

She smiled at the memory of the bathroom door meeting. The expression of shock and fear on his face had amused her at the time. However, after some thought, she realised exactly why he had reacted that way. How had Fumiko Hamaura been able to inspire that level of fear, she wondered? As she waited, she opened her shoulder bag and pulled out Ian's photograph. It was a good likeness she thought, but not quite the seemingly haunted man she had seen that morning.

Chapter 6

On his first day, Ian's feelings were mixed. He felt strange wearing a suit again after so long in casual clothes and was nervous about returning to a work environment after such a long break. Getting off the bus he hurried through the gates and approached a large group of Americans standing around the door of the gate reception building. At first he thought that the check-in process must be a very complex one, requiring extensive procedure. As he neared the desk, he realised that the problem was sheer inefficiency. Finally, as his turn came, he was confronted by a woman in her fifties, with heavily dyed bronze hair, poorly applied make-up and grotesquely long fingernails.

"Yes darlin', wot can I do for you?"

"My name is Ian Vaughan and I am due to start work here today."

She rummaged through some papers on her desk. "'Ere Audrey 'ave you got the 'New Start List' for this week?"

Audrey stopped what she was doing and checked through some papers in a desk drawer.

"No, I'm sure I saw it in your in-tray this morning."

"Well it ain't 'ere now," said the bronze hairdo.

Looking back at Ian she asked, "Wot's yer name again?"

"Ian Vaughan. If you contact a Mr Lambert he will know all about it."

"Mr Lambert is the Site Director. I can't disturb 'im."

"His secretary perhaps?" Ian replied, becoming a little annoyed.

"You'll 'ave to wait 'til I've dealt with the team behind yer," she said, showing signs of being flustered.

"No, that will make me late for my appointment with Mr Craine. Will you please call Mr Lambert's secretary, now."

The woman leant to one side, looking at the next person in the queue, and was about to invite them to step forward when Ian moved to block her.

"If you turn round and look at that sheet of paper on the floor behind you, you will see that it says 'New Start List' at the top."

Turning and looking she said, "Oh." Then stretching the fabric of her dress to almost bursting point she bent and picked up the paper. "Wot's yer name again?"

After three attempts of typing it into the computer she finally succeeded.

"Oh, yer on a green badge," she said, obviously puzzled. "I don't fink that's right."

"As I am going to be in charge of the expansion project here, I would expect to be given a green badge until Mark Parish hands over my permanent pass."

Glaring at him she pressed 'print' on the computer and pulled a plastic wallet from a box, thrusting the pass into it. "There," she said.

"Many thanks," replied Ian, turning and picking up his briefcase. As he got to the door he heard her say to her colleague, "Toffee-nosed git, who does 'e fink 'e is?"

Oh joy, he said to himself. On site five minutes and made an enemy, as if I haven't got enough of them already.

Ian's meeting with the head of site security, Mark Parish, had not been as friendly as he had hoped. "I'll say my piece now before Mr Lambert puts in his pennyworth," Hawkins said, after giving Ian a perfunctory handshake. "As far as I'm concerned, you're here under false pretences. Had we known what you have recently been involved in, you would not have been allowed anywhere near here. I'll tell you now, the Director is most annoyed, and has tried very hard to cancel your appointment. Sadly, someone with more clout insisted that you stay."

"The assessment is that the risk of Red Brigade reprisal is small," replied Ian, trying to play down the situation.

"Huh. That's not the briefing I received. Anyway you're here now and have a job to do."

The Site Director, Colin Lambert, had been even more scathing in his remarks. "We are here to provide counter-intelligence support, not play guardian to CTC agents who have made enemies." Ian was about to protest about being called a CTC agent, when he realised it was that title which had kept him in post. Eating humble pie he left the Director's office and made his way to the 'Human Resources' department, who were, thankfully, much more welcoming.

"You won't be using Mr Jeffery's old office in the main building, we understand that the Director has insisted that area be used for other personnel. You are rather isolated I'm afraid, in a Portakabin," the HR manager explained, with a concerned expression on her face.

The rest of Ian's week went well. The contractor, though behind schedule, was co-operative and producing good quality work. The Project Foreman, Jack Craine, was obviously good at his job and impressed Ian. His MoD colleagues too were friendly and helpful. Possession of a permanent pass meant there was no longer any need to call into reception on his way on and off the site. Even his Portakabin office was well sited, being alongside the contractors, and with a spectacular view out towards the Eddystone Lighthouse. During the day he was frantically busy, trying to pick up the threads left by his predecessor, and in the evenings installing himself, and his few belongings, into the studio bedsit. The only other disturbing thing had been a team of eight Japanese computer operators, who were receiving training on the site. When he had first seen them it was fortunate that he was in the company of the security chief, Mark Parish.

"I was told last week that there was going to be another one, maybe two, joining them," Hawkins had said. "They all seem to be very industrious, they work on to about seven, eight o'clock every evening." That had been on the Tuesday, and the next morning, he had seen the lady from his hotel checking in through reception, with the other Japanese. Now able to justify her presence in Kingsbridge, he felt strangely more comfortable.

Ian picked up the telephone a week later, the same day that flight F1589 had sighted the flare, and dialled Commander Campbell's direct number. His reports to Campbell's office were now almost routine. Normally he would just check in with Mrs Fitzgerald, and today, as usual, it was she who answered the phone. "Ah, good afternoon Mr Vaughan, if you can just hold on for a minute or two I know the Commander wants to pass on some news to you."

Ian's heart sank. "Have this Red Brigade pair shown up?" he asked, despairingly.

"Oh no, I believe it is some good news for you. Hold on, I think the Commander is coming down the corridor."

Over the phone Ian could hear a muffled conversation followed by a click then Campbell came on the line. "Mr Vaughan, how are you?"

"Very well, thank you. Mrs Fitzgerald said you had some news for me."

"Yes, indeed I have. Earlier today I was informed by sources in America that you are to receive the full bounty reward for the identification and, shall we say elimination, of Miss Hamaura and that man Madadhah. The sum, I am told, is quite considerable and may lead you to consider retirement even."

"Good heavens, I had no idea that there was such a thing nowadays. I thought bounties went out with the Wild West."

"Oh no, even in this country there is a system of reward for information and assistance for the arrest of certain criminals."

"Really?" replied Ian, now even more shocked. "When is this, er, reward going to be paid, do you have any idea?"

"I understand that the President's office have instructed that payment is made immediately."

Ian laughed. "Do they need bank account details?"

"No, we already have those from your wife, and have passed the information on," replied Campbell.

"You have informed Sarah?" asked Ian.

"Yes, I was speaking to her only an hour ago. Sadly the news has not changed her view on the current situation. We had tried phoning you first, but your line was engaged."

"How is she?" asked Ian.

"I understand that they are all very well indeed and appear to be settling into village life with great enthusiasm. Your wife did say that you had written with the address of the site. Very wise of you not to use the lodging address."

"She didn't say anything else?"

"Only that she was still determined on pursuing a divorce. I am sorry, I had hoped that by now she would be reconsidering that decision."

"I got a letter from our solicitor yesterday stating that Sarah was still going ahead with it. I just wonder what the girls are making of this."

"According to our watchers, they seem to be perfectly happy at the moment, enjoying all the new things around them I would think."

"Thank you for letting me know, I feel unable at the moment to phone their cottage, probably because I don't want to annoy Sarah any more than necessary," Ian said dejectedly.

When the call was over, Ian slipped on his weatherproof site jacket and, picking up his briefcase and shopping bag, ran across the car park to the main building, through horizontal rain. Entering the building through a side door he walked along a short corridor to the post room.

"Have you any mail for me? The name is Ian Vaughan."

The pale, but pretty lady mail clerk smiled back at him. "Yes, I think we have."

She turned to the rack behind her, and from the slot labelled PROJ. UPGRADE/ SUP, pulled out a handful of letters. "Here we are, they came in the afternoon post."

"Thanks very much, must fly, otherwise I'll miss my bus again."

Thrusting the letters into his briefcase without looking at them, he rushed back out of the building and ran to the bus stop. In

Kingsbridge he walked up to Lime Grove to buy provisions, for the week, at the supermarket. Laden with shopping, he slowly walked up Cookworthy Road, crossing to climb the slope up to, and through, the central car park, emerging in Fore Street breathing heavily from the exertion. Putting the shopping bags down, he flexed his shoulders to ease their stiffness and looked about him. The black car outside of the hotel attracted his attention, and whilst he was looking, the porch lights of the hotel illuminated the oriental guest as she came out of the building and slipped gracefully into the back seat of the vehicle. The manager, carrying her suitcases, loaded them into the boot of the car, and patted the car's roof as a sign for it to pull away. Something about the car was familiar, but Ian couldn't place it. Then it moved off in his direction, to cruise past him, giving an excellent view of its passenger leaning forward giving instructions to the driver.

*　　　*　　　*

As the high pressure weather system moved away southwards it brought south westerly winds to the Scottish waters as Cassey's yacht approached the outer isles. His arms-paying passengers had kept themselves to themselves throughout the voyage, but they were probably aware that they had been under constant watch since coming on board. The sinking of the trawler was still starkly etched on his memory and he was not taking any chances. He wondered whether, in spite of Iwaki's actions, there were survivors from the trawler. Gavin had said that the trawler skipper had appeared to be sharp enough to suspect a double-cross.

Putting these thoughts to the back of his mind he stared north picking out the few shore lights on the Island of Tiree. The beam reach, with the wind coming at right angles to their course, had the sixty foot two-masted ketch bounding along at nine knots. On the hour he had gone below to update the chart and enter the log. Running the dividers along their planned course, he concluded that they would be dropping off their 'guests' in about twenty two hours.

Cassey had been involved in gunrunning for years, but had never felt as nervous as he was with this deal. Those other bastards you could trust, because they were known. This sly Japo was something else. Nobody knew who he was, or with whom he was working. Someone had mentioned the Red Brigade, but the American connection had said something about Koreans. Well, tomorrow he was going to search them and the boat, thoroughly. No little slant eye was going to sink his boat.

They had passed south of Mull some hours back and were in sight of the Isles of Scarba and Jura, when Cassey summoned Iwaki up into the cockpit. The man did not look well, and had been suffering throughout the voyage with seasickness.

"I'm goin' t' be with just one of yer at a time, and search each one of yer and yer baggage. Do yer understan'?"

Iwaki nodded, but said nothing.

"If any one of yer objects, you're dead. You got it?"

"You think we do same to you as we did to trawler?"

Cassey nodded.

"Okay, I understand, we will co-operate, no problem," said Iwaki. "We each carry pistol and broken down M4s with ammunition and target assist. There is just one slab of C4 in my rucksack."

"We'll bag all yer ammunition and drop it off down the road a bit. Trust me, it will all be there."

Below deck, in front of Cassey, Iwaki explained what had been agreed, and ordered that no tricks must be tried.

Throughout the rest of the voyage the three terrorists were invited to stay in the cockpit with the helmsman and an armed crewman. Below Cassey and Gavin checked the boat from stem to stern, searching under the floors, to check the bilges, and every available space they could think of elsewhere. The boat was clean.

After barrelling between Scarba and Jura with the tide, they changed course towards the north-east and calmer water. A final meal was followed by several glasses of Irish whiskey. It was a reasonably inebriated Japanese trio who were ferried ashore at the head of Loch Melfort, out of sight of the few cottages along the road. The parting had been very friendly, in spite of the search.

On the beach, however, Hamaura predictably started to complain about the treatment, only to be sternly silenced by Iwaki. "Would you trust anyone who you had seen do what we did to Raymonde and his crew? Eh? If you had not searched, I would think you to be complete fool, stupid man, not fit for this important operation."

Hamaura hung his head, he was getting annoyed with Iwaki's continual criticisms. Soon they would be led by Murata-san. Things would change then.

Turning towards Kimelford Iwaki strode off, followed by Kimura, with Hamaura still nursing his ego, some yards behind. After half a mile they saw the dinghy pull away from the shore. Estimating where it had landed they climbed down the bank onto the rocky shore and, after a short search, found the bag containing the ammunition. Cassey had kept his word, and added a bottle of Jameson's whiskey into the bargain.

It was as they clambered back up to the road that it happened. Kimura, carrying the ammunition, stumbled, and in doing so badly twisted his right ankle; within moments it was swelling alarmingly, and he was unable to put much weight on it. Cold water from the loch eased the pain and swelling slightly, but it was obvious that the long night march to Oban was not possible for him.

Hoping to attract the attention of Cassey's boat Iwaki climbed down to the beach again, only to see the yacht's masthead light disappearing into the distance. As he got back up to the road he found Kimura sitting alone amongst the baggage.

"Where is Hamaura-san?"

"He will be back soon."

Iwaki was about to pursue the questioning when an old Toyota estate car was seen rolling quietly along the road towards them. The driver's door was open and Hamaura was pushing the vehicle whilst steering with his left hand.

"Mmm. Well done, Hamaura-san," Iwaki said, patting him on the back.

"People are very trusting here," he replied. "They did not lock it, only problem was steering lock. One hard twist of steering wheel and problem solved." He grinned triumphantly, raising his arms and flexing his biceps in comic strongman style.

Iwaki and Kimura chuckled.

It was Hamaura again who impressed by hot-wiring the car and starting the engine first time. With Kimura in the backseat and Iwaki acting as navigator they drove round the head of the loch past Melfort village then turned left towards Oban.

"Why we not go all way to Glasgow in this car?" asked Hamaura.

"If owners find car missing in next few hours, police will be looking for car," Iwaki explained. "We only go to Oban and hide car there. Then we take train as Japanese tourist. There are many such tourist here in Scotland at this time of year."

It was just getting light as Kimura and Iwaki settled themselves on the seats by the shelter of the bus stand opposite Oban railway station. After a few minutes Iwaki got up and strolled across to the harbour's edge and, leaning on the railing, took in the seafront view. He liked what he saw. A solid town, quiet and peaceful he thought. The soft rust-red stonework of the buildings was in keeping with the ambience of the area, the only exception being the garish bright red roof of the pizza restaurant across the small bay.

Hamaura, after ten minutes of driving around, found the perfect spot to dump the car. The car park in Lochavullin Road, opposite the supermarket, had two large coaches parked in it that would give complete cover from the road. Any passing police car would have to drive right into the car park before being able to see the stolen vehicle. Stalling the engine to stop the car, he got out after hurriedly inspecting the inside to ensure that nothing was left behind to give any clues as to who had stolen it. In his haste he failed to check the gap between the back seat cushion and the seat back. Had he done so he would have found the Takashima Exploration badge that had slipped from Kimura's hip pocket as he had wriggled to find a comfortable sitting position the previous night.

The 0811 train from Oban to Glasgow Queen Street passes through some of the most beautiful scenery in Scotland. The sunny morning, enhancing each vista, silenced the three travellers, who were now just content to stare from the train in wonderment. By twists and turns the carriages weaved their way up past Dalmally, Loch Awe and Loch Lommond, before reaching Glasgow.

* * *

As the three terrorists trudged their way across town to Glasgow Central Station, strong and gentle arms transferred the unconscious Brigitte from her stretcher to the on board sick-bay berth for a medical examination. Behind her, also on stretchers, Charles Raymonde and Paul le Garde, lay barely conscious and too weak to speak.

On arrival in the search area the ICGV *Tyr* had taken overall control of the search. It said a lot for the Icelandic fishermen out there that night for their perseverance in maintaining a constant search for those in distress. None of them would complain for the next time it maybe themselves that were in need of rescue. The coming of dawn had brought no success and *Tyr*'s captain ordered the search to move into the next box sector east. After four hours the trawler *Faskruosfjorour* reported sighting a life raft some two miles south of her position and the *Tyr* altered course and increased her speed to twenty knots. On arrival at the scene she hove to, lying beam on to the raft, to give it protection from the wind, and lowered a boat and crew to investigate. Within moments of arriving alongside the raft the crew reported it to be empty, but from a Canadian trawler named *Le Martinpêcheur*. Towing the raft alongside the *Tyr,* both craft were lifted inboard and the search resumed. Almost immediately the sharp-eyed crew of the *Kaskruosfjorour* reported a second raft sighted one mile off their port bow. This time the *Tyr*'s boat had returned with the survivors.

It would be a further twelve hours before Charles Raymonde and Paul le Garde were able to answer questions and reveal what had happened. By the time the *Tyr* had returned to port all antiterrorist organisations on both sides of the Atlantic had been informed of the forced voyage and sinking. In response to a request from the British CTC, the survivors were detained for further questioning. As soon as the news of the rescue, and the survivors' initial statements had reached London, Chief Inspector Jackson of the Counter Terrorist Command, together with Lieutenant Commander Morohashi had been dispatched to interview them. The Icelandic authorities also agreed that only a brief press release be issued, stating that most of the crew of a trawler in difficulties had been rescued.

"They didn't call each other by name, but those two were definitely the two youngest men. The other one, who seemed to be in charge, was older; maybe in 'is forties. 'E is not in any of these photographs," informed Charles Raymonde.

Chief Inspector Jackson sighed and looking at Morohashi said, "Have you any idea who this third man could be?"

She shook her head. "No, I am so sorry, I have no idea. We know that after their release in Tokyo, they must have had much help, but our intelligence regarding this group is very small."

There was a knock on the interview room door.

"Come!" shouted Jackson.

"My name is Fredrickson. I'm police artist. I come to do drawing of suspect for you," said the bearded young man who entered the room.

"Right. Let's go next door and see what le Garde can remember," Jackson said, standing up and striding from the room.

In the adjoining interview room, Paul le Garde groaned as the two officers entered. "Not more questions. I 'ave already made statement to Icelandic police. I 'ave told them that we were forced at gunpoint to take them to sea. We 'ad no choice! Why you people keep asking same questions? Why you not out there trying to find and arrest them for murder of my bother and my friends, eh? We are not the terrorists!"

"Do you recognise any of these people?" asked Jackson, ignoring le Garde's complaint.

Le Garde glanced at the photographs, and then looked more closely again. "Yes. Those two are two of the men that forced us to take them out into the ocean. You know who they are?"

"Do you recognise anyone else in those photographs?"

"No, monsieur, I do not."

"Do you recall any of their names?"

"I 'eard this one call that one," le Garde said, pointing to Kimura's photograph then Hamaura's, "something like Yorikun or Yoshikun. When I called 'im by that name I thought 'e was going to kill me, 'e looked so fierce."

"Yoshi-kun. That would be close friend name," explained Morohashi. "He would consider it to be very impolite for you to use that name."

Le Garde shrugged.

"What did he tell you to call him?" she asked.

"'E told me to call 'im Shujin."

Morohashi looked disappointed. "That just means 'master'."

" Does it? Huh. Le bastard," replied le Garde. Then his face lit up as he remembered something else. "I did ask 'im," he continued, pointing to Kimura's picture, "what I should call their boss, and 'e say *u-ray* or *urray* maybe, then 'e laughed and said it would be best for me to say 'sir'. Pig huh?"

Morohashi nodded and gave a half smile.

"Excuse me Chief Inspector, but can I talk with you outside?" she asked.

Jackson gave her a surprised look. "Alright, but I haven't finished asking my questions."

"It will not take long."

Outside in the corridor Morohashi walked a few yards away from the door. Then turning to Jackson, said in a low voice, "The name he was told to use for the boss is actually pronounced *yurei*; it means 'ghost'. This name has been picked up by our intelligence network, in connection with North Korean terrorism. Our people think it is nickname rather than code name, but it is unusual for us to use such a name."

"You think this lot are now associated with the North Korean terrorist threat?"

"It would be a natural ideological link, even though North Korean communism is possibly more severe than Red Brigade ambitions," Morohashi answered. "We have suspected for some time that North Korea has been training terrorist groups operating in Japan."

"Right, get that off to Tokyo while I ask what he knows about this arms' shipment they are supposed to have had with them," said Jackson. "I also want to know whose bally yacht they are using."

Back in the interview room le Garde was unable to answer Jackson's questions regarding the yacht, except to give a rough idea as to the course it took on leaving. When Morohashi came back into the room Jackson started to ask about the arms' shipment. Here both officers were amazed at the detail le Garde could remember, about the types of weapons and the explosives.

"What I cannot understand is why they did not come back to finish us off," said le Garde.

"It was a risk they had to take," replied Jackson. "If another vessel was nearby, well, it could have been something like the *Tyr*. Good thing you didn't let off flares straight away. That would have brought them back."

"Also there aren't many sharks in the cold North Atlantic to eat the corpses; so if anyone had come across bodies with bullet holes in them, it would have been obvious piracy, not just an accident," added Morohashi.

Both men turned to her with expressions of surprise.

"You are right Chief Inspector. Charlie 'e say not to send up flare. 'E say maybe they think we all dead," said le Garde, still looking at Morohashi in astonishment.

"Your mate Charlie seems too au fait with this lark for my liking," replied Jackson. "We'll be talking to him again, that's for sure."

"'E was not so au fait that he could keep my brothers and the others alive, monsieur."

"When you get mixed up with terrorists you must expect to get hurt," replied Jackson, "I see from your statement that their boss man, and one of the others, were not good sailors."

"No, monsieur, those two spent most of the voyage below in their bunks groaning. This one," he said, picking up Kimura's picture, "'e was strong in the stomach, and spent much time moving around, and seeing what we were doing. 'E seemed nice guy, eh."

"He has killed many times before, Monsieur le Garde. He was in prison for plotting further murderous acts," informed Morohashi.

An hour later they returned to interview Charles Raymonde.

"You say they came to your house," said Jackson. "Why do you think they would do that?"

Charles Raymonde shrugged.

"It is because you have worked for them before, isn't it?"

"No monsieur it is not. I 'ave never seen these men before."

"Maybe not these men, but you have worked for this terrorist organisation before. That is how they knew where to find you," snapped Morohashi, unimpressed by his denial.

"I demand to 'ave a lawyer present. We are not the ones who blew up *Le Martinpêcheur!*" Raymonde shouted back. "I lost my close friend Matthew, young Philippe and two other good men to those murderers, and you accuse me of working with them! You are both insane."

"How did they get to your house?" asked Jackson.

"They 'ad a four-by-four, 'ired I think," Raymonde replied, closing his eye trying to recall what he had seen. "Yes, I remember seeing Ameaux la Voiture Louer on the rear window. They 'ave place in St John's."

The interview continued for a further two hours, but nothing was learnt regarding the yacht, future plans of the terrorists, or their destination. It was late evening before both officers had filed their reports to London and Tokyo.

"That artist worked very hard, but the two images he got bore no real resemblance to each other, both men described him very differently," remarked Jackson. "Mind you I don't think either man would have thought to study his face in detail. - I can't see any reason to stay on here. We're not going to get any more out of those two."

"What about the woman, Brigitte Pascal?" asked Morohashi.

"Even if she told us of a previous contact with this bunch, it would be very hard for us to build a case. No, let's leave with what we've got for the present," he replied.

"I was thinking, maybe she would have a better memory of what their leader looked like," she said.

"Good point, we will ask our Icelandic friends, or the Canadian authorities to follow that one through. I am more concerned about where these bods landed in the UK, and what connections they've got."

"Yes, you are right Chief Inspector. By the way, what are bods?"

"Oh," he chuckled. "It's short for bodies. Slang speech really. I'm sorry I shouldn't use such words, it must be very confusing."

"Sometimes. Is 'bunch' also slang, when you refer to this group of men? It seems to be a strange application of that collective noun."

"Wow. After this is over, would you mind staying on to teach my son and daughter English as it should be spoken?"

She laughed. "I do not think Chief Superintendent Ishii would approve the leave time, I am afraid."

"Pity, the wife and I would have been most grateful. I can't blame our kids, it's the other kids at school that, at their age, they want to copy."

"Peer pressure is a very strong influence," said Morohashi, wistfully. "Sometimes I am grateful that I am not married with children to worry about."

"You are single?" replied Jackson, sounding surprised.

"Oh yes. You are looking at a career girl, Chief Inspector."

"Of course. It would be nigh on impossible to achieve your rank as a married woman in anyone's navy."

"Maybe married, a woman could make it, but with children, well, I would have my doubts."

*   *   *

In Oban Sergeant Hanson and Constable Kier stood alongside the stolen vehicle studying a name badge.

"You found this between the back-seat cushion and the backrest you say?"

"Yes Sarge."

The car had been reported missing at seven o'clock that morning and had only been spotted at 3 p.m., after the two coaches hiding it had taken their tour passengers to Glencoe for the afternoon.

"Seems strange to me, maybe old Miss Milman has given someone a lift recently."

"Could be Sarge. Shall I bag it or bin it?"

"Better bag it and be sure," Hanson said, looking up and waving his arms. "At last, here's the recovery truck. I'll leave you in charge of that, while I get back to the station."

"Okay Sarge," the young constable replied, before saying under his breath. "Yeah, back to the station and another cup of tea and slice of Mrs McDonald's cake."

At the station, true to form, Sergeant Hanson had gone straight to the canteen, bought a cup of tea, and was sat at a table, carefully unwrapping a large slice of Mrs McDonald's lovingly made fruitcake. Silently blessing the many and varied attributes of Mrs McDonald, his thoughts were rudely interrupted by Constable McKay. "No chance that either Baird or Lockhart nicked that car Sarge."

"Oh really, why not?"

"Baird is in Glasgow visiting his father, and that little tearaway Lockhart is in bed with the mumps. Poor sod, you want to see the size of his neck. It was difficult not to laugh."

"Damn it, I felt sure it would have been one of those two," replied Hanson. "Get on the computer, and see if we've got any other joyride specialists on the books that operate out of town."

"Right Sarge," replied McKay, then stepping past Hanson's table joined the queue for tea.

"Hey Constable, you don't have time for that. Get on with that computer search, chop chop." Reluctantly, McKay ambled out of the canteen to get on with the task set.

Returning to his tea and cake, Sergeant Hanson had just taken a large mouthful of his landlady's finest, when Sergeant Black sat himself opposite.

"You were not at Mr Amery's briefing Hamish." Hanson shook his head. "Why? You missed a treat."

Swallowing the mouthful well before he had extracted the full joy of the flavour, Hanson replied, "I was out looking at a stolen car over by the supermarket. What earth-shattering news did I miss today? Have the Triads set up headquarters in the local takeaway?"

"Close Hamish. It appears that the CTC in London reckon that a group of Japanese terrorists could be heading our way. Apparently they are thought to be responsible for blowing up a Canadian trawler out in the Atlantic, after having transferred to a yacht."

"Any names?" asked Hanson.

"No, nothing mentioned by Desperate Dan."

Fishing in his pocket, Hamish Hanson retrieved the plastic bag containing the name badge. "Found this stuffed between the seat and backrest in that stolen car."

"Who does the car belong to?" asked Black studying the badge in the bag.

"Old Miss Milman, out by Melfort Loch."

"Better get this up to Amery sharpish. You could get promotion yet Hamish. You'll still talk to us lowly ones though, won't you?"

"Bugger, the first moment I've had for a tea break and this happens."

"Get used to it Hamish, senior officers have a hectic existence," said Black, to the retreating rotund form of Hanson.

It was a delighted Chief Superintendent Daniel Amery, who had half the station staff scouring the beach along the north shore of Loch Melfort by 6 p.m. Though there had been a high tide since the landing, the search party did find the tracks where Iwaki and his companions had come ashore, and partial signs of the search the three had made for the ammunition bag. In addition, there were boot prints, in the flowerbed beside the spot where the car had been parked, and in the roadside verge, that matched some of those found on the beach sites, but did not match any footwear in the Milman home.

"We were dead lucky it hadn't rained," said the lab assistant, as he made a cast of the print.

"Yes, weren't we just," said Black, looking over his shoulder. "Let us hope that it's not the old lady's nephew and a couple of his mates up here fishing, eh?"

The lab assistant gave him a dark look. "That's what we like about you, Sergeant, always the optimist."

*   *   *

Interview notes of the sinking of the trawler and discovery of the badge had been e-mailed to Penny Heathcote just as she was about to leave for the evening. By 7p.m. she had spoken with the car hire company in St John's, and established that a returned four-by-four vehicle had been hired in the name of Takashima Exploration Inc, via Robertson Air. Further investigation had revealed that Robertson Air had transported three 'engineers', and their equipment, across Canada from Vancouver Island, using secondary airfields. A very nervous Aidan Robertson offered to go straight to the Vancouver police department, to confirm the identities of his passengers, once the pictures had been e-mailed.

Heathcote was just about to send the report to Commander Campbell when she received the three images of the third man. She printed them off and sat looking at them for some time before realising that separate features from two of the images appeared to have been combined in the third image. Immediately she contacted Reykjavik to identify the source of all three, and learnt that the combined image was the one drawn under instruction from Brigitte Pascal. Lifting the phone she dialled her flat, to speak to Morohashi.

The call clicked through to the answerphone. "Umeko-chan if you are there will you please pick up the phone," Penny said, and waited a few moments. She was just about to repeat the message when the phone was answered, and a breathless Umeko asked:

"Is that you Penny-chan? I am sorry to keep you waiting, but I have only just got back from the airport."

"Oh gosh, I forgot, sorry; before you take your coat off could you hop into a taxi and come round to DELCO?"

"Yes, of course, I will come as soon as possible," said Umeko Morohashi, putting the phone down without waiting for any response.

Morohashi had to wait some time, before she was able to hail a cab. Arriving at DELCO, she was surprised to see Penny waiting for her, just inside of the reception.

"We've got three sketches from Iceland, reported to be from descriptions given by Raymonde, Le Garde and the final one from Brigitte Pascal. I need you to study them and tell me what you think," said Penny as she hurried Umeko along the corridor.

"I saw the ones from Raymonde and Le Garde. It looked as if they were two completely different people."

"Yes, that is what I thought. Have a look at all three and see what you think. Then we need to look at some ticket office CCTV footage from Glasgow."

Penny explained about the badge found in the stolen car and her track back, revealing the terrorists' route. "I then took a guess that they would travel by train, and checked with the ticket office at Oban. Three oriental men caught the 0811 train to Glasgow Queen Street this morning. The staff at Glasgow Central could not have been more helpful, but they cannot be expected to remember, probably just one of the gang, buying tickets. That is why we have to sit and go through the CCTV."

Umeko Morohashi took half an hour studying the artist's work to come to the same conclusion as Penny. "Penny-chan, I think Brigitte Pascal's is probably the best likeness. See the way the eyebrows in her picture are the same as those from Le Garde's, yet hairline is nearer to the Raymonde recall. By the way Raymonde is taller than Le Garde, so hairline maybe more obvious. There are other cross comparisons as well."

"Excellent, that was the conclusion I had come to, but I needed someone else's opinion."

"Now, I've been checking train timetables and think that they would have been able to make any train from Glasgow after twelve o'clock midday. There are two cameras operating, you take one, I will take the other, after I have sent this picture off to your CS Ishii in Tokyo and Chief Honeywell in Vancouver."

It was nearly 11 p.m. when Umeko suddenly stopped her recording and wound back to replay. "That man is Kimura," she said, "but, he is only buying one ticket. That is very odd."

"Are you sure it is him, these cameras are not exactly magazine quality?"

"Oh yes, I am very sure," Umeko replied. "He has habit of pulling on his right ear lobe when he is nervous. It was very obvious when he was being questioned after his arrest, so a note was made on his file."

Penny leaned across watching the replay. "Very clever, they are buying tickets individually, to stop being recognised as a group. Oh yes, very smart."

Two minutes later it was Penny who stopped and replayed part of the recording. "What do you think of this?"

"It is not Hamaura, but could be this other man."

Penny put the recording on slow forward. After a few seconds the clerk reached across to his left to pick out a timetable. The figure at the counter moved his head to follow the clerk's hand. Penny froze the image.

"Hairline and eyebrows are similar to the Pascal sketch," said Umeko.

"Yes, I think that is our third man. By the way, he called himself, Itoh, when he was in Canada. It would be highly unlikely for him to use his real name, I would think."

Twenty minutes later they had placed all three men to be on the 1440 to London Euston.

Penny dialled Campbell's mobile. "Sorry to bother you, sir, but I thought you had better know that Hamaura and his sidekicks are in the country and, according to Lieutenant Commander Morohashi and myself, they arrived in London at approximately 1915 hours this evening."

"Thank you Penny. Can you contact DS Weaver and his team at Ishihara's house and alert them? Also can you warn the phone tapping crew to pay special attention to all calls, not just his. Every word must be recorded."

"Yes, sir, I will get onto it straight away. By the way sir, was Arnold Schaeffer at that embassy do this evening?"

"No, I learnt from Kline that Schaeffer had been recalled. He went back last Tuesday, family tragedy apparently," replied Campbell. "The new liaison man arrives next week, hopefully he will be as good as Schaeffer. Getting back to Hamaura, can you and Miss Morohashi come to my house, late tomorrow afternoon? I would like to receive all of the details, but do not have time to get into the Yard."

"1700 hours, sir?"

"Yes, that will be fine, hope you don't mind. Oh, and can you e-mail your report to Chief Inspector Jackson? I believe he is on tomorrow."

Campbell's house impressed Morohashi greatly. It was not the elegance of the house itself, or its beautiful furniture, but the whole comfortable atmosphere that seemed to pervade every part of it. After a quick tour of the conservatory with all of its exotic plants, they had briskly walked around the beautiful back garden, before taking tea on the lawn. As soon as their report had reached the CCTV recognition part, Campbell had ushered them inside to the study, in order to view the images on his computer, via a direct link with the DELCO mainframe.

"There has been no further information to report from today's events, other than a couple of phone calls regarding bales of wool cloth, sir," said Penny Heathcote.

Campbell was about to respond when the doorbell rang. Glancing at his watch he leapt to his feet and, opening the door to the study, said, "Could you show my guest into the lounge, please Mrs Clayton? I will be there shortly."

Back in his seat he said, "Now where were we? Ah yes, bales of wool cloth; strange phone call for a Saturday."

"Not for Ishihara, sir. It appears that he does a lot of business with small UK wool cloth traders, whose staff involve themselves in what they call 'pavement trading' out of normal office hours. It basically means that they use their own money to buy some cloth, then sell it through people like Ishihara," explained Penny. "Every weekend, that we have been monitoring his phones, it's been the same. We have checked on shipments with Customs and they tie up."

"Have we checked every one of them?"

"No, sir."

"Then I think we should," said Campbell. "What better way to hide contact information, than amongst the plethora of normal business."

Penny put her hand to her mouth. "Oh my God, of course," she said. "He's probably been passing information by this method for years, with such a pattern established, who would pick it up?"

As Morohashi and Heathcote left, on their way to DELCO offices, Campbell checked his hair and tie in the hall mirror and opened the lounge door. "I am so sorry Caroline. Here I am late on our second date, and in my own home as well."

Chapter 7

Ian had sat on his bed for two hours trying to decide how to approach Sarah about the news from Campbell, regarding the 'bounty' payment from the US government. One of the letters he had collected that evening had come from her solicitor and contained the basic case for separation and annulment. He felt hurt and annoyed that things were going this way and he could do nothing about it. If only they could talk without fighting. Finally he picked up the phone and made the call. The happy-sounding voice, as she answered, had him feeling full of hope, only to have it dashed once she recognised his voice. Explaining the reason for his call she quickly returned to her recent snappy hostile tone, stating sharply that she did not want anything to do with, as she put it, 'Blood Money'. For the remainder of evening he sat and worked out what it would mean to them, and slowly realised that even settling all of their outstanding bills and redeeming the house mortgage, he could afford to buy a yacht more than three times the price of the one he had seen, and have change from his half of the money. The knowledge made him feel light-headed, and a little scared. Should he commit to buying a boat that Sarah and the girls had not seen?

The second letter from her solicitor, received the following morning, settled it for him, and he made his offer for the boat. Within three days he had received acceptance of the offer and had a surveyor's report giving the yacht a clean bill of health. Thus it was a very excited Ian Vaughan who stood in the boatyard, watching as the Saltram 36 was lowered into the water.

"What are you going to call her, Mr Vaughan?" asked Hugh, as he unhooked the crane strops.

"Her previous name I quite liked, but as the owner is transferring that to his new boat, I thought I would call her *La Mouette sur le Vent*."

"That sounds nice. You gonna do it proper, you know, full registration an' all that?"

"Yes, I will. I know it's a bit of a palaver but it's worth the hassle."

"You got the forms an' all?"

Ian held up a waterproof document bag that held all of the ownership documents and registration form.

"Aw right."

Using the mooring warps, Ian and Hugh pulled the yacht clear of the carry hoist frame and secured her alongside the waiting pontoon.

As Ian stepped aboard, he looked up, and saw DS Weaver making his way towards him.

"What news?" asked Ian.

"They are believed to have landed in the UK yesterday, and are somewhere in London, we think."

"I thought that airports could pick out known criminals?"

"They can and do, but this bright bunch arrived in a remote sea loch in Scotland by sailing boat. Stole a car to get them to Oban, then came the rest of the way by train."

"Magic, you would think that governments would have learnt from the 'Kinoko Kumo' stunt wouldn't you? Huh. I suppose it's a big ask to monitor the whole of the coastline," Ian said dejectedly. "What now?"

"All the effort at the moment is to get Murata handed over to the Yanks as soon as possible," replied Weaver. "With luck, his little army will follow him. Campbell asked me to ask you, whether you will change your mind and come back to the safe house, until they are out of the way, that is."

"Did you come all the way down here just to ask me that?"

"No, this time you are just a side issue. Tokyo believes that someone else is out to get a group of Japanese computer specialists undergoing some form of software training. I've been sent down to the group based here to do the liaison with their protection team."

"That's not going to be easy. If it is the crowd that is on the same site as me, they are staying right in the middle of Plymouth."

"Not from tonight they're not. We've moved them out, to a small hotel we've taken over, near Modbury."

"Why not just cancel the training and get them back to Japan?"

"It seems that what they are doing is of vital importance to Japan's security. Don't ask me what. I would be the last to know."

"You said the group here. Are there others then?"

"Yeh, there's another at Portsmouth."

"Have you met Mark Parish, the site security chief?"

"No, I am meeting with him on Monday morning, first thing. Why?"

"Oh, nothing. It's just that he does not like too much in the way of site risk."

"Who does?" said Weaver.

"Are you going to be staying down here?"

"No. After I've set things up with the team, and Hawkins, then I'm back to London. Are you going to join me?"

Ian shook his head. "No, but I will consider the idea."

After a couple of beers on board, Weaver left, leaving Ian wondering whether to resign and beat a hasty retreat, or stay and not be scared off by some remote threat. It took him some hours weighing the pros and cons of staying or going, but finally he decided to stay. According to the last meeting with Campbell, the guys that were after him would first of all attempt to rescue their leader, Murata. Regarding the other threat, surely the place to take a shot at that group of computer buffs would be when they were in transit, or at the hotel. Anyway, their enemies did not seem to be the lot that he should be worried about.

Glancing at his watch, Ian realised that he had left little time to purchase charts, new lifebuoys and flares. His provisions for the rest of the weekend he had brought with him but, checking round the boat and its inventory, he had realised that several items needed purchasing. Focused now on the need to get organised, ready for the morning's early departure, thoughts related to his own and the site staff's safety were put to the back of his mind.

By the end of the day, and £478 worse off, Ian felt tired, but very satisfied with his purchases. On the spur of the moment he decided to eat ashore and got a taxi to take him round to Plymouth's Sutton harbour area. Where Vauxhall Street meets Notte Street he found 'The Eastern Eye' Indian restaurant and over a leisurely dinner, planned his sail from Plymouth to Dartmouth.

Leaving the restaurant, he walked up towards the city centre, and on Royal Parade managed to hail a taxi. It was dark when he returned to the marina, Weaver's visit had disturbed him, and he hurried to be safely back on board the yacht. Deciding on a nightcap he opened a bottle of Scotch and poured a generous measure, the alcohol relaxing him, sufficient to get him tucked up in his new sleeping bag and drifting into sleep.

The speed of the attack was alarming; desperately he tried to swing his right arm and reach out with his left, to grab the knife hand, but was trapped unable to move. Panic was overwhelming him as he fought to free himself of the restraints. The face, holding such a terrible expression of hatred, now blocked out everything. Then the face suddenly changed to a macabre image, as the left eyeball leapt out of the socket to dangle on the man's bloody cheek. Both of the eyes became lifeless, the right one staring blindly at some faraway object.

Heart pounding, his whole body soaking in the sweat of fear, Ian Vaughan sat up in his berth, cracking his head on the bulkhead, fighting the zipped-up sleeping bag that bound his arms to his sides. Now wide awake, breathing heavily, he frantically looked about him in the darkness. Slowly his brain caught up, as the nightmare was recognised for what it was. He groped in the dark and found the unfamiliar spotlight above his left shoulder and turned it on. Easing his body out of the sleeping bag and tunnel of the quarter berth, he tried to calm himself, but still the image of Yamada's death face haunted him. Standing, he had to hold onto the chart table for support, before carefully picking his way across the cabin to the locker above the portside settee, and reaching inside for the bottle of Scotch. Apart from a half bottle of red wine in the hotel in Washington, and some drinks on the flight home, he had not drunk alcohol since that evening in Bosham, a lifetime ago. He looked at his wristwatch; it was three o'clock and still dark. Sipping at the Scotch, he thought again about the wisdom of what he was doing. Was his desire to take on this gang of terrorists going to put others seriously in danger's way? Would getting these people locked up again actually save his marriage? It seemed that regardless of the outcome Sarah wanted out, so why was he risking so much to try and save the relationship? The thought of the divorce filled him with anger; no, no he didn't want them locked up; he wanted them dead, and no longer able to threaten either him or his family. The dawning of that realisation at first shocked him, but the more he thought about it the more he realised that it was his true motivation. He poured himself another drink.

When he had rushed down the airbridge steps to meet the girls and Sarah, just those few weeks ago, it had all seemed complete and at an end. Four members of the gang were dead, and their leader in prison, along with the only other known member. Now it seemed that the gates of hell had opened, and all its hounds let loose upon his trail. Unconsciously he reached up with his right hand, and ran his index finger along the groove in his left shoulder, gouged by a bullet from Yamada's gun on that hot afternoon on the Potomac. Yes, left to Campbell and his men, the gang would probably be arrested and imprisoned; on the other hand, if he found them, he would kill them.

When he woke he was stiff and cold. He had fallen asleep sprawled in the corner of the cabin settee. Getting to his feet his head started to ache. Not used to the alcohol, he was suffering a hangover. Boiling a kettle of water, he made a mug of coffee before successfully testing the yacht's shower, located in the midships heads compartment. After a breakfast of porridge, he dressed and climbed on deck to ready the yacht for sea.

It was ten o'clock when he cast off and, taking the tiller, he guided the yacht through Plymouth Yacht Haven, then once clear turned it through 180 degrees and westward, passing Mount Batten Tower. Coupling the autohelm to the tiller, he adjusted the setting to get the yacht pointing directly into the wind, then hoisted the mainsail. Five minutes later he had her skipping along at five knots on a southerly course with Drake Island to starboard and the yacht aiming for the entrance between the long Plymouth breakwater and Bovisand. Disengaging the autohelm he now had the yacht back under his control, revelling in the renewed experience of having a boat's tiller tugging gently at his fingers. Whether it was the excitement of being aboard his own yacht again, or the sheer exhilaration of being under sail, but for the first time in months he felt a sense of utter joy. Once clear of the breakwater, Ian put the yacht through its paces; tacking through the wind, close reaching, beam reaching, broad reaching and running before, then gybing. In the perfect wind conditions of a force three to four the Saltram 36 performed immaculately. Setting the mainsail boom just below the centre line she would lay perfectly hove-to, a great benefit that enabled the helmsman that chance to check on the chart, or brew up. Lashing the tiller to windward had the yacht describing graceful circles, another virtue that allowed the checking of the chart. Her long deep keel, though slowing her in the tack, meant that she held her course well and did not instantly luff up into the wind at the least gust. Ian was a distance cruising sailor, rather than a racing enthusiast, and the boat appeared to have all of the attributes he could wish for.

By two o'clock in the afternoon he was sailing past Hope Cove and Bolt Tail when, ahead of the boat, he could see that the surface of the water was disturbed with tiny wavelets. Reaching into the port-hand locker he pulled out a small bucket containing a mackerel line with feathered hooks. Controlling the tiller with the crook of his right knee he fed the line over the stern, letting it pay out several metres before making it off around the mooring cleat. After a few minutes he tested the weight of the line and found it to be quite heavy. Hauling it in again he found two sizeable mackerel caught on the feathered hooks. By the time he reached Bolt Head, both fish had been filleted and cooked, one for lunch with a squeeze of lemon, and the other ready to be made into a pâté. Lunch was enjoyed in the cockpit, immediately after the change of course bringing the yacht onto a broad reach, as it crossed the approaches to Salcombe.

More by luck than good judgement Ian arrived at the entrance to the River Dart approaching slack high water, and started the engine for the passage upstream to Dartmouth and Kingswear. Organising a marina berth for a week was no problem, and neither was the journey across the river by water taxi. To get from Dartmouth pontoon to Kingsbridge on a Sunday evening by bus was, however, tedious in the extreme. The answer would be to get a car, but then the problem was where to park it.

*   *   *

Whilst Ian was quizzing his landlady about safe and secure parking in Kingsbridge, Iwaki was sat in the back of a white van, insisting that his allegiance to the party's cause was as unswerving as ever. "If I am to secure the necessary money to conduct the attack, we must first secure the release of Murata. I explained all this to General Namgoong and General Sakoung; they both agreed that this should be the way ahead. If, after attack, British are able to track source of funding, it will lead back to Murata faction. Operation must not be known to be our inspiration."

The beady eyes of his inquisitor stared at him suspiciously. "What if Murata is taken to America before you can effect his escape?"

"Then I will have failed the party, and will accept its punishment."

"Our source inside Metropolitan Police say Murata will be taken to US Air Force base at Eastfield-cum-Welton. You any idea where that is?"

"No, but it is easy to find out. Do you know when?" asked Iwaki, surprised that US military were involved.

"In two or maybe three days' time," replied Dho. "No one knows which of three convoys he will be taken by."

"I wonder why they not use London Airport or British air force base near London," Iwaki said, more to himself than to Dho.

Later that evening Iwaki left the van and made his way across the field to the back of the industrial unit behind Crowhill Farm. Tapping the agreed signal on the back door, it was opened by Hamaura. Iwaki entered and stood still waiting for the door to be closed and the light switched back on. The single low-wattage bulb illuminated a small area of a textile warehouse, cleared just sufficient to allow room for the three to sleep and sit. Kimura lay on a sleeping bag with his injured ankle up on a large roll of Egyptian cotton. The unit was one of four that Ishihara used from time to time, though this one was actually leased to a Greek friend, who was also in the textile trade. Not being mentioned in Ishihara's accounts under storage facilities it had been missed in the surveillance operation.

"Get me that road atlas we bought at station."

Kimura twisted sideways to reach into his rucksack and took out an AA atlas of the British Isles and gave it to Iwaki.

Turning to the index he found the village that gave the airfield its name and turned to the page.

"Mmm," exclaimed Iwaki, making a noise like a low growl in his throat. "So long way from London. Why they make such journey?"

"What journey?" questioned Hamaura.

Iwaki informed them of his meeting with North Korean agent Dho, and the intelligence regarding the extradition plan for Murata's transfer to American hands. The three sat pondering the question of why Eastfield-cum-Welton for some time before Kimura exclaimed:

"They are going to hold him in Guatanamo. By sending him from US airbase the British need not be informed of final destination. If Murata-san taken from Heathrow his destination must surely be another civil airport in America, like Washington or Baltimore."

Iwaki and Hamaura nodded their agreement. "Well done Kimura-san, you have surely guessed correctly," Hamaura said. "They will treat him like al-Qaeda terrorist, and shackle his feet and hands; we must succeed in saving him from such dishonour."

"We will attack at the airfield," said Iwaki. "We do not have time to learn which of the three convoys he will be taken in. Tonight we travel to this place, and study layout."

After packing their few belongings, the three left the warehouse and walked the two miles to the council estate, where two garages had been rented for the storage of their arms and two Mitsubishi Warrior half cab trucks.

By dawn both vehicles, shrouded in camouflage netting, were parked amongst trees on a slight rise overlooking the airfield.

"I think this base has very few personnel. Maybe only used as refuelling for transport aircraft to other places in Europe," observed Iwaki.

Standing at his viewpoint he could not see any aircraft, either on the apron or in the hangers. The base obviously had a low operational status, but the fuel tanker discharging its load into the site tanks suggested that some activity took place here.

Actually the base should already have been closed. The British press had identified it as an airfield used for the 'rendition' flights; taking terrorists to places where possibly torture could be applied to extract information. Such was the political and public outcry that the US Government had thought it politic to close the base. Typical of most press-inspired shock horror exposés, once the closure decision had been announced, the press core decamped from the airfield entrance and peace returned. With no one monitoring the actual pace of the closure, the CIA planning team had gained permission to extend the operating period to allow for Murata's transfer. CIA thinking was that a remote airfield would be the easiest way of getting Murata to Guatanamo, where he could be held with virtually no risk of escape. In addition, as the crime was one of terrorism, the American public would prefer a military court to hear the case. The public criminal process appeared, for many, to be too lenient. Aware of the Guatanamo link, Campbell had presented a strong argument for the perimeter of the airbase to be guarded by British police for at least the 48 hours surrounding the event. The CIA, however, rejected the suggestion, on the grounds of keeping the whole process 'low key'.

At 0800 hours the security on the gate changed, with the three marines being replaced by four and a sergeant. The perimeter guards set off, with their dogs, on the six mile visual check of the perimeter fencing. As the day progressed the two-hourly security cycle became clear. Leaving Kimura to rest his injury and maintain a monitoring watch, Iwaki and Hamaura drove into Lincoln. A hardware shop and three garden centres provided them with all they needed, whilst the out of town electrical suppliers were happy to demonstrate the television set from which Iwaki obtained the weather forecast for the next three days. The final call, at a supermarket for food supplies completed their trip, and they returned, accepting that they had been caught several times on

CCTV, but confident that none of the footage would be viewed by the police, until after the event.

The following morning started with the same pattern of events, until 1100 hours, when three British police cars arrived at the main gate together with two grey, unmarked vehicles. Iwaki watched, intrigued by the meeting that was taking place. All of the occupants of the police vehicles were uniformed officers, but from the other two vehicles emerged three men and an oriental lady, all in civilian clothes. Shortly, the base commander and his staff joined the group. The meeting was obviously to discuss the arrival and transfer arrangements, and Iwaki was just beginning to lose interest when the man in the light grey suit, who appeared to be in charge of the British contingent, stepped from the circle and started to point towards the field and wood where they sat.

"They are going to search this area shortly," Iwaki said. "We will move away until time for attack is close."

Intentionally they had confined their movement outside of the vehicles to a minimum. Even the calls of nature had been conducted in a small stream that ran down the eastern edge of the wood. By the time the sixty police officers had arrived to conduct the search, the three men were two miles north-east of the base under the flight path of any approaching aircraft.

"How you know plane will come this way?" asked Hamaura.

"Planes always land and take off into the wind, if they can," replied Kimura. "Weather forecast you saw yesterday showed south-west wind for next three days."

Hamaura nodded and looked down at the road atlas book. "Ah yes, I see now."

* * *

"I am praying that Hamaura and his little group have not had time to obtain intelligence concerning this move," Campbell said to the base commander. "Hopefully their local support will be wrong footed by the decoys."

"You still reckon that the area search is necessary?" replied the base commander.

“I want to be sure that we have taken all the precautions that we can. I still believe that we should bring in a perimeter guard. You say that the aircraft will arrive early this evening and will be checked and refuelled overnight for an early morning departure?”

“Yeah. That’s the plan. You drop this guy off at 0700 hours, an’ we’ll have him in the air by 0710.”

Campbell nodded, and looking at the Chief Superintendent from Lincoln asked, “Do you have enough men to do a thorough search before it gets dark?”

“Yes Commander. They are well into it already, nothing so far. There has been some recent vehicle movement in and out of the copse over there, but our local lads are confident that it’s lampers doing a bit of coarse shooting for the pot.”

“I want six armed officers up in that wood throughout the night. Anyone turn up there, I want them arrested. Understood?”

“Yes Commander, but what happens if it’s say a courting couple?”

“Then her parents will be pleased to learn that their daughter’s moral welfare has been taken care of.”

The group of men laughed heartily and began to disperse.

“What are lampers?” asked Morohashi.

“Oh,” replied Campbell. “They are men who go out at night to shoot rabbits. They take a lamp or torch and shine it at the rabbit. Rabbits freeze when looking straight at a powerful light and present an easy, static target.”

“Did security hear any shooting last night, sir?” Morohashi asked the base commander.

“Sergeant! Did any of the guards hear any shooting last night? You know shotgun, that sort of thing.”

“I’ll ask, sir, if you don’t mind waitin’.”

“I doubt if they did Lieutenant Commander, lampers normally use high-power air rifles, which would not be heard at this distance,” commented Campbell.

Ten minutes later the sergeant returned. “Nothin’ heard last night, sir. Sometimes we only knows they been there ’cause we see the headlights as they drive off.”

“Thank you, Sergeant.”

"Will the plane be put into a hangar overnight, sir?" Morohashi asked.

"Sure, we'll need to put it in there to do the checks, then around 0600 hours we'll tow her out for refuellin'," he replied. "Don't worry mam, there ain't no way anyone unauthorised will get anywhere near that plane."

As the sun was setting the USAF C17 Globemaster roared over Iwaki and his two companions. "We wait until just before dawn. You know what to do?" Both men nodded. "Good; you are sure you can hit the target?"

"Oh yes, that is no problem," replied Hamaura confidently.

* * *

It was 2.30 a.m. when DS Weaver stopped outside of DELCO and reached across to open the car's passenger door for Morohashi.

"I'm not too sure whether to say 'good night' or 'good morning' to you," he said.

She smiled. "In Japan we would say it should be 'good morning'."

"Ah, then *OHAYO*."

By 3.15 a.m. they had reached Belmarsh Prison and made themselves known to the officer in charge of the convoy operation.

"The Gatwick decoy is ready to leave in the next couple of minutes, and that will be followed by the Heathrow one. Then the real thing leaves ten minutes later and will take the usual route to the Old Bailey before cutting back and heading north."

"We will leave with the Gatwick convoy until it gets onto the M25 then as it turns south we will go north and fall in behind the real thing on the M11," confirmed Weaver. "You know, I will be so glad to see the back of this guy."

"This is Inspector Hancock. He will be in charge of your man's escort."

Nodded greetings exchanged, Hancock made his excuses, and left to make his way to the lead car.

"Would you like to drive?" Weaver asked Morohashi.

She looked surprised. "You don't mind a woman driver?"

"It wasn't that exactly, it's just that anyone looking at our car following a police convoy with me driving, and not overtaking it, would correctly assume that we are part of the convoy. Having a woman driving they may assume that she is probably too nervous to overtake it," Weaver explained, feeling pleased with himself for thinking up the idea. "I will pretend to be asleep."

"Englishmen, like Japanese, do not think highly of women drivers, do they?"

"It's not that, it's just that women are more cautious," replied Weaver, now regretting he had made the suggestion.

Morohashi strode round to the driver's side and got in. As she adjusted the driver's seat and mirrors the Gatwick convoy appeared up the approach road from the prison, and roared past them.

The traffic lights on the main road changed to allow the convoy free passage. With outriders on motorbikes, also blocking the road, the lead police car and convoy swept out onto the dual carriageway and turned left towards the A205. Morohashi felt nervous, and hesitating, pulled away some distance behind the rear escort car. By the time she had reached the traffic lights they had turned against her.

"Good move. That should make it conclusive that we are not part of this game," said Weaver, with genuine admiration.

She considered confessing but thought better of it.

By the time the convoy had reached the A2, Weaver, head back and eyes apparently closed, and Morohashi, now feeling a little more comfortable at the wheel, had caught up, and were following at a respectful distance.

"We have a motorbike following us," said Morohashi.

"Yes I know," replied Weaver. "We picked him up just as we joined the A205. Let's see what he does when we part company with the guys in front."

At the interchange with the M25 motorway the convoy carried on across the flyover to take the southern carriageway to Gatwick while, as planned, Morohashi took the first slip road down onto the northbound carriageway.

"That got him confused," chuckled Weaver. "I thought he was going to fall off. Let's hope he has taken the bait and follows the decoy."

As they joined the trickle of traffic on the motorway, Morohashi accelerated the car confidently out into the fast lane, then, when they were out of sight of the junction put on the siren and blues.

"If he changes his mind, I want to make it as difficult as possible for him to catch up with us."

Weaver smiled. "When we've seen Murata off I'll stand you a good lunch at a nice restaurant I know at Hemingford Grey. It's on the way back."

"Let us get the job done first, then see what time we have," Morohashi replied. It was not that she did not want to lunch with him. He was actually quite nice company and keen to practise his basic Japanese. There was something else stopping her from immediately accepting his invitation. Since the meeting yesterday, at the airfield, she had felt apprehensive and certain that something had been missed.

With the siren and blues going they were waved through the ticket barrier at the toll and were soon through the tunnel and flashing towards the M11 motorway. At the interchange just before the Stanstead exit she cut the siren and lights and headed up the slip road turning right onto the roundabout bridge section and stopped with all four wheels on the pavement.

"Are you checking for motorbike Willie?"

She nodded.

"Hmm. What are you going to do if he comes past?"

"Warn the airbase that an escape attempt is likely."

"Excellent," said Weaver. "That should surely cover all the points."

An hour passed and there was no sign of the motorbike, Morohashi relaxed a little.

"It looks as though he took the bait and followed the convoy to Gatwick," she said. "Our convoy should be here shortly."

Had she adjusted her rear-view mirror a few degrees, she would have seen the front wheel of the motorbike just in view, parked on the grass verge beyond the Department of Transport's yard entrance off the A120.

As the convoy swept under the bridge, five minutes later, Morohashi started the car again, and completing the roundabout circuit headed down the slip road, and within a few minutes had joined the convoy a few yards behind the rear police car. The motorcyclist had started his machine as soon as Morohashi started down the slip road. Taking the bike onto the bridge where Morohashi had just parked, the rider raised his visor and, taking binoculars from his jacket pocket, confirmed that the unmarked police car, he had nearly caught up with two miles down the road, had joined the convoy. The mobile phone call to Iwaki was brief, but signalled the start of the attack procedure.

* * *

The fence patrol was now two hundred yards past where Iwaki and Hamaura lay.

The rain had been falling steadily for the last hour. Hamaura reached out cautiously and, with a set of heavy-duty wire cutters, snipped through a link in the fencing. The noise sounded deafening to the two men, and both stared anxiously at the guard and his dog, but neither turned nor appeared to react in any way. Hamaura adjusted his camouflage cloak and hood. Standing slowly he leant against the fence post and snipped through the wire higher up, then carefully started to unthread it from the mesh.

Ten minutes later both men lay, one each side of the taxiway, cutting out a six foot by three foot turf strip. Laying these to one side they dug out the soil beneath and spread it thinly around the area. By the time the dim light of day had touched the north-east end of the runway and taxiway both men were hidden in the shallow trenches covered by the grass turfs. Alongside Hamaura was his M4A1 rifle, with grenade launcher, and a case containing a set of four steel balls for the French game of petanque. The other side of the taxiway Iwaki was armed with his M9 Beretta pistol in its waist holster. Alongside his trench lay an extending ladder that they had painted a muddy green the previous evening.

At 0655 hours the convoy transporting Murata arrived at the airbase main entrance and was let through, and ordered to follow a military Jeep that led them to the side of the C17 aircraft. Three tough-looking Marines took charge of Murata, one signing the handover sheet.

"That's a hell of a size aircraft for just four passengers," said Weaver, with some feeling.

"Hell no," chuckled the base commander. "That bird's also carrying a Canadian C2 Leopard Tank and a maintenance crew back to Toronto. They just pulled out of theatre in Afghanistan."

"Oh right," Weaver laughed. "I thought they might be entertaining him with a couple of games of basketball on the way back."

As the handover process continued Weaver found himself studying Murata. To Weaver he looked very frail compared to the arrogant stance he had held during his appearance at the Old Bailey.

A second Marine undid the handcuffs and passed them to the prison guard. Then picking up an orange-coloured overall from the tarmac thrust it at Murata. "Hey, put this on."

Murata looked at the overall for a few seconds then with a sigh put it on. "Hold your arms out," the Marine ordered. A heavy set of handcuffs was clipped over Murata's wrists, and then shackles applied to his ankles; both sets connected with a link chain that prevented Murata from raising his hands above his mouth. With a Marine at either side, Murata was walked away towards the aircraft steps.

"You can drive back," said Morohashi, feeling relieved, but still strangely anxious.

"Sure," replied Weaver. "You up for that lunch?"

"Yes, thank you, that would be nice," she replied a little distractedly.

"There is a lovely old manor house in the village. It houses a fascinating collection of quilts. If it is open to visitors today, I think you will find it very interesting."

Morohashi smiled, her eyes fixed on the prisoner, as he was being helped up the steps. As he disappeared from view she turned and walked back to the car.

"Are you okay?" asked Weaver.

"Yes, I am fine. No, I am not fine, I think something has been missed," she said turning and walking back to the group of American officers watching as the C17's engines were started.

"Excuse me, sir!" she shouted over the roar, to the base commander. "Has anyone checked the runway in the last hour?"

"No, but you think we should?"

"I am very surprised that no attempt has been made to free this man you are taking. There is still some chance whilst he is in this country."

"Sergeant Hammell!"

"Sir!"

"Take a Jeep and two armed men and drive down the taxiway and runway. Anythin' suspicious radio back."

"Sir!" replied Hammell, snapping to attention and saluting.

"Okay, Lieutenant Commander?"

"Thank you, sir."

Morohashi watched as the Jeep sped away down the taxiway with a soldier looking out either side. At the end of the taxiway the Jeep crew reported that all was clear then started out along the runway. The search completed, the base commander ordered the aircraft away and the group watched as it lumbered the mile down the taxiway.

"That Jeep and soldiers should be going down the taxiway in front of that plane," Morohashi said loudly. The base commander turned and glared at her, but said nothing.

*   *   *

As the huge aircraft came towards them, both men felt threatened by its sheer size and power. Timing was critical. The attack must be made just before the aircraft started its turn towards the runway. Hamaura held his breath, his stomach churning with nerves. Would this work? Would he hit the target? So much depended on him being able to stand and throw the balls accurately. He had almost blown it when the Jeep had come along. When it had stopped just after it had passed him, he had almost broken cover to attack it.

Slowly he raised his head and peered again through the slit, beneath his turf covering, at the massive aircraft approaching. When the wings pass over the white marker, is what Iwaki had said. He must not move until then. On and on the plane came, getting bigger and bigger in his vision. Then the starboard wing spread its shadow over the marker and, throwing back the turf, Hamaura stood and threw a steel ball straight into the outer starboard engine's turbine fan. Even before it had struck its target a second ball was on its way.

The bang was very loud, as were the subsequent bangs and explosions. The engine pod started to gyrate, then, as Hamaura's third ball went into the inner starboard engine, it too began to disintegrate. Both pods were now gyrating dramatically and vast amounts of debris was being blasted out of the rear nozzle. The sudden loss of power on the starboard side, combined with the confusion caused by the noise and violent shaking of the whole aircraft, delayed pilot response momentarily. Powered only on the portside engines the aircraft slewed just a few feet to starboard putting its starboard undercarriage off the narrow taxiway, and onto the wet soft ground.

Flight Lieutenant Cortez and his co-pilot had both been looking left towards the runway intent upon making the turn without putting the aircraft's wheels off the somewhat narrow taxiway. As a result neither had seen Hamaura stand and launch his lethal attack.

"Shut down everything!" yelled a frightened Dwain Jenson, the co-pilot. "Shit I said this old bird was not up to such heavy lifts. She didn't sound right when we came in to land."

Cortez looked back over his shoulder. "Go down to the personnel bay and see if anyone is hurt," he ordered to Lutman, the loadmaster.

"Tower this is Flight Lieutenant Cortez, flight GH224, we have just experienced massive engine failure to our starboard engines. I am evacuating all personnel from the aircraft. We are checking for any casualties at this time and will report. Out."

At that moment leaking fuel from the ruptured fuel lines ignited on the hot engine casings and flames licked the underside of the aircraft's starboard wing.

Turning to his co-pilot Cortez shouted, "Get down below and give Lutman a hand evacutin' the guys down there, and stop soundin' like a child for fuck's sake!"

At the cargo level Lutman had opened the internal door to the cargo bay, and was checking that the passengers were unharmed when he heard Jenson shouting, "The engines are on fire get everyone off the plane!" as he half ran, half fell down the internal steps.

"Open the crew door, that'll be quickest," replied Lutman, now getting a grip of the situation. "Everyone unbuckle and make their way over here. Don't run!"

Murata, being shackled, and somewhat shaken by noise and vibration, was slow to respond. His guards however had moved instantly, providing a shield, so when the two stun grenades came through the doorway the effect on him was relatively minor.

When Jenson had pushed the crew door open he had been surprised to see a short man standing close by, dressed in a camouflage cloak. It was the last thing he saw. Hit by two rounds from Iwaki's M9 his body continued its forward motion falling from the aircraft to the ground. Throwing two stun grenades into the cargo hold, Iwaki ducked and covered his ears. A third grenade, thrown up the step access to the cockpit door, rendered Cortez unconscious.

With the arrival of Hamaura both men got the ladder in place and were in the cargo bay inside thirty seconds. Kicking bodies out of the way, and shooting those that were showing any signs of movement, they made their way across to Murata. Hamaura kneeling on one knee hefted the shackled man over his shoulder in a fireman's lift, whilst Iwaki, having executed the three Marine guards, searched them for their keys. By the time the two military Jeeps, with armed men, were halfway down the taxiway, Hamaura had reached the perimeter fence and was pulling a groggy Murata through the gap.

"Well done," said Kimura as he let the wire mesh fall back into place. "You take him to the nearest truck and put him on the back seat. I will take care of the Americans and cover Iwaki-san."

The two Jeeps were no more than fifty yards from the plane as Kimura raised his M4 and fired a short burst, hitting the driver of the right-hand Jeep, which promptly swerved and rolled over killing two more of its occupants and throwing the others out like rag dolls, to be winded and injured as they hit the tarmac with force. Seeing the first strike, the driver of the other Jeep swerved to bring the vehicle out of sight behind the plane as Iwaki leapt from the aircraft and ran towards Kimura. Dragging the wire mesh aside with his left foot Kimura fired at the legs of those assembling on the other side of the plane. Screams could be heard as three of the men fell to the ground wounded. Iwaki did not stop after clearing the fence, but kept running towards the getaway truck, and clambered in alongside Murata. Kimura, now walking backwards away from the fence was firing as he went. Reaching the truck he climbed into the tub at the rear and banged on the roof for Hamaura to get underway.

Driving fast along the perimeter track their truck came into view of the only soldier to escape uninjured. He opened fire, but only succeeded in hitting the truck twice, neither of which caused any problem.

* * *

On the airbase apron the party seeing off the plane had watched its progress for half the length of the taxiway before losing interest and starting to disperse. The base commander, coming over to Weaver and Morohashi, smiled. "Now, you have a safe journey back to London. Please give my best wishes to Commander Campbell when you report in."

"We most certainly will, sir," replied Weaver. "Would it be possible to use your washr…"

"Binoculars quickly," said Morohashi. "Something is happening down there."

Weaver had been aware that her entire concentration had been on the progress of the plane. He fumbled in his jacket pockets and, after catching the binoculars in the lining, finally removed them and handed them to her.

Hurriedly focusing the glasses she searched along the underside of the starboard wing just as a loud bang was heard.

"There is someone down there!" she shouted. "I cannot see from here what he is doing, I think he has thrown something at the plane." A second load bang was heard and the aircraft veered off the taxiway onto the soft ground.

"Where's Sergeant Hammell and that Jeep?" shouted the base commander.

"Sittin' at the west end of the runway, sir, waitin' for the plane to take off, sir," replied his orderly.

"Get them on the radio and have them back here pronto. Then radio the gate and get their Jeep up here with as many armed men as they have."

The commander turned to Weaver and Morohashi, but they were already running towards their car. Weaver got there first and leapt into the driver's seat and started the engine. "We can't get involved on their airfield, and anyway we would not get there in time," said Weaver, as Morohashi slammed her car door.

The car's wheels spun, smoking, as they raced away towards the gate. Morohashi grabbed the road map, and sought a route that would take them to the nearest point at the end of the runway.

"Turn left outside the gates then take a right hand fork through the village, it will lead to the road passing near to the end of the runway."

At the gate, even though the vehicle approaching had police lights and siren going, the guard kept the barrier down, moving to stand in front of the car with his hand raised.

Holding up his warrant card Weaver yelled, "Stop pissing about and open the bloody barrier you idiot."

Then from the guardroom a voice boomed, "Open the barrier, Private!"

Now running back to the gate controls he pressed a button. The barrier slowly started to rise. It had barely got halfway before Weaver launched the car at the gap, and was off down the road, accelerating the vehicle up through the gears.

Morohashi had never been in a car travelling so fast. At each bend in the road her heart was in her mouth, her hand out holding onto the dashboard. Weaver dropped the car into fourth as he scythed through the pinch point in the road, with its sign welcoming careful drivers. In the village itself, women grabbed at their children as they stepped back from the edge of the narrow pavements. The driver of the brewer's dray lorry slammed his cab door closed, and quickly leapt to the safety of the gap between his vehicle and the car parked in front. With siren screaming and the alternating red and blue lights flashing in unison with the flashing bright headlights, their car had cleared the village in just under twenty seconds, leaving the inhabitants frightened and annoyed.

"Go left at the next junction," Morohashi instructed.

"When is that?" asked Weaver.

"Just round this right-hand bend I think."

Dropping the car through two gears to third Weaver flicked the car right and floored the accelerator, powering the vehicle out of the bend. Then he hit the brakes hard, moving the car across to the right-hand side of the road and going down to second gear. Morohashi thought the car would turn over at the speed it was doing, but instead it power-slid into and through the corner to accelerate again off down the lane. Trees blocked his view of the next bend and Weaver braked hard again to slow the car as again he took the vehicle to the wrong side of the road in order to get the straightest line. As the sightline opened up he hit the brake even harder, stopping the vehicle a foot from the front of a large farm tractor, towing a trailer. Flinging the car into reverse he spun the wheels and the car shot backwards, then heaving on the wheel he reversed it into a field entrance and stopped. Throwing the car door open he franticly waved to the tractor driver to get past quickly, shouting, "Come on you stupid bastard, can't you see we're in a bloody hurry, come on get a move on!"

Mud spattered up the sides of the car as they powered back onto the lane almost clipping the rear of the farm trailer as it passed them. Through the bend and for some way along the next straight section, mud and gravel could be heard, above the noise of the engine, striking the bottom of the car as the clods of mud came off the tyres.

Mud on the road at the next bend almost had them in the ditch and, in panic, Morohashi dropped the map book.

"We must look for a track on the left," she said as she groped for the book on the floor between her legs.

Just in time she regained her sitting position before Weaver threw the car left, between two trees onto the track the gang had used. Recent rain had made the surface soft and slippery and Weaver needed all of his skills to keep the car on the track and avoid getting stuck. Suddenly clearing some low scrub there in front of them parked across the track was the second Warrior truck Iwaki had driven in.

"Shit! Hold on, we may hit it!" shouted Weaver. The car slewed and bucked under hard braking, miraculously stopping inches from impact. "Phew, that was bloody close."

Getting round the obstruction took time and a lot of bad language, but eventually Weaver cleared the area and got the car barrelling headlong again in pursuit.

The district nurse, driving sedately along Witch Hazel Lane, almost fainted as the unmarked police car, which she could hear, but could not see, either in front or behind her, suddenly appeared, in a spray of mud and grit, from the hedge at the side of the road, only feet in front of her. Braking, and snatching at the wheel her little car skidded gently off the road to drop its nearside front wheel into the ditch before stopping. Rosemary Crofton sat stunned and trembling for several minutes before realising, with some embarrassment, that her driver's seat felt rather damp.

Weaver had seen a fleeting glimpse of the nurse's car as he fought to react to the sudden arrival in the lane.

"Jesus Christ, that was bloody close," he said, then looking in the rear-view mirror again, he continued, "I think they're alright. I don't think they hit anything solid, just went up on the grass."

Hamaura had been similarly surprised by the sudden arrival at the lane and had put the Warrior on two wheels as he overreacted. The effect was to slow him down a bit, enabling the faster-moving police car to gain on them swiftly. He was beginning to regain his confidence when Kimura banged on the rear window of the cab and pointed to a spot behind them. Glancing in his wing mirror Hamaura saw the flashing lights behind him and pushed the accelerator to the floor. It was no contest, however. After three bends, in which Hamaura had almost crashed, the police car had closed up. In the tub at the rear of the Warrior, Kimura sat up and smiled at the two figures in the car behind and waved. Then raising his M4 carbine he fired a short burst at the driver's side of the car. The third bullet smashed through the windscreen, hitting Weaver in the throat, severing his jugular, and smashing his vertebrae. He died instantly.

The police group, which had been stationed overnight in the wood, found Morohashi, holding her left collarbone and with blood dripping from a cut on her forehead, beside the wreck of the police car and a bailer, in the field. Seeing the gun she had shouted a warning but too late. Weaver had braked hard, and still had his foot on the brake pedal when he was hit. As the car slowed it had left the road, run up a small bank and through the hedge to be stopped by the farm bailer parked at the edge of the field. The impact with the bailer had the effect of dislocating her left collarbone as the back frame to the bailer came through the windscreen cutting her forehead as the car stopped.

Chapter 8

At the time Murata's prison van entered the Dartford Tunnel, Chief Inspector Jackson was standing just to the left of Ishihara's front door. To his right was a fully kitted armed officer holding a battering ram. To the right of him were six Specialist Firearms Officers (SFOs) in their black uniforms, each armed with a Glock 17 pistol and a Heckler & Koch MP5 sub-machine gun.

"Make it one hit," Jackson whispered to the ram holder. "This is not a courtesy call."

The man nodded and smiled.

"Right, let's go then."

The ram smashed into the door at the Yale lock level with such force that it sheered the main bolt and ripped the six secondary frame locks from the frame itself. A further kick and the now twisted door opened wide enough for the team to charge in.

"Front bedroom!" yelled Sergeant Khan.

A uniformed WPC pushed past Jackson and ran up the stairs. By the time Jackson arrived in the bedroom a terrified Jirou Ishihara was standing facing the wall with his hands raised touching the picture rail, whilst an SFO searched him. At the other side of the bed his wife, sobbing with fear, was being searched by the WPC. Moving back away from the couple the search officers ordered both to turn round.

Jackson stepped forward and said, "Jirou Ishihara alias Takumi Ishihara I am arresting you under the United Kingdom's antiterrorism laws ..."

Unlike a drugs bust, the SFOs did no more than search for other occupants of the house. The real search needed to be much more delicately done by a CTC team experienced in the art of uncovering the clandestine world of the terrorist.

"There is evidence that the garden shed has been used by a group very recently, Chief Inspector," reported Khan. "There are six bedrolls there and some plates and eating utensils."

"I'll come and have a look right away," replied Jackson. "How the hell did a group that size exist without us knowing for God's sake? We've had round the clock here for weeks, both front and back."

The garden shed was very large, the size of a normal garage. Inside what would usually have been ranged around the walls, had been stacked at the back of the shed. Two lawnmowers were piled, one on top of the other, watering cans and garden tools were stacked in one corner and held in place by a length of rope tied to the shed frame. The six bedrolls were neatly stacked against the side wall under the window.

"Where is the rest of it I wonder?" mused Jackson.

"Sir?" asked DS Carter, the other CTC officer at the scene.

"You know, garden furniture, kids' bikes, that type of thing."

"Round behind the shed, sir," replied Carter. "Except they don't appear to have kids."

Shocked neighbours gave a picture of a polite and friendly couple that had lived in the house for ten years. No one appeared to have either seen or heard anything of the group who occupied the shed.

The dustbin revealed a large quantity of food wrappings and cans. Checks suggested that this amount had been discarded during the last four days. Forensic would later find toenail clippings between the floorboards of the shed and a discarded North Korean cigarette packet amongst the garden tools; but otherwise the shed was clean, too clean.

Back in the house Jackson walked through to the front doorway. "Alright Constable tell the team to get in here and start."

After the initial shock of being rudely awoken to find themselves looking down the wrong end of a MP5 gun barrel, the Ishiharas proved to be stubborn under further interrogation, and Jackson prepared himself, and the interview team, for the long haul.

It was late afternoon when the information regarding Murata's escape and the death of DS Weaver came through to Jackson. Gathering the CTC team together, he informed them of the event and outcome, then reminded them all of the importance of maintaining exact professionalism in both the interviewing of the Ishiharas and in the search of their property.

"You know as well as I that the slightest relaxation of the rules on our part will virtually guarantee the freedom of this pair, who, I have no doubt, are as guilty as hell. So be thorough, but be very careful."

Two hours later he found himself outside the front door of Weaver's parents' home, together with WPC Tucker. "I'm sorry you are the one that has to help out with this. The local nick has promised to send their victim support team a bit later, but at the moment they're having to deal with a nasty house break-in at an elderly couple's home."

"That's alright, sir. Having been on the receiving end of this type of news myself, it's possibly not as daunting as it would be for some."

It was the first time Tucker had seen Jackson handle anything requiring extreme delicacy, and she was very impressed. His image was always of a man as cold and as hard as steel, but the way he broke the news, and the tenderness in the way he conveyed his own and the team's sympathy, was a marvellous example of leadership.

Tucker took care of the tea making and clearly written notes for the couple, regarding the return of their son's body and belongings. Jackson told the parents as much as he could with regard to the case. "I would like to tell you more, but I am afraid that this case is far from over and security is of vital importance. We would appreciate it if you would avoid making any statement to the press. It could be that they get wind of this event, but I am hoping that you will not be bothered in any way by them."

The arrival of the victim support team gave Jackson and Tucker the opportunity to make their apologies, and leave.

"What lovely people, and so brave," Tucker said as she moved the car out into the evening traffic.

"Yes, they are, and they definitely don't deserve that type of news," replied Jackson, the hardness, or was it bitterness, returning to his voice. "We are going to find this Murata and his little gang so help me, and when we do, I'm going to do everything I can to make sure that those little bastards are locked up here for the rest of their natural."

Tucker glanced sideways at him and saw, in his glowering expression, determination and a ferocity that reminded her of her own feelings, so long ago.

Caroline Tucker left New Scotland Yard at the end of her shift feeling tired and sad. As she walked towards St James's Park underground station, she wondered how Campbell's team must have been feeling. Jackson had been very quiet on their return to the Yard, and had gone straight to the lifts without even saying goodnight. Taking the tube train to Monument Station, she got off and walked slowly across London Bridge, stopping halfway to look down at the river and, almost unseeingly at *HMS Belfast* and, behind the battle cruiser, Tower Bridge. A light gust of chilling air from the river brought her out of her solemn revere, and standing straight, forcing her shoulders back, she walked briskly across the rest of the bridge to her little flat by Borough Market.

She took a shower, then, in her nightdress and dressing gown, cooked an omelette and threw some salad leaves and a slice of tomato around it on the plate. She did not recall tasting any of it, nor the glass of red wine she had drunk. The television news had nothing about the incident, and she felt relieved that Campbell and Jackson, with their team, would be able to get busy trying to track these monsters down, and not have to waste time answering the stupid questions of the press. As the programme changed she flicked through the channels, but found nothing that could hold her attention. Though tired she was unable to consider going to bed, so she busied herself tidying the flat and doing some ironing.

It was close to 11 p.m. when the downstairs buzzer went. She ignored it. Maybe they, whoever they were, would go away. It went again, and reluctantly she turned off the iron and walked through to the intercom.

"Who is it?" she asked.

"It's Alec, can I come up? I want to be sure that you are alright."

"Can you wait a few minutes, I am not dressed to receive visitors."

Standing at the street door to the building, Campbell felt rather conspicuous. Why was it this lady had him doing things on the spur of the moment? Jackson had merely said in passing that Caroline Tucker had been a great help at Weaver's home. Why had he assumed that she would be upset following it? Was it because he knew she had been the recipient of a similar visit, when her husband and sons had been killed? No, if he was to be honest with himself. It was that, after being bewitched by her at the embassy dinner, where she had sparkled like an exotic jewel, they had sat at supper in his house, talking like two poker players, each unwilling to show their hand. He had been fearful of frightening her away. She had skilfully avoided any show of feelings. Was it the sensation of being in some kind of limbo that had brought him here, where he could risk destroying a relationship before it had really started?

Caroline took five minutes to throw on some clothes and quickly brush her hair. When her flat doorbell rang she realised that she was trembling. Trying to control herself, she crossed the small hallway and opened the door. Standing on the landing was an exhausted-looking Alec Campbell, pale and dark-eyed.

"Sorry I took so long," she said. "You look absolutely done in. Come on through. Can I make you a coffee?"

"I didn't want to put you to any trouble, I just wanted to make sure that you were okay, after the news about Weaver. I didn't know until an hour ago that it was you who went with Chief Inspector Jackson to see the parents."

"I would be lying if I said I was okay. It is strange really, I hardly knew him, but I felt so sad when the Chief Inspector told me what had happened. Is the Japanese officer he was with, alright?"

"I saw her a couple of hours ago. She was very lucky to come away with minor cuts and bruises, and a dislocated collar bone," Alex Campbell replied. "I told her to take the next few days off, but she insisted on being at tomorrow's meeting at DELCO. Tough young lady that."

"I'll make that coffee, I was going to have one anyway, and you look all in."

He didn't move, he just stood there, looking at her with a very caring expression on his face. Whether it was Weaver's death or the meeting with his parents or her sense of utter loneliness, she didn't know, but she found herself suddenly crying like she hadn't done for years.

"That's it, let it all out," he said, taking the one step needed to stand close to her and take her in his arms.

When she recovered her composure he got her sat down in an armchair and, seating himself at the far end of the settee, talked with her for hours. Occasionally they just sat in silence together. It must have been during one of those periods that she fell asleep, for in the morning she found herself covered with a blanket, her head on cushions. A note was on the coffee table, written in his neat hand, 'I'll come back for the coffee some other time. Alec.'

Getting out of the chair, she went to the kitchen and made breakfast, then showered and changed. She felt emotionally empty, but in another way full. In spite of the grey clouds over London, her spirits were high, as if she was in sunshine. Pulling open the drawer of her dressing table, she took out an envelope with HR DEPARTMENT written in bold letters on the front. Her resignation had been written as soon as she had returned from the supper at Alec's house.

* * *

Kimura had seen Weaver's head and torso collapse forward onto the steering wheel and the car leave the road. Banging on the cab roof again he had made a karate chop gesture then brought his hands together as if striking dust from them. Hamaura had raised his fist in salute. Iwaki was, however, distracted in getting Murata's shackles off and removing the orange overall.

Having freed Murata from his restraints and got him dressed in everyday casual clothing, Iwaki ordered Hamaura to find some woodland where they could abandon the truck out of sight. Crossing the Market Rasen to Lincoln railway line they came across the perfect spot. Turning the vehicle off the road Hamaura drove the Warrior down the muddy track deep into the wood. The adrenalin created during the attack was wearing off and all four men sat silently for several minutes as the realisation of what they had achieved became a reality in their minds.

Iwaki was the first to speak. "Shortly they will have helicopter up looking for us so we stay here in this cover. We must each take a side of the wood and keep lookout until dark when we will go cross-country to town of Lincoln."

Leaving Lincoln, one at a time, they used local trains the following morning to get them close to London, then buses to cross the city as far as Wimbledon where they regrouped and took a train to Alton, arriving late the following evening. At the warehouse things were much as they had left them, and with Hamaura and Kimura acting as lookouts, Iwaki and Murata sat for the first time to discuss the future.

"I was wondering when you were going to tell me the price of my freedom," said Murata. "There must be a price, even when you are helping a friend."

"Murata-san it is not correct to say there is a price, true freedom is rarely bought," replied Iwaki. "As you know, I have close relation to our friends and supporters across the western sea. These friends of ours require our help with problem."

Murata sat silent and impassive waiting for Iwaki to continue.

"Britain and America are putting great effort into cyber warfare. Many times have our friends' systems been compromised by such means. As you know, missile guidance programme, reaching satisfactory development stage, but General Namgoong fears that soon West will break code and destroy software again." Iwaki straightened his back and looked searchingly at Murata for some reaction. "You can understand why so important to stop such things happening."

Murata nodded his head. "What plan do you have in mind? It must not be as stupid as that young hothead outside, who only deals in revenge with no other objective."

"There are many Japanese defence workers here in this country being shown special computer software for code breaking. They are also being trained in how to use such technology to, how they say, er, 'hack into' our friends' computers," Iwaki explained. There was a long silence before Iwaki continued, "Comrade Dho believes it will take force of forty men to make sure western forces' plan is destroyed. They must strike at just one location to ensure that particular threat is eliminated."

"Do they have such force here in this country?" asked Murata surprised at the numbers.

"No, only six, and twenty more will arrive very soon. Comrade Dho hopes that we assist."

Murata frowned and shook his head.

"Comrade Dho reminded me that he has given you much assistance in past," said Iwaki, not pleased with Murata's reaction.

Murata glared at Iwaki. "Comrade Dho does not need to remind Tadashi Murata of his debts!"

"You will assist him then?"

"Let me see Comrade Dho's plan. Maybe we can achieve with smaller force."

"Maybe."

"Forty men too much for attack. Such force no way to retreat after operation complete."

"I do not think Comrade Dho would have such idea. To bring such a force into action would be very high risk of discovery and difficult to command," replied Iwaki, slightly angered by Murata's anticipation of the strategy. "I will contact him and arrange meeting, Murata-san."

Murata sensing the annoyance asked, "If we are involved in one section of this attack, who will be in command?"

"As I said, Murata-san, I do not know detail, only that our support would be welcomed."

The two men sat in uneasy silence for a time until Murata suggested that the lookout was changed.

*   *   *

The afternoon meeting at DELCO was a very sombre affair. Campbell looked unusually tired and strained. Lieutenant Commander Morohashi sat staring into the distance, her eyes dark-ringed and red. Lorna had sat her down for two hours during the morning in a counselling session, but felt that for once she had not been of much help, and many more sessions might be needed.

Jackson, back to his icy, cool self, was taking the lead.

"We are getting nowhere with the Ishiharas at the moment. I had hoped that she would crack, when I first saw her, but now, I don't know," he said, before turning to Penny Heathcote. "Lieutenant, what we need is a breakthrough from his textile transaction records."

"We may have something there, sir," replied Heathcote. "We went back five years on the accounting records from his house, to establish a trading pattern. The analysis of that showed that by far the greater part of his business has been the export of quality wool cloth, from this country to Japan. The second most popular item is pure cotton, normally from Egypt, but also destined for the Japanese market. The only other item, in any consistency and quantity, has been viscose; imported from Russia, and divided here for re-export to a variety of destinations in Japan.

She paused as she turned over some papers to find the sheet she wanted to refer to.

"Fortunately for us, Mr, or Mrs, Ishihara, is a very orderly bookkeeper. So it was possible for us to tie nearly all of the transactions to shipping documents."

"You say nearly all. Were there any significant transactions where shipping documentation was missing?" asked Campbell, speaking for almost the first time that afternoon.

"Yes, sir, there was," replied Heathcote, smiling broadly. "He paid two large sums of money, $15,000 and $40,000, for three rolls of red silk to be shipped from Japan to Vancouver. The payment was made eight days after Hamaura and Kimura were released, and was made in US Dollars, not Yen or Sterling."

"Do we have the bank details?" asked Morohashi.

"Yes, we thought that CS Ishii would enjoy following those up."

"Oh yes, he will be delighted," replied Umeko Morohashi, grateful that at last some lead had been found regarding the group's funding arrangements.

Together Campbell and Jackson sat up straight in their seats. "I suspect that you have another item of interest," said Campbell.

"Yes, sir. On the same day an order was sent out to the States for the supply of the following." She put a slide onto the overhead projector and turned on the lamp:

10 bales of brown silk. (6C – 4/ 10)
6 bales of orange silk. (20/4PL2- SG's)
27 rolls of white silk.(491059M-9/1225846U24)
27 rolls of green silk.(2300M4-A1/1808) (ATA/GL)
100 spools of white silk thread.
100 spools of green silk thread.

"I am a little confused," said Jackson. "What is it that drew your attention to this order?"

"Well, sir. One, the order was very vague for a material such as silk. The dye identification alone would be much more specific. Two, I discovered that the figures in brackets were absolutely meaningless when I checked with London merchants. Three, and most important of all, was that the United States has not produced silk in commercial quantities since the 1720s. Apparently the silk worms smuggled out of China did not like American mulberry leaves enough to make it viable."

"Oh, well done, Lieutenant, very well done," said Jackson.

"That is not all, sir. The value of the order was $27,080, a lot more than the silk would be worth," Heathcote said triumphantly.

"I assume that the payment was made from here?" said Campbell.

"No, sir. We know that it was made, but there is no entry regards payment. My guess is that the encashment of the first transaction mentioned will be in US Dollars, and be from the $40,000 sum mentioned."

"Are these the only silk shipments?" asked Campbell.

"No, Commander. Over the period we have studied, Ishihara has made three such deals, all with the States."

"The French Canadian trawler skipper was paid in counterfeit money," interjected Morohashi.

"Do you have any idea what the order is really for?" asked Jackson.

"I suspect that the brown silk is C4 explosive. The orange I don't know yet. The white and the green are possibly Beretta M9 pistols and M4 A1 US forces' issue carbine rifles. The rest, ammunition."

Jackson and Campbell stared at each other with expressions of amazement.

"They would not have paid for that in dud cash," said Jackson.

"The orange silk is possibly stun grenades," said Morohashi. "The SG probably stands for stun grenades. Hamaura and Kimura used those when they attacked the plane."

"They couldn't have brought that lot from Oban," said Jackson.

"Only a small amount of the shipment was for them," said Campbell. "The majority was for the Irish group, whoever they are, who Hamaura and his chums transferred to in mid Atlantic. Voyage paid for with an arms deal, very tidy."

"That's what we thought too, sir," said Heathcote. "Also as mentioned in my report to you at the weekend, sir, Mr Robertson, the pilot who flew them across Canada, seemed sure that the men that this Itoh introduced as local staff, were Korean, which seems to reinforce the ideological link with the group."

"Yes, thank you for reminding me," said Campbell. "Anything else?"

"Just one thing we are following up, sir. Very occasionally he instructs a delivery to, or collection from, a warehouse at a place called Crowhill Farm. We are trying to establish where that is."

"Why does that stand out Lieutenant?" asked Jackson.

"Well, sir, it is not one of his regular warehouses, and this one doesn't appear in his books. We've had the others searched this morning. Nothing unexpected was found."

"Let me know what you find."

"Of course, sir."

"The next thing on the agenda is, what are they going to do now? Take out Vaughan, do you think?" asked Campbell.

"First they will get Murata to a place of safety. It is also possible that he was injured during the escape and may need medical attention," said Morohashi, wincing as she moved her left arm on the table to pull a glass of water towards her.

Penny Heathcote looked across at her, eyebrows raised questioningly.

"I am fine, Penny, thank you."

"We alerted all of the hospitals within a radius of fifty miles, but nothing came back, except two Chinese takeaway cooks with burns," informed Jackson.

"I am concerned that there appears to be a Korean involvement in this particular Red Brigade operation," said Campbell. "I am also aware of the concerns of our friends in Tokyo, with regard to the two groups of computer software specialists in training over here." Campbell reached forward and, taking hold of the flask, poured himself another coffee. "The MoD has made us all too aware of the importance of the work these teams will be expected to do upon their return to Japan, in terms of infiltration of North Korean cyberspace." He took a mouthful of the coffee. "I recall that the previous attempts to achieve this were uncovered by North Korea and vicious steps taken to close that route. Our assessment concurs with that of Tokyo, in that agencies of North Korea will attempt to disrupt any plans to hack into their computer systems."

To those in the room it seemed that Campbell was talking more to himself than endeavouring to inform or promote a discussion.

"Would you excuse me for a few minutes, sir?" asked Lieutenant Heathcote, after a few moments during which there had been complete silence.

"Something important?"

"I think I may be able to improve on the information regarding the arms delivery in Vancouver, sir. It would probably rattle Mr Ishihara, if we could tell him exactly where the shipment was sent too."

Campbell nodded his agreement, and then continued now sounding positive and instructive. "We must locate this Crowhill Farm, just in case it is used for something that is of interest to us. Chief Inspector, can we get DS Carter working on that immediately."

Jackson nodded and left the meeting room.

"Lieutenant Commander Morohashi, what do you think will happen once Murata is tucked up safely?"

"If they are working alone, I think they would try to take out Ian Vaughan, then hide until the heat is off," she replied.

"That's what I think as well. If only he would agree to come back to the safe house."

"There is another possibility, sir, and that this is a joint operation involving North Korean interests. Due to current sanctions, North Korea has very limited hard currency. Murata's group, on the other hand, appear to be in funds, and well connected in this country and the States. I can't imagine what the deal is exactly, but I believe that we cannot ignore the possibility of a joint operation."

Before Campbell could answer Jackson came back into the room. "I think Lorna Pennington has tracked down that Crowhill Farm," he said. "Seems to be on one of these small industrial estates that appear to be springing up outside of every town and village. This one is not far from Birmingham Airport."

"Have you got Carter and a team organised?"

"Yes, sir, they are on their way. I've told them not to involve forensic until we can be sure that it is of value."

"Yes, you are probably right, it does seem to be a long shot," replied Campbell, stifling a yawn. "Tomorrow morning I would like to review the Bristol surveillance operation, and can you ask Inspector Hemmings to join us, I need an update on the Leeds situation concerning that mosque. At 1100 I would like you to join me in a visit to Eastfield-cum-Welton airbase, to try and learn how they made the attack."

"I've got that address," announced Penny Heathcote excitedly, as she re-entered the meeting room. "Oh, sorry, I didn't mean to interrupt."

"It's alright Lieutenant," said Jackson, smiling. He liked Penny Heathcote, because of her enthusiasm and consistent cheerfulness. "Carry on, tell us all."

"Well, sir, it came to me just now as I was reading the actual order and realised that there was no address for delivery. I have just been and checked with the other orders, and they were the same, no delivery address. Then I saw it. The numbers 491059 and 1225846U24 alongside item three were the same as those on previous orders, but the commodities appeared to be very different. I thought at first it was a postcode but that didn't tie up, then I realised that it was latitude and longitude. There is your address, sir, Prince's Gardens Business Park, Unit 24," she said triumphantly. "Oh, and according to item four on the list, it was to be delivered at 2300 hours on the 18th July."

"Brilliant, young lady, brilliant," said Jackson. "If, as you say, the place has been used more than once, it may well be a terrorist cell meeting point. Let's hope it is. Can you get that off to Vancouver? CI Jarvis is the man."

"Commander?" said Morohashi.

"Yes?"

"Are you going to put some protection around this Ian Vaughan?"

"Yes, we are," he replied. "Why do you ask?"

"It is just that I would like to volunteer myself for that task, I feel I cannot achieve much being here."

Campbell sat back and considered her proposal for several moments. "I see some merit in having an observer there who could instantly identify members of the gang, but I do not think it would be the best use of your skills. Unless you are well concealed you might well become a target. We don't know how good a look they had of you in the chase from the airfield. Let me think about it for a time, with Murata now free I am going to try and get Mr Vaughan to return to a 'safe house'."

Half an hour later the meeting broke up without any decisions being made with regard to search priorities. News broadcasts had been put out, with photographs of Hamaura and Kimura and an identikit image of Iwaki, but no names or details were given other than 'in connection with an incident in Lincolnshire', and a warning not to approach the suspects.

*　　　　*　　　　*

The base commander had been rather distracted during Campbell and Jackson's visit. In his office, frequent calls from the States interrupted the meeting they were having. Eventually they had been escorted to the damaged aircraft; now back out of public view in the hanger. At the scene of the attack Sergeant Hammell pointed out the trenches and handed to Campbell the petanque ball that had remained unused on the ground beside Hamaura's hiding place.

"Simple, but mighty effective, sir," said Hammell, taking the ball back. "They shot and killed the three marine guards, and two of the tank maintenance crew, plus the co-pilot. Shit, what a mess this has been."

"I am surprised how few men there are based here," said Campbell.

"Well, sir, this base was due to close down two weeks ago, and was only kept open to handle this flight. Most of the men have been posted. I should'a been in Afghanistan by now."

"I see," said Campbell. "That explains a great deal, thank you."

As Campbell spoke, Jackson's mobile bleeped. "Jackson." There was a pause as the person on the other end imparted some information. "Right, get Carter to go down there and check that one out. Tell Lorna to keep at it, if necessary we check out the ones in the north of Scotland."

Turning to Campbell he said, "Lorna Pennington has come up with another Crowhill Farm, this one near to Alton in Hampshire. I've ordered Carter to get down there. It is apparently leased to an Egyptian textile merchant."

"That sounds more promising than the Thai furniture warehouse," replied Campbell. "I hope Scotland isn't an option, the overtime will cripple our budget."

On the train back to London, Campbell and Jackson reviewed the morning's meeting with Hemmings regarding the Bristol situation, and discussed deployment of protection teams to look after the two Japanese training groups. It was just before their train entered Kings Cross Station when Jackson asked, "Did you hear that WPC Tucker has resigned, sir?"

"No, I hadn't."

"Bloody shame, she was damn good at her job and very reliable. I don't suppose we can persuade her to change her mind?"

"Oh, I doubt it, Chief Inspector, she always struck me as being very strong-minded. I'll have a word with HR and see what they can do."

"You or I shouldn't have a word then, sir?"

"Oh no, best leave that type of thing to HR. I'm sure they can find better words than we can," replied Campbell, anxious, but at the same time hopeful at the news. "Ah, here we are, Kings Cross. I need to have a word with Ian Vaughan when I get back to my desk."

* * *

Murata had been pacing about like a caged lion for the last hour. Iwaki watched him, curious as to why such a man seemed to need to expend so much energy in the thought processes. Dho was due to arrive at any moment, but it was obvious to Iwaki that Murata was not ready for such a meeting.

Suddenly there was a rapid banging on the rear door. Iwaki was there, turning the handle in a flash. Outside Hamaura stood pointing to the end of the building. "Police in two cars," he said. "We must go quickly."

The group hurriedly stuffed sleeping bags and other personal items into their rucksacks and gathered outside the back of the building near a gap in the fence. Listening at the door Iwaki heard the front shutter being opened then, turning towards the group, pointed across the meadow beyond. Five minute later, from the cover of the far hedgerow, Kimura reported on police movement. Iwaki was stood a few yards away with Murata, talking to Dho by mobile phone. "He was just about to drive onto site when he saw police cars. He will meet us at top of that field and take us to safe location."

Murata acknowledged the message with a nod. "Good fortune shines on us Iwaki-san. A few minutes later and all would have been lost," he said with a flash of excitement in his eyes.

"Another police vehicle has arrived," announced Kimura. "Police dogs!!"

Now there was panic as the group began to scramble up the steep hillside to the lane and, hopefully, rescue. Behind them they could hear the barking of the dogs as they picked up the scent and pulled at their leads to take up the chase. One of the handlers saw a movement on the hillside above and let his dog off the lead. The Alsatian sprinted away across the meadow to the hedge, where only minutes ago Kimura had raised the alarm. Scenting their trail again the dog ran swiftly, closing the gap at an alarming speed. Murata's group were straggled out a little with Hamaura puffing at the rear, taking fearful glances over his shoulder at the pursuing animal. Targeting Hamaura the dog was about to attack and bring him down, when the crack of an M9 was heard above the snarling and the dog dropped to the ground dead.

Hamaura had also stopped, and seemed frozen to the spot staring at the poor animal as it lay almost at his feet, lifeless, blood trickling from the wound in its chest.

"Hamaura. Come now!" shouted Murata, holding the M9, ready to shoot the young man if he disobeyed. "Go through there quickly."

Shaken out of his apparent trance, Hamaura panted the last few paces to a gap in the fence and fell down the bank to land in a heap at the feet of Comrade Dho, who stood by the rear door of the Transit van.

"Get in quickly," ordered Dho, reinforcing his command with a kick.

As Murata leapt into the vehicle, the doors were closed, and two seconds later it started to move off.

* * *

"All right, Lee darlin'?" she said handing over a red pass to the young Chinese postman. "'And it in at the gate on yer way out."

"Sure thing," the postman said, and leaving the reception block, leapt into his van.

Ian Vaughan, working with Jack Craine, the contractor's site manager, was measuring up the area, as there appeared to be a drawing discrepancy. Ian looked across at Craine and raised his eyebrows. Craine smiled and shook his head. The visitor escort seeing the exchange came across to them.

"You saw that, eh?" he said quietly, so as not to be overheard. "I sometimes wonder why I am here. Anyone on a red badge should be escorted, but not according to her."

"Does make you wonder doesn't it," replied Ian.

"It's even funnier than that. You see, the lad that came in is not Lee, but Chang."

"Really?"

"Yeah, I spent several years out in Hong Kong in the services, and got used to telling them apart. Sometimes it's not easy," said the escort. "It's a waste of time telling her though, you just get a mouthful of abuse, and told to mind your own business."

Ian thought about mentioning the incident to Mark Parish, the site security chief, but decided that, as he was not exactly flavour of the month, it would be better to leave things alone. Back in his office there was a message for him to contact Commander Campbell.

"Murata has escaped, and he and his little gang are probably coming after you," said Campbell.

"I thought special precautions were being taken to avoid him getting free?" replied Ian, his heart sinking at the news.

"They successfully attacked the aircraft he was in, during its run along the taxiway, before take-off. I'm sorry, but I feel you must come back to the safe house."

"No, I am not hiding away, besides the chances of them finding me down here are very remote. Murata is a marked man, they will need to get him safely away before they think about me. I remind myself daily what the other two look like, so I will see them before they see me. Apart from Murata, who only saw me for a few minutes, if that, the other two will have no idea what I look like."

"It has been taken out of my hands. They are seeking a replacement for you at this moment and as soon as he arrives you will be relieved of your post. I am sorry, but there are too many lives at stake."

"Damn, I suppose it was pressure from Lambert. Well when this guy shows up I will hand over to him, but I am not going back into the safe house. I'm staying down in Kingsbridge," replied Ian testily.

"I cannot force you to stay at the safe house, all I can do is advise you that we cannot, at this time, offer adequate protection to you down there. We just do not have the resources."

"That's fine by me. Do you still want me to phone in daily?"

"Oh yes, of course. If you do see any of them, get in touch immediately."

When the conversation ended Ian went for a long walk around the site perimeter to calm himself down before he met anybody. In his present mood it was likely that he would not be very polite. The really frustrating thing was that he was enjoying the work he was doing and, with the money from the States, he didn't need an income immediately, but he did need some normality to occupy his days.

It was two days later that he was summoned to a meeting in Colin Lambert's office. "This is Mr Chater, who will be taking over your work as from tonight. Make sure that you hand over all of the information in a satisfactory way, and make sure you hand in your pass on leaving."

Chater looked highly embarrassed as he shook Ian's hand. "Call me Bill, I've had a look round so there shouldn't be too much that I will be asking," he said.

"Well, we better be getting on with it," replied Ian. "I would hate to extend my presence here beyond normal hours. Make sure my pay is in the bank on time will you, Lambert?" he continued, walking out of Lambert's office with Chater close behind him.

"I've been told by others that this is not your fault," said Chater as they walked across to the Portakabin.

"No, I am the victim of circumstances, and I suppose Lambert is too: for reasons of security I cannot explain the problem."

So there it was, a new career over almost before it had begun. The handover had been smooth, thanks to Ian's good record keeping and progress reports, plus the full co-operation of Jack Craine. "I'll be sorry to see you go, you are damn good at the job," he had said, as he walked with Ian down to the main gate.

In the reception building Mark Parish took Ian's pass, and sounded almost genuine when he wished Ian good luck. Shirley Withers, the receptionist with the dyed bronze hair, gave a sneering smile as she looked on.

* * *

Campbell had been expecting the call from Chief Superintendent Ishii, anticipating that it would be to announce the recall of the injured Morohashi. To his surprise Ishii announced that the Japanese Government were sending a Detective Inspector Ariyoshi to work with Morohashi, in the hunt for Murata and his group. Campbell was soon to learn that the diplomacy had already been done, and he was 'requested' to give all possible assistance. When Ariyoshi arrived from Washington, he and Morohashi met Campbell at DELCO.

"You are both aware that our laws prevent you from carrying weapons," said Campbell. Both nodded.

"That is good. I have been requested to offer any assistance I can, but I insist that neither of you take any action without informing us and agreeing it with this office first. Do you fully understand that? Anything you do whilst you are in this country must be within our laws. Is that understood?"

"Yes Commander, we both fully understand our position here," replied Morohashi. "We have been discussing the situation regarding the tracking down of Murata and his group with Chief Inspector Jackson. We understand that at present you have protection teams covering both of the sites where Japanese staff are located."

"Yes, that is correct, and I make no secret of the fact that it is stretching our resources beyond the limit. In fact we have had to request the Kingsbridge police station to take over the job of keeping an eye on Ian Vaughan."

"Did he refuse your offer of a safe house then, Commander?" asked Morohashi.

"Yes, he did. We made a mistake when he went to work at the Yealmstoke Head facility. We signed him on as a CTC agent temporarily, and armed him. The idea was conceived before this Korean threat arrived and the possibility of Murata's group joining in with it. We thought that if Murata were freed then Vaughan would become an immediate target, so we set up watchers around him and, just to cover all eventualities, set him up as well. Now of course those watchers have had to be redeployed to fill gaps elsewhere. Vaughan is therefore potentially vulnerable and at present he has probably only part-time protection, and none at all if he chooses to put to sea in this new boat of his."

"Why you not remove his CTC status and disarm him, sir?" enquired Ariyoshi.

"Because he point-blank refused our safe house offer, and I can't bring myself to leave him out there without any defences," replied Campbell. " Also we have – "

A knock at the meeting room door stopped Campbell continuing.

"Your secretary on the secure phone, sir," said Lorna, her head just showing around the door.

"Would you both excuse me for a few minutes?"

Morohashi and Ariyoshi made their way along the corridor to the coffee machine. Selecting the black coffee option Ariyoshi said, "Can't bring himself to leave Vaughan-san without any defences? That seems very strange."

"Ah, you thought so too," said Morohashi. "When I was working with Lieutenant Heathcote, she showed me the file on Ian Vaughan. SIS, who the Commander really works for, believes Mr Vaughan would make a good agent. The report from the training school stated that he showed good promise."

"You think Campbell is treating this case as a field trial for Vaughan-san?"

"He is like Ishii-san, a spy master. Don't be fooled by the polite English speaking and gentlemanly manners," said Morohashi. "By leaving Mr Vaughan dangling like bait on a hook,

Campbell is covering two possible areas that Murata will attack. He has the computer teams heavily protected, which would be his primary concern. His secondary problem, one of far less importance to Britain, is Ian Vaughan's safety; for Campbell it will be like watching a cockfight. If his bird wins, it will be taken home and fed well. If the other bird wins Campbell will throw a cloth over his bird and have it buried."

"But Vaughan-san is married man yes? With two children."

"His wife is wanting a divorce," replied Morohashi.

Ariyoshi shook his head and sighed.

The two stood in silence for a few minutes, sipping their drinks.

"What are we doing here Morohashi-san? What use are we?"

"None at this time, but when Murata shows his hand we will have much to do. We know how he thinks when carrying out attacks, here they have no experience of such things."

The door opened to Campbell's office and he waved at them to indicate that he was ready to continue the meeting.

"We have just heard from the CIA that their source in Pyongyang believes an attack may be made at Portsmouth," informed Campbell. "Given that there is another potential target I suggest that we reinforce both places with your expertise. Which of you goes where is up to you. Just make sure we have your contact details so that we can inform the leaders of the respective protection teams."

"Isn't Plymouth where Mr Vaughan is working?" asked Morohashi.

"He no longer works there. The site director was not prepared to take the risk of him continuing on the site after Murata was freed. I quite understand, especially after the escape attack and the apparent wanton killings."

"Has Vaughan-san left area?" asked Ariyoshi.

"I don't think so, he has a boat down there, which I think he will spend some time on."

A further interruption from Lorna brought the meeting to an end and Morohashi suggested they both lunch at a small Italian restaurant nearby. During the meal they discussed which of them should go where.

"I need you to help me in Plymouth area before you report to the team at Portsmouth," said Morohashi. Ariyoshi looked at her questioningly. "I think Murata may let Hamaura and/or Kimura loose to attack Vaughan. If we plant listening devices in his apartment maybe I can listen out for any problem there. The lady who owns the house could be in danger if Hamaura chooses to get into the building and wait for Vaughan."

"You think Murata would do such a thing before attack? That would draw much attention to area."

"Yes and act as distraction or diversion to the main attack."

"We must put this to Commander Campbell, Morohashi-san. We cannot do that without his acceptance of plan."

Chapter 9

The hooded figure at the entrance to the alley watched the woman check that she had securely closed the brightly painted front door, then struggle with two large canvases, and a folio case of mounted prints, down the front path. At the gate the woman turned left, and he peered around the corner of the house that concealed him, to check that she was indeed leaving. At the sound of a car starting he broke cover and walked to where he could see her drive away. As the battered MG Metro accelerated out onto the road, in a cloud of oily exhaust, the man darted into a side alleyway that led to the rear of the terrace of cottages. Checking that he was not being observed he vaulted the low courtyard wall and knelt at the back door. The lock was a simple five-lever type and he had the door open within two minutes, triggering the beep of the burglar alarm. Hurrying through to the front door, and the burglar alarm keypad, he tapped in 0767 and the beeping stopped. Again he wondered why people had their alarm keypads so close to their front doors. Any patient burglar could see what code was tapped in, simply by using a pair of binoculars.

Carefully he climbed the stairs, aware that any noise might alert the neighbours to his presence. The old lock on the door presented no problem and within a minute he had gained entrance to the bedsit. A quick glance around gave him the impression of a neat and tidy person, nothing obsessive, just well organised and clean. It took him twenty minutes or so to find suitable locations and fit the listening devices. Finally he used the kitchen stool to reach the loft hatch and placed the booster transmitter on a joist in the roof space. Replacing the stool he pulled out his mobile phone and dialled a number and let it ring three times then cancelled the call. Walking over to the bedside lamp he spoke quietly, reciting a haiku poem he had learnt at school. Fleetingly he remembered his teacher extolling the writings of the poet Basho, who had perfected the simplicity of the 5 – 7 – 5 syllable form of a haiku poem.

Summer Grass
All that remains
Of a warriors dreams

The phone, set on silent in his hand, vibrated, alerting him to an incoming call.

"Morohashi-san?" he said quietly.

"Good signal, you better leave, I think he will be returning soon."

A final check that all was placed as he had found it and DI Masato Ariyoshi slipped out of the cottage unseen, to throw the hood back, and merge looking like a tourist into the bustle of Kingsbridge Fore Street. Idly he tried to remember whom the general was, whose death in battle Basho's poem referred to. 'Ah, yes, General Yoshitsune.'

Across town in Union Road, Morohashi was sat in their hired car watching as Ian Vaughan, after shaking hands with the car salesman, climbed into the little Ford van he had purchased.

* * *

"The area of low pressure will move north-east overnight, bringing clearer skies and occasional showers in the south-west of the country. The outlook for the next few days is for more settled weather as high pressure takes over from the continent…"

Ian turned off the radio and went downstairs to knock on his landlady's door. "Hi Miranda, sorry to bother you."

"Come in, fancy a coffee?"

"No I can't stop, I just called past to tell you that I will be away for a few days, sailing."

"Lucky you, where are you off too?" she asked.

He almost told her the truth. "Oh just along the coast, maybe Fowey or Falmouth if the weather's right." If anyone asked she would misdirect them quite unintentionally and therefore give the genuine appearance of honesty.

"Anything you need me to look after while you're away?"

"I don't think so, I'm not expecting any callers or deliveries."

After loading the van with his kit and provisions, Ian walked round to the hotel for lunch. Selecting his favoured corner seat, he picked up the menu and was glancing at it when he saw her, out of the corner of his eye, come into the restaurant. He found himself staring at her as she looked around, apparently deciding where to sit. Yes, most definitely, she was very beautiful. Suddenly she looked straight at him and smiled. Feeling slightly embarrassed at being caught staring, Ian returned a nervous smile back before fixing his gaze back at the menu.

She had waited three days since planting the bugs. Apart from classical music, and occasionally his humming, there had been nothing to listen to. Then she had heard his conversation with Miranda Cox, and had swiftly driven round to park near the cottage. Hurrying through the back alleys she stopped half hidden to observe him loading the van. When Ian had locked the vehicle and walked to the hotel, Morohashi had decided to make the contact.

"Not on site at Yealmstoke Head today?"

Ian looked up in surprise. "Er, no I no longer work there," he blurted out, getting to his feet, immediately annoyed with himself for divulging so much information.

"Oh really. What do you do now?" she asked.

"I'm taking some time out from work."

"I also not working at this time, I have to wait for others to finish before I can start again. So I am on holiday too," she said, thinking quickly.

"What do you plan to do?" Ian asked.

"I honestly do not know. I was hoping to get some sailing in, but I do not think anyone would charter a boat to a woman sailing alone."

"You surprise me, I thought you would be visiting London or Bath to see the tourist sites."

"Oh no, I have been visiting England for many years. You do not see the real England in such places."

Ian glanced at his watch. "I came here to have just a quick lunch, you are welcome to join me, but I am a little pushed for time."

"Thank you, I am getting very tired of eating alone," she replied, sitting down opposite him. "My name is Umeko Morohashi, please call me Umeko."

"I am Ian Vaughan," he shrugged. "Ian." They shook hands across the table.

"Do you sail at all?" she asked.

"Yes I do."

"Do you have your own boat, or do you sail on a friend's yacht?"

"I have recently acquired my own yacht," he said, allowing a hint of pride to enter his voice.

"You are very fortunate, in Japan I have to share with my father on his yacht, which is not so convenient, as he insists on where we go and for how long," she laughed, shaking her head.

The waiter came over, and they ordered their food.

As the meal progressed Ian found the conversation becoming easier. This lady was as far removed from Fumiko Hamaura as one could possibly be. Despite the outward soft appearance though, she gave the feeling that she possessed a very strong personality beneath the surface. There was a hint of command experience in the way she chose her words, which Ian found intriguing. Obviously not in charge of the computer boffins, she did not seem to fit as being one of them either. Who was she really? Why had she approached him? That was strangest of all. Ian, though not aware of Japanese women's behaviour, was reasonably confident that they would not make such an approach. He decided to take a gamble.

"Look, I'm taking my boat out for a few days. If, as you said, you would like to do some sailing…" he let his voice peter out.

"Oh that is very kind offer, but I could not spoil your holiday."

"You would provide me with some company, and it would also mean that you would not be eating alone."

She laughed at the last comment. "How about I come sailing with you for a day?" she said, as if on the spur of the moment, but wished that it were Ariyoshi who was the good sailor and not she. Why, she thought, do I have to be partnered with a man who suffers from seasickness when looking at ripples in a puddle?

Ian thought about his plan for a visit across the Channel to Morlaix. Glancing again at his watch, he quickly calculated that he was in danger of arriving at the difficult entrance to Morlaix late afternoon at best, maybe even when it was getting dark. That was the plan but, now this mysterious woman had arrived on the scene, the visit to Morlaix must wait.

"Yes. Okay. Can you get to Salcombe Harbour Office quay at nine o'clock tomorrow morning?" He didn't want her to know where he berthed his yacht.

"I will be there," she said, smiling radiantly.

After settling his bill, Ian made his excuses and left. Arriving in Dartmouth he took the lower ferry across to Kingswear, then drove round to the marina car park and unloaded the van. When all the gear was stowed and the yacht ready for sea, he placed a short mobile phone call to Campbell's office telling Mrs Fitzgerald that he was going sailing for a few days. Dropping the lines off he slipped the throttle lever back, feeling the prop shaft turn and the yacht's stern kick a little to starboard from the prop walk. When steering almost any long-keeled, single propeller boat, the term 'going astern' is a very general description, and Ian silently thanked the previous owner for installing a bow thruster, which, with careful use, got *La Mouette sur le Vent* pointing in the right direction. Once clear of the marina, and off lying moorings, he put the yacht on course downstream, leaving Dartmouth and its Britannia Naval College astern, and headed for the open sea.

It was late evening as Ian steered the yacht around Salcombe bar, then, turning north, passing Mill Bay to starboard, he motored the yacht straight to the visitor moorings in the area known as 'The Bag', where he was fortunate to find an end pontoon vacant. Having prepared fenders and mooring lines on the way in he put the yacht gently alongside, and stepping onto the pontoon, soon had *La Mouette sur le Vent* secured.

The sound of the powerboat, being started up on the other side of the pontoon at seven o'clock next morning, woke Ian with a start. He had overslept; hurriedly he washed, dressed and breakfasted in time to cast off and head for the harbour master's quay just before half past eight. Ian was returning from the harbour master's office, having paid the mooring fees, when he saw her standing at the far end of the pontoon. Her long jet-black hair, tussled gently by the breeze, hung halfway down the back of a blue and white striped polo shirt. A pair of light blue slacks and deck shoes finished off the almost fashion model image. He smiled as he came up to her.

"Good morning Umeko, would you like to step aboard?" he asked, pointing to his yacht.

"Thank you, is this yours? I have been admiring her. Colin Archer concept, yes? Pointed at both ends."

"Yes, along that style. You know your yachts."

"*La Mouette sur le Vent*. Umm, a very interesting name."

"The gull on the wind."

"Ah, I see, how lovely. My French is not very good at all. Did you name her?"

"Yes. There's a bit of a story to it. The name itself is not my original idea, that was someone else's."

"You can tell me the story as we go along."

"No, I wouldn't bore you with that," he said picking up her bag and swinging it over the yacht's guardrails.

Nimbly she stepped up onto the side deck and, collecting her bag, made her way along the deck and down into the cockpit.

"If you stow your bag in the forward cabin, I will sort out a harness and life jacket for you," he said, eyeing the mooring lines and planning the sequence for casting off.

Leaping aboard he went below and, pulling the back of the main cabin starboard settee away, revealed a locker in which the four, collar-style, life jackets were kept. Selecting one he went to hand it to her.

"Oh, you have your own," he said surprised.

"Yes," said Umeko, thankful for the loan of Penny's lightly used sailing kit. "May I be cheeky and ask whether Frenchman's Creek is in range of a day's sailing?"

"Gosh, that's the Helford River, maybe eleven to twelve hours away." To himself he thought: yes, you clever little thing you, selecting a destination just beyond that informed to Miranda Cox. How did you know?

She looked disappointed. "Pity, I am admirer of your author Daphne du Maurier. When I was assigned to this team I planned to visit Frenchman's Creek, but it will have to be some other time. Maybe when I go to Jamaica Inn."

"I think so, it would mean us staying overnight there otherwise."

"Would you mind?" she asked, as if on impulse.

Ian was surprised by the question, or was it a request. "Er, no I wouldn't mind, er, it's up to you, I mean, you, you hardly know me." Inwardly he cursed at being outwitted again. Was it the pretty face and shapely form? God, he was going to have to be careful.

She laughed. "You could be just as much a threat to me on board for one day, as you would be over one night. I do not believe in werewolves. Anyway it is not a full moon."

He went to laugh, but suddenly a thought struck him. "Have you been sent along by my wife?"

She frowned with annoyance. "No I have not. What makes you say such thing?"

"I'm sorry. It's just that she is demanding a divorce. Look, let's get underway and I will tell you the whole sorry saga."

She stood not moving, apparently weighing whether to stay or leave.

"I said, I'm sorry. It's just that life has not been straightforward for me of late," he said, regretting the obvious mistake. "Look, please forget I said anything."

There was a few moments' pause as they looked at each other then she nodded. "Okay, but understand I know nothing about you, or your wife," she replied, sounding very convincing. She had studied his file in detail, and had learnt a great deal from Commander Campbell. It was the Commander's assurance of Ian's loyalty to his wife that had given her the confidence to spend time sailing with him, alone. The job was dangerous enough without the risk of an amorous target.

The continental high-pressure system that had pushed north overnight brought with it sunshine and a Force 4 southerly breeze; ideal conditions for a swift sailing passage into Cornish waters.

During the rest of the morning Ian spun a yarn about his family being kidnapped by a gang of drug smugglers, who were being pursued by the police. In the story he had been forced to sail the gang to Spain. He then went onto tell her about the miscarriage and apparent breakdown leading to the divorce demand. He had practised and practised the story to such an extent that it sounded absolutely true.

"Wow, how horrible for you to have your life turned upside down by such people," she said, admiring his invention and presentation. "I now understand your question of me earlier. Please believe me, your wife has nothing to do with me being here."

The atmosphere between them almost restored, they sailed on, happily holding those cultural exchange conversations one does with people from abroad.

It was exactly at seven o'clock that evening when Umeko dropped the loop of mooring rope over the buoy and Ian gave the engine a brisk but short run astern.

"Okay, while I lift the buoy up with the loop, can you thread that free warp twice through the ring on top of the buoy and then back on deck?"

He watched as she ably carried out the task, ending by feeding the warp so that both lengths, to and from the yacht, were equal.

"Thank you, that's just what I needed," he said, as he released the buoy and recovered the looped warp. "Let's hope this is the right buoy and we don't get disturbed."

"It is the number the man told us was his," she said, making off both ends of the rope around the foredeck cleats.

"If you want to freshen up, I will inflate the dinghy and we will go ashore for a meal."

She looked around at the wooded banks of the river. "There is somewhere to eat around here?"

"Yes, we passed the entrance to the creek while you were searching for the buoy."

They enjoyed the meal at the Shipwright's Arms in Helford village, and the walk down to see the huge fuchsia tree near the ferry landing. The stroll back round the head of the creek to the jetty, where they had left the dinghy, was full of the scents of wild flowers and distant cornfields. The evening's conversation had been light and fun, but she had been aware of his eyes darting towards the doorway every time anyone came into the pub.

With the tide ebbing he had kept close into the shallows, out of the main current, as he rowed them back, going out to deep water upstream of their mooring. Letting the dinghy float gently down the stream to the port side of the boat, he made off the dinghy's painter on the amidships cleat, then helped Umeko aboard. She declined a warm drink and, announcing that she would turn in for the night, disappeared into the forward cabin.

Sipping at a measure of Scotch and with a cup of coffee at his side, Ian sat out in the cockpit, listening to the lapping of the water on the yacht's hull, and thinking about his delightful companion. Why was she here? What was she up to? All day he had been racking his brains with this problem. He was sure that she had engineered the meeting and the trip out sailing, but he could not understand why. His first thought had been that she was part of the Murata faction, but had that been the case she would never have got onto the Yealmstoke Head site with the rest of the Japanese team. The divorce idea was quite obviously wrong, so what was it? Finally, coffee cup and glass empty, he went below and after a visit to the heads, stripped off shirt and slacks, to replace them with the tracksuit he always used for sleeping in.

The bump along the starboard side woke him instantly. He looked at his wristwatch, 2.30 a.m. Another few bumping sounds announced that someone was coming aboard. Immediately he felt the chill of fear sweep over him as he strained to hear their movements along the side deck. His hand searched under the pillow and retrieved the pistol. He had closed and locked the companionway hatch. Would they break it in or try a more stealthy entrance? Then a more terrifying thought occurred to him, had she opened the forward hatch for them? Sweat ran down his spine from the back of his neck. Then the unwelcome visitors stomped down into the cockpit. Ian estimated that there were only two of them. Their clumsy movements suggested that they weren't assassins, more likely thieves that had failed to spot Ian's dinghy, tied onto the opposite side of the yacht to their own.

Quietly, he had eased himself from his sleeping bag, and was carefully sliding himself out of the quarter berth when he saw her standing between the chart table and the galley sink, gun in hand, staring fixedly at the companionway hatch. At that moment he realised why she was there.

"You sure this is that bastard Keating's boat?"

"It's 'is soddin' moorin' innit?" came the reply.

Ian pushed his pistol back under the pillow.

"I'll giv' 'im fifty fuckin' quid fine, the bastard. I'll kick this bleedin' 'atch in for a start."

"Don't be stupid, Brian. You'll 'ave that lot upstream awake."

"Wot they gonna do, eh?"

"Look, just nick the electronic stuff, and let's get out of 'ere. If Cheryl finds out that I left the kids on their own again, I'll get anuver kickin' from 'er old man, so bloody get on wiv it, quietly."

Carefully Ian reached over and, putting his hand over the gun, pushed downwards, shaking his head. Stepping back she lay the weapon on the port-hand settee and returned her gaze to the hatch. A thin flexible steel blade was being inserted and carefully worked along the gap above the top washboard, until it found the catch. By using a slow sawing action the operator worked the blade over the catch, releasing the top hatch, and pushed it forward. Swiftly he removed the washboards, then turning himself round, came backwards down the companionway steps.

"Give us an 'and, Ed," Brian said looking up into the cockpit. "You know more abou' this stuff than I does." Then he gave a sharp intake of breath and appeared to collapse.

His mate, wondering what had happened, put his head and shoulders through the hatchway to get a better view, only to find himself being grabbed by his shirt collar and pulled down the steps to the cabin floor, where, with Ian's knee in his back, he had his right arm, painfully, twisted up behind his shoulder blades.

Taking some sail ties out of the bottom chart table drawer, Ian grabbed the youth's left arm and, after tying both his wrists together, pulled him to his feet and dragged him up the companionway steps and into the cockpit, to a chorus of shouts and threats. Forcing the lad to sit, he tied both ankles together before grabbing the terrified youth's collar again and saying in a cold frightening hiss, "What is your name, cretin?"

"Eddie Crouch," the youth replied timidly. "Wotcha gonna do wiv us?"

"The temptation to take you out to sea and drown you is high on my list," Ian replied, his face very close to the youth's and the grip on the collar tightening.

The youth appeared to shrink. "If Cheryl doesn't know where you are, I don't suppose anyone else does," Ian continued in a threatening whisper.

"For fuck sake mister, we was only nickin' some gear like. I bet it was insured," Crouch answered, almost in tears, his bruised knees hurting from the descent of the companionway steps, and his bowels feeling uncomfortably loose with fear.

A whimpering sound from the companionway steps signalled the arrival of Brian, wrists bound.

"Officer Morohashi, would you put him down there while I secure his ankles?"

She didn't need to put him down, the youth virtually collapsed, and offered no resistance to Ian as his ankles were tied.

"If you look in the top drawer of the chart table, you will find my mobile phone, could you bring it up?" It was then that he realized she was wearing only a T-shirt and a pair of very brief knickers. "You had better get some warmer clothes on as well."

Whilst she was gone Ian reached into the cabin and unclipped a torch that was kept alongside the flares. He flicked it on and pointed it at the two captives; both were weedy, scrawny examples of mankind. He then turned the beam towards their dinghy, lying alongside.

"It's nice to know that ours was not the only boat that you targeted this evening," he said, almost conversationally. "You have quite a haul there. I'm sure the police will be delighted to clear up, oh, five or maybe six cases in one go."

Turning the torch back onto the youths, Ian noted a somewhat relieved expression on Eddie's face at the mention of police. Until that moment the prospect of drowning had been featuring large in the lad's imagination

"Here is your mobile, sir," said Morohashi. She had picked up instantly Ian's address to her as 'Officer'. "Unfortunately there does not appear to be any signal here."

"Okay, I will radio the coastguard at Falmouth and get them to contact the police," Ian said, edging past her and descending into the cabin.

The sergeant, who had recognised the pair of boat thieves instantly, took a statement from Ian and carefully listed the haul of electronic equipment from the youths' dinghy.

"You say they thought that this was Colonel Keating's boat?"

"Yes, apparently he fined one of them fifty pounds."

"Yeah, that'll be right. The Colonel's a JP and chairman of the bench," the Sergeant said, with an expression on his face suggesting that Christmas had come early. "The magistrates are gonna love dealing with these two, oh yes."

By eight o'clock, Ian and Umeko were back on board the yacht and Ian was preparing a cooked breakfast.

"Obviously you are not that interested in my company or the enjoyment of sailing. So who are you, and what are you?" he asked. "Somehow you don't come across as being police."

Umeko explained her real title and the link with the British Counter Terrorist Command.

"Interesting," Ian said, placing a plate of bacon, eggs and sausages in front of her. "Let me guess, you are not my minder. You are just following me about because I may well be good as bait to attract Hamaura's brother."

She looked sheepishly back at him. "When I learnt that you were going sailing I could not watch from a distance. So I had to kind of invite myself aboard. I am sorry, but these people must be stopped, over the years they have been responsible for many deaths, as you know."

"What does Commander Campbell think of this plan? Was it his idea?"

"He thinks that you are a target. Our problem was, that no one knows where Murata and his gang are at this time. When Murata escaped, my orders were changed. There is a separate threat to the team of Japanese computer experts at Yealmstoke Head. We thought that I could cover both this way."

"Weaver, the poor sod, told me that there was no connection between Murata and those wanting to get at the Yealmstoke group."

"No, there is nothing to suggest that there is. We are not really sure who is leading this other threat. At the moment there is another computer team here in your country, we cannot cover it all. We took a gamble that Murata would learn where you were working, and hoped that he didn't know that you have left the site. There is chance that he will seek you out there or at Kingsbridge." She sounded desperate, or was it frustrated. "Commander Campbell has men at Yealmstoke and the other site, I am just doing what I can."

"Does Murata know that I was there in the first place?"

She shook her head and shrugged her shoulders, leaving Ian confused as to what she knew and what Campbell knew.

"You don't know in other words."

"We know that they were able to get very accurate information regarding Murata's extradition route; so it is very probable, they will be able to track you down, and take their revenge," she retorted hotly. "If you want to put me ashore, go ahead, but I will tell you now, you have been lucky so far, but lucky is all you have been, and that is not enough against these people."

Ian held her hostile gaze for several seconds. She was right, he had been lucky, so far. A sniper could take him out at any time, so what exactly was he doing out on his own, without any protection? Suddenly the safe house seemed to be his only option, but that would mean giving in, admitting that they could wreck his marriage and life with impunity. Sod that.

"I'm sorry, maybe it was being seen purely as bait that annoyed me."

"We considered close protection, but that is often too close, and the enemy just gear up to take it out as well," she explained. "By acting more as a watcher, from a short distance away, you are able to see a wider field. However, for it to be really successful it is better not to have looks of recognition or association between watcher and watched."

"I see, so my sailing plans really did blow it."

She nodded. "Yes, your boating activity, so soon after we set things up, meant a complete change of plan. So I disobeyed orders and put myself in the firing line, close to the target," she said with some feeling, glaring into Ian's now cold blue eyes.

"Welcome aboard," he replied. "Tea or coffee?"

She was thunderstruck for a moment by his response. Then the rather perverse humour of his reply struck her and she laughed. "Tea, please."

Breakfast was consumed in silence, whilst each was considering how to proceed. Clearing the plates and cups, Ian filled the sink with hot water and started to wash up.

"May I help?" she asked.

"Were you serious about seeing Frenchman's Creek?"

"Er, yes, I was, but, well …"

"Right, you grab a shower, while I finish up here."

An hour later Umeko found herself being rowed up a narrow, wooded creek, under a clear blue sky.

"Daphne du Maurier took a few liberties with her storylines. Her French hero, for example, would never have used this creek. It completely dries out at low tide."

"But at high tide, everything is green and there is birdsong and romance," she remarked. "It appears to be a very secret mooring. This far into the creek, it is difficult to imagine being seen from the main river. Not so much, as you say, artistic licence."

"Before the tide turns I'll show you another site of interest."

Leaving the creek, Ian rowed the dinghy further upriver to an isolated, but substantial, stone quay. Alongside, he held the dinghy close to the stonework while she scrambled ashore, then followed her.

"This is Tremayne Quay, built for the visit of Queen Victoria. Probably paid for by the locals, who were not rich in those days. She never actually arrived here, as it was raining. Must not get the royal topknot wet."

"Topknot?"

"Oh, sorry, it's a slang expression for a tuft of hair on one's head. Your English is so good, I tend to forget, and stray from English as it is taught."

"Mmm, topknot," she repeated, and giggling, tapped her head.

"On the way back to the boat, I would like you to consider how far your close protection extends in terms of distance of travel," Ian said.

"You have plans to sail further away?"

"I really was planning to sail to Morlaix, in France, when we met the other day. Your request for a day's sailing caused me to postpone that idea. Now, however, things have changed."

She stood looking across the river, obviously wondering what to do. Suddenly she turned and looking straight into his eyes asked, "Why do you want to go to Morlaix?"

"It is because I got slung off the job I was doing, thanks to Murata and I cannot visit my children or try and patch up my marriage, thanks to Murata, and I am hoping that if I am at sea I stand a better chance of seeing him coming at me than if I am on land."

"And?"

"I wanted to play with my new boat."

She continued to stare at him questioningly.

"For God's sake woman, do I need a list of reasons a mile long?"

"We will sail back to Kingswear, where you moor the boat, and I will check with Commander Campbell. If he agrees I will go back to the hotel for more clothes. I will then return to Dartmouth, and cross to you on the water taxi."

"Of course you know where I moor the boat. You probably know what size shoes I take."

"Size nine. Shall we go?" she asked, smiling slightly.

*   *   *

The day following Murata's narrow escape, DS Carter knocked on Jackson's office door.

"Come! Ah yes, what is it Carter?"

"Some interesting finds from the Crow Hill Farm Unit, sir," replied Carter. "Hidden behind some rolls of cotton fabric, we found a set of records and a telephone with an answerphone system linked. The records included phone bills showing frequent calls to Japan and a number near Richmond, Virginia."

"The other records?"

"All in Japanese, sir. I've arranged for a translator, who should be starting work on them in the next hour. Forensic have got all they can from them. Mainly fingerprints that match the Ishiharas'."

"Was there any indication as to who the fourth man is?"

"Not yet, sir. We have identified the prints of Murata, Hamaura and Kimura amongst the twenty or so recent prints in the area, but apart from the Ishiharas' none come up as known to Tokyo or us. Shall I take that Richmond number along to the Commander? I think he will be interested in discussing it with the FBI."

"I'm sure he will. Let's go and find."

In Campbell's office, Carter's prediction was confirmed.

"You are right Sergeant, I will be very interested to talk to the States about it. I think that this may well prove to be the centre of a very complex web that this group have managed to weave. The records, you say, go back some years."

"Yes, sir, over ten years. What I felt was strange about them, was that they were kept in suitcases. Something about it has me thinking that they were kept as evidence, rather than just record," said Carter. "It's hard to explain, sir, but I think it was as if they were to be used as some form of currency."

Carter's intuition was surprisingly accurate. Ishihara's wife had maintained the record realising that should they need to prove their loyalty to Murata, such items would be an obvious written record of their hard work. On the other hand, should they need to realign themselves with the Yamamoto faction, the records, combined with their personal knowledge, would enable them to deliver virtually the whole of Murata's American and European network. Noriko Ishihara intended to live to a ripe old age regardless of her anarchistic beliefs.

"That is a very interesting observation Carter. If you were correct their value to us would be immense. Chase that interpreter up will you, and bring in a second one, we need to get an urgent assessment."

"Morohashi, sir. Why not use her on this translation stunt?" asked Jackson.

"Of course, good idea, it will get her out of harm's way as well," Campbell responded enthusiastically. "I'll phone her straight away, in fact she and Ariyoshi might as well join in with this."

Failing to get through to Morohashi's mobile Campbell tried the number Ariyoshi had given him. It was answered straight away.

"Ah, Detective Ariyoshi, Commander Campbell here, we urgently need to have both yourself and Lieutenant Commander Morohashi back at DELCO, to translate some documents we have found. How quickly do you think you can get here?"

There was a pause whilst Ariyoshi explained that Morohashi and Vaughan were sailing together.

"She is what!!?" Campbell replied loudly. "Sailing with Vaughan! Good God whatever possessed her to do that? Get in contact with her as soon as possible and get her back here."

There was a brief explanation from Ariyoshi, which Campbell only gave half an ear to.

"That may be so. Now we need both of you here to assist, so please return as soon as you can." With that Campbell switched off the phone, shaking his head in exasperation.

"Did you hear that? The silly girl has only joined Vaughan on his yacht. Damn it, if Murata had turned up she would have been right in the middle of it, and after her experience with Weaver, oh!! How can you possibly bring in protection when you are standing right next to the target?" Exasperated, Campbell tossed his mobile phone onto the desk where it landed with a thud.

*　　　　*　　　　*

Ariyoshi and Morohashi returned to the DELCO office the following morning, to find most of the translation work completed. Ariyoshi had been waiting in the marina car park when *La Mouette sur le Vent* had glided into her berth the previous evening and they had driven straight to London.

"Good morning Lorna."

"Hello. They are waiting for you in the meeting room. The Commander will be along after lunch."

"Thank you," Morohashi replied, smiling to herself. Lorna's dull act was perfect.

Morohashi was relieved that Campbell would not be there until later. She needed to find out how annoyed he was. Ariyoshi had given her the impression that they were likely to be sent home in disgrace.

Penny Heathcote greeted her warmly. "Hi, Umeko-chan, I'm so glad you're back to give me a hand with this. These direct translations don't read very easily. By the way the Commander wants to see you in the interview room immediately after he arrives. I think he wants to express his concerns about your safety."

"Does he want me off the case?"

"Oh no, I think he is just worried that you will get shot. You had a very close call when DS Weaver bought it, and standing next to Mr Vaughan did put you at risk," Penny said, trying to be tactful. "Anyway we had better get stuck into this stuff and see if we can make sense of it."

"What is in the brown envelope with all those American stamps on it?" asked Morohashi.

"The Kinoko Kumo enquiry report from Washington. Someone in either the FBI or White House organisation photographed the full report and had it sent to the Ishiharas," replied Heathcote.

"So Murata and Hamaura will know exactly what happened, and what part Ian Vaughan played in it."

"Yes, had he been CTC or FBI then it would have been different. Probably they would have just accepted that the organisation was responsible. A private citizen is somehow different, that makes it personal."

"And there he is out there on his own," said Morohashi.

Penny Heathcote noticed tenderness in her concern. "He is being watched over, Umeko-chan," she said. "They will look after him for you," she added mischievously. She thought she could detect a slight blush in Umeko's cheeks.

Umeko Morohashi tried hard to give the impression that she had not heard what Penny had said and, picking up the top sheet of the translation, stared hard at it, frowning. It took her some minutes before she could settle into full concentration.

Whilst Morohashi and Ariyoshi worked from the original *Kanji* writing, Penny sat annotating the basic translation. A picture was appearing of a significant network of contacts and informants.

"More than ten years of operating without even the hint of investigation into what they were doing appears to have made them very complacent," commented Morohashi. "They have not even bothered to disguise their contact names with a code, or maybe they have." She flicked back a few pages and compared two contact notes. A few more pages and she checked again. "This will take time, but I think there is a rolling name system being used. Say you make your contact in January, then you use the name Seiko, in February Yoshi, March Yukiko and so on. If the wrong name is used then the recipient will know that you are not a member of the group."

"That is very clever," said Penny, then after some thought she asked, "What happens if a group member makes a contact in early March, then the papers are discovered by the authorities and a second contact is made by them, also in March, using the same name?"

Morohashi had been continuing her search to confirm the pattern. "You are right Penny-chan. It is not a monthly rollover it is with each contact. See here in July, three contacts to same number and each time a different name logged and a tick placed beside it." What had first appeared to be a sizable army of people was, after three hours of intensive work, reduced to eleven. These were spread from Yemen, across Europe and America, to Japan.

"I would think that these are the cell hubs, and with each contact point there is a small group of individuals dedicated to the cause," said Ariyoshi. "I cannot imagine that there is only one person involved at each contact point."

"Yes, yes," said Morohashi excitedly. "That is why there are exactly the same number of names at each contact. All the numbers are mobile phones, nothing strange in that for modern small businesses. Then other phones are used to distribute the message throughout the rest of the group, probably also using rolling name system. That way each recipient would act as the identity security, and when genuine instructions are received everyone knows what is going on without having to hold a meeting. No physical contact needed."

"Guaranteed that the phone purchasers' names and addresses are false, and that each is a pay as you go," said Penny. "These are going to be a nightmare to track down. Oh no, has anyone answered calls to that phone found at the farm?" There was a shaking of heads. "The next thing you must do," she said looking at Ariyoshi and Morohashi, "is listen to the messages received on the answer-phone."

Lorna put her head round the door. "Morohashi-san, Commander Campbell would like a word with you."

Morohashi, looking nervous, stood and made her way to the door. "Good luck," said Penny.

"We have dealt with the regular contact numbers," said Ariyoshi. "What about these?" he asked, lifting a small pile of contact sheets and starting to look through them. A quarter of an hour passed in silence, then, "Here, this is very interesting. It is a message to DHO requesting them to contact brother. DHO is not initials, nor does brother mean associate company as translator suggested. Dho is very common Korean name. I believe that Ishihara was asked to make contact with someone named Dho."

"What?" said Penny, with a note of alarm. "Did you say Korean?"

"Yes, Dho is like your Smith I believe."

Penny was on her feet and out of the room almost before Ariyoshi had finished the sentence. At the interview room she knocked on the door and waited.

"Come in," she heard Campbell say.

Entering, she was relieved to see both Campbell and Morohashi smiling.

"Sorry to interrupt, sir, but I thought you'd better know that we have made a link with a Korean by the name of Dho."

"Check with MI5 to see if they have anything on him," said Campbell. "Is there any phone number mentioned?"

"Yes, sir, it appears to be a landline."

"Excellent, get a trace on that, and we had better set up a stakeout. Can you contact Chief Inspector Jackson, and request him to join us? You know I think we may have a breakthrough at last."

* * *

The number traced to a riverside yard on the banks of the Itchen at Southampton. Within four hours DS Carter, and two detective constables from the Southampton police station, were sat in the offices of a stainless steel fabrication company that overlooked the neighbouring yard.

Keeping well back from the window, Carter studied the front Portakabin on the neighbouring site. He could see into the two rooms within the unit quite clearly and was satisfied that it was not occupied. In the corner of the first room was just a packing case on top of which was a pair of shiny boots that reminded him of police training college. The rear Portakabin was apparently windowless and stood between the front, probably office unit, and the river. A door of this unit was on the end, and as his high-powered binoculars ranged over it, he noted the hasp and staple unit, with its padlock, securing it.

Carter thumbed Campbell's number on his mobile.

"We're all set up here, sir. I think this yard has only just been occupied as there is an agent's board announcing that the site was 'let by' a firm called Needham and Blake. There doesn't appear to be anyone here at the moment, in fact the only sign of habitation is a pair of shiny military-style boots on top of a packing case."

"Leave the two constables to keep an eye out for any movement, and get round to these agents and see what you can learn from them. I doubt if they are involved in anything other than property letting, but you never know," instructed Campbell.

"Right, sir, I'll get on it straight away."

"Oh, make sure that you frighten them enough to stop them warning their client of your interest," said Campbell as he finished the call.

It was almost 8.15 p.m. by the time Carter had tracked down the address of the nearest partner of the firm. Joseph Blake's house, near the beautiful village of Crawley, was well constructed and maintained. Georgian double fronted, in brick, it was set some way back from the road, up a wide gravel driveway. What looked like a stable block could be seen through a gateway to the right of the house, with a walled garden to the left. Carter was impressed, very impressed.

The ring at the doorbell eventually brought Blake's son, who after giving Carter a sneering superior look, shouted, "It's for you Father!" then walked away from the door leaving Carter feeling that he should really have used the tradesmen's entrance. Carter was now singularly unimpressed.

The door to the dining room opened and Carter could hear the buzz of dinner conversation. A medium height, rather stout man appeared, and looked at Carter enquiringly.

"Yes, what is it?"

"Are you Mr Blake of Needham and Blake Commercial Property Agents?"

"Yes. If it's a problem with any of our lettings contact the number on the board and our manager will send somebody out."

"I am Detective Sergeant Carter of the Counter Terrorist Command," replied Carter, showing his warrant card. "I would like to talk to you about a letting you have recently secured in Southampton."

"See me in my office tomorrow afternoon, I am entertaining guests at the moment. It will have to wait," said Blake, making to return to the dining room.

"We can either talk here, now, or I take you to Southampton police station for questioning, Mr Blake. The choice is yours."

By 9.30 p.m. Carter was sat interviewing a, now nervous, Joseph Blake, and his equally nervous Lettings Manager at their Winchester offices.

“It seemed all above-board,” said Marcus Hornby-Taylor. “Their company lawyer, a Mr – er let me see, – ah yes, er Takumi Ishihara, came down on the 10th July, to sign the lease. Takashima Exploration, he informed us, needed the yard for the storage of some light equipment.”

“Did you carry out any checks?”

“Well er, we established that a lawyer by the name of Takumi Ishihara practised in Japan. He explained that the company was newly formed, and was going through the ‘tedious’ process of registration in Japan,” replied Hornby-Taylor. “His business address tied in with the details he left with us.”

“Yes, the only problem for you is that the real Takumi Ishihara died of stomach cancer some months ago, and his heartbroken wife committed suicide,” informed Carter. “What has happened is that the gang, we are hunting, has stolen his identity and has used it in connection with a major terrorist plot.”

Blake put his head in his hands and swore.

“Right,” continued Carter. “This is what happens from here on.”

Chapter 10

The negotiations had lasted three days during which it had been revealed that General Namgoong's son had been placed in charge of the Korean group. Iwaki had assumed that Murata would feel obligated to the North Koreans for their assistance in his escape and would agree to provide some funding and supply weapons through his dissident Irish contacts. The problem was that though Murata felt obligated, his sense of obligation was overridden by his ambition to become the undisputed Red Brigade leader. Murata, unaware of the real world fame the Kinoko Kumo attack had given him, believed he still needed to prove to the world that he was the true leader of the reborn Red Brigade. Namgoong, however, was not prepared to play second fiddle and it was only when Iwaki suggested the two target idea that a breakthrough was made.

What had been agreed was that the total group be divided into two commands. The first led by the son of General Namgoong was to target the site at Portsmouth whilst the group under joint command of Murata struck at Yealmstoke Head, with Dho acting as his second in command, in charge of the Koreans involved. Namgoong had readily agreed to Murata's idea to strike at both targets simultaneously, basing his support on the London bombings of 2005. "The world knows how attacks at same time was too much for security services here to handle even with long-term surveillance of suspects."

At the end of the negotiations it was Iwaki who found himself to be the loser. His personal ambitions had one by one been sidelined in favour of Murata and with each turn in fortune his resentment had grown.

The other person dissatisfied was Yoshi Hamaura. He had made it plain that Murata now owed him, and he wanted the head of Ian Vaughan before prancing onto the political stage in support of North Korea. Seeking fresh air and solitude he had left the claustrophobia of the rear Portakabin by a door opening onto the riverbank. As he paced backwards and forwards rebellious thoughts built in his mind. The sound of the door opening again had him turning and walking back cautiously towards it.

"Teiji-kun des-ka?"

"Hi, hi," confirmed Kimura. "Yoshi-kun, what is your problem?"

"Simple, already we are being hunted. If we succeed with the raid, and achieved their political goals, we would have to leave this country never to return, leaving the killer of my sister and your cousin alive," Hamaura answered bitterly, poking Kimura aggressively with his finger. "Also who will be the hero eh? Not Teiji Kimura or Yoshi Hamaura or his sister Fumiko, no! It will be the great Tadashi Murata," he said bitterly emphasising Murata's name. "The one who got himself arrested, and tried in court, accused of petty crimes. He will actually have achieved nothing compared to Fumiko's victory in America."

"Keep your voice down."

"We are alone out here."

"How you know that? How you know that Murata-san will take all glory for himself? In jail did you have any glory? No, even the burglars treated you with contempt, you told me so yourself. I owe Murata-san much in obtaining my release. To free me from the perverts I was with in that prison was the greatest gift any man could give me," Kimura said quietly, his voice shaking with emotion, his mind recalling the humiliation he had been forced to endure. "You have only one man that you want kill, I have five, and I want each of their deaths to be after a year of agony." In his mind he ran through the names of the five who had attacked and raped him during his time in prison.

Hamaura was shaken by the intensity of his cousin's words. The two men stood silently for a time staring out over the waters of the River Itchen.

"Calm yourself Yoshi-kun, before you return to the cabin. Do not risk making an enemy of Murata-san." With that Kimura walked away leaving Hamaura to continue his pacing, now somewhat subdued.

Putting his disquieting thoughts to one side, Hamaura looked around him at the dark shapes of the surrounding buildings. It was as he looked up at the first floor of the neighbouring building that he saw it, the glow of a cigarette, as someone drew on it to inhale the smoke. Then it was gone. He waited tense, wondering whether he had been seen. Then the cigarette glowed again. Hardly daring to breathe he watched for a few more minutes, and then the person opened a window and tossed the cigarette butt out. Hamaura waited and watched, sensing rather than seeing the person standing looking out over the yard. Ten minutes had passed before the flicker of a cigarette lighter cupped behind a hand briefly lit the face of a man. Stealthily he made his way back to the door of the cabin and knocked gently. Kimura opened the door and after Hamaura had stepped in and closed the door behind him, he switched on the light.

"Murata-san, we are being watched. There is someone standing in the dark up in the office, over the fence. They were smoking and I saw the light of the cigarette."

"You are sure it is not a watchman doing his rounds?"

"Yes, they were standing still, I watched for long time."

"Do you think they saw you?"

"I do not know. It would be difficult, I think."

Murata thought for a few moments, considering Hamaura's information. "We cannot take risk, not now all is agreed with Dho-san. Take the binoculars and have closer look."

Hamaura returned in the space of three minutes. "The man is standing alongside a tripod with large binoculars mounted on it."

"Pack your things; we will leave by that loose fence panel Dho-san showed us," ordered Murata. "When we are clear, I will contact him with warning, and ask him to meet us near football stadium."

Silently they gathered their kit together and checked that they had left little sign of their presence. Just as they were about to leave, Murata said, "Hamaura-kun, you did well to see and warn us. Do not think that I have forgotten your desire to bring retribution down upon this man Vaughan, but all in good time, eh?"

The deep purple of the eastern sky heralding the dawn hurried the gang through the fence, to appear five minutes later along Southampton's Mill Street, casually walking towards the St Mary's football stadium.

*   *   *

Carter returned to the stakeout only minutes after Kimura had quietly closed the Portakabin door. After the interview with Blake he had gone back to his hotel room and tried to get some sleep. Unable to settle he had showered and dressed then, opening his laptop computer, had written up the interview report, before deciding to check on the stakeout team.

"Anything happening?"

"No sir, not a movement," replied PC Payne, removing another cigarette from his pack and lighting up.

"What the hell do you think you are doing Constable?" demanded Carter, snatching the cigarette from Payne's lips and stubbing it out on the floor. "Have you lit up standing here before?"

"Well, yeah. They haven't been there so what's the problem?"

"Do you think the front door is the only one they can use, eh?" Carter replied, angrily. "Do you think they will come walking in without first checking that it is safe to do so?"

"Sorry, sir, I didn't think."

"No, you didn't. Well think on this. If we haven't seen any sign of life by sun up in twenty minutes, we are going in to have a close look. According to the agent's plan there is a door at the back of each of those cabins. If we find that they have used them, then you can look forward to doing crowd control at every home fixture for the next five years."

At four thirty, Carter took a quick look through a grill that had once been attached to an air conditioning unit. In the dim light he could not make out any sign of occupation, but it was with great fear that he tried the door handle to the back door of the riverside cabin. It opened and, pushing it wide, he looked nervously round the doorframe; to his relief the cabin was empty. About to step inside he looked down and stopped, staring at footprints on the linoleum floor covering.

"Payne, look at this."

PC Payne stepped forward and, following the direction of Carter's finger, stared blankly.

"You will note, Constable, that those footprints were made by the mud in this yard and that they are still wet. What does that mean, Constable?"

"It means I am doing crowd control for the next five years?"

"Bloody right it does!" shouted Carter. "This is the second time this gang have slipped through the net and, as sure as hell, no one is going to hang it on my record."

Carter, for his part, reacted swiftly calling for backup, then contacting Chief Inspector Jackson, who in turn instigated the rapid establishment of roadblocks along all routes out of Southampton.

In London Campbell was incandescent with rage, and was on to the Chief Constable of the Hampshire force within two minutes of putting the phone down from Carter. Jackson, who was in Campbell's office at the time, could not remember ever seeing his boss so angry. When the telephone conversation was over Campbell swung round on Jackson and said, "We agree to extradition, and he gets away, we track him down to Alton, and he gets away. Now at Southampton some stupid plod sends out smoke signals to tell Murata that he is under surveillance! Are we a nation of incompetents?"

"The escape at the airbase was really down to circumstances, sir. After all the base was due for closure and had very few personnel to adequately deal with that type of attack," said Jackson. "Also you can hardly blame anyone for the Alton fiasco. Agreed the Southampton thing is bad but these things do happen."

"Rubbish, Chief Inspector. We were weak in allowing the airbase route. That should have been through Heathrow. We were weak in not insisting upon perimeter policing at that base; both errors made, thanks to our political masters. Carter should have used greater stealth at Alton, I told him that when he returned here. Then he makes the same mistake at Southampton! That's bad Chief Inspector, too bad. I am considering that young man's future with this team."

Jackson looked shocked. It was the first time that Campbell had ever suggested that he would take direct disciplinary action. Previously any slackness was left to him to deal with. "He was on to me immediately, sir, and did a lot of bullying to get the road blocks established quickly."

"Shutting the door after the horse has bolted you mean!"

Campbell stood up and turned, glaring out of the window at the view towards St James's Park. "I've got petty politicians using underhand methods to protect their fat salaries and solid gold pensions, I've got diplomats bringing their own police in here wanting to take a slice of the action. At least Chief Superintendent Ishii seems to be playing a team game. He, by the way, has informed me that the intelligence services in Tokyo suspect that their computer team at Portsmouth are the target. That fits in with Murata and his band being in Southampton. I am not trusting Morohashi or Ariyoshi down there; I want them here, assisting Lieutenant Heathcote with any analysis work to be done."

"What about protection at Portsmouth, sir?"

"I have been on to the MoD requesting a unit to proceed there immediately and establish an armed guard twenty-four seven. They have agreed to despatch a platoon of fifty marines from Lympstone barracks in Devon."

"When will they arrive, sir?"

"They are setting off tomorrow morning. That, I understand is the quickest they can respond."

Jackson raised his eyebrows, but did not comment about the delay. "Could you leave Carter to me, sir? I have a feeling that there is more to his actions than meets the eye."

"Yes, of course, but I want to have a full report," said Campbell, turning back to look at Jackson. "By the way, I would like you to take over the monitoring of the watch keepers on Vaughan and his wife. The team in Derbyshire seem to be coping all right, but that is probably because Sarah Vaughan and her daughters have hardly strayed from the village. Ian Vaughan, however, has eluded our watchers again by going to sea. Fortunately he submitted a passage plan to HM Coastguard. We have alerted the French authorities. I suspect that he will be safer there than in home waters."

"No sign of a mend in that relationship then, sir?"

"Apparently not. WPC Tucker has been keeping in regular contact with Sarah Vaughan, and has reported to Mrs Fitzgerald that, if anything, Mrs Vaughan is even more determined to break the marriage up. The watchers report that a Mrs Johnson-Lacey is a regular visitor, and I have the distinct feeling that she is at the root of the break-up, despite what Mrs Vaughan claims."

"It's not that she's got her eyes on half of his reward then, sir?"

"Apparently not. According to a phone call we monitored she doesn't want any of it."

Back in his own office Jackson was just about to pick up the phone when there was a polite knock on the door.

"Yes Tucker, what can I do for you?" Jackson said, smiling.

"I just came to say goodbye, Chief Inspector."

"God, have you worked your notice already?"

"I had some leave to come."

"Damn, I was hoping that we would have time to talk you out of this move."

WPC Tucker smiled. "As nice as it is to feel wanted, I really feel that I have to move on. It has been a pleasure driving for you and the Commander."

"You're having a farewell drinks do, I suppose?"

"I really don't know that many people, sir."

"Oh, well all the very best to you Tucker. The Commander and I will miss you," Jackson said, standing and reaching over the desk to shake her hand. Did he detect a slight moistening of her eyes? "Are you all right?"

"I'm fine, sir. Goodbye," she replied, blinking rapidly as she turned to go.

"Okay. Goodbye and good luck."

The phone call adjusting the reporting arrangements made, Jackson was sat considering how best to deal with DI Carter, when Campbell entered.

"Oh, good evening, sir. Did Tucker come and say goodbye to you?"

"She did this morning, when she drove me into work," replied Campbell. He stood for a moment or two, staring into the middle distance remembering how sad he had felt at the time. "I came to tell you that Vaughan is moored up in Morlaix. Their local police have put a man on him."

"Oh, right, sir. You reckon that will be enough?"

"Yes, I'm reasonably confident that Murata will not have been able to follow him."

* * *

Caroline Tucker's last day had been full of handing in uniforms and signing of forms before being escorted to the public exit of the building by a junior from the HR department and bade a frosty farewell. She walked all of the way home along the embankment and across the Millennium Bridge, all the time running over in her mind the memory of the last few days. Alec Campbell had been wonderful; not once had he pressured her or questioned her decision to leave. All he had said was that he would miss her driving him. It seemed as if he was pleased for her, but unwilling to influence her in any way. She was still confused in her own mind with regard to their relationship, if that is what three evenings in each other's company could be called. The early part of the embassy dinner had, she must confess, made her heart skip. Then had been that brief conversation with Jackson that had brought her back to earth. The evening at Alec's home had done nothing to help, neither had his late call at her flat. Twice, during the long walk, she was nearly run over as she crossed a road, her mind elsewhere. The second time she had even been aware of her hand on the car bonnet, fending it off, as the driver screamed abuse at her. Then suddenly she was there, entering the key code to gain entry to the lobby. In her flat, she dumped her handbag and light cardigan on the armchair and, after washing her hands, poured herself a glass of wine. The sound of the buzzer seemed miles away, but loud enough to penetrate her consciousness. Pressing the communication button she asked who it was, to be told that it was a delivery of flowers. The young Asian boy was completely hidden by the bouquet he was holding. Caroline signed the delivery chit and returned to her flat, searching amongst the blooms for the message card, finding it tucked behind a sachet of plant food stuck to the cellophane wrapping. She opened it and read, ‘Picnic in Knole Park, Saturday, pick you up at 10 o’clock. Alec.’ Maybe then her life would start again, either with him or, as before, alone.

*   *   *

Dho cautiously drove the van into the stadium car park and was about to turn the vehicle round and drive away when he saw Murata appear from behind a low wall at the end of the disabled parking area. As he drove nearer he saw Murata duck out of sight as a police car raced past the car park entrance with siren blaring and lights flashing.

“We believe your base is known to police,” said Murata as he leapt into the back of the van. “Hamaura saw someone, in office next to yard, keeping watch.”

“There has been news flash on local radio,” replied Dho. “They named three of you, yourself, Hamaura and Kimura. Radio say they have set up roadblocks around the town and all trains and buses are being checked.”

For the next two hours Dho drove around, trying to find a route out of Southampton that was not guarded, but failed.

“We should abandon the van and walk out of this place,” said Murata. “They cannot be watching every footpath and alley.”

“Are we going to walk all the way to Plymouth?” asked Iwaki, sarcastically.

Murata swung round on him angrily. “Of course not. Once we are clear we can obtain transport.”

“That is very unlikely to succeed,” interjected Dho. “There is countrywide search for you.”

“What about stealing boat?” suggested Kimura.

Iwaki and Hamaura both shook their heads, memories of unpleasant sea voyages still fresh in their minds.

Dho turned into a side road and parked the van behind a removal lorry, out of sight of the main road. “That is very good suggestion. Sailing boat would not need much fuel so no need to go to filling point. Also many, many boats out on water here in Solent area. Sailing very popular.”

"And who will sail it?" asked Iwaki, hoping that his question would end the discussion.

"I have supporter who knows," replied Dho. "She not far away. I will make call."

Michelle Goodwin was the product of the nineteen eighties miners' strike. Her father, a fourth generation miner, had been drawn into the more militant wing of the union from a very early age. His father, a mild-tempered man, had been killed in a pit accident when Brian Goodwin was just entering his teens. His mother, a hard-bitten woman, also from a mining family, instilled in her son a hatred and distrust of management that influenced and stunted his educational direction throughout his school life and beyond. At the age of nineteen he was to appear on security and police records as a rabble-rouser and violent ringleader. Though possessing a high IQ, he never became involved in the intellectual or negotiation side of the union, preferring the militant group as an enforcer. Several short terms in prison only served to deepen his own and his family's hostilities and feelings of resentment towards, what they considered, an unfair capitalist society. At a communist rally in France he met and got drunk with Carol Hook, who conveniently had her own council flat near to the pit in which he spread his message of injustice. Michelle, born nine months later, was raised in this highly charged political atmosphere, where she lived more as a spectator than a member of the family. From the age of seven she was frequently left on her own, whilst her parents went off to spread unrest amongst factory workers and labourers. At the age of fifteen, her father, who strangely she idolised, was drowned after falling, or maybe being pushed, from a cargo ship on the River Mersey. The police investigation was brief, and a quick inquest returned a verdict of death by misadventure. The mother, who had never loved or really cared for her daughter, soon found another man, who made it plain that Carol was not welcome. Continuing the pattern of irresponsibility Carol's mother soon left to join a band of travelling eco protesters led by her new lover. Shortly afterwards Carol was put into social care, and it was during this period that she was introduced to sailing, under a scheme supported by a local philanthropist. She thoroughly enjoyed what was really the first recreational experience in her life. Probably she would have turned her life around then had it not been for a meeting with Darren Shelton, Dho's errand boy. Soon she would become involved in the minor workings of Dho's network of informants. Now she was about to move up into the big league.

Murata and his group stared dismissively at the girl, as Dho introduced her.

"You can sail a yacht?" asked Hamaura sneeringly.

"Yeah, why?"

Murata was trying to form an opinion. The girl in front of him did not at first glance impress. The Doc Martin boots, part covered by frayed combat trousers below a dirty green T-shirt gave more the impression of a boy than a girl. Her face bore an unhealthy pallor, not improved by the studs and rings in her lips, nose and eyebrows. Her arms bore tattoos, as did her neck. The finishing touch to this unsavoury being was bright orange and green spiky hair. Yet the eyes held Murata's with confidence and the suggestion of intelligence.

"How you know about yacht?" asked Murata.

"Me an' Darren lives on 'is boat an' we goes out wi' old Arthur 'oo owns the sailin' boat next to us. Alright?"

"You go far in this sailing boat?"

"Yeah, down to Poole and Weymouth. Wotcher wonna know all this for?"

"Could you sail us to Plymouth, without running aground or getting lost?"

She thought for a moment. "Yeah, as long as you pay me. I don't do charity."

"You can, er, navigate?"

"Yeah, old Arthur taught me, an' 'ee's been sailin' all 'is life," she said looking wistfully away across the road. "Doubt if 'ee will be doin' anymore though. We 'ad to get an ambulance to 'im last Sunday. ' Ee was coughin' up blood poor bastard."

"Could this Arthur's boat take us all to Plymouth?" asked Dho.

"Yeah. I would fink so. Be a bit tight though," she replied looking round the group assessing the load. "I gotta ask 'im first though, I ain't nickin' 'is boat for yer, no bleedin' way." She paused. “Me an’ Darren are going in to see ’im tonight, I’ll ask if I can borrow it.”

Murata was just about to insist on taking the boat without permission when she said:

“It’s alright. I knows who you are, I won’t go tellin’ no one. I’ll just make it right wiv Arthur.”

“Will you need to bring this Darren?”

“Darren, he going to take van to Plymouth for us,” said Dho. “We will arrange meeting place when we know about boat.”

Murata steered Dho to one side out of earshot from the rest.

“Do you trust her?” he asked.

“Yes, she has worked well for me. She knows nothing of our mission, and will merely deliver us to Plymouth, avoiding movement by road and risk of roadblock.”

Murata nodded his agreement and the two returned to join the others.

“You mention pay,” said Murata.

“Yeah,” she replied and sniffed. “I reckon that it will take, maybe three days to get down there, an’ three back. I fink fifty quid a day plus food is fair. Alright?”

Murata smiled and nodded. “Alright, your ‘fifty quid a day’ it okay.”

* * *

Ian enjoyed the warm weather whilst moored in the locked basin at Morlaix. The sail across the English Channel had gone well with sufficient changes in wind strength to have him reefing the sails, then, as a lull came, letting out the reef again. Traditional and heavy she might be, but well behaved and balanced, definitely a boat that would look after you in any weather. The only vaguely disappointing thing was that he missed his new found sailing companion. Her pleasant company and obvious sailing skill had made the Helford River trip a very enjoyable time. As he sat in the cockpit, with a chart on his lap, planning the next day’s sail to Cherbourg, he wondered whether they would ever meet again. She had been very apologetic about not joining him, but apparently there had been some development in the Murata case.

Now for the first time since his return from the States, and away from Sarah's hostility, he felt relaxed and more aware of things around him. That man, for example, who had borrowed the harbour master's berthing board and receipt book, was obviously one of his watchers. The way he had stood, struggling to keep his balance on the rocking finger pontoons, made it obvious that he was not used to the water. Then reaching across for Ian's money he had exposed the butt of a pistol wedged into a shoulder holster. However, it was nice to know that there was someone out there keeping an eye on him.

Here he was again, cautiously walking towards him.

"Bonjour monsieur. You are to leave us, eh?"

"Yes, I need to get more practice at handling this yacht. I have not owned it for many days. I will not learn by sitting here in Morlaix, as nice as it is," replied Ian.

The man nodded. "Where do you plan to go? Round to Brest?"

"No, the other way, probably Cherbourg, the weather is changing," Ian said pointing up to the sky. "Mackerel sky and mares' tails make lofty ships carry low sails. It will be too rough for the Chanel du Four without a strong crew."

The man looked at him in total bemusement. "When are you leaving?"

"On the high tide tonight."

The man shrugged and turned to gingerly make his way back along the pontoons to the shore. Once in the harbour master's office Ian could see him talking to somebody on the telephone, gesticulating wildly.

He had just finished preparing the charts and setting the yacht's Yeoman Plotter system, when his mobile beeped.

"Hello?"

"We understand that you are making for Cherbourg tonight." It was Jackson's voice. "It would help if you kept us informed directly, to avoid any confusion."

"I didn't want to disturb you all, you seem to have a lot to do just now. Is there any news on where Murata may have got to?"

"We think, in fact we're pretty sure that he is in the Southampton area. It is surrounded with road blocks at present and we are slowly closing in with house-to-house searches."

"Not an easy task with all of the options he has available, road, rail, ferry or even small boat."

"We've got road and rail well covered," replied Jackson. "As you can imagine there are a lot of very unhappy motorists down there at the moment."

"Any sightings?"

"Yes, too many, we're being run ragged chasing shadows. Nearly every oriental in the town has been pinned up against a wall and questioned."

"You didn't mention small boats," said Ian.

"We've got the docks and ferries covered, but apart from the Operation Kraken team we don't have the manpower to check small boat movements as well." Jackson paused for a moment or two. "Bearing in mind his previous modus operandi a small boat could well be his choice of transport. How does one check every craft in an area like the Solent where there are thousands of them?"

"I assume you've blitzed the area with posters of the men?"

"Yes we have, but I don't think we've covered marinas," replied Jackson. "Thanks for that."

"It would also be a good idea to ask owners to check on their boats to ensure that they are still safely on their moorings. At least contact marinas and ask them to check. A few radio announcements should cover most of it."

"You should be in charge of this," said Jackson, as he added another note to the ever-lengthening list. "Given a choice what would you nick if you were Murata?"

"If I had friends that could meet me just outside of the cordon, and give me local safe refuge, I would go for a power boat. If I was thinking to go any distance, I would not want to risk road accident or police roadblock, and choose a yacht and sail there."

"Why choose a yacht for the longer journey?"

"Refuelling. Few power boats go very far on a tank of fuel, so you then risk being recognised when you come ashore to fill up," replied Ian. "The big power boats with a good fuel range have normally got sophisticated antitheft fitted as part of their insurance requirements. I doubt if these guys are up to that standard regards boat theft. So it would be something on the small side if it was power."

"That's very interesting. We think that they may have an interest in attacking something in the Portsmouth area. It would explain their presence in Southampton."

"Have you contacted the coastguard? They may well be able to offer some help. That chap, er, Saints, was brilliant in working out where I was being forced to go, the last time Murata was on the loose."

"We are getting in touch with them at the moment as it happens. Thanks for all of that. Oh, by the way, before she left the force WPC Tucker visited your family a few times. The last thing I heard was that all was well and the children seemed to be very happy in their new location."

"Any comment about how Sarah is?" Ian asked.

"Not much except that she still appears to be set on a divorce. Her friend, Mrs Johnson-Lacey, is a regular visitor. Tucker wasn't that sure that her presence was a good thing, but they are old friends, and it is her house that your wife is living in."

"I just wish we had never known the woman," said Ian with some feeling. "What I cannot understand is why Sarah pays so much attention to her."

The arrival of someone in Jackson's office brought the conversation to a close and left Ian sat, staring blankly at the forward bulkhead, thinking of Sarah and the girls. Would Murata's capture and permanent imprisonment make any difference to how Sarah felt? If Murata was shot and killed would there be any change? The more he thought about it the firmer became the conviction that she would still blame him for the loss of their unborn son and the near loss of her life.

The ping on the yacht's clock, marking the hour, brought his thoughts back to the present and the planned voyage to Cherbourg. Checking the almanac for the lock opening times he decided that four hours' sleep and a meal would just work out with the lock free-flow timing. Nestled in the quarter berth he was soon fast asleep.

The wind was getting up and Ian found himself struggling as he prepared the boat to cast off. Setting the propeller turning gently astern a single breast rope held the yacht close to the pontoon allowing Ian to release the other mooring ropes. Jumping aboard he freed the yacht by undoing the ferryman's hitch around the starboard winch, securing one end of the breast rope, and *La Mouette sur le Vent* now started to move sedately backward clear of the finger pontoon as Ian watched the loose end of the breast rope slide along the side deck and out through the midships fairlead. Still keeping an eye on the rope as it unwrapped itself from around the pontoon cleat he used the bow thrusters to get the yacht pointing in the right direction. Hurriedly he recovered the breast rope and, returning to the cockpit, steered the yacht out into the main channel and through the open lock. It took six scrambled journeys round the deck to bring all of the mooring ropes and fenders back into the cockpit, but once they were there the coiling and stowing operation was conducted calmly.

The Morlaix river snakes down to the sea for nearly four miles before passing into the estuary with its vast area of oyster beds to either side; yachtsmen then find themselves faced with a tortuous period of piloting to follow a safe channel through the off-lying islets and rocks. It was only when clear of these that Ian felt confident to turn the yacht into the wind and hoist the minimum of mainsail. Back on course he now set the jib then used an increasing amount of staysail until he balanced the yacht, taking pressure off the tiller. The night was very dark and the wind appeared to be increasing beyond that forecast. Rain soon began to lash down depriving Ian of any real visibility. Setting the autohelm he went below to check his position and obtain an accurate course to steer; back on deck he now concentrated as hard as he could on lookout duties. Half-hourly checks on position and course also gave fleeting opportunities to change his neck towel for a dry one or make up a packet soup. The dawn was high, the band of cloud on the eastern horizon blocking the sun's light foretelling that more rain was to come. The wind had eased a bit, bringing slightly smaller waves to attack the yacht's stern as it was driven hard past the north-west coast of Guernsey. His course during the night had been parallel to the eastbound shipping lane and several times he had seen the starboard lights of cargo vessels making up the Channel. Visibility was now improving, and Ian felt it safe to go below to prepare some breakfast. Coffee and porridge restored his dwindling energy levels and now, sitting feet up on the starboard cockpit seat, he just enjoyed the exhilaration of a fast broad reach passage making eight knots over the ground with the flood tide easing as it reached its height. The change in tidal direction for the next six hours would mean the boat's progress would slow considerably as it fought against the ebb.

*　　　　*　　　　*

Reluctantly Hamaura and Iwaki lowered themselves nervously into the small inflatable dinghy and, gripping its sides, clung on as Michelle put the outboard in gear and set off from the quay out into the waters of the River Itchen. It took twenty minutes for the little craft to bob along, upstream to the Macwester Seaforth's moorings, where it bumped alongside the yacht and the two reluctant passengers clambered unsteadily aboard. Their experience of sailing from Icelandic waters to Loch Melfort was nothing compared to what they were soon to endure. Arthur, fearful of his yacht's safety, had wrung a promise from Michelle not to put to sea until the current low-pressure weather centre had moved away and gentler winds prevailed. Explaining this to Murata, though, had produced an angry reaction and a demand for immediate departure.

"It ain't safe goin' out into the Channel in wevver like this when I am the only one who knows how to sail," she said.

"We go now!" shouted Murata, moving to strike her, his eyes full of fury.

Holding up an arm she said, "How about we go across to Newton Creek, it's quiet there an' there ain't no one goin' to bother us when it's blowin' old boots an' pissin' down wiv rain." She and Darren had visited the Isle of Wight's ancient harbour on several occasions with Arthur and she felt confident that she could enter there, especially at high tide.

The comment was enough to stay Murata and lowering his hand he turned to Kimura and said gruffly. “You help her.”

Fearful now of her passengers and anxious not to damage Arthur’s boat Michelle took great care with preparation for the short voyage. Eventually Kimura dropped off the mooring warps a little before two in the morning. It took four hours to motor down Southampton Water to Calshot and south-west down the Solent to the narrow entrance of Newton Creek against the flood tide. On arrival Kimura picked up the buoy pendant at the third attempt and thankfully passed the loop over the port bow cleat.

“We’ll ’ave to stay ’ere until tonight I should fink. Shouldn’t get any bovver ’ere though.”

It appeared that everyone was turned in and fast asleep so it took Ken Fallon, the harbour master, some time to get any response. Below, only Iwaki had woken at the sound of the approaching craft; creeping out of the stern cabin and keeping low out of sight, he had crossed the cockpit to the main cabin, where he was starting to shake Michelle into wakefulness as Fallon knocked on the yacht’s hull.

“Surprised to see old Arthur out and about in weather like this. Is the old devil down below?” said Fallon to a dozy-looking Michelle as she struggled into a fleece jacket for protection against the wind and rain.

“’E’s fast asleep,” she replied, yawning. “’E was ’ittin’ the gin shortly after we got ’ere, so we won’t be seein’ ’im till tea time I shouldn’t fink.”

“He’s a daft old sod, the doctor told him especially to lay off the booze. Anyway it will still cost him £10 a day to stay here.”

Michelle went below and, poking Iwaki, indicated she needed some money. Returning to the deck after a couple of minutes, she noticed that Fallon was looking curiously at the stern cabin window.

“’Ere’s the tenner. We should be out of ’ere tonight, back to ’is moorin’ I would fink.”

"Yeah right, here's your ticket, er, give Arthur my best," replied Fallon showing signs of wanting to leave quickly.

In fact what Fallon had seen was the face of Hamaura glaring at him from the stern cabin. It was only a fleeting glance but enough for the harbour master to see that it was an oriental face and add two and two together accurately.

"'E saw sumfin'," said Michelle to Iwaki, when she returned to the cabin. "All of a sudden 'e was rushin' off. Normally 'e wants to talk all bleedin' day."

Rapidly screwing a silencer onto his pistol barrel Iwaki pushed past her and gaining the cockpit saw Fallon, now at least twenty feet away. Taking aim he kept pulling on the trigger until with his fifth shot he hit the unfortunate harbour master in the back of his skull, killing him instantly.

"Oh, Gawd, we're in the shit now. Oh Gawd you bleedin' gone an' killed 'im. What we gonna do now? Oh shit, I don't want no more o' this. You put me ashore, I'll hide for a bit. I won't say noffin, 'onest I won't," said Michelle tears of fear running down her cheeks, her hands trembling.

"Be quiet," ordered Iwaki, slapping her around the face. "Get down there and get dressed properly, then we leave here, you sail, we help. Go!"

Blindly she stumbled down the companionway steps into the main cabin to find herself face to face with Murata. Unlike Iwaki he did not look annoyed, though the burn scar down the right side of his face made it impossible for him to appear gentle or kind. "Please understand," he said, "Iwaki-san, he had no choice. If that man got back to shore we would all be dead by end of this day."

"They wouldn't kill yer," she heard herself say, "They's want to arrest yer again that's all."

"We will never be arrested again," said Kimura, sitting in the starboard double berth. The chill in his voice adding to Michelle's fears. "We would rather die."

What little colour Michelle's complexion had disappeared and she collapsed fainting into Murata's arms.

On deck Iwaki coolly watched the launch continue across the water in almost a straight line, heading for the westerly arm of the creek. Just beyond a muddy spit of land the launch pinballed off a moored powerboat, crossed the creek and ran aground at the head of a narrow field drainage channel, the engine stalling as the propeller dug into the mud. Iwaki stood almost motionless for half an hour, watching for any signs of life or reaction to the launch's grounding, but there were none; the wind and rain swept creek remained deserted.

When she came round she found herself alone in the cabin and noises coming from on deck. Slowly her brain cleared and she realised that their intention was to get underway. Carefully she sat up, then got to her feet and climbed the companionway steps into the cockpit.

"There's no way out of 'ere," she said to no one in particular. "The tide is too low see, an' this boat will go aground."

Almost instantly Murata was by her side, brought by the sound of the word 'aground'. The Kinoko Kumo attack was almost ended before it had begun by a yacht running aground. That had made him very sensitive to the possibility of it happening again.

"What you say?"

"I said you can't get out of 'ere yet 'cause the tide's too low."

All activity stopped and the gang hurried below out of the rain to hold a conference.

Unable to understand a word of what was being said, Michelle, realising that she was starving hungry, rummaged amongst the stores and spent the next half-hour nervously producing a spaghetti and tuna dish; and wondering why nobody had raised the alarm after the shooting. By the time she had finished, Hamaura had been told to take up a lookout position in the cockpit, whilst the others set about cleaning weapons and preparing for what they thought would be the inevitable fight to the end. Pushing Iwaki and Kimura out of the way Michelle thrust the sleeping bags at Dho and silently converted the double berth back to a dinette. Setting plates on the table she served the food, putting the kettle onto the hob for coffee.

During the meal Hamaura found himself to be almost constantly stared at by Murata. When the harbour master had knocked on the yacht's hull Murata had woken immediately and carefully raised his head to get a good view into the cockpit, his gun held hidden, but ready. The angle of sight also allowed a view into the stern cabin where he saw Hamaura stand and glare out through the cabin window at their visitor. Murata knew it was Hamaura who the harbour master had seen; yes it was Hamaura who had so carelessly given them away. So unlike his sister, who was so cunning and careful, but also, so alike her in many ways such as their shared hatred of the world. The question was, could he, Murata, afford to keep this reckless revengeful fool nearby or should he send him away? Unaware of what Murata had deduced and was contemplating, Hamaura just felt uncomfortable, and as soon as he had cleared his plate he excused himself and returned to replace Iwaki as watch keeper.

"We should be able to get goin' in about annover ten minutes."

Her words cut through Murata's thoughts.

"We can go now?" questioned Murata frowning.

"Yeah in a bit, yeah. Oh you fort we was 'ere for good. No, tide is comin' in see an' that means the boat will get through the channel."

"I well understand about tide," Murata snapped back.

"Oh, anyway, I'll get fings ready."

On deck it was still raining and there did not seem to be a soul about on any of the other boats. Whilst Michelle had been getting the meal, she had frantically thought of what to do next. Realising that they would never let her escape alive she had decided to sail them to Plymouth and hope that they would let her go there. She thought of Arthur, as he had looked the previous evening, lying on a hospital bed with wires stuck to his chest and tubes up his nose and in his hands. She was going to bring Arthur's boat back to him if it was the last thing she ever did. Decision made, she swiftly removed the sail covers and stowed them in the cockpit locker on top of the fenders.

Starting the engine she frowned at the fuel gauge. "We ain't got a lot a fuel left, so we'll 'ave to sail most of the way."

Iwaki sat watching, sighed and nodded. "We know," he said with deep resignation.

The tide flooding up the Western Solent, combined with a still strong Force 7 gale meant progress was very slow. Almost as soon as they had cleared the shallows Michelle had got Kimura to hoist the mizzen sail and then let out a fair amount of the genoa, causing the craft to heel over some twenty degrees before gathering way and shouldering the waves aside to head directly at the Beaulieu shore. As she sailed the ketch on a series of tacks down towards the Needles Passage she could not help wondering whether Arthur would appreciate the way she was handling his boat. Approaching a line between Yarmouth and Lymington she noticed that the tide was turning and, with now growing confidence, she took the yacht as close as she dared to the island shore before calling Kimura to tack the genoa again as the yacht turned and charged out of the Solent past Hurst Castle and through the narrow channel into Christchurch Bay. Here the waves were significantly bigger than before and within minutes Michelle could hear the groans of seasickness sufferers and the crash of the heads' door as someone scrambled in, to spend some hours with their head in the basin.

Kimura, Michelle noticed, seemed to come alive in the rough conditions and asked to take the wheel. Nervous at first to allow a total stranger to take command of her friend's precious boat she soon realised that the man had a natural flair for helming. Off Mudeford they tacked once more to gain sea room and it was then that Murata came up into the cockpit and announced that he wanted her to steer for Cherbourg.

"Many people will search for us along this coast when they find dead man. You take us across English Channel then we go west."

Chapter 11

A chilling knot of fear had grown rapidly in his stomach the moment he had seen the oriental face glaring menacingly at him through the stern cabin window. In milliseconds his brain had linked the face to those being sought in Southampton and the fear had almost paralysed him. The fact that the girl was mixed up with this crowd seemed to fit; she had always been a rude little cow, together with her yobbo mate Darren. Why old Arthur had taken them under his wing was a complete mystery to Ken Fallon, but now he needed to get away without them suspecting he had rumbled them.

Taking the cash he had fumbled a bit in writing the receipt and almost forgot to cast off his breast rope from the yacht before putting the engine in gear. Turning immediately to port he nearly ran the craft aground and only by thrusting the throttle lever hard astern, spinning the wheel then thrusting the throttle full ahead again, had he got the craft speeding to starboard, but was then too late to cut across the yacht's stern, and had to steer round the next boat on the line of buoyed moorings before he could head back to the yard. Fallon had patted his pockets for his mobile phone, before remembering that out in that part of the creek there was no signal anyway. His launch was running back passing Arthur's boat and, as he glanced towards it, he had seen the top of a man's head appearing from the companionway hatch. Seconds later he heard, but failed to assimilate, a ping and wining noise, then a thwack, a low poing, another thwack as bullets from Iwaki's gun hit the launch, then nothing. His dead body had fallen forward over the wheel then back in a tangled heap into the bottom of the launch. The craft running uncontrolled and at speed parallel to the line of moorings created considerable wash, setting the moored boats into a lively jig. On board *Cloudless Skies* Jenny Edwards was tossed across the double berth, where she was reading a book, almost onto her husband. Surprised and a little alarmed at first both recovered and giggled before cuddling each other and settling back to start a conversation about her parents' fortieth wedding anniversary.

It was just over two hours later that it happened, the peak of the tide had just been enough to lift the launch clear of its muddy resting place and the ebb to gently float it back towards the line of moored yachts. The thud on the hull woke the Edwards from their siesta and caused Jonathan to leap up and, without putting shoes on, scamper up the companionway steps to the cockpit. On deck he saw the harbour master's launch sliding down the port side of their yacht. Grabbing a boat hook from the cabin roof he hooked the stern quarter of the launch and pulled it back alongside. It was then that he realised the heap of clothing was in fact the body of the harbour master.

"Jenny, don't come on deck, just get on the radio to the coastguard and tell them to get the police launch here pronto. It looks as if Ken, the harbour master's been shot."

Jenny gasped and went to come on deck.

"I said don't come on deck! Get on the radio now!"

Stopped in her tracks, she slowly processed the information and reached for the radio microphone. "Solent coastguard, Solent coastguard, Solent coastguard. This is yacht *Cloudless Skies, Cloudless Skies, Cloudless Skies,* over."

"Cloudless Skies, Solent coastguard, please go to channel 67, over."

"Going to 67."

Jenny hurriedly punched 67 on the keypad and depressed the microphone button again. "Solent coastguard this is yacht *Cloudless Skies* there has been a shooting here in Newton Creek and we urgently need police attendance, over."

"Is there still shooting activity taking place? Over."

"No all seems quiet, over."

"Please confirm your position, over."

"We are four or five boats down on the south-west arm inside the entrance to Newton Creek, over."

There was a pause in communication whilst the coastguard made contact with the police, requesting officers attached to Project

Kraken to attend urgently. Project Kraken was established to handle marine crime, and the officers dealt with anything from boat and equipment theft to people smuggling and terrorism. Carrying the police stop and search powers to inshore waters made them an effective unit.

"*Cloudless Skies* please stand by we have requested the police launch to attend."

"*Cloudless Skies* standing by, out."

Clipping the microphone back onto the radio unit she went two steps up towards the yacht cockpit and asked, "Is he dead, Jonathan?"

"Yes, sadly he is. Don't come any further love; it's not a pretty sight. Could you put the kettle on I could do with a cup of tea?"

"Yes of course, is there anything else I can do?"

"No, I don't think so. I've got the launch tied up alongside. I don't want to touch anything until the police get here."

Jenny was quite shaken when Jonathan came down the companionway steps. He was terribly pale and obviously very upset by what he had seen.

"It's awful Jenny, such a mess. The only way I knew it was old Ken was that I saw him in the launch a couple of hours ago, doing the rounds, collecting mooring fees."

"Don't tell me any more. The whole thing has made me feel ill," Jenny replied, sitting trembling on the bench by the chart table. "As soon as the police have been I want to go home, away from this. I could never come back here again, we will have to find another quiet spot to moor for our long weekends." As she said this tears started to run down her cheeks.

* * *

"You said you saw the harbour master making his rounds earlier on. What time was that?" asked PC Jason Porter, his warm Welsh baritone voice resonating around the cabin.

"Oh, must have been about midday I suppose, yes, I remember glancing at my watch," replied Jonathan Edwards, confidently.

"You didn't hear any shots fired?"

"No, not a sound. Someone in a powerboat charged up the creek in a hurry, but apart from the wind and rain that was all we heard."

"When was that?" asked PC Mark Winters, as he put down his cup of tea and picked up his notebook.

"Oh four, five minutes after we saw Ken pass by in the launch."

"Then the next you know the launch has bumped alongside you and you radioed the coastguard," said Porter.

"Yes, I went straight up on deck, wondering what it was that had bumped us and saw it was the launch. I didn't think there was anyone on board at first and thought it had just come free of its moorings. Then I saw the pile of clothing and Ken's hand," Jonathan explained, turning his head away and holding a handkerchief over his mouth as he started to wretch.

"It's alright, sir. You take your time. Shall I get you a glass of water?"

"No, I'll be alright," said Jonathan, swallowing hard and taking a few deep breaths. "It was when I looked a bit closer that I saw what was left of his head."

"Yes it's not a pretty sight. We think there were several shots fired as there is fresh grazing and gouging on the launch."

At that point other officers arrived and, using small semi-inflatable ribs and dinghies, the team started to visit the other vessels moored in the creek. Thoughtfully a female police liaison officer had been sent to stay with the Edwards and gently talk them through their experience again, more as part of counselling than statement taking.

The vessels further up the creek were quickly dealt with as none of them had anyone aboard and according to the local yard had not had their owners on board that weekend. The line of craft downstream however, were visitors, some on the visitors' moorings, and three others in the anchorage. According to his receipt book, Ken Fallon had collected fees from two yachts near to the entrance channel that day before he was shot. In the last entry the space for the boat's name was left blank. His book also showed that the previous day he had collected fees from two powerboats further down the line of moorings, one of which was *Liquid Assets.*

"Can we come aboard?" asked PC Porter. "We would like to ask you a few questions about any boat movements in the last, say twelve hours."

"Stan! There's a young copper 'ere wants to come on board and ask questions," said Gracey Bevins turning from the sliding door to the cabin and shouting over the noise of the television football commentary.

"What questions?"

"Sumfin' abou' boat movements."

Hauling his somewhat obese form from the port-hand settee Stan Bevins peered out at the bedraggled policeman. "It's simple mate, when it's rough they goes up and down and when it's calm they don't."

Porter gave the man a tired look and shook his head. "What we want to know…"

"It's alright lad come on board," Stan interrupted. "'Eer, step inside and slide that bleedin' door to."

Porter shook the rain off his cap and stepped into the cabin, sliding the door closed behind him.

"Put the kettle on Gracey luv, we could do with a cuppa," said Stan, before turning to PC Porter and asking, "You got ID?"

Porter showed his warrant card. "Police Constable Porter."

Pulling a notebook from his pocket Porter took down the couple's details and name of the boat.

"What do you want to know lad?"

"When did you get here, sir?"

"Oh let's see now, musta been about two o'clock on Friday. Just before this bleedin' rain started," replied Stan. "Why?"

"Did you see any boats arrive say last night or early this morning?"

"Yeah, a yacht came in about six maybe half past this mornin'. Just made it before the tide dropped too low. Made a right cock-up of pickin' up the moorin', 'ad to 'ave three or four goes at it and when he picked it 'e was almost pulled over the side, 'cause she didn't stick it in reverse quick enough," Stan chuckled at the memory.

"Just the couple on board?"

"Yeah I think so."

"No, there was four or five of 'em," interrupted Gracey. "Must 'ave been just after old Ken went by in the launch, they was all up there messin' about."

Porter's ears pricked up straight away. "Which mooring are they on?"

"They were on that one just astern of us," answered Stan, pointing at a buoy between them and the next moored craft. "They left way before high tide, I was surprised they didn't get stuck in the entrance. Buggered if I would pay a tenner for what, six, seven hours."

"Can you describe the yacht?"

"It was quite old, centre cockpit, with two masts. Had a dark blue hull; been looked after well though, you know, clean."

"Can you remember the name?"

"No, sorry mate," replied Stan.

"It was *Weighward Lass*," informed Gracey, pouring Porter a second mug of tea. "I think I've seen it in 'ere before, we come 'ere quite often, it's nice an' quiet see."

Stan Bevins looked at his wife with surprise. "Cor, you don't miss much do yer?"

"I don't sit around all day watchin' the bally telly," she retorted, poking him in the stomach with her finger.

Porter smiled and said, "That's very interesting, Mrs Bevins. If you'll excuse me I'll just go outside and radio that in, won't be a moment."

It took an hour to trace the yacht's name to its normal mooring on the River Itchen and another half an hour to get the address of the owner. When the police learnt that the owner was in hospital and currently undergoing surgery for the removal of a tumour, Chief Inspector Jackson ordered a full marine search, to take in the waters surrounding the Isle of Wight and adjacent harbours such as Portsmouth, Langstone and Chichester.

"All three of the Hampshire police launches are out searching, and we've alerted harbour masters and marina managers to look out for the boat and report as soon as it is seen, sir," said Jackson, over the phone to Campbell.

"You think they will stay that close after murdering that harbour master?" replied Campbell. "Surely they would want to put some distance between them and the murder scene? That is assuming of course that it is Murata and his bunch."

"Down here they reckon it to be unlikely that they would go out into the Channel in this weather, sir, and we can't put out an 'all ships' notice via the coastguard in case they're listening in."

"Yes, I see your point. We could warn the harbour masters and marina managers in all the Channel ports though. I'll get my team up here to deal with that, you've got enough on your plate at the moment."

"Thank you, sir. Could you also contact Ian Vaughan, I think he's sailing up towards Cherbourg. If it is them he needs to be warned."

"Leave that with me, Chief Inspector, I think you are right, he needs to be warned alright."

*　　　*　　　*

Ian Vaughan was exhausted by the time he had entered the western end of Cherbourg Harbour's Grande Rade. He knew he had another half-hour's sail before he could drop anchor in the Petit Rade north of the marina wall. The Grande Rade itself offered some protection and he took advantage of this to go below and slip a pre-baked pie into the oven to heat through. As he passed the chart table he noticed his mobile phone was showing a missed call. Picking it up he unlocked the keypad and searched for the call details and found that it was Campbell's office. Going back into the cockpit he called the number.

"Campbell," came the brisk reply.

"It's Ian Vaughan, you called me?"

"Yes, we did. There has been a development at Southampton. We now think you were right and Murata and his little army got away by water. We are not one hundred percent sure, but believe they have employed the services of a young couple that borrowed a friend's boat to take them down Southampton Water and the Western Solent to Newton Creek. We now think that the harbour master there got a glimpse of them, and was on his way to report when they shot and killed him."

"Oh my God the nightmare continues," said Ian.

"Indeed it does," replied Campbell. "The locals' thinking is that the English Channel is too rough for them to consider crossing at this time, and it is more likely that they have just holed up in another harbour in the Solent area."

"What are they sailing in?" asked Ian.

"I'm told that it is a MacWester Seaforth, about thirty-six foot long I understand."

"Right, well that's more than capable of crossing the Channel in these conditions. If I had just bumped off the local harbour master I would want to put more than a few sea miles between me and the scene of the crime. Do you have the name of the boat?"

"Yes, it's called *Weighward Lass* as in weighing anchor, it's not registered formally, not even on the Small Ships Register."

"When did the shooting take place?" asked Ian.

"We think between 1200 and 1300 hours, though it was not discovered for a further three hours by which time this yacht had left the creek," said Campbell. "Where are you now?"

"Just sailing across the Grande Rade of Cherbourg Harbour."

Campbell was quiet for a moment or two. "You are confident that they would not recognise you?"

"Yes, the only one that has seen me before is Murata and then it was only for a very short time and I've lost a lot of weight since then."

"I was going to suggest that you place yourself under the protection of the French police, but if you are sure Murata would not recognise you if your paths crossed then I will ask you to do us a favour and keep a lookout for them over there."

"Sure, no problem. If they left say around 1300 hours I wouldn't expect them to turn up here until say 0200 to 0300 hours tomorrow at the earliest. I'll be at anchor just outside of the marina here, so if they go in for fuel or to tie up I will see them," said Ian.

"Apparently they would have been unable to leave Newton Creek until shortly after 1500 hours. Depth at the entrance would not have been enough for them until then," informed Campbell.

"Right, well that shunts the timing back to 0400, 0500 hours local time here. I might get some beauty sleep."

"The other piece of news that might be of interest to you is that Mrs Johnston-Lacey has been to your bedsit in Kingsbridge asking where you are."

"Nobody told her I hope," replied Ian.

"No, in fact your landlady had her driving halfway round Cornwall searching for you."

"When I left I didn't tell her that I was sailing over to France. In fact I intentionally told her that I was heading along in the Falmouth direction. I wonder what Rebecca wants to talk to me about."

"I did ask your wife in the hope that she had changed her mind regarding your marriage future, but she has no idea, and I regret to inform, is still determined on divorce. I am sorry that things have worked out this way."

The conversation continued for a few minutes more until *La Mouette sur le Vent* arrived at the entrance to the Petit Rade and Ian was required to prepare the yacht for anchoring.

There was a large Dutch yacht at anchor some way out from the marina wall leaving just enough room for Ian to anchor closer in where it was more sheltered. A hot meal and a good tidy-up of the cabin and navigation area would leave him, he estimated, with about six hours of sleep before his watch should start.

The rattle of flailing halyards and cracking of flogging sail woke him two hours later than he had planned. The noise was from the Dutch yacht as she fell back towards the main channel having weighed anchor. Cursing his own tardiness, Ian hurriedly washed and dressed then prepared breakfast, all the time taking glances out of the companionway looking for any craft in the channel. After clearing away and washing up he went on deck, now convinced that, if Murata had crossed the Channel to Cherbourg, he had missed him. He needed to know for sure and opened the deep port-hand locker to haul out the small Avon dinghy and two-horsepower outboard. Inflating and launching the dinghy took some time and it was a slightly breathless Ian that locked the hatchway and clambered down the side-boarding ladder to the little dinghy bobbing alongside. Three pulls on the starter cord and the outboard engine burst into life and Ian directed the dinghy towards the marina entrance. In the shelter of the marina he was able to throttle back and carefully take in his surroundings. The marina was almost full and it took Ian time, checking the names of each of the vessels moored. On leaving the third line of berths he turned the dinghy towards the fuel jetty where a ketch was just casting off and turning in his direction. On the yacht's foredeck a scruffy looking girl with bright orange hair was coiling the mooring warps and lifting the fenders inboard. As the two craft passed each other, the man at the helm turned away, bending down to open the cockpit locker presumably in preparation to receive the warps and fenders.

"Excuse me, hey excuse me, can you help!" A young woman's call from the end of the finger pontoon to his right diverted his attention away from the yacht. "We've just lost two of our fenders and they are floating away over there," she continued, pointing towards the fuel berth. "Could you rescue them for us?"

Ian waved an acknowledgement and altered course slightly to intercept the errant fenders. Two minutes later they had been retrieved and he turned the dinghy and was heading back towards the lady, trying at the same time to make out the name written across the stern of the ketch, but the yacht's fenders tied to the pushpit obscured the name.

At the pontoon end the lady's husband had joined her and after receiving profuse thanks Ian asked, "Did either of you notice the name of the blue-hulled ketch that just went out?"

"Oh you mean that Seaforth? No I didn't look at the name, she was in fine condition though. We used to have one, lovely sea boat, take you anywhere," the man said nostalgically. "Fancy a coffee or something?"

"No thanks, I need to get back to my boat, I've forgotten something important."

"Oh well, thanks again."

Pushing off from the pontoon and opening the engine throttle wide Ian steered for the marina entrance cursing himself for forgetting his mobile phone and for being distracted by the woman's request for help. The little two-horsepower outboard, however, was no match for a thirty-eight horsepower BMC inboard diesel driving a large three-bladed propeller, and by the time Ian had reached the entrance and could see into the Petit Rade, the Macwester was out of sight somewhere in the Grande Rade.

"I've just seen a Macwester Seaforth leaving Cherbourg. There was a young woman with bright orange hair, probably in her early twenties, on board. I couldn't get a look at any of the other crew," Ian said to Mrs Fitzgerald over a bad phone line. "Could you pass the message onto the Commander or Chief Inspector Jackson?"

"How can we get hold of you again?"

"It will take me half an hour to get underway to follow them, hopefully you can get back to me before then."

"Thank you Mr Vaughan, I will try."

Starting the yacht's engine, Ian then plugged his mobile phone in to recharge the battery before going on deck to check the run of the anchor chain over the windlass spawl then started the process of weighing anchor. To the solo yachtsman an electric windlass is an essential item for low-hassle anchoring, and Ian again thanked the previous owner for his forethought. Checking that the anchor chain run to the mouth of the hawse was clear, he started the windlass, hurried back to the cockpit and slowly motored the yacht forward, as the windlass effortlessly wound in the anchor chain. A small dip of the bows indicated that the anchor had been pulled out of the seabed. Putting the yacht's engine in neutral Ian went forward to see, seconds later, the anchor clear the water. Stopping the windlass

Ian quickly stowed the heavy CQR anchor on the stemhead and inserted the locking pin that held it in place. Already the yacht was being blown towards the deep-water channel, its bows paying off to starboard, as Ian briskly made his way back to the cockpit.

Since clearing the marina Ian had kept a good lookout towards the eastern entrance to the Grande Rade and was confident that the Macwester had not left by that route. Holding binoculars to his eyes he searched the waters of the Grande Rade for any sign of the yacht, without success. He was gambling now as to which way the Macwester would have gone on leaving the western entrance. If it were returning to English waters then it would have gone north, on the other hand, if it was staying on the French side of the Channel it would continue along the coastline until it arrived at the Alderney Race. Ian shook his head; if only he had sat in wait on board *La Mouette sur le Vent,* instead of impatiently taking the dinghy into the marina, he would probably have had clear sight of the yacht, and seen its name clearly enough to be sure that he was chasing the right vessel. Now he was at least three quarters of an hour behind it and with a horizon of only four miles at sea he was out of sight of it. Hearing the sound of his mobile ringing he leapt down the companionway steps and grabbed it, removed the charging lead and returned to the tiller.

"Ian Vaughan."

"Jackson here, you say that you saw a yacht fitting the description of the one we are searching for?"

"Yes, a Macwester Seaforth, it had a dark blue hull and the female crew on the foredeck had bright orange hair. I didn't manage to get a look at the man helming the boat or its name."

"Pity, there is a remote possibility that it is the boat we are after, but all the advice here is that they would not have taken on a Channel crossing in last night's weather conditions," replied Jackson. "You didn't see anyone else on board? We have a witness that said she saw four or five people on deck in Newton Creek."

"No I didn't. I was not best placed to see into the boat at all," Ian paused trying to recall the moment again. "Maybe the others had been dropped off ashore."

"Yes, that would make sense. I'll get onto the French police straight away and get them to make enquiries at the marina."

"I doubt if they would come all the way across the Channel to sail straight back again, so it is probably best if I try and search west of here, I'm confident that they didn't leave by the east entrance and go north."

"I'll contact the Channel Islands and get them to alert the harbour authorities," said Jackson. "I think we've got enough eyes on our own coastline to pick them up. If you see anything don't try and take them on, we think they've got enough hardware to do a rerun of the Second World War."

"No, I'll contact you if I see anything, bullet dodging is something I don't want to repeat."

* * *

The previous evening, aboard *Weighward Lass,* Michelle was still recovering from the shock of seeing a man shot dead, and was only just aware of a growing sense of exhilaration as her confidence in helming the yacht grew. As the hours passed, and the yacht charged on a beam reach out of Christchurch Bay into the English Channel, she felt detached from those around her and, for the first time in her life, in tune with something she felt was truly magical. Needing to visit the heads, she asked Kimura to take the wheel for a short time and, as soon as she returned, he had been happy to hand it back to her and go below to attend to Iwaki and Hamaura, who were again suffering *mal de mare*. As he left, the one they called Murata-san clambered up into the cockpit and sat looking out to sea, apparently deep in thought.

"You know course to steer?" he asked suddenly, destroying her sense of isolation and peace.

"Yeah," she replied. "I put the co-ordinates in for Cherbourg entrance as a waypoint, an' the computer gave me the course, simple really. 'Ow's yer mates down below? That 'Amaura was well sick."

"They do not enjoy the sea."

“This Kimura bloke, ’e’s okay. I fink ’e may be good at this sailin’ bit.”

“Kimura-san, you should say. It is very impolite you say bloke.”

“Oh. You really from Japan?”

“Yes.”

“Darren ’e says you’re the bloke who sorted that fing in America.”

Murata nodded.

“Cor, I bet they want yer real bad.”

By luck rather than knowledge and good judgement Michelle sailed across the westbound large vessel traffic lane at the correct angle and safely between a refined spirit vessel and a large container ship. During the rest of the crossing, she and Kimura shared the task of helming, whilst Murata and Dho saw to food and drink supplies.

It was getting light as they approached the entrance to Cherbourg and it was a nervous and fearful Michelle that steered the yacht through the entrance and turned it into the wind to lower the sails. A quick study of Arthur’s almanac had revealed where the fuel jetty was, and they slowly motored into the marina and tied up against it an hour before the staff came on duty.

Michelle stood on the side deck and desperately looked around for help only to find the area deserted. All thoughts of returning Arthur’s boat back to him had disappeared hours ago in the middle of the Channel; all she wanted to do now was escape. Being amongst this group was terrifying, their cold ruthlessness apparent in their every move. Standing there she measured the distance across the pontoon to the ladder up to the fuel pump stands. Could she make it? Climb the ladder and get behind the lift crane before they realised she had gone?

“Not a good idea,” the voice behind her said.

She whirled round to look into the cold dark eyes of Iwaki standing close to her shaking his head, a sneering smile showing faintly on his face. She shuddered and wondered how he had got that close without her being aware.

"What's not a good idea?" she said, her voice unable to disguise her guilt.

"You were thinking of leaving us here," he replied calmly. "We could not allow that." Again the smile returned.

"No I wasn't, honest," she protested.

"Murata-san wishes we all stay out of sight in cabin until fuel worker arrives."

Reluctantly Michelle went below to sit between Dho and Hamaura until the clatter of feet on the pontoon alongside indicated the arrival of the staff.

At a nod from Murata, Kimura reached over and gently tugged on Michelle's sleeve jerking his head in the direction of the companionway. On deck under the nervous but watchful eye of Kimura, they took on one hundred and seventy litres of diesel, paying in crisp new euro notes. Immediately the receipt was handed over, Kimura started the engine and ordered Michelle to cast off. Apart from a woman standing on the end of a pontoon and a man in a small dinghy, there was no one about. Silently she mouthed the word 'help' as the dinghy came close, but the man was looking intently at the yacht's hull and she failed to catch his eye. Now they were out at sea again and she had been ordered to sail north-west into the middle of the English Channel then westward, ensuring that they were out of sight of land and the majority of shipping. The wind had eased, and, though the sky was overcast, it was not raining, making a windward voyage under full sail a more pleasant experience than had been endured by Iwaki and Hamaura the previous night. Progress, however, was strangely slow, and it was a bewildered Michelle who plotted their midday position, unaware that by holding the mizzen sail too close to the yacht's centreline it acted like a brake, and when sailing a ketch to windward it was often better not to use the mizzen sail at all.

*　　　*　　　*

On leaving Cherbourg's Grande Rade Ian Vaughan decided to try and hedge his bets by steering a north-westerly course until he came close to losing sight of the few yachts making towards the Channel Islands. By doing this he felt he could also look out to the north and north-west maximising his search area. Now with a steady westerly Force 4 wind blowing, *La Mouette sur le Vent* was romping along at eight knots under full jib and mainsail heeled at fifteen degrees utilising her fullest waterline length. The carefully considered plan was frustrated by the Saltram's ability to sail closer to the wind than the bilge-keeled Macwester and two knots quicker through the water, which was about to save Murata from being identified, tracked and captured. The slow speed of the Macwester and its less efficient bilge keels meant that its windward performance was far worse than that of the long deep-keeled Saltram. In addition sailing against a tide meant that both yachts were sailing a more northerly course than their compasses indicated. Though this made little difference to Murata's plan of reaching the centre line of the English Channel before striking westward, it took Ian too far north, and almost out of sight of the yachts inshore, too quickly to bring the Macwester into view north-west of him. Now only able to see the mastheads of the inshore yachts Ian tacked the yacht back towards the shore.

Within minutes he picked up the twin masts of a ketch as it tacked away from him following a course close into the shore. During the next twenty minutes Ian used all the skill at his disposal to get the maximum speed from his yacht. Then, confident that he would see the hull colour through binoculars, he set the autohelm and with the glasses in hand made his way forward, leant against the forestay and peered through them at his quarry.

The heaving bows of his yacht made it difficult to hold the binoculars steady, and it was several seconds before he was able to establish that the hull was white, and the ensign Dutch. Disappointedly he returned to the cockpit and tried again to place himself in Murata's position. How would he have acted? What course would he have taken? Now his confidence in the yacht he sought having departed from Cherbourg's Grande Rade by the western entrance was beginning to fade. Had he missed seeing them go east, or with the tide starting to run against them, had they chosen to double back once outside of the western entrance?

After half an hour on the new course his mobile phone showed he was in signal distance again and he dialled Campbell's number.

"Commander Campbell's office," answered Mrs Fitzgerald.

"It's Ian Vaughan, Mrs Fitzgerald, is either the Commander or Chief Inspector Jackson about?"

"I'm afraid not, they are both in Portsmouth. Can I relay a message for you?"

"Yes please. Can you tell them that I have lost touch with the yacht, which may have been the one they are seeking. It is possible that it went either east of here or due north back to the Solent."

"I will pass that on immediately. Is there anything else?"

"Yes, can you tell them that I will continue my search further west, just in case, and unless I find anything, I will return to Kingsbridge in a couple of days."

"I will tell them Mr Vaughan, bon voyage."

A further two tacks brought the Saltram close to Omonville-la-Rougue, a small, quiet harbour not far from Cap de la Hague. Scrambling below to the chart table he pulled the almanac from the bookrack and studied the entrance details to the small bay and harbour. Careful to avoid going too close, and spoiling his next tack out into the Channel, Ian got close enough to confirm that the blue-hulled ketch had not put in there. Now the question was, would Murata risk going through the Alderney Race, and amongst the Channel Islands where his details were sure to be circulated, or would he decide to stay out at sea in the English Channel and head for Brest or some small port around the Brittany coast?

A long tack took the yacht well clear of the infamous tide race between the little island of Alderney and the French coast at Cap de la Hague. Ian held the course until he had almost reached the eastbound large vessel traffic lane, before turning again in the general direction of Guernsey. He decided that at the next tack he would carry straight on, heading for the English coast, and leave the search to the professionals. Hungry now, and with the sea all around him deserted, he hove the yacht to and went below to prepare a late lunch. The wind now no more than a Force 3 he took his time in preparing a small feast, which he ate leisurely under a cloud-veiled sun. By the time he had washed up and cleared the galley it was late afternoon, and after a session at the chart table working out a course to steer, he freed off the backed jib and setting both headsails and full main brought the yacht round onto a course of 340 degrees. For the next ten minutes he tweaked the sails until he achieved that balance of 'light weather helm' that allowed the yacht to reach its full potential in such a pleasant breeze.

He was well clear of the shipping lane as darkness fell and settled back feeling more relaxed now he was away from large vessels charging at high speed across his track. At midnight he adjusted his watch back to British Summer Time, checked his position and entered up the log, then relaxed back in the cockpit for another hour's watch keeping. In the early hours it is hard not to doze off when you are alone on deck. The trick Ian had learnt over the years was to give oneself a series of small tasks to perform during each hour, in order to keep the brain active. A check in the bilges for excessive water, sail trimming, a walk forward to check the anchor locking pin, or reefing line tail coils, all helped to pass the time and improve alertness. The 0100 position check he combined with a brew up and had just finished his mug of tea when suddenly out of the inky blackness of the cloudy night he saw the grey loom of sail some yards away off the starboard bow. Whatever it was, was not showing any navigation lights and it was therefore difficult to judge its distance away. Hurriedly unhitching the autohelm Ian hauled on the tiller, turning the yacht hard to starboard and in doing so narrowly avoiding a collision, as the two yachts rushed past each other, like two jousting knights. Reaching forward he went to grab the torch from its tray under the sprayhood to shine it at the other yacht, but the turn had put *La Mouette sur le Vent* in danger of gybing. Grabbing the mainsheet tail he jerked it from the jammer jaws, then let the sheet run out through his fingers allowing the mainsail boom to swing out over the starboard side whilst angrily shouting:

"Show some bloody navigation lights, idiot!"

Ian's struggle to avoid either a collision or a crash gybe meant his only view of the other vessel was a blur of sails and a white face staring back at him from the yacht's centre cockpit.

A moment later the yacht was gone into the inky blackness leaving Ian a little shaken and annoyed as he now hauled in the mainsheet and brought the Saltram back on course.

Taking the torch he pointed the beam over the port quarter in the hope of at least getting a reflection from the sails or sight of the yacht's wake, but the sea seemed to be empty again. Several minutes passed as he searched the waters around him without success, and reluctantly returning the torch to its tray, he sat back, trying to recall the angle of turn and relative speeds. The result of his thoughts were cold comfort indeed, had he not seen that faint image of the other yacht's sails, the impact would have been at speeds of around ten knots with a combined weight of maybe fourteen or fifteen tonnes. He considered for a few moments the horrific consequences of such a collision in the middle of the English Channel at night, then forced his mind to concentrate on sailing and watch keeping. On the hour he went below to bring the chart up to date, taking his current position from the GPS-linked Yeoman Plotter, and put the kettle on again for another, this time much needed, hot drink; back on deck he quickly searched the seas around him in time to see the lights of a large vessel approaching from the east. Going below again he took a close look at his AIS unit, which, according to the target read-out on the screen, showed that it was the Le Havre to Rosslare ferry travelling at twenty-one knots. The ferry would pass some distance astern of him, but he guessed it would be pretty close to the unlit yacht. On deck again and back in control of the helm he now split his attention between the compass, wind instruments, and the ferry. After a further ten minutes the ferry was well past a line astern of him when its bridge searchlight came on, vividly illuminating a yacht that appeared to be almost under the ferry's bows, accompanied by five loud blasts of her siren. The reaction aboard the yacht was predictable and Ian revelled in the sight of sails flogging uncontrolled as the person on the helm turned her desperately to port for fear of being run down.

Even after the ferry passed, its searchlight still illuminated the wallowing ketch, now tossed about by the large ship's wash that was threatening to swamp her. After a few minutes, during which time the ferry's watch keepers, Ian supposed, had satisfied themselves that the ketch was still safely afloat, the searchlight was extinguished and the ferry ploughed on towards Rosslare, but not before Ian heard a radio message, sent to the yacht, clearly pointing out its deficient lighting and poor watch keeping.

* * *

Aboard *Weighward Lass* the day had slowly improved with the calmer weather. Michelle was still unable to find the reason for their slow progress, but, as no one else seemed concerned, she set about following Murata's instructions and sailed the ketch to the centre of the English Channel then westerly until they could strike north for the coast just east of Salcombe. Apart from three yachts crossing their path some miles away they saw no other vessels during the hours of daylight, and were totally unaware of the coastguard and police helicopter search for them being conducted some fifty miles north-east of their course.

Around mid afternoon Murata came up into the cockpit with a chart of the South Devon coast and a piece of paper with co-ordinates written on it.

"Where is this?" he demanded, thrusting the chart and paper at Michelle.

She spread the chart out along the cockpit seat and crouched over it.

"I need the long ruler from the chart table," she said.

Murata rasped out an order and Hamaura cautiously went below to return minutes later with the rule.

Running her finger down the left side of the chart, her hand stopped at the 50 degrees north line; from behind her ear she retrieved the soft pencil she used for chart work and drew a faint line across the chart. Working along the scale at the top of the chart she stopped at 03 degrees 26 west and, repositioning the ruler, drew another faint line down the chart. Where the two lines crossed she pressed a little harder forming a darker pencil cross.

"There, that's it, just there. We meetin' someone then?" she enquired.

"Yes," Murata replied. "When do we get there?"

"I'll 'ave to work it out."

After ten minutes at the chart table she looked up. "I fink if we goes straight there an' this wind stays the same we should be there by ten o'clock tonight. But if we goes down the middle like, an' then turns up like that," she said indicating the comparative options on the chart, "we probably won't make it till say, two firty, maybe free in the mornin'."

A discussion followed between Murata and Dho for several minutes before Murata confirmed that they stick to the original plan, putting the ketch near the meeting point in the early hours of the following morning. Darkness had fallen and Michelle had just seen the yacht through a turn, bringing them back onto a starboard tack, then handed the helm over to Kimura, who with Murata would hold the course for the next hour. In the cabin below, Michelle struggled out of her sailing jacket and threw herself down on the port-hand settee and fell asleep almost instantly, exhausted by the events of the last two days. At some time during her sleep she was disturbed slightly by the jangle of a flapping mainsheet and sails, and a faint cry.

The next thing she knew was being shaken awake by Murata demanding to know whether to turn for the target co-ordinates.

"We must be close to meeting place, check chart."

Unsteadily she sat up and turned towards the chart table. It took her several minutes to collect her thoughts and set about plotting their position.

"We are maybe hour and a half away. If we change course now we should be able to make it," she told Murata, yawning and flexing her shoulders to try and ease their stiffness. "Tell Kimura-san to steer 345 degrees."

Without making any acknowledgement Murata climbed up into the cockpit and with Kimura on the helm tacked the boat.

Iwaki and Hamaura had retreated to the stern cabin some hours ago, tired but not feeling ill. Now with the yacht on the port tack Michelle eased herself down onto the starboard dinette seating and was just closing her eyes when a bright light illuminated the yacht's interior and a ship's siren was blasting loudly. Seconds later she was on deck shading her eyes from the searchlight's glare and screaming at Kimura.

"Turn to port!! Turn to port!! Quickly you prat!! Now!!! Now!!!"

Pushing a confused Kimura out of the way she spun the wheel and the yacht turned away from the path of the ferry as it thundered towards them. Its bow wash tossed the yacht up and almost onto its side floundering as Michelle grabbed Kimura's arm. "Undo the rope on that winch. HURRY!" she shouted, pointing to the foresail sheet around the starboard winch, then she reached for the engine start key and turned it. The engine slowly cranked into life and as it did so she opened the throttle to drive the yacht forward away from being drawn in by the large ship's eddying wash and smashed against her side.

"Now get that rope round that winch and pull it in tight!" Her voice, now almost a scream, was enough to get Kimura leaping into action again. The sight of the ferry's hull towering above them transfixed Dho and Murata, both seated at the rear of the cockpit.

By now they were almost halfway along the ferry and only just holding clear of the drag affect. To Michelle the seconds seemed like hours, her ears filled with the sounds of rushing water from the wake then the thunder of the ferry's engines before the ship finally swept clear of them leaving the yacht bouncing in the choppy wake. Almost immediately a stern warning was heard broadcast from the ferry concerning lack of navigation lights and poor watch keeping. Then the harsh light was extinguished and they found themselves stumbling around in the dark trying to untangle knotted running rigging.

"'Ow many times did I tells yer to keep looking behind yer!" Michelle screamed at them. "Yer fucking useless arseholes, we'd be dead if they adn't seen us!"

Kimura raised his hand to strike her, but she got in first drumming her fist onto his chest shouting, “You’re a bleedin’ idiot who don’t do wot ’e’s told! Leave the bloody steerin’ to me, you’re too bloody dangerous.”

Again Kimura raised his hand to strike her, but was stopped by Murata. “No Kimura-san, she is quite correct, we are very fortunate to have escaped without harm.”

Then patting Michelle on the back he said, “You are right, we failed you, but we must get to meeting place. Please help and then you can sail home.” Five minutes later Michelle was back in the cockpit with a course to steer, her hands still trembling as she grasped the wheel, nausea from the shock welling up inside her. Behind her Dho and Murata were back in serious discussion about the raid. After a few minutes Kimura reappeared in the hatchway by the wheel.

“Here, drink this,” he said handing her a small glass.

“What is it?”

“Brandy, it will make you feel better.”

Suspiciously she sniffed at it, and then drained the glass in one gulp. “Thanks.”

Chapter 12

The white van splashed down the muddy potholed Devon lane with Darren Cripps at the wheel peering into the near-horizontal rain looking for the gateway to Wahidi Naraiman's house. Idly he wondered how Michelle was managing with the boat, amazed that she had got it across the English Channel to Cherbourg. The road suddenly dipped down a steep incline towards an old stone bridge, beyond, which was a T-junction. He looked down at the scrap of paper on which he had scribbled directions and, after almost hitting the low bridge parapet, he hauled on the steering wheel to take the van to the right. Five hundred yards on the left the note said, though he felt it was nearer half a mile.

The gateway cut back into the bank had tall stone gateposts with black cast-iron gates and looked both repelling and impressive. Darren squinted to make out where the bell push was. Seeing a grey panel set into the high stone wall to the left of the entrance he leapt from the van and ran across to it. The panel comprised a speaker grill and call button; pushing the button he waited, hopping from one foot to the other, as if to dodge the raindrops. A minute passed and he pressed the button again, unaware that a CCTV camera was already studying him from a tree behind the gate.

"Who is it?" said a crackly disembodied voice from the grill.

"Darren Cripps. Open the bloody gates, I'm gettin' bleedin' drowned out 'ere."

"Who sent you?"

"Dho. Comrade Dho."

Almost immediately he heard a click from the centre of the gates and the whirr of an electric motor. Running back to the van he climbed into the cab and selected first gear, as the gates slowly opened towards him, only narrowly missing the van's front bumper. The driveway was maybe two hundred yards long and snaked up the hillside between established woodland. As it crested the rise Darren found himself driving across a wide clearing in the centre of which was an imposing modern, but traditional style, house. Hopping out of the van he was running towards the front doorsteps when a tall African called to him indicating he was to enter by the side door.

"Wipe your shoes," the man said, as he stopped Darren from walking beyond the doormat with a hand the size of a dinner plate thrust at Darren's chest.

"'Ave yer got a towel or sumin' I'm bleedin' soaked through 'angin' around at your soddin' gate."

"Stay there," the African ordered, and left what looked like the utility room of the house, with washing machines and tumble driers. One machine was slowly turning and Darren idly watched as the curious load tumbled round inside. As the machine's sequence ended Darren stared open-mouthed on seeing three fifty-pound banknotes stuck to the glass door of the unit.

Moments later the African returned with a towel and passed it to Darren, who busily dried his hair, face and arms. "I'm 'ere to see a Wa-hi-di Nar-ai-man," Darren said, saying the name very slowly as he read from the scrap of paper.

The man looked up at a camera suspended from the ceiling and nodded. On one side of the camera a green light came on. "This way."

The corridor led past the kitchen and dining room where they then turned left and down some steps to a large well-furnished lounge with enormous windows overlooking a lawn. Beyond, the land fell away towards more woodland, barely discernable in the failing light and heavy rain. To the right of the lounge a glass-panelled wall looked into a large indoor swimming pool. Darren stood open-mouthed looking about him.

"Stand up."

Darren looked in the direction of a sofa and watched as a young pretty blonde got to her feet, slowly wrapping a satin dressing gown around her naked body. Her dark, drug-dilated eyes looked uninterestedly at him as she stepped away from the sofa. Then a tall lean Middle Eastern man in his forties stood and turned to face Darren.

“You have a package for me?” the man asked, his voice sounding both inquiring and threatening at the same time.

Still looking at the girl Darren replied, “You able to do the meetin’?”

“I will stay there fishing for one hour only.”

Darren shrugged his shoulders and sniffed. “I’ll get the package,” then turning to the African asked, “You got a brolly, mate?”

Outside in the van, Darren lifted the floor mat on the passenger side, and removed a section of the floor, reaching down into the cavity below he lifted out the package. “You want to check it ’ere or in there?”

The tall African shouldered Darren out of the way and producing a flick knife, made a short slit in the wrapping. As he withdrew the knife a small amount of cocaine puffed out, and the man put some on his forefinger and raising it to his tongue licked it off.

“Dho says it’s best Columbian.”

“If it isn’t he will have to swim ashore,” came the deep-voiced reply. “The gates will open when you get there.”

After negotiating the narrow bridge Darren drove the van up the hill and along the lane to the main road, there he turned right then left along another narrow lane. At the fork coming in from the right he stopped just in time to avoid a boy racer hurtling along without lights in the gathering gloom. Swearing profusely, he put the van in gear again and turned in the same direction as the small car, expecting to see it in a ditch, or decorating the front of a farm tractor at every bend. At the top of a steep incline he turned right away from the Avon valley snaking up the hill then down into Kingsbridge. Skirting the harbour he took Embankment Road out to New Bridge, then the first turning left that ran along the edge of a village. Looking in the rear-view mirror he could see a car’s headlights behind him, so finding a wide field entrance he pulled off the road to allow it to pass. He waited for a few minutes to allow the other vehicle to get well in front before pulling away again to drive about a mile and a half up the lane, then he reversed into a field entrance on the left. Lights off he sat waiting as instructed, expecting another vehicle to appear with the men he was to take towards Plymouth. A slight movement to his right had him turning his head. The oriental face, close to the side window staring in at him caused him to jump with shock.

"Shit, what the fuck!" he shouted in fear, and then realising who the man was, opened the door and said, "Shit mate, what did you bloody creep up on me like that for? You want to give me a fuckin' heart attack!"

"Open door, please," the man said pointing towards the rear of the van.

Pulling the key from the ignition Darren walked to the back of the van where two other men were waiting; unlocking the rear doors he opened them and stood back as the three climbed in, weighed down with rucksacks.

"You take us these places," said the little man, who had frightened Darren with his sudden appearance, handing over a map.

"Right, yeah. 'Eer, you lot been campin'?" he asked.

"Sorry no understand."

"Oh. Don't worry mate, you could 'ave been stayin' at the bleedin' Hilton for all I care."

In the cab, on his own, Darren tuned the radio to a local pop station then pulled out of the field entrance and onto the lane back in the direction he had come from. In Kingsbridge he took the route out through West Alvington to where the road forks for Plymouth. At Modbury he turned right into Scalders Lane stopping some way along to let the team of saboteurs out. He had, for some reason, expected them to go towards a building or house but instead they leapt over a field gate and disappeared into the darkness. The rear doors opening and the rocking of the van indicated the return of the group. Starting the engine Darren waited until one of his passengers banged on the cab bulkhead before pulling away to drive back to the main road then he turned right, up the hill to Brownston Street, where again he waited alongside a field. The next stop was near the junction of Yealmton Hill and Bowden Lane in Yealmton before moving out to a lane just west of Pipers Cross. Here Darren's curiosity got the better of him and after waiting a short while he quietly opened the door and went to the field entrance through which the group had disappeared. There silhouetted by the luminance from Plymouth's street lighting was a mobile phone mast. Returning to the van the group found their driver leant against the vehicle's bonnet smoking a cigarette. The final stop was at Staddon Heights, where the group spent the best part of an hour before returning to instruct Darren to take them to a wood near to the West Lodge, Holton Junction, on the Kingsbridge road.

"Can't 'ang about anymore mate I gotta pick up Dho see."

"You leave us there, then go," replied the group's leader, frowning his annoyance at Daren's implied demotion of their importance.

This time the leader rode up front with Darren and after they turned right at the junction directed him to take the first turning left, then left again, at a small crossroads. Shortly the narrow lane passed through an area of dense woodland near the far side of which Darren was ordered to stop.

"You go now pick up Comrade Dho. Hurry or you be late!" said the man as he leapt from the passenger seat onto the grass verge.

"If I am it will be your bleedin' fault prat!" shouted Darren in reply as both the passenger and rear doors slammed shut in unison. Slamming the van in gear he pressed hard on the throttle as he let out the clutch and, wheels spinning, showered the group with mud and grit as they started to cut a path through the wood's ground cover. At the next junction Darren, guessing more than knowing, turned right into a narrow lane, where the hedge scratched at both sides of the van, to arrive at the village of Ford, where he turned right again back over the small crossroads to the main road. Fortunately at that time of night the Devon roads were deserted and Darren made it to Slapton Sands with a few minutes to spare.

Parking the van in the car park, halfway along the beach, facing out to sea he sat with eyes glued to his watch waiting for the exact moment when those out to sea would be looking for his signal. At precisely 3.30 a.m. he flashed the headlights three times, then sat and waited with growing anxiety. What if his watch was wrong? Was he in the right car park? As the minutes passed so his concerns grew exaggerated by his fear of Comrade Dho; he had seen what happened to those who failed in their duties. After ten minutes he got out of the van and walked down to the water's edge in time to hear the soft grounding of a small dinghy as it hit the beach some ten yards away to his right.

As he walked towards the sound Dho appeared from the darkness.

"You have completed your tasks?" Dho asked.

"Yeah, all done like you wanted."

"That is good. Get your things, you are going to sail back with Michelle, she needs help return boat to old man."

"Oh, right," replied Darren, vaguely relieved that his part in this dodgy business was over.

It was then that the wiry Japanese man called Iwaki joined them. "I'll get my gear then," said Darren, anxious to escape Iwaki's seemingly hostile stare.

A short, lean, but strong Middle Eastern man rowed Darren away from the beach and somehow located the black-hulled powerboat, at anchor, two hundred yards offshore. As he boarded the boat the man called Murata, and one of his men, took his place.

"You sorted fings out wiv Michelle mate?" Darren asked looking down at Murata.

Murata looked up at him and nodded. "Yes, she was pleased with final arrangement," he replied.

"Sit there while we get the rest ashore," said Wahidi Naraiman, indicating the leather seat next to the helmsman's. "You were on time, I like that."

"You don't be late for Dho, I'll tell yer," replied Darren, pleased by the small praise.

"Take my advice friend, and sail across the Channel and find some way to hide the name of the boat or sink it. The entire police force is looking for it."

"How do they know about this Murata bloke and the boat?" Darren asked.

"Apparently there was a shooting where they anchored overnight," replied Naraiman. "You do not listen to the news broadcasts on the radio?"

"No, too soddin' borin', I like me music."

"When you get on board search the whole of your boat, they may have finished with your services," advised Naraiman.

Darren turned pale. "Oh shit. Look 'ow about we pick up Mitch an' you drop us off near where you're goin'."

"You will leave your boat to drift?"

"It ain't our boat see, we just borrowed it."

Believing Darren to mean that he had stolen *Wieghward Lass* Naraiman decided to make a possible recruitment. "You cannot return to Southampton just yet. I will let you stay ford a few days until police stop looking. Maybe you will prefer to work for me, eh."

An hour later they came alongside the yacht and made fast whilst Darren jumped down onto the yacht's side deck.

"All right Mitch?" he asked.

The hard slap round his face caught him totally by surprise and had him sitting down hard on the cockpit bench. "What was that for? Did they give you some grief?"

"Grief? I'll bloody say they did. They only gone an' killed old Ken Fallon." Darren looked blankly at her. "You know, that bastard 'oo takes yer money in Newton Creek."

"You're fuckin' jokin'," replied Darren, now fully aware of their predicament. "Get your kit quickly, we gotta leave this boat, I don't care what you promised Arthur. Chances are 'e's dead anyways."

"No, I said we was gonna bring it back an' that's wot I'm gonna do."

"Wot an' spend twenty years in the nick? Don't be a stupid cow, get your kit an' let's get off this, now."

She glared at him for several seconds.

"Look, the chances are they bleedin' planted sumfin' that would blow us to bleedin' bits."

"Wot an' you bin gabbin' away, an' not telling me that, you shit."

Below, Michelle hastily gathered up her things and was aboard the powerboat in less than two minutes.

Darren was about to follow her when Naraiman stopped him, and handed him a hacksaw. "Look in the engine compartment. You will see a pipe for the engine cooling water. Cut through it, you will have time to get off." Turning to the large African he said, "Get the Dan Buoy and those horseshoe lifebelts and throw them below. When he comes back make sure the hatches are closed, we do not want any flotsam left."

*   *   *

At about the same time Murata stepped ashore on Slapton Sands, Ian was slipping into his sleeping bag with *La Mouette sur le Vent* secured in her marina berth. Sleep came almost immediately, a dreamless sleep born of exhaustion that was enjoyed through to midday when the crew on the yacht alongside awakened him with their laughter and chatter. After a shower and some lunch he contacted Campbell's office and spoke to Mrs Fitzgerald.

"Any news from Portsmouth?" he asked.

"Not that I am aware of, they are still searching for that yacht I spoke to you about," she replied. "You had no sighting I presume."

"I chased around after some lost causes off the French coast, then was forced to accept that if the yacht I saw in Cherbourg was theirs, then it had sailed straight back to England and not along the French coast as I had gambled on."

"It seems strange that we haven't found it. The search has been truly massive in the central Channel area. Anywhere from Lyme Bay to Eastbourne has been covered by helicopter and police and custom's launches. Every harbour and marina has been thoroughly searched," commented Mrs Fitzgerald.

"Maybe they went east into the Seine Bay to Ouistreham or Deauville. They could have even gone to Le Havre, that's a big enough place to get lost in."

"The French authorities have been very co-operative and we are quite sure that the yacht didn't put into any of those ports. The Channel Islands have not reported any sightings either."

"I am beginning to think that they sunk it like they did with that charter boat they hired, when Murata started his little games over here."

"That is what Chief Inspector Jackson believes. The Commander on the other hand thinks that Murata and his men have been dropped off and the two who borrowed the yacht told to sail it to some location where it will act as a decoy," she replied, with her emphasis placed upon the Commander's theory.

"A thought has just occurred to me," said Ian. "Last night I had a very close encounter with a yacht sailing without navigation lights. To be honest I was far too tied up with avoiding a collision to get a good look at the other craft. I didn't associate it with Murata as it was on a course south-west and way to far west too be dropping people off at Portsmouth, but now I come to think about it the yacht must have tacked because the Le Havre to Rosslare ferry almost ran it down; they may well have seen enough of it to identify it."

"You think the couple would have sailed that far west to divert us away from Murata's location?"

"I don't know, but it might be worth making enquiries of the watch keepers on board the ferry."

"I will get the Commander's special team to follow that up. On another subject, I had a call from your wife asking if I knew where you were. It appears that her solicitor wrote to you over a week ago with a settlement proposal for the divorce. She wants to receive your response as a matter of urgency as Mr and Mrs Johnston-Lacey have offered to sell her the cottage she is staying in. I got the impression that she is very anxious to proceed with the purchase."

"Did you tell her where I was?"

"No, I just said that you had taken a few days off to go sailing."

"Thanks, apparently Mrs Johnston-Lacey has been down here looking for me. I suppose Rebecca has got some scheme that necessitates the urgent disposal of the cottage and she wanted my agreement," said Ian. "I suppose I better get back to the bedsit and see what this is all about."

Ian had got almost to his van before he remembered that he was unarmed. He stood for several seconds debating whether or not to return to the boat and collect the pistol before finally deciding that it would be best not to be without it. On board he found the gun and checked to see that the magazine was full and the safety catch was on before changing into the trousers with the pocket holster.

Miranda Cox was out in the front garden when Ian arrived.

"Hi, welcome back Mr Popular with the Ladies," she said with a wry grin.

"Huh, do you mean Mrs Johnston-Lacey?"

"Yes, very Gucci, and most upset that you were not at home. In fact, on all three occasions her expensively perfumed form graced this very humble abode, she gave me the distinct impression that it was my fault you were away enjoying yourself."

"My wife's friend has a very high opinion of herself I'm afraid. Personally I can't stand the woman, or her husband."

"Well, I get the impression that she fancies you a great deal. Her type doesn't dress that provocatively unless they are out to seduce," she said teasingly.

"It's not my body she wants, it's my signature on a divorce settlement that would enable my wife to purchase their Derbyshire cottage."

"Maybe that as well," Miranda replied, grinning broadly. "I promised to phone the hotel the moment you returned."

"Please don't," said Ian, his face a picture of fear and concern. "The last thing I want is any contact with the woman who has been brainwashing my wife into filing for divorce."

Miranda looked interested.

"I'm not going to go into the details with you. It's too complicated, but suffice to say that the lady is trouble with a capital 'T' and I am just going to rush in, get the post and get back to the boat as fast as I can."

"I'll give you half an hour's head start."

"Oh come on, please."

"Alright, one hour."

Ian glared at her. "Thanks a bunch, friend."

"It's alright, your secret return is safe with me."

Within ten minutes Ian was back in his van and driving back to Dartmouth and the ferry to Kingswear. On board his yacht he sat himself at the chart table and started to go through the assorted mail from the bank until he came to the letter from Sarah's solicitor. The covering letter referred to Sarah's wishes regarding purchase of the Derbyshire cottage and the urgency in sorting out the overall settlement to achieve this aim and provide the children with a more settled life. The detailed proposal was really quite simple with regard to the distribution of the remaining cash from the sale of their property and division of the remaining savings. Basically she and the girls got three quarters of any monies plus a demand for a generous maintenance settlement, with the proposal that this should be a one-off payment from his reward. Then came a passage regarding access to the girls; here was the bit he had been trying to put out of his mind, this was the stumbling block to the whole thing. He didn't care too much about the financial settlement, it would still leave him enough to live on for a few years, but the severe limitation of access to his daughters he could not accept.

Reading the letter and proposal again made him feel extremely angry, sufficiently so for him to write back immediately stating quite simply that he would not accept either the division of wealth or size of the maintenance settlement and under no circumstances would he accept such limitation of access to his daughters.

Posting the letter 'Recorded Delivery' at the post office in The Square he sensed an impending war and feared what it would do to his lovely daughters. If only he had not agreed to stay away until Murata and his gang were caught and locked up. Replies to the letters he sent to them were now few and far between, and he had the sense that he was losing them forever. It was with these depressing thoughts that he left the post office and started to make his way back to the boat, walking away from the ferry landing and past the station. He crossed the road twice as a way of checking whether he was being followed, and felt reassured enough to take the left fork down to the marina car park entrance. He had just crossed the railway track at the level crossing and was strolling across to the pontoon access building when his mobile phone rang.

"Hello."

"Campbell here, Mr Vaughan. I've just been speaking with my secretary regarding your recent sailing experience."

"Did you get any more information from the ferry?"

"Not yet. What I would like, is for you to come to London as soon as you can and take us through your voyage using the appropriate charts."

"You're in luck," replied Ian. "I was so late last night and have had divorce issues distracting me today so haven't had time to rub out the plot on my own charts."

"Marvellous, how quickly can you get underway?"

"In about half an hour I should think, I'll get the first train I can. Where do you want me to meet you?"

"Give me a call when you are approaching Paddington Station and I will have someone meet you. We are running this from one of our sub offices, which maybe tricky to find." What Campbell meant was that he was not prepared to give out the address whilst on an unsecured line, particularly a mobile.

At Paddington Station Ian suddenly felt out of place as he strode down the platform, surrounded by smartly suited men and elegantly attired ladies, with himself dressed in an open-neck denim shirt, pale cream trousers, deck shoes and carrying a white canvas kit holdall and a plastic tube containing the charts.

"Mr Vaughan?"

The grey-uniformed chauffeur was tall and at first glance gave the image of genteel respectfulness. A second, more focused glance revealed to Ian a more muscular torso and the cool hard eyes of a man trained for more serious action than just driving a car.

"Who sent you?" Ian asked.

"Commander Campbell, sir. I have been asked to take you to your hotel in Chelsea."

"Where is your car?"

"Just over there, sir," answered the chauffeur, now with an expression of mild amusement hovering around his eyes. "The Commander said you would be cautious. Shall I take your bag, sir?"

"Yes, thank you," replied Ian, suddenly keen not to be encumbered with the bag. Putting his hand in his pocket he gripped the pistol butt and felt strangely reassured.

At the apartment block behind DELCO Publishing, Ian followed the chauffeur up the steps and into the reception lobby.

"The Commander's visitor, Mr Vaughan," he announced to the receptionist.

"Oh, come this way sir," she said, giving Ian a warm smile.

Ian thanked the chauffeur and picked up his bag and followed her through a badge-activated door then along a short corridor to enter a room fitted with an array of equipment similar to that he had seen at his training establishment.

"I am now going to check that you are who you say you are," the receptionist said, placing Ian in front of a retina scanner.

When the checks were completed, Ian was shown to a comfortable bedroom with its own shower room and toilet. The tough-looking waiter who had shown him up from reception put a menu in front of him.

"Not a great choice I'm afraid Mr Vaughan, but the quality's good."

"I'll have the steak and new potatoes if I may," Ian replied, before asking, "When do I meet the Commander?"

"Commander Campbell has asked me to tell you that Lieutenant Heathcote will call for you at 0830 hours."

"Okay, thanks."

At precisely 0830 the following morning the street door to reception opened and an attractive redhead entered and walked straight up to Ian. "I'm Lieutenant Heathcote, Commander Campbell has asked me to escort you round the corner to our offices. He will join us a little later," she said, presenting her identity badge.

"How do you do Lieutenant," replied Ian, taking in the smart raincoat over a silver-grey dress and immaculate medium-heeled black shoes.

The walk to DELCO was short and conversation limited to the weather and pleasantries about his journey up from the West Country. Commander Campbell arrived an hour later to find Ian in the meeting room looking over his charts with a cup of tea in his hand.

"Ah, you are being looked after I see," Campbell said, striding across the room to shake Ian's hand.

"Thank you, yes, your staff have been very kind."

"You've met Lieutenant Commander Morohashi, I understand," said Campbell turning to usher Umeko towards Ian, "and you know Lieutenant Heathcote; she is our intelligence analyst assigned to this operation."

Ian gave a small bow to Umeko. *"Konichi-wa."*

She smiled, and returning a slightly deeper bow replied, *"Konichi-wa Vaughan-san."*

"I have just briefed my team at the Yard and must now outline the situation to all of you," announced Campbell. "This morning I had the Prime Minister on the phone again and the Foreign Secretary, both emphasising the pressure the American government is putting them under to find and arrest Murata and his gang. Inevitably the actual work is ours to carry out and we must leave no stone unturned in our search for them. It is with that in mind that I have asked you, Mr Vaughan, to join us."

Campbell turned and, indicating a seat to Ian, said, "What I would like is for you to take us through your recent voyage to France and back, with particular emphasis from the point at which you arrived in Cherbourg."

Ian took them through his voyage, explaining his arrival at Cherbourg and his passing a ketch, which could have been *Weighward Lass*, and the distraction caused by the lost fenders.

"Leaving the western entrance I tried to cover as many options as I could by steering this course," he said, standing and pointing to a line on the chart. "When I could hardly see the mastheads of the yachts inshore I tacked, here. Then seeing a ketch-rigged yacht sailing closer inshore I went in closer to investigate, along this track. It wasn't the one. I then realised that I really had too many options to cover and as I was within mobile phone range, I called your office Commander, and left a message with Mrs Fitzgerald." Campbell nodded an acknowledgement. "Having eliminated that vessel I changed course again and took a look at Omonville-la-Rogue harbour, just in case they had put in there, as it's a quiet place, then, I sailed on down here," he ended pointing to the mark on the chart where he had stopped for a late lunch.

"Excuse me," said Lieutenant Heathcote, producing a set of dividers and measuring a distance off the chart's side scale. "You were about five miles offshore when you made your first tack and with a maximum of four miles horizon it might have been possible that they sailed really close inshore just below your horizon, but I think that is unlikely." She stood back a moment, in thought. "What is more likely is that the yacht you passed in the harbour was just over your horizon to the north of you."

"What makes you suggest that Lieutenant?" asked Campbell.

"Well, sir, they had just fuelled up, which would indicate that they were planning a long voyage. My guess is that they either sailed back to somewhere like Chichester Harbour or even Brighton and our search missed them or they headed for Portland and Weymouth or even Lyme Regis and after landing had the yacht taken back out to sea again and scuttled."

"We did include Lyme Bay in our search area Lieutenant."

"Yes, sir, but after dark we only had surface craft available due to an incident concerning a fishing boat."

Just then the door opened and Lorna peered in. "Excuse me Commander, Penny, I have the ferry company on the phone for you, they've got hold of the watch keeper you wanted to speak to."

Penny Heathcote left the room, leaving the three of them looking at the charts, deep in thought.

"Why do you have two positions marked here?" asked Morohashi.

"I had hove to whilst I got some lunch, that gap is the yacht's drift whilst I was eating," Ian replied.

"Um," she smiled at him, "A long lunch I see."

"At what position did you have this near miss with the unlit yacht?" asked Campbell, aware that there was something more in Morohashi's smile and comment than mild humour.

"About here, sir," replied Ian pulling his gaze from Morohashi back to the chart. " I would think around 50 degrees north 3 degrees 20 west."

"That is a good way south and west of our search area, sir," said Morohashi.

"Yes. It is more likely that Lieutenant Heathcote's assessment was correct and they went north from Cherbourg, and we have either missed them, or they sank the boat to avoid it being found."

"That would tie in with Tokyo's information about a target in the Portsmouth area."

"Are you sure they meant Portsmouth and not Plymouth?" asked Ian.

Campbell and Morohashi both looked at him wide-eyed.

"Get Lorna to get you connected to Tokyo on the secure line and check that out please," Campbell said to Morohashi. "We may have made a very big assumption."

As she left the room Ian said, "I hope my comment hasn't sent you off on a wild goose chase."

"Everything tells us that wherever the attack will be, it will come in the next couple of days. We need to take every step necessary to ensure we are guarding the right target."

The door opened again and an anxious Lieutenant Heathcote rushed in. "From the sound of it the yacht that was nearly run down by the ferry could well have been the one we are searching for. Their watch keeper could not see the whole name but the second part was either lass or lassie, he didn't make a note of it. His description also makes it seem highly likely; he confirmed it had a dark blue hull and the old-style aluminium folding radar reflector that, unsurprisingly, didn't show up on their radar screen. Apparently there were four people panicking around in the cockpit one of whom he felt sure was a woman."

"Anything else?" asked Campbell.

"The mainsail had what could have been a Seaforth logo on it and below it the number twenty-three. I understand from the owner's son that it was the last one built and that ties in with the number."

"That sounds very much like it," said Ian. "It may be profitable to check Dartmouth, Salcombe and the marinas in Plymouth." He looked up to see Campbell with an odd expression of enquiry and amusement on his face. "Oh, sorry, I was getting carried away there, for the moment."

"It's easy to get caught up in the excitement here, Mr Vaughan," said Campbell, then, turning to Heathcote he said, "Maybe not the diversionary tactic I thought. Yelmstoke Head, do you think?"

"It could be, sir, but it could also be the *USS Omaha*, she is in Plymouth on a courtesy visit."

"I don't know her," replied Campbell.

"She is the last build of the Ticonderoga Class, sir, a cruiser, very powerful, has been lead ship in the Indian Ocean piracy operation for the last three months."

"I thought Tokyo were pretty certain that the target was the computer boffins."

"When we caught up with them in Southampton, Murata may have decided to switch targets, sir. It would match the profile of some of the Red Brigade's earlier attacks, when intelligence indicated targets other than those actually hit."

"Um. I am not so sure that it can happen as quickly as that," said Campbell. "They will have done surveillance and got transport and weapons in place for the Portsmouth plan. He would be reluctant to discard such an investment. Look at the way he went ahead with the Kinoko Kumo attack after their yacht was damaged." Lieutenant Heathcote frowned and was about to argue the case when Campbell said, "Mr Vaughan, you reported to Mrs Fitzgerald that the yacht you almost collided with must have tacked in order to come close to the ferry. What course would that have put them on?"

"Approximately north-west sir," Ian replied unaware that he was now using the subordinate 'sir'.

"Could you indicate it on the chart for us?"

Ian plotted where he thought he had taken avoiding action and then, basing his assessment on time and approximate course, drew a circle on the chart. "Somewhere in that area I would think."

Lieutenant Heathcote leant over the chart and started plotting another course. "This is the course of the ferry, sir, taken from their log. The positions are GPS so they should be accurate." The line just touched Ian's circle. "Can you point out roughly where your yacht was at the time of the incident with the ferry?"

Ian studied his logbook, then his chart. Opening the dividers again and measuring off the side of the chart he stepped off a distance and marked it. "There, that's where I was when the incident with the ferry happened."

The Lieutenant drew a line from Ian's mark to the point where his circle touched the ferry course line. "Was that roughly the angle from which you observed the incident?"

"Not as far round as that, more there," Ian replied, drawing another line.

"Okay, so that would indicate their course as being more northerly. You presumably looked out for them when you arrived in Dartmouth?"

"Well not specifically, but as I was tidying things up on deck and hosing off the salt, no other boat came in."

"Maybe they went into Salcombe, sir. That would be a good place to start a search I would think," Heathcote said.

"Why go into a harbour? They could have dropped off Murata, if it is his little army on board, at several points along that coast," said Ian.

"Good point, they probably know by now that we are looking for them, and would avoid harbours," she acknowledged.

"It would also explain why they were sailing without navigation lights at night," added Ian.

"Yes, sir, I now understand. We do need him on the team."

Ian looked up and glanced from one to the other. "Who do you need?" Ian asked puzzled by the subject change.

"I'll be talking to him later, Lieutenant, on that matter," said Campbell hastily avoiding answering Ian's question. "I want to get enquiries underway from Plymouth round to Torquay, just in case they haven't tumbled to us. It is possible that the target is still Portsmouth, but they had to go that far west to get clear of our search area. Helicopters quartering the seas are pretty obvious."

"If that is the case, sir, then the computer personnel will be out of the way the day after tomorrow. They are having a day off at Bletchley Park and being given a tour of the wartime huts and shown the 'enigma machine' then it's onto GCHQ."

"When are we moving them up there?" asked Campbell.

"First thing Wednesday morning, sir. All the teams involved will be there, it's also a type of wash-up meeting."

"I want that moved forward to tomorrow evening, for both the teams at Yelmstoke Head and Portsmouth, get Lorna to help sort the accommodation. Ah, here is the Lieutenant Commander."

Morohashi had entered the room and was looking a little nervous. "I am sorry to report that Tokyo cannot give a definite answer to our question. The information came from an agent inside North Korea. They will be unable to make contact due to the dangerous situation of the agent. Chief Superintendent Ishii says that earliest contact would not be before tomorrow evening."

"Damn," said Campbell. "This means that we will have to cover all of the bases and arrange protection for the Cheltenham visit. Our resources are stretched already, and the army has told us that with their overseas commitments they cannot provide any more troops on an immediate basis."

"Exactly how many are we up against?" asked Ian. "There are the four on the boat seen from the ferry. Would they have any other support here in the UK?"

"The dog handler at Alton said he saw four men running away from the warehouse, and maybe there were one or two in the van used to make their escape," informed Lieutenant Heathcote.

"My fear," said Campbell, "is that there is a cell of North Korean agents here, who we have failed to pick up on our radar. We know that there are several North Koreans who have come here to escape the regime, but how many are truly genuine is anyone's guess."

"Was there something specific that both of those sites were working on?" asked Ian.

"Yes," replied Campbell, "Some time ago we broke the North Korean missile project coded message pattern; both teams have been tracking messages and interpreting them independently then comparing results. They are now sufficiently consistent for us to be able to design our own computer-based translation programme. This would not only allow us to send false messages but actually corrupt their computer-based decoding programme."

Ian whistled. "I assume that the work is not yet completed."

"Correct, Mr Vaughan. There is still a great deal to be done by both teams that requires their specific understanding of the language, allied with a complete understanding of the North Korean military command structure."

"Are we totally reliant upon these teams for this work?" Ian asked.

"Neither we nor the Americans can muster sufficient experts to complete the work in time. Our intelligence suggests that independent missile launch programmes will be completed by the North Koreans and downloaded at each missile site in about two weeks from now. Once that is done we would not be able to corrupt their software."

"I am beginning to wish that I had rammed and sunk that yacht yesterday morning."

"I think that would have only solved one problem, Mr Vaughan," replied Campbell. "Lieutenant Commander, can you contact your team leaders immediately and tell them that they are to be ready to move to Cheltenham by 1600 hours tomorrow. Lieutenant Heathcote can you get Lorna to rearrange the coaches for them, if you would."

After another hour, during which Campbell and the team contacted local police forces in Devon and requested they check on marinas and moorings, the meeting broke up.

As Campbell walked back down the corridor towards reception with Ian at the end of the day, he asked, "Are you available to have some dinner with me this evening?"

Ian was a little taken aback. "Oh, yes, er, thank you, that would be great."

It did not surprise Ian to find that the venue for dinner was Campbell's club. The doorman directed Ian to the cloakroom where he was issued with a blazer and tie.

"I regret, sir, that you will be required to dine in the bar. A dark lounge suit is the minimum requirement for the members' dining room in the evening."

Ian smiled. "Of course."

Campbell arrived five minutes later looking somewhat harassed. "I'm sorry to keep you waiting. Shall we go through to the bar? I have arranged a private room for our meal as I don't want people to overhear our conversation."

Ian raised his eyebrows. "Sounds very cloak and dagger."

"I suppose it is in a way. What would you like to drink?"

The excellent dinner and pleasant conversation somewhat lulled Ian into believing that the evening was really just a social nicety, so he was unprepared for Campbell's question, delivered as soon as the waiter had brought in the coffee and liqueurs.

"How would you like to come and work for me in SIS?" Campbell asked, whilst looking carefully at Ian's facial reaction.

Years of delicate contract negotiations had taught Ian the art of deadpan response, but even then he only just held onto a mild smile, and took care in putting his glass onto the table beside his armchair before looking directly at the Commander.

"I would not have thought that my background qualifies me for SIS/MI6 work. I'm not a great academic, university yes, but my foreign language skills are poor," he replied.

"We employ people from a wide range of backgrounds, but all of our operational officers have those skills that you have in spades. They are all loyal, resourceful, and have skills other than purely intelligence gathering and data analysis," said Campbell, pleased that Ian had not rejected the invitation out of hand. "Despite what you say we know you to be intelligent enough for the tasks we would give you. We also have a good idea of how you respond in a critical situation. You took on most dangerous adversaries, when you were hijacked, and did not appear to flinch. Not just that, but you followed through, even after you had escaped, with what the FBI consider to have been brilliant evaluation and advice."

"Very flattering, Commander, but frankly I have no desire to find myself looking down the wrong end of gun barrels again. Also I have a wife and two daughters to consider."

"Very, very rarely operational officers find themselves in such danger. The circumstances leading to your exposure to gunfire were almost unique," said Campbell. "Regarding your personal situation, am I to understand that you and your wife have reconciled your differences?"

"Well no, but I am hoping that in time she will come round and we can patch things up."

Campbell looked thoughtfully at the glass of single malt whisky in his hand. “I’ll tell you what. How about you joining our training programme? It lasts for up to nine months, and at the end of it, we will know for sure if you are suitable, and you will know whether you still have a marriage to consider. How about it?”

Ian got to his feet, walked across to the window, and looked down onto the busy street below. A whole range of thoughts rushed through his mind. What else did he have to do for the next few months? He couldn’t spend all his time sailing; he would need to find something more constructive to do. Was it likely that Sarah would change her mind? She seemed very definite about the divorce. If the divorce went through with the recently proposed settlement, he would need a job. What about his ambitions to find and run his own business? Probably couldn’t do it without Sarah anyway, her support would have been essential in the hard years of start-up. An image entered his mind of Fumiko Hamaura spitting the hatred of extremism, mindless of the cost in human lives.

Turning away from the window he walked back to his chair and slowly sat down. “Okay, I’ll give it a try. No, I’ll do my best and hope to come up to standard.”

“Excellent! First thing in the morning I want you to return to Devon with Morohashi and settle your affairs there. She is to brief the Japanese team down there and get them safely away to Cheltenham. Then I would like you to return to our DELCO offices while we check what level of security you can be given initially.”

“It will take me a couple of days, the boat will have to come out of the water as I doubt if I will be able to get back to it if I’m doing this training.”

“Report to the DELCO building next Monday then. We’ll take it from there,” said Campbell, reaching across to shake Ian’s hand. “Welcome aboard.”

As Campbell stood at the window watching Ian hail a taxi to take him back to the apartment behind DELCO’s offices, a distinguished grey haired man entered the room.

“Is he joining up Alec?”

“Yes, Sir Andrew. I think we can safely say that we have the Funchal observation covered.”

Chapter 13

Rain had started to fall again as Murata and Dho reached the van and climbed in. Dho, in the driver's seat, started the engine and reversed the vehicle round to face the car park exit. "We are going place called Kingsbridge where I show you plan to get mail van," said Dho, before crunching the gearbox into first and pulling away.

"Mail van? What purpose is mail van?"

"Each day there are mail van deliveries at place they call Yelmstoke Head, where your country's computer hackers are being trained so that they can destroy our legitimate defence weaponry."

"I see; you think we capture mail van and use it to get into this Yelmstoke Head."

"That is correct, Murata-san," replied Dho. "Van is big, easy get eight men inside."

Murata nodded thoughtfully. He had not taken an active part in any of his faction's attacks for several years and now the prospect of close combat drew close he realised that he no longer relished it, especially in an unprotected van.

"Is there somewhere for us to rest?" asked Murata. "My men not enjoy voyage, as you know."

"It is all arranged. House empty today. Owner on holiday."

It was getting light as they squeezed through the hole in the fence and crossed the garden to a slate-hung house that stood alone on the hill overlooking the town. Dho produced a key from his pocket and, opening the back door, stepped cautiously into the kitchen, and removing his boots stood listening intently. Satisfied that the owners had not returned unexpectedly, he then signalled to the others to follow. Closing the back door and locking it, Dho crossed the kitchen and opened the door to the cellar, reached inside and turned on the light.

"We sleep down there, too much risk we are seen if we use rest of house."

Murata started down the cellar steps and was pleasantly surprised when he got to the bottom and looked around him.

"Hamaura-kun come here, you will like this."

The cellar walls had been plastered and decorated, in one corner was a dartboard, in another a television with a stack of DVDs alongside it, but the crowning feature was a full-size snooker table.

Hamaura's eyes widened when he saw the table and spied the cues on a rack on the opposite wall. "Ah fantastic," he said, making towards the rack. "You remember Nagano-san's house in Osaka."

Murata nodded his head and smiled. "Iwaki-san you did not know young Nagano. He lived in house with mother and younger sister. Whole living space like this, to sleep they put futon on floor under table."

"Ah so. Is it his sister who is still in prison in London?" asked Iwaki, with a subtle hint of sarcasm.

Murata's face darkened with anger. He had no wish to be reminded of that fact by Iwaki. "I think of her every day wasting her life there. Unless they move her we have no chance to set her free, security very high level."

Tension between the two men had been building since the escape from Alton. No argument had taken place or comment made, it was just their body language that showed the growing hostility.

A clicking of snooker balls broke the cool silence that had descended on the room, as Hamaura made his opening shot, unaware of the friction Iwaki's question had produced.

"Hamaura-san we play later, now rest," Murata ordered. Reluctantly Hamaura replaced the cue and bent to open his rucksack.

"Iwaki-san here is key, I must check on men dealing with communications. Please lock door after me, I will return at 1400 hours with food, be ready at door," said Dho, handing Iwaki the key to the back door of the house.

The two men climbed the stairs leaving the others to make their sleeping arrangements. In truth, all of them were exhausted, Hamaura and Iwaki from almost constant seasickness throughout the voyage, whilst Murata, Kimura and Dho were suffering from pure lack of sleep. At no time, whilst they were sailing, had any of them had more than one hour's rest at a time.

Iwaki followed Dho out through the fence to the van parked in the back lane.

"Be careful Iwaki-san. Murata-san still has loyalty of those two young bloods. Hamaura is brave but stupid, Kimura is cunning and very dangerous."

"I know well those two young bloods as you call them Comrade, be assured, I will not endanger this operation, but I find it difficult to work under anyone who has no real direction of purpose. Neither Murata nor that cowardly Yamamoto has any true motivation, both are only interested in their own petty status. They act just like Yakusa shateigashira, only fit to run small town pachinko parlours and prostitutes."

"General Namgoong and General Sakoung believe Murata-san's plan and attack in United States was brilliant," responded Dho, "and damage to America's electric supply system amazing achievement for such small team. President Huckle shouting that death of Hamaura's sister and Madadhah great victory against terrorism is only typical Western propaganda. We know that attack has had great effect on American peoples, they now fear Murata-san as much as they did bin Laden."

"We have been in hiding since release of those two from prison and have had little chance to hear news," replied Iwaki, surprised by Dho's statement and praise of Murata.

"It was over a week before the Americans admitted to the full extent of the damage done. Their Mission Creek power station will never operate again, costing them many millions of dollars," informed Dho. "In Japan there are reports that many young radical thinkers are seeking to join Murata's cause. Since his escape he is being seen as the new leader in the fight to remove the corrupt monarchy and capitalist regime."

Inwardly Iwaki's heart sank a little with the recognition that for now he must content himself with being still just a lieutenant in the movement and not its commander. The 'Kinoko Kumo' operation had obviously been far more successful than either Higashi or Ishihara had understood and reported.

"Comrade please can you obtain newspaper, we need such information."

"Of course, I thought you already knew of his great achievement, I will bring all I can. I must leave now it is important we are not seen here," replied Dho opening the driver's door of the van and leaping in.

Iwaki stood for a time in the kitchen considering what he had just been told, then in his normal shadowy way went down into the cellar.

"Murata-san."

Murata, standing brushing some dirt from the back of his jacket, jumped. His was still not used to or comfortable with the way Iwaki appeared to just materialise.

"Iwaki-san, you surprised me."

"Comrade Dho is bringing newspapers with him when he returns telling the world of the great success of the Kinoko Kumo attack."

"I heard reports from Ishihara-san, whilst in prison, but was not allowed access to newspapers. A chance to read the reaction will be rewarding my friend," said Murata, surprised by Iwaki's use of the words 'great success'.

Shortly after 2 p.m. Dho woke them holding two large plastic bags full of takeaway Chinese food. In near silence the group settled down to eat. Dho had guessed correctly that during the period at sea none of them had eaten sufficient. As the last grains of rice disappeared from the aluminium packs conversation started up.

"Dho-san, I understand from Iwaki-san that you have newspaper telling of reaction to Kinoko Kumo," said Murata.

"Yes, here," replied Dho, handing over several newspaper cuttings. "Ishihara-san gave the early ones to me during time you were in prison. When you were freed I got Comrade Byoun to collect newspapers. His English good."

The rest of the afternoon was spent in careful reading and discussion about the newspaper articles. It was in the early evening that Dho again set off in search of food, to return an hour later with more takeaway. Only after the evening meal did the atmosphere relax sufficiently for the snooker table to provide the centre of attraction.

The rattle of the back-door handle had Iwaki moving swiftly, but silently, up the cellar steps to peer carefully round the kitchen door, which stood slightly ajar. Iwaki froze momentarily at the sight of a young policeman standing on the back step, squinting as he looked through the glass into the kitchen. A squawking from the policeman's radio caused the officer to step back and raise the radio to his mouth.

"What was that Sarge?"

The radio squawked again.

"I'm up at the outlaw's house, so I'm not far away." Another squawk could be heard. "What was that?" the question was repeated. "Oh I'm just checking the doors whilst Ann's parents are away."

With that he started to walk round the side of the house and was soon out of view. Iwaki slipped into the kitchen and stealthily through the house to the lounge at the front, which had the curtains drawn closed. Very slowly he eased a corner of the curtain to one side just enough to watch as the policeman got into his car and drove away.

"Kimura-san we must clean mud off kitchen floor and hide boots." Iwaki had heard Kimura creep along the hallway and had not even found it necessary to turn and look at the young man, knowing by the faint sounds of the approach who it was.

"Straight away?" asked Kimura.

"No. Please ask Murata-san and Comrade Dho to come here," Iwaki requested, as he stood staring at a china display cabinet in the corner of the room, deep in thought. "We clean up kitchen later."

Murata and Dho arrived curious as to why they had been summoned.

"Kimura-san told you of police visit?" Iwaki asked.

"*Hi*, he said police checking house secure," replied Murata.

"That is so. He just checked door, but I think house belong to friend or relative, so he will return maybe tomorrow to check again."

“Maybe,” said Dho, looking puzzled. “If door is locked and we stay hidden in cellar he will go away again, but I agree, we must be very careful to avoid being discovered.”

“Of course,” replied Iwaki. “If he found door broken and that china and other things stolen?”

Dho frowned, not understanding, but Murata nodded and smiled in agreement.

“Yes, yes, very good, that would have police out here away from town centre. Very few police in small town like this. Such a robbery would take many away from normal duty. Yes Iwaki-san, very good.”

“Now we must clean mud from floor and hide boots,” said Iwaki leading the way back into the kitchen. “If we leave early morning on day of attack and wait outside town until right time, maybe we could find good place to watch them running about, it would be good entertainment.”

In the cellar Dho opened Ordnance Survey map OL20 out on the snooker table as the rest gathered round. “We are here,” he said jabbing his finger at a point just west of Kingsbridge Quay. “Every morning Royal Mail van leave depot here and take route to Plymouth this way. He stop at Aveton Gifford and Modbury before he call at MoD/ DCF Yelmstoke Head.”

“We take van at this place?” asked Hamaura, pointing to Modbury.

“No, there too many people in street at Aveton Gifford and Modbury and too much traffic to make clean getaway,” answered Dho. “We think best place here in Kingsbridge when van leave depot.”

Murata leaned forward and studied the map more closely. “We must see this place today. What time van leave?”

“Every weekday at exactly 1100 hours. They seem very good discipline .”

Murata looked at his watch. “In two hour time. Can we find place to watch?”

“Maybe we have to park outside depot, but better we park up street a little.”

Dho left at quarter past ten to collect the van from where he had hidden it, returning twenty minutes later. The others ran, crouching, down the rear garden path and, under snarled commands form Murata, leapt into the van, closing the doors as it pulled away.

Entering the town via West Alvington Hill they turned left at the quay roundabout, driving up Fore Street before turning right along the one-way system to Belle Vue Road that led into Church Street. A delivery truck pulled away from outside of Giovanni's and Dho swung the van into the space.

"Very good place to see from," said Dho. "Mail depot over there, you see where small red van go in." Kimura and Iwaki in the front, alongside Dho, nodded.

Outside of the depot cars were parking and leaving regularly providing almost constant access to one or other of the parking bays. At precisely 1100 hours a LDV Convoy van nosed out of the depot entrance and into the traffic heading down Bridge Street to the Quay roundabout.

"Please follow," requested Murata, who was sitting in the back of the van.

Dho started the engine and pulled out to follow the Royal Mail van at a good distance. At Aveton Gifford they watched as the mailbags were taken from the post office and thrown under the mail van's half-raised rear shutter onto the existing pile. At Modbury the traffic prevented them from stopping to view and they had to wait halfway up the steep hill for the mail van to pass them. Careful not to follow too closely along the narrow lane the Royal Mail van had turned down, Dho explained, for the first time, where his small team of explosive experts were in hiding. Half a mile away from the Yelmstoke Head site Dho swung the van through a field entrance and stopped.

"Over there is the MoD/DCF place. In a moment you will see van arrive at entrance," informed Dho as he took from his jacket pocket a pair of binoculars. "Here Murata-san, look through these."

Murata raised the glasses to his eyes just in time to see the mail van swing through the main gate. Stopping at the barrier the driver got out and went into the reception building to re-emerge a few minutes later waving something at the soldiers manning the gate.

As the postman closed the van door the barrier opened and he drove through, then turned right to take the van round to a side door. Taking a bag from the space alongside the driver's seat the postman pulled open the side door to the building and went inside. After five minutes he came out again with another bag and a box, which he loaded into the mail van, via the rear shutter. Driving out he merely handed something to a black-uniformed MoD security guard and drove back down the way he had come, passing Murata's group a few minutes later.

"Are there always soldiers guarding this place?" asked Murata.

"No, they arrived maybe two days ago," said Dho. "They are no problem, they raw recruit only, not hardened soldier."

"I see five of them, is that all?"

"No Murata-san, there are eight altogether. Maybe other three behind building. Next group arrive midday, they will stay guard only two hours before another change."

"So within short time maybe twenty-four soldiers can be here," said Hamaura.

"Do you have trained sniper in your team, Dho-san?" asked Murata.

"Yes, Comrade Byoun is top marksman."

"There is tree in field to right of site, from there he should have good sight of both front and back of building," said Murata, handing the binoculars back to Dho. "See for yourself."

"You think to place him there to take out any opposition to our arrival?"

"Correct Dho-san. We must place him there before dawn, but he must walk last mile from back there. We cannot take chance to bring van this close at night."

"We must go to place where Comrade Byoun is hiding and bring him back here to show him. He must check and confirm that location is suitable range for weapon he carry," put in Iwaki, not wanting to be left out of the organisation of the attack.

"Good, Iwaki-san," said Murata, then turning to Dho he asked, "We go now, please?"

Dho reversed the van out of the field entrance and started back the way they had come. Cresting a rise they could see a long way down the lane, and in the distance, coming towards them, a police car. "You two in back, quickly," he ordered, slowing the vehicle to allow more time.

As the two men scrambled into the back of the van Dho put on a pair of sunglasses and a flat cap. To the sergeant and police constable driving past them he looked like any other young farmer going about his business. Near the woodland hideout south of Holton Lane Dho drove the van into a field entrance on the left of the road just before a road junction. The field had recently been harvested and the surface was firm enough to take the van without it bogging down. Reversing it close to the field side of the high hedge and out of sight from the lane Dho got out of the vehicle and stood signalling towards the woodland across the field. Almost instantly two men appeared, carrying something between them. As they got close the others saw that the two men had brought a camouflage net, which they promptly threw over the van, adding to its concealment.

"We not stay," said Dho to the tough-looking man pegging down the netting.

"There is message from Comrade Namgoong saying they are delayed."

The group hurried across the field and into the wood where the Koreans had established a camp.

"How much delay they suffer and why?" demanded Dho.

"He say vehicle bringing their weapons from Bristol hiding place broke down. He want delay one day."

Dho turned to Murata and explained the problem. "Comrade Namgoong wanting one day delay. Shall we delay or continue as planned?"

"Yes," interrupted Hamaura. "Delay is too much risk we are discovered in house."

The planned day was, by his calculations, an auspicious one; even the date, calculated by numerology reduced to the good fortune number of eight. Hamaura was now concerned but he dared not mention such superstitious ideas as a reason to proceed.

"We must consider carefully," replied Murata, surprised by Hamaura's ardent interruption. "I still think that simultaneous attack is best plan. Is there risk the owner of house will return?"

"I do not think so. Note in milk bottle say house empty two week. That is why we chose that house," replied Dho. "Cellar hiding place was bonus."

"The extra time will allow better planning," said Murata, his mind considering how best to take the mail van without attracting attention. "When Comrade Byoun is satisfied with his sniper location then we return to house and hide until time for attack. We run too much risk driving around."

As Hamaura went to protest again against delaying the attack Kimura grabbed his arm and shook his head. "It is best this way Yoshi-kun. Every detail must be perfect or we will fail."

*　　　　*　　　　*

Vaughan sat up late that night wondering about the decision he had just made. Doubts were already creeping into his mind as his hopes for a change in Sarah's feelings began to return. Lying on the bed staring at the ceiling he thought that at least he would not be involved anymore with the Murata capture. If the gang was going to be anywhere in the West Country it was much more likely that they would seek the anonymity of a city like Plymouth rather than a small town like Kingsbridge, especially with all the police posters and TV coverage. Surely they would know about the search and hide rather than come looking for him. At some point he must have fallen asleep for it was getting light when, stiff and cold, he woke, to find himself still fully dressed on top of the bed. Having stripped off and slid under the duvet his sleep seemed to have lasted only seconds before the phone rang with the early morning call.

It was the tough-looking chauffer who strode into reception and asked for him at the desk. In the car sat a demure Lieutenant Commander Morohashi talking quietly on her mobile. When she had finished the call she turned to Ian.

"Good morning Ian-san, how are you today?"

"Very well thank you, and you?"

"Oh quite well. I am looking forward to seeing the lovely countryside again."

Ian uncharacteristically found himself wanting to sit staring at her, as she sat alongside him, dressed in a classic cream satin sleeveless dress, wearing no discernable make-up, except for lipstick, and no jewellery, but giving the immediate impression of graceful beauty, wealth and class. Beside her Ian felt like a tramp, in his clean but crumpled shirt and slacks. Glancing down he spied the immaculate black medium-heeled shoes on her neat little feet and thought of his own salt-stained deck shoes. He wondered whether they should travel together or whether he should find a seat in another carriage altogether. As it happened the decision was taken away from him due to the previous train being cancelled and therefore theirs being packed out. It was only by chance that Ian saw a single seat available for her. "You take that I will go and grab a coffee at the bar. Would you like one?"

"No thank you Ian-san, I am fine."

At Newbury a few people got off and Ian secured a favoured corner seat from where he could monitor passenger movements. Alighting from the train at Totnes he was surprised not to see Umeko get off as well. He felt disappointed as he crossed the footbridge to leave the station on the north side and walk round to Weirfields, where he had left the van two days before. He had been looking forward to having another chance to talk to her about Japan and all of the other subjects they had covered on that sail back from the Helford River, but she had more important things to do, he remembered.

On the train he had made a list of all the tasks he had to complete before returning to London and on the drive to Kingswear he checked through them in his mind, trying to ensure that he had not missed anything. At the yard the manager was surprised by his sudden request to have *La Mouette sur le Vent* lifted out and scrubbed off.

"She hasn't long been in Mr Vaughan, do you think she needs a scrub so soon?"

"Sadly she will be out of the water until next season," replied Ian. "I have to work in London for a few months. I'll go down and clear out the kit I need and the stuff I shouldn't leave on board, then she is all yours."

An hour later he was putting the small amount of rubbish he had accumulated into the bin when he overheard the yard hand talking to the foreman.

"Boss says *Mouette* is to come out tomorrow. I thought that bloke Vaughan was gonna sail all year round."

"Maybe 'e's got to deal wiv sommat else."

"No, it's that oriental bit of crumpet," the lad replied. "You could see 'e fancied 'er. Cor I bleedin' did an' all, sexy little thing with that long black 'air." The foreman shook his head and bent to pick up the end of the hoist strop. "That's the problem with these sex bombs," the lad continued. "They entice yer into bed then demand you gives up all yer pleasures and marry 'em."

"Oh of course yeah, that's 'ow it was for you and Deb's wan' it. Or maybe it was because you put 'er in the puddin' club," remarked the foreman, coupling his statement with a friendly punch to the lad's shoulder. "Maybe you should pass on your wisdom to Mr Vaughan 'e's just over there."

"Oh shit, do you think 'e 'eard me?"

"Like as not, you bleedin' talk loud enough."

As Ian walked away from the bin, back towards the pontoons, he saw out of the corner of his eye the lad scuttle out of sight behind the office. Well, he thought, with a smile, the lad's got taste.

He paid in advance for the lift out and scrub plus the winter storage fee, then, checking that he had cleared everything from the boat, walked over to the van and drove down to the ferry to start his journey to Kingsbridge. It had clouded over and rain had started to fall as the ferry loaded, turning the river to a flecked slate grey. Ian noticed that already house lights, on the Dartmouth shore, were coming on as the ferry hovered in midstream waiting for the eastbound one to cast off. The last shoppers, huddling under umbrellas, scurried along the narrow pavements as he drove through the town, trying to avoid splashing them. A lorry was struggling up the steep hill past Britannia Naval College and Ian was grateful for the two traffic lanes available on his side of the road. The road between Halwell and Kingsbridge was busy and the thick clouds overhead indicated that it would be dark before he could arrive at the bedsit.

Miranda Cox was disappointed to learn that her tenant was leaving so soon. "I had thought that you would be staying a lot longer than this," she said. "I was just getting used to having you around and then you go and leave me, was it something I said? Or was it that Johnson-Lacey woman on your trail."

Ian laughed. "No, it was nothing you said, or the dreaded Rebecca, in fact, though I will be leaving I would like to continue renting. You see I will be away training for a new job and will be dropping by when I'm given time off."

"Oh right," she said, sounding relieved. "I feared I would have to go through the advertising and interviewing stunt again."

"No you won't need to do that, but I would like you to check from time to time that my books and charts are okay and not getting damp at all."

"Sure, no problem, I'll keep the mattress aired as well," she offered.

"That would be great, thanks. I'll pay you six months in advance and settle up with you at the end for heating costs if that's alright with you?"

"That will be fine."

Ian avoided the hotel for an evening meal, not wishing to appear like a stalker in the eyes of Umeko Morohashi. His fridge was almost empty and the freezer yielded only a fillet of cod, so he contented himself with a very simple meal of cod and what he could salvage from a now old bag of potatoes. Having dealt with the boat and his accommodation all that was left to do was arrange redirection of post and inform his bank of a change of address. The rest of the evening he spent unloading the van of items from the boat and taking them up to his room before almost literally falling into bed to sleep soundly till morning.

* * *

As Ian trudged backwards and forwards to his van Commander Campbell was on the telephone to Chief Superintendent Ishii.

"Obviously we have launched a search for the yacht, both air and sea, off the Devon and Cornish coast, but so far no sightings have been made. It is possible that the ferry sighting was inaccurate, it was at night and searchlights do distort detail. Your agent is confident that Portsmouth is the target?"

"Yes, he is. We have learnt to treat his information as reliable," replied Ishii.

"Thank you, we can now concentrate our defences."

"There is one other important piece of information our agent gave us last night and that is that General Namgoong's son is leading the attack. I am therefore surprised that active support from Japanese persons, even if they are Red Brigade, is being accepted. As you probably know, Japan and Korea are ancient enemies, we now do much business with South Korea but North Korea looks on Japan with much suspicion."

"I see, so you do not think that Murata and his gang are involved," said Campbell.

"It would be very unusual for them to be so closely associated as to take part in same attack as someone like the General's son. Maybe they have only provided financial support or arranged weapon supply."

"The weapon supply is a strong possibility according to information we have obtained from some documents found at a warehouse used by Ishihara," said Campbell. "It would mean that somehow they got them across from Ireland, but anything is possible."

Superintendent Ishii's assessment was, in part, correct, and in fact the protracted negotiations between Murata and Dho had started with Namgoong as sole leader of the fighting group and attack planner, and Murata providing the funding and weapons. This followed the original plan, proposed by Iwaki in North Korea, that also included Kimura and Hamaura joining him in supporting a single attack at Portsmouth by Namgoong's team, once Murata had been set free.

"I have received reports from Ariyoshi-san and Morohashi-san that you wish them to return to your headquarters once they have briefed technology group leaders and seen them off to Bletchley."

"Yes, we have brought that visit forward in view of the situation. Our feeling is that an attack is imminent and we wanted to minimise the staff on site at Portsmouth, especially those associated with the decoding exercise," explained Campbell. "All non-essential staff will work from their homes until ordered back on site."

"This will delay the decoding programme surely," commented Ishii. "Will they be able to complete the work in time?"

"I really don't know," replied Campbell. "What I do know is that our Ministry of Defence is preparing two other sites for that purpose, which they informed me earlier, should be ready to receive the teams after the visit to Bletchley Park tomorrow."

"That is good to hear Commander. Thank you for passing that information to me, you will appreciate our great concern regarding this issue."

"If our roles were reversed Chief Superintendent, I know that I would be asking the same questions and expressing the same concerns," replied Campbell.

After the call, Campbell made his way to the operations room where Chief Inspector Jackson was co-ordinating road closures around the Portsmouth site.

"The only weak spot is this crossroads here, sir," said Jackson pointing to the south east corner of the site. "We can't close off those two lanes because of access to the hospital just here. We have therefore put in place concrete barriers across the road that leads to the main gate. They are large enough to stop any attempt to ram their way towards the main gate."

"What about this barrier?" asked Campbell, indicating a point at another road junction to the west of the site.

"There we've installed a staggered barrier and placed an armed personnel vehicle 100 metres further back which will block the road should anyone try to go through the barrier without the appropriate pass."

Campbell nodded his approval. "Well we've done what we can, let us hope that it is enough to put them off. By the way has everyone going on site for the next week been issued with the new pass for tomorrow?"

"Yes, sir, they have, and we have arranged for a different daily pass to be issued at the reception area each evening from 4.00 p.m. If anyone forgets theirs they won't be allowed back on site the next day."

"What if the pass is stolen?"

"Each person has been told his or her own individual list number, sir. They won't be allowed through without quoting it and it being checked."

"Thank you Inspector. If there is any, I repeat, any, event associated with this you are to contact me immediately on my mobile."

"You won't be at home tonight then sir?"

"No, I'm dining out with a friend."

Outside in the street Campbell hailed a taxi. "Borough Market please."

*   *   *

Darren rolled over, eyes closed, but his arm reached out to encircle Michelle; with his hand finding only the crumpled duvet, he opened his eyes and blearily looked around the bedroom. It was their second night at Wahidi Naraiman's house and so far things had gone well. Michelle had almost accepted that Darren was not to blame for what happened in Newton Creek, but she was still cool towards him. He was hoping that a second good night's sleep would put her in a more amorous mood and was disappointed that she wasn't beside him. Thinking that she had gone to the bathroom he lay back, with arms behind his head, staring at the ceiling thinking of Naraiman's offer of work. Five, ten, then fifteen minutes passed, and still she had not returned. Curious, he got up, pulled on a T-shirt, and crept along the landing towards the bathroom, where he found the door open and the room in darkness.

"You in there Mitch?" he asked in a whisper. There was silence, so he tiptoed back to the bedroom, closed the door, and turned on the light. That was when he discovered that her clothes were missing. "Oh shit, she's done a runner," he muttered to himself. "What the fuck do I do now, Naraiman will be well pissed with this."

Fearful of the Afghan's reaction to Michelle's disappearance Darren sat on the edge of the bed and tried to work out what to do. It took him all of five minutes to realise that his only chance of survival was to escape himself, but how? Indeed how had Michelle escaped? Looking around the bedroom for some clue he checked the window to find the catch fastened so she must have left from another point in the house. Beginning to panic now, he grabbed his clothes and hurriedly dressed except for his boots. It was as he was picking up his comb and wallet from the bed that he noticed the duvet cover was missing. At some time in the night when he was asleep she must have slipped it off somehow, without waking him. He stood staring at the duvet, shaken that she could have done that without disturbing him; then he remembered going to the toilet earlier in the night, she must have taken it off whilst he was out of the room. He shook his head. Cunning little cow, he thought, I wonder what she did with it? Maybe it was still in place. He tried to remember the layout of the house and realised that the bathroom window overlooked the indoor swimming pool. Tying his bootlaces together, Darren hung the pair around his neck, stealthily opened the bedroom door and crept along the landing to the bathroom, closing and locking the door behind him. Switching on the light he stood for several seconds, blinking until his eyes got used to the brightness, then, careful not to slip on the ceramic floor, crossed to the window, which stood open to the night air. Immediately he could see the knot of the duvet around the casement's lower hinge and noted the windowsill had been cleared of jars of cream, tubes of toothpaste and other bathroom paraphernalia. Returning towards the door he switched off the light, then, with caution, returned to the window and looked into the darkness below. As his night vision returned he could see that the duvet hung low enough for a person to get onto the pool roof without needing to drop and risk falling through the glass roof lights. Smiling to himself, he grasped the window's central mullion and swung a foot up onto the sill, heaved himself up, and, feet first, started to slide his body through the open window. He had got halfway when he was stopped by his belt catching on the casement frame; frantically he heaved with his elbows to try and pull his body back enough to release the belt. He was now sweating profusely, and with rising panic becoming less cautious about noise. Feeling the load come off the belt he reached down and eased it over the frame's edge and resumed his exit until a rattling of the bathroom door handle froze his actions.

"Get downstairs and have a look around outside, Mnamad," Darren heard Naraiman say.

Grabbing the duvet with his left hand he pushed the rest of his body up and back with his right, clearing the sill. It was as his right hand grasped the duvet that he felt the movement that caused him to look at the knot around the hinge. As his eyes focused, he saw the end pass through the bind and the duvet unravel, releasing him into freefall, down and through the glazed roof light below.

Mnamad, at the foot of the stairs, heard the crash and rushed through the lounge and into the swimming pool area. Darren's body floated near the surface bent backward at an unnatural angle from the lumbar region, where his backbone had been broken as his body struck the edge of the pool, his eyes wide and staring with lifeless fear.

"He is dead," said Naraiman, now standing behind the African. "The girl won't be far away, they must have been running away together, we must search straight away. When you find her, kill her, we will lose their bodies out at sea."

As Mnamad stepped off the patio onto the lawn, playing a powerful torch onto the surrounding woods and hedges, Michelle was over a mile away, stumbling across a newly ploughed field towards yet another hedgerow. Though she didn't know it she was just north of the little village of Ashford. Her guiding light had been the night-time glow of Plymouth and it was with some surprise that, on looking to her left, she could see the shapes of houses in the village below. A few paces more brought her to a gap in the hedge leading to a narrow lane. Breathing heavily, she paused, weighing up whether to leave the safety of open countryside for the restriction of a lane.

As Darren had surmised, she had feigned sleep waiting for him to pay a visit to the toilet, then hurriedly took off the duvet cover and stashed it under the bed. It was not long after his return that his breathing pattern told her he was fast asleep again. Slipping out of bed she had gathered up her clothes and shoulder bag then tiptoed to the bathroom. With nail scissors she had cut down the duvet side seams, unfolding it into a long sheet. A simple half hitch knot, around the lower casement hinge, appeared to hold when she tested it, so she threw the long tail out into the darkness and returning to the door turned off the light. Like Darren she felt rising panic as she heaved herself up onto the windowsill and, feet first, slid her body out into the darkness. Unlike Darren she again tested the knot by wrapping the tail around her leg and trapping it between her feet, then gently transferring her weight to it whilst holding onto the central mullion. The knot and material appeared to hold her weight, so, pulling her shoulder bag clear, she lowered herself down and onto the pool room roof. Standing with her back to the wall she edged along to the corner of the main house where, reaching round the corner, she could get hold of the rainwater downpipe and climb down it to the ground. She had already worked out that to travel by road would risk Naraiman and his sidekick catching up with her quickly using their vehicles; on foot, in the few lanes that existed, it would not be long before she would be found. Travelling across country, with plenty of cover, she felt she had a much better chance of getting completely away.

The houses weren't far away and she decided to make for them, hoping that she could get help there or find somewhere to hide. She stepped onto the lane and walked as quickly as she dare, in the smothering darkness between the hedgerows. After a hundred yards or so she detected a light area ahead of her, and increasing her pace made towards it. Suddenly she found herself at the edge of a main road; to get to the houses, and possible safety, she must cross it, but she could not see any path or road leading to them. Turning left she started to walk along the main road in search of a way into the village. She had only gone fifty yards when a car rounded the bend behind her, catching her like a frightened rabbit in its headlights; she turned and went to run, an act that immediately looked suspicious. As the car stopped a few yards in front of her she then saw the illuminated police sign on the roof and breathed a sigh of relief.

"What were you running away for, when I came round the corner eh?" asked PC Hicks, as he walked round the back of the car, shining his torch at her.

"I fort you were someone else," she replied, "I fort you were this Nar-ai-man bloke an' 'is minder. I won' t' report a murder."

"Do you now? Well, we better get you into the car where I can take down the details."

* * *

"She's back," said Miranda, as Ian descended the stairs the next morning.

"Who, Rebecca?"

"Yes, Mrs Gucci, I saw her looking in a dress shop window at the bottom of Fore Street ten minutes ago. Hardly her style I would have thought. If you hurry you may catch her."

"Oh, ha ha ha," replied Ian. "Well I won't be shopping in Kingsbridge this morning, I will go to Dartmouth instead. Don't you dare tell her that, promise?"

"Promise, but you better hurry, it looked as if she was coming this way."

As Ian, in his van, turned left from Waterloo Road into Church Street, heading north towards Halwell, an immaculately attired Rebecca Johnson-Lacey emerged from the alleyway and turned along the path to Miranda Cox's cottage, her high-heeled Jimmy Choos tapping loudly on the Yorkstone paving.

"Is Ian here?" she asked, her tone somewhat demanding.

"Good morning, no he's not," replied Miranda, annoyed at the abruptness of the question.

"When do you expect him to return?"

"Not for some months, I am told that he is undertaking some work-related training in London."

"Do you have an address for him? I really do need to contact him most urgently."

"No I am sorry, I don't, I would suggest you contact him via his wife."

"She has no idea where he is either. If you see him tell him that his wife has suggested a very reasonable settlement and he should accept it now instead of being so damn selfish and mean," replied Rebecca haughtily, before turning on her heels and strutting briskly away before a stunned Miranda could think of a suitable response.

"You bitch," she ended up saying to an empty path, before closing the door.

*　　　　*　　　　*

Dho kept lookout, while Murata and the rest of his gang loaded their gear into the back of his van. Iwaki had previously carefully packed the china from the cabinet then rifled through all the drawers and cupboards in the house, collecting jewellery and things he thought may be of value, and placing them in another box. He was now adding the finishing touches by using a nail bar to force the back door from the outside leaving it open and obvious. Crossing the back lane with the boxes, one at a time, he handed them over the hedge to Kimura, who then secreted them some distance away, by a gnarled oak tree, before covering them with some polythene.

"They will find them eventually," Iwaki said. "Here are your boots Kimura-san throw those old boots from the house out into the long grass. If they use dogs they will not follow your track into the field, only our tracks to the van, so they will think we have taken everything with us."

Kimura had already worked out why he had been ordered to use the gardening boots from the house, but was polite enough to acknowledge Iwaki's unnecessary explanation with, "Ah so," and a smile.

This time they drove away from Kingsbridge over the rise and down towards Collapit Bridge. The lane took a sharp right at the bottom of the hill, towards the bridge, but almost immediately Dho took another right turn up the lane leading to West Allington. At the top of the steep hill above Easton he pulled over into a field entrance.

"We will be able to watch the police play from here," he said pointing down the slope towards the house they had just left.

After ten minutes or so of inaction Murata started to talk them through the attack again. The previous day had been spent confined to the cellar, going through, time and time again, his plan, each element being explained with care, until everyone in the gang knew exactly what their individual part was and whose actions theirs would assist.

It was the stealthy Iwaki who was tasked with the taking of the mail van whilst Murata, Dho, Iwaki and Kimura were detailed with the task of herding all of the staff of both floors into the first floor restaurant area, assisted by two of Dho's men. Hamaura was to guard the main entrance. Byoun was to start taking out the perimeter guards, once the gang had entered via the side door. All Japanese staff were to be handed over to Murata and Dho for questioning about the location of their computer hard drives and the location of the central computer within the building. Only Murata and Comrade Dho were to execute any of the oriental staff involved, should that be necessary in order to quickly obtain the information required. Dho's men were to deal with any demolition required and destruction of the main computer. All recovered hard disks were to be retained and taken to North Korea.

By the time Murata was satisfied with members' recitation of their individual and joint tasks it was approaching half past nine, and the sun had turned the van into an oven, even with the driver and passenger windows wound down.

It was just before quarter to ten when Kimura saw the roof of the police car moving along above the lane's low hedgerow.

"Ah, here come our policeman," he said, bringing the group's full attention onto the back of the slate-clad house.

Twenty minutes later two other police cars arrived at speed and the group of officers went inside, after a short conference near the back door. The dog van arrived next and the handler's head could be seen moving backwards and forwards along the back lane as the dog tried to follow their scent. Another white van arrived with a forensic team to search for fingerprints, to laughter from the gang as they looked on.

Murata patted Iwaki on the back. "Good, very good, maybe every policeman in the town is down there, intent on looking for a common burglar."

"Mopping cellar floor and steps may stop them from searching that area too thoroughly," replied Iwaki. "Are you sure you wiped every snooker ball and cue, Hamaura-san desuka?" asked Iwaki.

"*Hi, hi,* Iwaki-san," confirmed Hamaura. "Also table and rests."

Iwaki nodded his approval, then glancing at his wristwatch, said, "We have only twenty minutes to get into position, *'ikemasho-ka'*?" he said, asking whether they should leave.

"Yes, we go now, let us hope that this moment is an auspicious one," responded Murata, as Dho reached forward to turn the ignition key of the van.

The van lurched as it reversed back onto the lane, causing Hamaura, who was just regaining his seat, to stagger. Sitting, he looked down at the spot where he had crushed something as he had tried to keep his balance. The form of a large harvest spider lay squashed against the floor, sending a surge of superstitious fear through Hamaura's body and mind.

CHAPTER 14

Campbell woke at the third buzz of his mobile phone; reaching for it, he sat up in bed. "Campbell here."

"Carter, sir, you said to phone with anything."

"What has happened?"

"Plymouth police are currently questioning one Michelle Goodwin, in connection with the murder of that harbour master, Ken Fallon, and the theft of a yacht."

"Who's in charge down there?" asked Campbell.

"An Inspector Maclaren sir, telephone number…" Carter conveyed the contact details and asked what Campbell wanted him to do next.

"I want you to get down there as quick as you can, taking those charts that Ian Vaughan left with us. See if she can point out where they dropped off Murata and his friends," instructed Campbell, "and Carter, go gently with her, I want her to co-operate as quickly as possible. You better convey that to Inspector Maclaren at Plymouth before you leave. Oh and Carter, try and contact Ian Vaughan when you get down there, he may well be able to help."

"Right sir. Do you want to involve the Japanese officer, sir?"

"No Carter, she has enough to do."

"Will you be coming in early, sir?"

"Yes, could you phone the pool and request a car for me."

Putting the phone down, Campbell showered, and dressing hurriedly made his way downstairs to the kitchen. The smell of kippers met him as he opened the door.

"Good heavens Mrs Craven, what are you doing up at this time?"

"I heard that wretched mobile of yours and knew you'd be off out with just a cup of coffee if I didn't set to."

Campbell shook his head. "What would I do without you?"

"Starve more likely, or die from eating takeaway meals," she replied, bustling through to the dining room to lay a place setting.

"Poached egg on top?" she asked as Campbell seated himself at the table.

"If it's not too much trouble," he replied.

Mrs Craven gave him a serious look, then turned and left the room.

Five minutes later she returned with a large tray with his breakfast and a pot of tea with two cups and saucers.

"Are you joining me?" Campbell asked. Occasionally she would join him with a cup at breakfast time if there was something she wished to discuss. Normally it concerned days off or holiday arrangements, but this morning it was very different.

"I wanted to be nosy and ask you if you enjoyed your dinner with Caroline Tucker?" she answered, her eyes bright with interest.

Campbell laughed. "Yes thank you, I did. We had a very pleasant and relaxed evening together."

"And?"

"And what?" he replied frowning.

"Oh you are exasperating," Mrs Craven said, almost huffily. "Are you going to see her again?"

"I don't rightly know. It's possible I suppose," he replied, intentionally teasing.

Finishing her tea, she got up and gave him another serious look. "If you let that lovely young lady go out of your life, well, it would be the biggest mistake you could make."

"Maybe Mrs Craven, maybe," he replied, looking up at her and smiling kindly.

"Well I must get on. I've had my say."

Campbell watched her leave the room and wondered how his household could possibly run without her to keep order, and to remind him occasionally that he had another life, away from the almost constant demands of the Service. Would it all change if Caroline became part of this sanctuary, that Mrs Craven had built together with his late wife?

Flashing blue lights reflecting off the lounge ceiling announced the arrival of his car. Swallowing the last mouthful of tea, Campbell slipped on his jacket, checked his pocket for wallet and ID, then, scooping up his briefcase strode towards the front door.

"I have a feeling that it is going to be a very busy day, Mrs Craven. Don't wait up."

She opened the front door for him shaking her head. "You got clean spare kit at the office?" she asked, frowning her disapproval at the sure indication that she would not see him for days, and when she did, knowing that he would look thoroughly drained and exhausted.

"Yes," he replied, smiling. "Full kit all present and correct." Sometimes, like now, he felt like giving her a peck on the cheek. It was just as if his mother was seeing him off to school.

Getting into the police car, he instructed the driver to take him to DELCO offices, then said, "In future, if you are assigned to collect me from my home, I would appreciate you not making it look like a police raid."

"Oh sorry, sir," replied the driver. "Cut the blues Trace."

At DELCO Campbell tapped in the reception door code, and checking that the door had closed correctly behind him, walked across to an innocuous steel cabinet and entered a second number to the door keypad, watched closely by the night security guard behind the reception desk. Holding the door to screen what he was doing from any passers-by, he put his right hand onto a palm identification pad whilst adjusting his position to come in line with the retina scanner. Checks completed, the door to the left of the cabinet opened and he passed through into a lift. On the second floor he made his way towards his office, but halfway along the corridor saw that lights were on in the conference room. Putting his head around the door he asked, "What is up with everybody this morning? First Mrs Craven, now you two."

"Carter phoned sir," replied Penny Heathcote. "So I called Lorna, just in case we were needed. Coffee sir?"

"Not just now thank you, but you carry on."

In his office Campbell hung up his jacket in the wardrobe and crossed to his desk switching on the screen of his computer. Password entered, he searched down the file list to Murata and opened it. Somewhere in this file, he thought, was a clue as to what Murata's next move would be; would he go for glory by attacking the *USS Omaha*, try to attack Yealmstoke Head or has he tracked down Vaughan? Maybe Murata was just running for cover in Ireland or rendezvousing with a ship in the Western Approaches. He started to read, jotting down notes as points of interest came to his attention. Reaching into his briefcase for a notepad, the one he had used when first interviewing Sarah Vaughan, his hand touched a photo frame. Pulling the frame from the briefcase he looked at the official photograph of Caroline and himself at the US Embassy and almost stood it up on his desk. "No," he said aloud. "No distractions Alex," and bent again to exchange the frame for the notepad.

Two hours later there was a knock on his office door. "Excuse me sir." It was Heathcote.

"Yes, Lieutenant, what is it?"

"In view of the girl giving herself up to the police in Plymouth, we have called off the search for the yacht sir," she said. Before Campbell could ask why she continued, "We spoke briefly with Inspector Maclaren who informed us that the yacht was scuttled sou'-sou' west of Start Point."

"Have you got a chart open in the conference room?"

"Yes sir."

"Right, let's go and have a look."

In the conference room Campbell found Lorna on the phone to Morohashi who had at the time, been checking out from the Kings Arms Hotel.

"Apparently the girl told them that she had been ordered to sail to a position 50 degrees north by 3 degrees 26 minutes west. There, a large black-hulled powerboat met them. Murata ordered her to wait at that position for her boyfriend Darren Cripps, then take the boat back to Southampton."

"Why was it scuttled then?" asked Campbell.

"It appears that this Cripps chap thought that the yacht may have a bomb on board, so they scuttled it and were taken ashore by a man called Naraiman who owned the powerboat," explained Heathcote.

"What happened then?"

"We don't know sir, except that the member of the gang who shot Mr Fallon, the harbour master, is called Iwaki and the others on board are Murata, Kimura, Hamaura and a man called Dho."

"Ah, a Korean link. So it is unlikely to be the *USS Omaha*, much more likely to be Yealmstoke Head. Can you get me Chief Inspector Jackson please?"

"You don't think that North Korea would want to attack a US warship then sir?" asked Lorna.

"Definitely not, they are ill-equipped to handle American retaliation at this time, no matter what their sabre-rattling suggests," replied Campbell. "No, they are aware of this cyberwarfare work and that is what they need to disrupt."

"Chief Inspector Jackson on the phone sir," said Heathcote, handing the phone to Campbell.

"Chief Inspector, I believe that both Portsmouth and Yealmstoke are to be subject to an attack. I need the rapid response team sent down from Heysham Power Station to Yealmstoke Head as soon as you can arrange it. Helicopters if you can. I believe time is of the greatest importance."

"All of that team sir? We did have a high risk category flag on that site sir," replied Jackson.

"We will have to take that risk Chief Inspector. If Murata succeeds with this, the fallout will have far wider reaching effects."

"I'll get onto it immediately sir."

"Yealmstoke is protected by a bunch of raw recruits Inspector. Willing, I have no doubt, but no match for Murata's little army."

Putting the phone down Campbell turned to Lorna and asked. "Was that Lieutenant Commander Morohashi you were talking to when I came in?"

"Yes sir."

"Where is she now?"

"She was just checking out of the hotel there, then is making her way back here, sir," replied Lorna, somewhat surprised at the sharpness of his tone of voice.

"Good, I don't want her involved in this, she was injured before and I don't want her repatriated in a body bag," said

Campbell, ignoring the expression on Lorna's face. "Can you get Carter for me please."

"Right away, sir," said Heathcote, snatching up the phone and dialling hurriedly. After several moments Carter answered. "I have the Commander for you, hold on."

Taking the handset Campbell said, "When you get to the police station I want you to directly interview this girl, you are to take the lead in the interview, not the local lads they won't know the questions."

"Got that sir."

"Concentrate on where the gang was landed. Her boyfriend may have told her something. Also find out where the boyfriend is and the whereabouts of a man named Naraiman." Campbell spelt the name out to ensure the right man was being sought.

"Do you want them brought in sir?"

"Ideally, yes, but tell the locals they must not risk the casual approach. Armed backup will be essential," advised Campbell. "How long till you get there?"

"About another hour, sir, according to PC Wheatley."

"I can't hear the siren going," said Campbell.

"I switched it off when the call came through sir," lied Carter, who had been enjoying a nap when his mobile rang.

"Tell Wheatley to get a move on, this has become very urgent."

"Right sir."

"Lorna, can you get me the site director at Yealmstoke Head, his name is Lambert I think."

When Lambert came on the phone Lorna handed the receiver to Campbell. "Ah, Mr Lambert, we have reason to believe that there is a significantly heightened risk of your site being attacked. We have a rapid response unit making its way towards you by helicopter. I would like you to arrange for all non-essential staff, especially the women, to work from home until further notice."

Campbell could sense the fear in Lambert's voice when he responded and guessed at the rising panic his message had caused. How quickly Lambert would react was difficult to judge, but Campbell guessed that the man would go into a funk before issuing any useful instructions.

"Lorna send a coded signal to Yealmstoke confirming that we are raising their security level to 'Amber', and copy it to MoD, Galbraith's office."

Putting down the phone Campbell stood staring at the Ordnance Survey map Lorna had set down alongside the chart. "A small part of England yes, but an absolute maze of small lanes and byways. What resources have we got down there?"

"I'll find out for you sir. If you want to transfer to the Yard ops room sir, I will get the information to you there," replied Lorna, as she picked up a phone and started dialling Plymouth Central Police Station.

"Thank you, I will transfer, could you inform Chief Inspector Jackson that I am on my way and to use mobile phone contact until I get there."

* * *

As Dho drove through the field entrance above the slate-clad house, that had been the gang's hideout, Ian was lowering his binoculars, having just watched *La Mouette sur le Vent* being lifted safely out of the water and onto her winter storage cradle. Parked on the South Embankment at Dartmouth he had walked a short way along the pavement to where he could get a clear view of the hoist basin on the other side of the river. Idly he wondered when he would be free to return to the yacht that he now, after such a short time, felt so at home aboard. Back in his van he checked his list, then started the engine and pulled away towards Kingsbridge and his bank. Approaching the Halwell junction his mobile rang. "Why is it always when you're driving?" he muttered as he braked hard and swung the car off the road into the entrance of a small industrial estate.

"Ian Vaughan."

"Vaughan, Campbell here. We've just learnt that Murata was landed ashore somewhere near to your location maybe two days ago."

"So it probably was the yacht I saw near to the ferry."

“It very much looks that way. Now look, I want you out of there as soon as possible. Get your things together and make your way to the Manor, you remember the address, yes?”

“Yes sir, I remember,” replied Ian, recalling instantly the training establishment he had visited before.

“Good, if you see any of them, hide, do not think of taking them on, just report their location as soon as you can.”

“Yes, sir.”

The phone went dead and Ian glared at it then put it back onto the magnet on the dashboard. “Sod it, bank, bedsit, then away.” Putting the van into gear he pondered on why he felt so reluctant to depart. It wasn’t the beautiful Umeko Morohashi, as lovely as she was. Could it be the lifestyle, the thought of being able to just go sailing when the weather suited? If Sarah would only accept sensible access to Clare and Louise, life, on the face of things, would be perfect. Why had he really accepted Campbell’s offer? Was it just because the continued survival of Murata and Hamaura’s brother presented a threat to him and his family? If so, he was joining just to conduct a vendetta, not a genuine reason to sign up for Queen and Country.

Ian still had not reached any satisfactory conclusion by the time he had parked the car in the Quay car park at the head of the creek in Kingsbridge. On the road into the town he had been careful to look around at the faces of people in the streets. Now on foot, he was being extra cautious by joining a group of people making their way towards Fore Street. He felt hunted, but not really scared, unlike the first few days after leaving the safe house. Crossing the road with the group he looked at their reflection in a chemist’s shop window, concentrating on those following his little party. Satisfied that all was clear he turned right, crossing the bottom of Fore Street and rounded the corner into Bridge Street heading towards the bank. A few yards along he stopped, ostensibly to look at something in a shop window, glancing back and then studying people on the opposite side of the road. At the corner by the Royal Mail depot he crossed the road and entered the bank. It took only five minutes to transact his business before he was striding out through the door to almost knock a startled Lieutenant Commander Umeko Morohashi off her feet.

"I'm so sorry, I was too intent upon reading this brochure," he said, feeling foolish and embarrassed. "Are you alright?"

"I am fine, Ian-san, no harm done," she replied, slightly amused as she saw him blush. "I was looking for an ATM."

"There is one on the end wall," Ian informed her, pointing to his left. "I thought you would be on your way back to London by now."

"I will be shortly, I had some reporting to do before I left and it was easier to do it from here so I told myself. Actually, I wanted to savour a few more hours here, I have so enjoyed my stay." she replied. Then she looked at him curiously, having noticed that he was staring intently over her shoulder at something behind her.

She had been standing with her back to the road and had not seen the Ford Transit van, parallel parked, blocking in three cars, outside of the Royal Mail depot. Ian had subconsciously noticed the van as he was leaving the bank and had also been aware of a man getting out of the passenger side and hurrying back to intercept a mail van leaving the depot. What triggered his change of attention from Umeko to the mail van was the opening of the mail van driver's door. His peripheral vision had picked up something, now confirmed, as he focused on the mail van now driving away with the man he had seen hurrying from the Ford Transit at the wheel. His eyes, now focusing on the white van, saw Murata looking back from the passenger side door window, the burn scar to the face leaving no doubt as to his identity.

"Don't look round!" he said, taking a hurried step towards her and embracing her. "It's Murata and his little army, they have just hijacked a post office van," he continued, talking quietly into her right ear and using her long black hair to hide most of his face whilst watching as the mail van followed by the white Ford Transit drove off in convoy.

"Quickly, we need to see where they are going," Ian said, releasing Umeko and running off in the direction of the quay.

At the roundabout junction he saw the back of the mail van disappearing along Ilbert Street and indicating to take the first exit out of the roundabout and head towards West Alvington.

As Umeko caught up with him she said, “I don’t have a car.”

“Mine’s over there in the car park, come on, let’s see where they are going, we can phone Campbell as we go.”

Picking his moment to run between two cars, he sprinted across the road past the information office and was fifty yards in front of Umeko by the time he reached his van. Unlocking the doors he looked up to see her in full flight, dress riding high on her thighs, her hands clutching her shoes and shoulder bag and her stockinged feet a blur as she raced towards him.

“What about the local police?” she panted, as she reached the car.

“Unarmed policemen in pursuit of that bunch would be dead in moments, they would have absolutely no idea of the kill mentality those men have,” Ian replied as he started the engine, and with wheels spinning accelerated up through the car park, frightening several people as he went.

“I forgot that most of your police are unarmed.”

Braking hard for the hump near the car park exit, Ian eased the van over it before driving hard to reach the road just in time to force the van into a gap in the traffic. Turning left up Ilbert Street he was able to speed up, slowing only to check that the next roundabout was clear before pointing the vehicle in the direction of West Alvington.

In the village itself they were forced to a standstill as the uphill queue allowed downhill traffic to come through the narrow section of the road. Moving off again there was no chance to overtake before the road junction.

“Left or right?” she asked.

“I doubt if they are heading for Salcombe. It’s unlikely they would hijack a mail van as part of a business takeover.”

Umeko gave him a dark look. “No need for sarcasm, I do not know this area.”

"Sorry I was well out of line with that," he replied, snatching a gap in the oncoming traffic to take the Plymouth fork, forcing an oncoming car to brake heavily and sound the horn.

"That is someone else you have upset today," Umeko said primly.

"Let's hope the list for the day includes Murata and his little lot."

It was not until they crested the hill above the Avon valley that Ian saw the mail van and Ford Transit ahead of them, crossing the bridge.

"There they are, get on the phone to Campbell, I bet they are heading for Yealmstoke Head."

Snatching up her mobile she dialled the number. "Nothing," she said, frowning at the screen. "Oh, no signal."

"Try mine," he said, taking it from the magnet and handing it to her.

"It's no good there is no signal on this one either."

"It's probably a blind spot, try again when we get to the top of the next rise."

At the bottom of the hill they caught up with a stream of traffic crossing the causeway and bridge across the River Avon, and with no chance of overtaking, Ian started drumming his fingers on the steering wheel in frustration. Reaching the roundabout on the north side of the river, their path was blocked by an articulated lorry that now led them slowly up the Aveton Gifford bypass. As they came abreast of the cricket pitch Ian held the van back from the lorry then accelerated hard, pulling out and passing the lorry as it came to the road junction leading back to the northern end of the village, regaining the left-hand traffic lane again after rumbling over some centre hatched markings. With a clear road in front of him Ian kept his foot on the accelerator and soon had the little van flying along at over seventy miles an hour. Passing Grove Park Farm they were fast catching up with two cars travelling considerably slower than them and by the end of the following straight Ian had caught them, and without lifting off passed both vehicles in the braking distance into the left-hand bend leading up to the Harraton road junction where the Bigbury road branched off. Rocketing through the bend and up the hill to the junction Ian could see, out of the corner of his eye, Umeko Morohashi furiously thumbing her mobile phone.

"Still no luck?"

"No," she replied. "Very strange to travel such a distance and not receive any signal."

"Jesus Christ!" he shouted in fear. They had reached the junction at high speed to find half their lane blocked by an MPV full of children, its adult driver staring, eyes wide in horror, as their van flew at him. In the opposite lane was a slow-moving petrol tanker lumbering up the hill from Modbury, fortunately hugging the kerbside, allowing Ian just enough room to flick the steering wheel right then left to round the front of the MPV and then avoid the tanker. "That was bloody close, are you alright?"

"What was he doing, pulling out like that?"

"He probably misjudged the speed we were travelling at and thought he could get out and be in front of that petrol tanker before we arrived."

"Ian-san, when we get in sight of their vehicle do not get close, DS Weaver made that mistake and died as a result."

"No, I just want to be sure where they are going so that we can call in the necessary troops to take them out."

Just a mile and a half south of Modbury, Ian sighted the Transit as it followed the mail van into a right-hand bend in the road ahead.

"There they are. We've got three cars between us and them that hopefully will keep up and allow us to follow at a safe distance," he said. "I know it is a strange thing to carry in England, but do you have any sunglasses in that shoulder bag of yours?"

"You think they would recognise me?" Umeko asked.

"It is unlikely that they would recognise you from the chase at the airfield, but I bet they have had people watching the computer group you were with," Ian answered. "I instantly recognised you the first day you came onto the Yealmstoke site, and that was from a distance of at least two hundred yards."

She turned and looked at him raising her eyebrows in surprise. "Okay I will put them on straight away. What about you?"

"If you wouldn't mind reaching into the glove compartment for me, they are in there."

Rounding the next bend, Ian looked to his right. "There, there is a mobile phone mast, we've got to have a signal now."

Umeko looked down at her phone. "No nothing."

"They've taken out the communication to the site. Site staff are not allowed to use their mobile phones from within the site boundaries so it won't be until Murata's little band take out the main switchboard that anyone will try to use them."

"What do we do?"

"Stop in Modbury and use the landline system from a shop," said Ian.

"What if it is not Yealmstoke Head but the *USS Omaha*?"

"I can't see them getting close enough to the *USS Omaha* in a Royal Mail van, without bringing a heavily armed response down on themselves."

In Modbury, Ian pulled up outside of an estate agent's office, and leaving the hazard warning lights flashing on his van, ran inside. "My name is Vaughan, Counter Terrorist Command," he announced, holding up his identity card. "I need to use your telephone, it's an emergency."

"You can try sir, but all of our telephones seem to be down," said a young man, looking at the handset of his telephone with a puzzled expression on his face.

"When did that happen?"

"Just a minute or two ago, I was talking to a client and the line just went dead."

"Thanks, I'll try next door, it may just be yours that is out."

As Ian turned to leave, a lady in a smart white chemist's coat hurried in. "Are your phones working?" she asked.

Ian brushed passed her and ran to the van, leapt in and started the engine. "They've taken out the entire telephone network for this area."

Morohashi looked stunned. "How could they possibly have done that?"

"No time to find out, what we need to do is get to Yealmstoke, but God knows what we can do when we get there."

At the top of the hill they found themselves three cars back from a slow-moving lorry. Ian swore, frustrated by his inability to overtake without endangering others, then a break came as the second car in the line indicated to turn left and the car in front of him slowed, allowing Ian to swing into the opposite lane and pass.

"That no doubt is another annoyed person," he said, shooting a sidelong glance at Morohashi.

"Without doubt," she replied. "The list gets longer by the minute."

It was as they were descending the slope towards the Erm Bridge that Ian noticed the whip aerial waving wildly on the lorry's cab roof.

"We've got to stop that lorry, it's got a CB radio on board. They won't have been able to take that out."

Morohashi looked at him questioningly. "What radio?" she asked.

"You know, 'breaker breaker this is Wild Man is anyone out there?' That type of radio."

"Oh," she replied. "Of course, yes, they should not be affected."

At the Ermington junction the car between them and the lorry turned right and Ian was now able to close up to the lorry, and by sounding the horn and flashing his headlights, finally had the lorry pulling into a lay-by near a farm entrance and stopping with Ian parked behind him. Leaping from the van, they both rushed along to the driver's door.

Suspicious of their intent the driver remained in his cab, door locked and window shut tight.

Ian held up his identity card, shouting, "Counter Terrorist Command, we need to use your CB Radio."

The driver's window lowered an inch and Ian repeated the message.

"What's up wiv your bleedin' mobile then?" responded the driver.

"The same as yours, no signal. In fact the whole area does not have any mobile signal."

Reaching to his dashboard the driver flicked his delivery clipboard to one side and picked up his own mobile phone and studied the screen.

"What about a phone box?"

"The same thing. Oh, for Christ's sake this is an emergency."

"Come round the other side."

Climbing up into the cab, Ian introduced himself and Morohashi then handed the driver his ID card for inspection.

"Right guv, what do you want to do then?"

"Are you in range of your home or base with that CB radio of yours?"

"Should think so."

"Where would that be?"

"Plymouth."

"Okay. Can you call them up please, and ask them to write down a message I want them to relay to someone in London."

"Alright, you used one these before?"

"VHF, I assume the principle is the same."

The driver reached down and selected Channel 19. "Breaker breaker this is the Tiny Trucker calling The Dovecote, are you listening in there Honey?"

Ian looked across at the driver and smiled. The man was huge, almost filling his side of the cab. "Tiny huh," he said.

The radio crackled and the driver's wife responded. It took ten minutes at least to convey the message and check that she had all of the details correct. They then sat chatting about gravel haulage issues until the radio crackled again and his wife confirmed that the message had got through. Campbell also relayed the message that an attack had been made at Portsmouth; she finished with "The man, Mr Campbell, insisted I tell you to wait for assistance."

"Sorry you're breaking up, thank you very much for your help," replied Ian, handing the microphone back to the Tiny Trucker. "How much do I owe you?" he asked.

"Nothin' mate, only too pleased to help, good luck."

"Cheers. Remember not a word to anyone, the last thing we need is any panic, okay?" The driver nodded, and with that Ian leapt down from the cab, grabbed Morohashi by the arm and steered her back to his van.

“Campbell is doing what he can but it appears that while the message was being relayed an attack had started at Portsmouth,” informed Ian.

“Ah so, maybe Murata has some other plan, and not Yealmstoke.”

“No, the more I think about this the more I am sure that it is Yealmstoke, and I reckon that the attacks were timed to synchronize with each other in order to split the response. Come on, let’s go and see what we are up against.”

*　　　　*　　　　*

Murata had just caught a fleeting glance of the man as he stepped out from the bank doors onto the pavement; something jangled in his thoughts, but he could not instantly recall what it was. The mail van was more pressing than a vague memory, and Murata turned his head to look back down the road, waiting for it to appear. His peripheral vision picked up the man embracing a woman, then the mail van was passing them with Iwaki at the wheel, and he ordered Dho to follow; the stranger now fading from his conscious thoughts. It was as they crawled in traffic across the narrow bridge at the place called Aveton Gifford that Murata’s subconscious pieced together the two sightings.

“Vaughan,” he said out loud.

Dho looked at him. “What did you say? I no understand.”

“Nothing, just a thought I had,” Murata replied, but in the pit of his stomach he felt a chill. Looking away, at the hedgerow flashing by, his thoughts were now engaged in desperately questioning his recall of the man who had wrecked his life’s most ambitious achievement. Why was he there? Was Vaughan to be his nemesis? Try as he might these thoughts would not go away. He kept looking into the nearside wing mirror to see if any car was consistently following them. He only relaxed as they turned off the main road and Dho had slowed the van whilst he checked to see that they were on their own.

Dho’s men were hurriedly stacking mailbags to create a wall against the mesh screen behind the van’s driver and another wall to block the rear loading shutter, leaving only the side loading shutter clear, when Murata and the others arrived at the field by the woods. Bags of explosive units for blowing doors were loaded in the middle and each man was issued with his weapons and spare ammunition.

"Comrade Seon will drive mail van and go to reception, he look much like regular postman," said Dho, proudly pushing forward one of his soldiers. Seon had been the motorcyclist who had followed Weaver and Morohashi when they drove from Belmarsh Prison following Murata's extradition convoy.

The body of the Royal Mail driver had been taken from the van and his shirt removed. Dumping the body in the wood where they had camped Comrade Seon washed the specks of blood off the shirt and put it on.

"Is Comrade Byoun in place?" asked Murata, knowing full well that he would be, but wanting to keep the appearance of command despite his growing inexplicable anxiety.

"He has been there since before dawn," Dho replied, testily.

"That is good Comrade, as I expected everything done in good order, thank you. Now we leave the young and fitter men to gain entry and we follow when they are inside main building."

Dho nodded and issued orders to Comrade Seon and the remaining two Koreans who promptly got into the mail van alongside Kimura and Iwaki. Hamaura was to go in with Murata and Comrade Dho, as Murata did not want the young hothead out of his sight.

Slamming down the side load shutter Murata signalled to the driver to move off and watched as the bright red van passed through the field entrance and turned in the direction of Ford village before climbing the hill towards Holbeton and Yealmstoke Head beyond.

"This is a good auspicious day Hamaura-kun," said Murata as he closed his door in the white van.

"Hi so desu," agreed Hamaura loudly, trying hard to banish the spider from his thoughts and at the same time rerun in his mind the mathematics that confirmed his fears that the day held bad fortune.

Each time he arrived at the number four, the most unlucky number, called *shi*, and sounding the same as the Japanese word for death.

*　　　　*　　　　*

Similar fears were exercising the mind of Site Director Colin Lambert. More than a month previously he had been requested to prepare a plan for such an event, but somehow he had not been able to evaluate his staff in terms their being essential to the basic running of the site. None of the main tasks of his highly skilled computer teams could be conducted from their domestic broadband connections without seriously endangering national security; therefore they would have to stay. As some of his senior code analysts were women it seemed that unless he closed the site completely, he should simply send the secretaries and clerks home.

Commander Campbell's telephone call and instruction had been swiftly followed by a similar call from the MoD's Executive Director in Whitehall, confirming to him that the security level had been raised to 'Amber', causing Lambert to rummage frantically through his briefcase for the notes he had made weeks before.

It was half an hour before he summoned his department heads and conveyed the message regarding the threat. It was the annoyingly bright Malcolm Cauldwell who stated the obvious initial measure.

"I would think our first action should be to download all our current data onto the Cheltenham mainframe and seal our mainframe room."

"Of course," responded Lambert, trying to convince everyone that he had assumed that as a first action, when in fact the thought had not crossed his mind.

"We should also warn our little army," continued Cauldwell. "We don't want them to be surprised do we?"

A ripple of nervous laughter ran round the room.

"My staff are halfway through preparing lunches," announced Bob Stokes, the catering manager. "What do you want them to do?"

"Oh yes, lunch. Um, well, we can't starve," said Lambert, the only one in the room to laugh.

"Until we know more about the threat, may I suggest getting my people to put out a large selection of sandwiches and say, some fruit, that those remaining on site can help themselves to? Then I can send all my people home, out of the way."

"Excellent," responded Lambert. "Can you see to that straight away? But try not to cause any panic, call it an exercise. Yes, that, er that, would be best, in fact everyone please instruct your staff in the, er... er, procedure as, er, only an emergency exercise."

In the end the decision regarding who should stay and who should leave the site was delegated to the individual department heads, leaving Lambert with the weighty decision of whether or not he should stay. With the time now approaching 10.45 that decision was going to be made for him.

In the outer office Lambert bent over Cheryl Jay's desk and said quietly to her, "Cheryl darling, there is a bit of a flap on. I want you to get your things together quickly and go straight home."

The affair between Lambert and his secretary, Cheryl, was the only reason that Shirley Withers retained her position at the gatehouse reception. Whilst doing a menial post room job, earlier in her career, Withers had caught the pair *in flagrante delicto* thereby ensuring her future employment prospects for the duration of Lambert's site directorship.

"What about tonight?" she asked, looking at him in that hurt way she always did when there was a change in their plans.

"Oh, I hope to be at the caravan as we arranged. This is probably a false alarm. Come on, hurry along, just in case."

"You'll be alright Colin?" she asked, picking up his fear.

"Oh I may well make a visit to the naval base, Stephen Pardew said he wanted another meeting about his network extension."

"I thought you told him we didn't have the manpower to take that on?"

"Well we are almost at the end of this Korean project."

Cheryl had completed her ritual visit to the ladies, to touch up the make-up and just tweak the hairstyle, and was, with happy thoughts of playing wife for a night, making her way across the car park as a Royal Mail van stopped at the site barrier and the driver jumped out to make his way into the gatehouse reception. Looking around her everything seemed perfectly normal as she waved to her friend Linda, who was also apparently leaving. At her car she opened the rear door and carefully placed her handbag on the back seat before picking up her sensible flat driving shoes and changing into them, placing her high-heeled pair on the floor behind the passenger seat. Closing the door she turned, and reaching for the driver's door handle paused at the sound of a cry from her friend Linda, who she could now see hurrying towards the gate. Looking at the gate she could see a soldier crossing the road from the gatehouse, where he had been standing moments before. He was looking curiously at his mate, now sat slumped, his back resting against the barrier pivot post. The soldier had just reached the middle of the road when he collapsed as if felled by some invisible axe. Linda now close to the body of the first soldier screamed and put her hand to her mouth moments before she too fell in a heap to the ground. Cheryl stood for several seconds paralysed by the sight of the three bodies lying lifeless on the ground, then turning back towards the building, ran as fast as her legs could carry her. She almost took the door off its hinges as she charged into the main foyer crying for help, shocking the ageing site visitor escort.

"There, out there, something is terribly wrong with them," she screamed, almost incoherently, pointing out towards the site gate.

"What?" asked the escort, trying to make out what she was saying and what she was pointing at.

"I think they have been shot. They are lying on the ground as if they are dead." Tears were now rolling down her cheeks and she was on the point of passing out.

The escort went towards the door intent on investigating.

"Don't go out there!" Cheryl screamed. "You will be shot!"

The escort faltered momentarily, then pushed his way through the door as a white Ford Transit van drove through the unguarded site entrance and past the open barrier, to bounce over the body of the second soldier before turning into the car parking area to speed towards the building's main entrance. Caught in the open, the escort stood no chance; Murata threw open the van door as the vehicle skidded to a stop, and shot him twice in the chest.

The only witness to the shooting was Cheryl who stood motionless, staring in disbelief as Murata entered the foyer followed by Dho and Hamaura.

"Comrade Dho, you take her to first floor eating area at front. We will clear this level and bring them to you," said Murata, roughly pulling Cheryl's swipe pass from around her neck.

Only the canteen staff and four of the secretaries had actually made it off site in time to miss the attack.

Chapter 15

Campbell was listening to the truck driver's wife when Jackson burst into his office in New Scotland Yard. "The Portsmouth site is under attack. They haven't got into the building yet but it seems as if things are a bit tricky down there. They came in from the east side, used a large lorry to bust through the fence."

Campbell held up his hand to stop Jackson's outpouring of information. "It seems as if Yealmstoke may well be hit as well and so far we have not been able to reinforce the defences there," Campbell responded, turning to face the Chief Inspector, revealing the handset held to his ear.

"Sorry sir, I didn't see that you were on the phone when I came in," said Jackson, as Campbell replaced the receiver at the end of the call.

"That's alright Chief Inspector. I was getting a message from Vaughan, via a CB radio link, from a truck driver and his wife." Campbell shook his head in amazement at the route of communication. "Murata appears to have hijacked a mail van and Vaughan is convinced that he is making towards Yealmstoke Head."

"What's with the CB radio?" asked Jackson.

"It appears that all telephone systems have been taken out in the area surrounding Yealmstoke. My call to that chap Lambert must have been one of the last to get through."

"That seems to have been far better planned than the strike at Portsmouth. They are able to give us a running commentary."

"Operations Room I think," said Campbell leaping to his feet. "We need to get the ETA for the rapid response team going to Yealmstoke."

"I've already got people asking that question sir, they should know by now."

As they entered the room a WPC wearing a headset raised her hand and said, "RRT ETA Yealmstoke one hour twenty minutes, they are just refuelling at Yeovil sir." Jackson frowned.

"I understand that the only fully crewed operational aircraft was already airborne and returning from another job when our call diverted it sir."

"Thank you constable. Has anyone heard any form of message from the Yealmstoke Head site?" asked Jackson.

There was silence, each person in the room looking around for a response.

"Hasn't that army unit got radio down there?" asked Sergeant Hunter. "Surely that's working?"

"Get hold of the barracks they came from and find out what equipment they were issued with. You're right it seems damn stupid to put soldiers in the field without independent communications," replied Jackson. "The Commander has heard that Murata is in that area and we think is responsible for taking out all telephone communication links," informed Jackson. "Tolman, get onto Plymouth and get them to send what armed officers they've got available out to Yealmstoke Head and tell them to try and link up with Mr Ian Vaughan. Got that?"

"Yes sir."

"We also need to know the extent of the communication blackout. Tell them that they need to establish a radio communication link to the site area as a matter of extreme urgency," said Jackson, before turning to another officer and asking, "What's the situation at Portsmouth, Holdsworth?"

"Five of the attackers dead, two wounded and in custody and three trying to get away in a four-by-four that is being chased down by the local armed response team as we speak sir."

"Excellent, keep us posted."

*　　　　*　　　　*

Comrade Namgoong had spent three days trying to plan his attack. Unlike Yealmstoke, the site at Portsmouth had very secure communication links that could not be taken out without first breaching the security fencing. There was also apparent radio linkage to the naval dockyard and the site was far from being an isolated location. His first plan had been to break through at the main gate and rush the main building, but twelve hours later a large contingent of Royal Marines had taken over all guard duties and their first action was to build two strongly defended firing positions protecting the main gate. The next day the roadblocks started to appear, and by the end of day three, access to the site's main gate by road was impossible. The delay in receiving the weapons shipment had been critical.

Namgoong sent two of his group to probe the woodland to the north of the site but without success; from fifty yards away it was obvious that the woods hid a large number of troops. The only vulnerable point was the south-east corner of the site; here there was a crossroads, which, for reasons that Namgoong could not understand, was left open to traffic from south, north and east. Somehow, he concluded, they must break through on that corner, or better still, just to the north of it, the problem was how to do that with only light vehicles.

The solution as to how the fence could be swiftly breached came when Namgoong's second in command, Comrade Kweon, was admiring the view from the burger bar car park opposite a public house. Watching a dredger unload in the harbour, it took only a moment to identify a heavily laden lorry leaving the site and driving north towards the A27-Eastern Road junction.

"Comrade Namgoong, there is our battering ram," said Kweon, handing the binoculars to his leader and pointing. "See the dredger and the lorries loading?"

"Yes Comrade, that is possibility, come, we go closer look."

Twenty minutes later the two were sat on the grass at the junction of Eastern Road with Anchorage Road, with their backs against the support post of a supermarket sign, watching the comings and goings at the aggregate yard.

"Will tomorrow be as hot as today?"

"Is weather important?" asked Kweon.

"Maybe, Comrade. You see all lorries coming out of yard have the driver's window down to cool the cab." He didn't elaborate anymore, leaving Kweon to puzzle over the significance of his statement.

*　　　　　*　　　　　*

At eleven twenty on the morning of the attack, Keith Willett was sat in his cab sipping hot tea he had poured from the flask his partner, Gemma, had stuffed into his holdall, along with a crumpled pasty and a crushed packet of crisps. The cab rocked again, spilling some drops of the tea, as another loader shovel of concreting ballast was dropped into his tipper's thirty cubic metre rear tub. In his newspaper he was reading about a journalist's investigation into the ex-Home Secretary's links with a terrorist gang, who had used his second home as a base. Trust that little bugger Parson to find that patch of dirt to dig in, he thought, the man must get leads from somewhere, no other paper has started on it.

The loader driver signalled that the tub was full, and Keith, tossing the remains of the tea out of the window, screwed the top back on the flask and put it in the bag, before climbing down from the cab to haul the tarpaulin cover over his load and secure it. Back in the cab again, he started the engine and drove off across the yard and out towards the Eastern Road. As the lorry ground its way towards the avenue of poplar trees that screened the yard, Keith saw the traffic lights turn to red, and braked. Resting his elbows on the large steering wheel he only saw a fleeting glimpse of someone darting from amongst the trees on his right towards his cab. Even the gun's flash, imprinted on the retina of his eyes, would not be translated into thought before he died.

Kweon was surprised how much the man he had just shot weighed, as he struggled to push the body across the cab and down into the well in front of the passenger's seat. He had just achieved the manoeuvre before the traffic lights changed and he set the vehicle in motion turning right away from the city. Under the A27 flyover Kweon pointed the lorry in the direction of Drayton, turning left at the T-junction to thunder along the Havant Road into Cosham. By the time he had reached the Cosham roundabout his nerves were beginning to jangle and it was then that he recognised real fear for probably the first time in his life. Concentration was beginning to get difficult and he almost drove straight on, only turning at the last moment, to drive the mammoth vehicle up the

London Road before forking left and up the steep road to the top of Portsdown Hill. Through the fog of his thoughts penetrated the sound of a siren, and looking in the wing mirror, he saw a police car racing up the hill behind him with lights flashing and siren screaming. Kweon reached for his gun and kept the lorry doggedly climbing the hill. The police car swept past, to enter the roundabout at the top of the hill and disappear. Relieved, Kweon checked his wristwatch. He was ahead of schedule by approximately ten minutes. Would the others be ready, he wondered, as he entered the roundabout to take the first exit? Seeing a lay-by on the right-hand side, he pulled over to wait. The area was deserted and he looked curiously at the obviously abandoned buildings on top of the bank to his right. It was Ishihara who had bought the two Izuzu four-by-fours at a second-hand dealers immediately after Iwaki's phone message announcing the operation. As the first one pulled up alongside the lorry, Comrade Li jumped out and climbed into the cab to act as armed support, his feet on the body of the dead Keith Willett.

"Comrade Namgoong behind, we go now."

The large truck lurched forward again, now accelerating as hard as it could to have enough momentum to ram the low but steep bank, take out the fencing and get clear enough to allow the following vehicles to follow through. Clearing the area surrounding the old Fort Southwick the road started a gentle descent towards the crossroads. There were no hedges here and Kweon suddenly felt exposed as the truck charged down the road in a way that would cause alarm to anyone who saw it. Everything now seemed to be going in slow motion, and as the moment came for him to turn the lorry to the right, and aim it at a grey power supply box, he had time to take in every detail of the grass bank, rust-stained fence posts and chain link fencing. The impact with the bank was much harder than either man could have imagined, and its force sent Comrade Li straight through the windscreen, together with most of the torso of Comrade Kweon. Forty-two tonnes of lorry and ballast develops amazing momentum when launched at a static object at sixty miles an hour. Though the bank had ripped off the front wheels and suspension, the truck still continued it's forward motion rearing up into the air and crashing through the fence, carrying the posts and chain link away. The wreck then skidded across the grass for a short distance before it's cab blew to pieces as an anti-tank missile hit it.

The leading four-by-four followed the lorry through the gap but was immediately caught in withering machine gun fire from a well camouflaged position to its right, which killed the driver outright, causing the vehicle to crash into the back of the truck. Namgoong's driver, witnessing the devastation in front of them, braked hard bringing his vehicle to a standstill with its bonnet just into the gap. The man, with an expression of absolute terror on his face, turned to Namgoong.

"Why do you stop!" shouted Namgoong.

"We cannot continue the attack with just three men Comrade leader; and you are too important to die here," said Comrade Sergeant Chang, the man especially selected to act as bodyguard to the General's son. "They knew how we would attack Comrade; with one hundred men we may have succeeded, but not this small force."

"How can I return, having failed the party and my father, tell me, how dare I return home."

Namgoong had not expected the blow that sent him unconscious across the seat.

"Drive that way," shouted Chang. "Hurry, they will be here any second."

The driver needed no second bidding, and reversing back onto the lane launched the four-by-four off towards Southwick in the hope of hiding among the maze of lanes that formed a web between Portsmouth and Alton.

*　　　　*　　　　*

Major Henry Neville and Staff Sergeant Smethurst's assessment and deployment expertise had been learnt in the cruel classroom of Afghanistan. It was they who had organised the road barriers, defended main gate positions and sited the camouflaged heavy machine gun position that covered both north-east and the vulnerable south-east corners of the site.

"Do you think we have covered all of the options, Staff?" asked Major Neville. "The woods at the back we've got men in, moving about enough to put anyone off and the zigzag road block down the hill is well covered. Captain Langley knows what he's up to."

"May I suggest sir, that we place the Javelin antitank just out of sight below the rim of the bank on the south-east corner of the building, just in case they try to smash their way through with something big and fast," Staff Sergeant Smethurst said, casually.

"Good God, did we bring one?" replied the Major.

"I thought it might come in handy sir."

Neville had looked at his Staff Sergeant and shook his head. "Good idea Staff, as you say, just in case they go for the spectacular."

Neville and his Staff Sergeant had established lookout positions on the south-east and south-west corners of the building's first floor that gave them commanding views of the approach roads and at least eighty percent of their defence positions.

It was the Major who had recognised that the lorry hurtling down the slope towards the crossroads was a real threat.

"Javelin, load and prepare to fire, potential attack at south-east corner. Eyes wide open everybody, they could be coming from more than one direction."

"Javelin loaded," came back the acknowledgement.

"HMG take sight to south-east corner and be ready to engage."

"HMG ready sir."

As the large truck burst through the fence sending concrete fragments and chalky soil in all directions, the Major ordered 'fire at will' and watched as the Javelin's missile flew rapidly and directly at its target to devastate it in a blinding flash followed by a ball of flame. Fascinated he watched as the truck's tub appeared through the flames to gouge a deep rut across the grass before being brought to a halt after some fifty yards.

The deep and rapid thud-thud-thud of the heavy machine gun indicated that there had been a pursuing force. Marines with L85A2 rifles moved from their position behind the Javelin team and made their way round the wreckage of the truck. As they approached the crashed four-by-four the Marine line on the northern side saw the second four-by-four drive off and opened fire, but without success. Those on the southern side found the two injured survivors of the first four-by-four and took them prisoner.

To avoid risk of friendly fire, the two police armed response vehicles and teams were parked up away from the site, to act as chase vehicles in the event of any escaping attackers.

At his control point, Major Neville picked up his radio again. "Cease fire. Chase teams, a second silver four-by-four is trying to make its escape in the direction of Southwick, all yours gentlemen."

*　　　　*　　　　*

At Yealmstoke Head a sergeant was instructing his new recruits in the art of building two sandbag defence positions to cover the main gate. An L7A2 general-purpose machine gun, minus ammunition, lay on the ground alongside each position. The remoteness of the site had caused some delay in establishing perimeter security. Few of the recruits had experienced tented accommodation before and the site director had been decidedly 'sniffy' about the soldiers using the offices' toilet facilities. The defence work completed to 'manual specification' the sergeant begrudgingly admitted that 'it would have to do for now' before ordering the men to get cleaned up and getting the staff sergeant to issue the ammunition belts.

About to sneak behind the gate reception building for a quiet cigarette the sergeant was hailed by Julia Fanshaw, head of the site's HR department.

"Excuse me, to save me going all the way to the Lieutenant's tent, can you tell him that we have received a warning from Whitehall to say that security has now been upped to Amber level."

"Certainly madam, anything else?"

"Oh, just that, as an exercise, we are reducing our staff on site to match that security alert level. You know, er, non-essential people. I of course will have to stay."

"Of course madam," replied the sergeant, instantly recognising the bureaucratic self-importance of an empire builder.

Having delegated the task, Julia Fanshaw returned to her desk to complete her draft of the advertisement for a second assistant.

It was as the sergeant entered Lieutenant Lyon's tent that the Royal Mail van pulled up at the barrier. Jumping down from the cab, the driver waved to the young soldier on guard and headed straight towards the door of the reception building. Inside, Shirley Withers looked up from her magazine. "Yes luv?" she said, not sure whether it was Lee or Chang she was looking at.

Comrade Seon gave a false mighty sneeze, and covering half his face with a handkerchief, blew loudly into it, whilst groping with his left hand in his trouser pocket for the site pass.

Withers, due to go on holiday to Mexico in two days' time, did not want her sunbathing and poolside tequilas spoilt by a cold. "Lee init?" she said. Seon nodded, then sneezed again. "'Ere yer are luv, 'and it in at the gate," said Withers, holding a red visitor's badge out at arm's length.

Audrey, returning from the washroom, saw the back of Seon as he hurried out of the door. "Which one was that?" she queried.

"Lee, love, 'ad an awful cold. I don't want none of that to take on 'oliday."

Seon hurried from the building and across the road to the van to find the young soldier beckoning towards the rear loading shutter.

"Open this up mate, I gotta look inside."

"Van full mail bag," Seon replied. "They all fall out."

"Just up it a bit, so I can see."

Seon unlocked the shutter and raised it to expose a layer and a half of mailbags.

"Okay mate," the soldier said, no longer interested. "I'll do the barrier for yer."

Shutter closed and back in the driver's seat Seon crunched the van into first gear and drove it around the perimeter road to the side road leading to the post room entrance at the east side of the building under the watchful eye of Comrade Byoun, perched high in the oak tree.

Comrade Seon was still amazed at the ease with which he had gained entry to the site as he raised the side shutter of the van and threw the few mailbags blocking the doorway to the ground. Silently his team jumped out and followed him through the unlocked side door straight towards the post room where Patsy Smith sat checking a mail rate for a package to America.

"Who are you?" she demanded to know. "I haven't seen you before, you got a pass?"

Seon pointed to his red visitor's badge.

"Well I haven't got much for you, you're a lot earlier than normal. Hang on I'll just tie up the bag, and there's a special to sign for."

Standing, she moved towards a frame with grey mailbags hanging on hooks from it, and turned her back on him. The blow with the pistol butt cracked her skull and rendered her unconscious, but had not killed her. Bending down Seon turned her body over and removed the pass swipe card from the plastic holder attached to the ribbon around her neck. The card he now had gave access to all sections of the building. In his haste Seon forgot to check whether Patsy was indeed dead.

Using Patsy Smith's pass Comrade Seon opened the coded doors to the corridors either side of the post room and disabled the electromagnetic activators in the head of each doorframe. Leaving Iwaki, and with the corporal and a private to clear Level 'B', Seon and Kimura rushed up the emergency stairs to Level 'D', and using the swipe pass again started to drive shocked and terrified staff in front of them towards the central link staircase and restaurant. As expected no one offered any resistance in the face of the heavily armed men, and the clearance of the three general offices on that level was quickly achieved. It was as they checked the meeting rooms and smaller offices close to the lifts and main stairwell that Kimura noticed the door sign 'Directorate Offices'. Instructing Seon to complete the shepherding alone, Kimura entered the outer office, which he found to be deserted. The locked door beyond offered little resistance to his four hard kicks and when it burst open he saw Lambert crouched in the corner quaking with fear; hauling the man to his feet Kimura studied Lambert's ID badge.

"You Director, you come with me."

Kimura, with his prize hostage, reached the head of the stairs as Murata was herding the last of the Level 'A' personnel through to Dho.

"Murata-san. This man Director. Senior man here."

"Ah so, maybe he know where Nihon-jin team is hiding. I will take him in here, you get Comrade Dho for me, then help Comrade Seon control people until Iwaki joins you."

As Murata roughly pushed Lambert into the Human Resources Meeting Room 2, Kimura stood aside to shepherd those from Level 'B' in the right direction. When all hostages from inside the main building were held in the restaurant, Iwaki and the two Korean soldiers left to bring in building workers, and deal with any military personnel not neutralised by Comrade Byoun. All three men were glad to get away from the screaming women who, with the male staff, filled almost every space within the restaurant.

Hamaura, standing guard at the main entrance, his back to the glass doors, did not see the small van pull up in the field entrance half a mile away and two people get out. Emboldened by the sight of the frightened women and impotent men being herded past him, Hamaura's earlier fears had left him, and he now strutted arrogantly backwards and forwards confident of success.

Vaughan and Morohashi's arrival was also missed by Comrade Byoun who was absorbed in the business of taking out one after another of the raw recruits guarding the site perimeter. The gate guard who had inspected the post van had been easy, as was the second man at the gatehouse. The woman too was a simple shot but her scream had alerted the guard nearest to him who had instantly dropped flat on the ground behind some long grass. Patiently Byoun had waited for the man to move, to be rewarded half a minute later as the young soldier rose on one knee and started to scan his surroundings sighting along his rifle. Smiling to himself, Byoun waited until the youngster had pivoted round, to be sighting straight at him before pulling the trigger and watching the soldier's head jerk back from the impact of the bullet and his body collapse in a heap on the ground.

That was when things started to become more difficult. Ideally snipers move after each shot in order not to give away their position. Byoun, however, was stationed up in a tree and though partially hidden by the trunk was in a location that could be generally identified. The two guards patrolling the rear fence line, on hearing the last two shots now had some idea as to the source and were peppering the tree with bullets. Moving alternately, each under covering fire of the other, they reached the side fence nearest to Byoun's tree; here they lay hidden by long grass, presenting no target for him.

The two young soldiers were sadly unaware of Iwaki looking out of the widow above and behind them. The breaking glass had both recruits turning enquiringly, only to be hit by a hail of bullets from Iwaki's automatic carbine.

* * *

Ian Vaughan had been sufficiently convinced of Murata's target to drive straight to Yealmstoke Head. Cresting the rise above the site, Ian stopped his van at the field entrance Comrade Dho had used previously for reconnaissance. As he got out of the van he clearly heard the third shot from Byoun's position. Raising his binoculars he saw immediately the mail van parked by the building's side door. As he watched he saw the young soldier come onto one knee and start searching for the attackers. Instantly the young man was thrown back, Ian swung to the right, searching for where the shot could have come from, but was then distracted by the cover fire from the two soldiers, as they used each other's covering fire for both men to reach the perimeter fence. At first he thought their fire was wild and random, but hearing the clatter as branches and foliage were constantly hit, his attention focused on the tree. A movement to the right of the trunk confirmed that a sniper was hidden there.

"Umeko-san, Murata's put a sniper up in that tree over there. Apart from killing the guards around the fence he is distracting those that are left from the real attack that is going on inside the building."

"What can we do?"

"Try and take him out for a start," replied Ian. "Are you armed?"

"No, it is back in the hotel," she looked sheepishly at him. "Well I am not supposed to carry a gun in your country, according to Commander Campbell."

"That didn't stop you waving one about when you were on my boat," Ian replied with some venom. "Well, come on, we shall have to win one for you."

Using the roadside hedge for cover, Ian, followed by Morohashi, started a crouching run down to where the road turned to the left almost level with the oak tree. Then the rapid fire from Iwaki's weapon rang out and had both of them ducking for deeper cover.

"I think that's our two soldiers taken out, I wonder how many are left. Jesus, what a mess," said Ian quietly.

Morohashi looked at him frowning. "Maybe it is their fire."

"No, different sound, different weapon."

Taking care to stay low and out of sight of both tree and building, they crossed the road and peered through the hedge towards the tree.

"I'm going to try and get closer," said Ian. "I couldn't hit a barn door at this range."

"No, wait for backup."

"The charge of the cavalry will get so much attention that a mouse wouldn't be able to get close to that tree. Look at the field of fire the top floor of that building's got. No one will have a chance of getting close until they run out of ammunition, and I bet that won't be for several hours yet, plus they've got hostages."

Finding a small gap in the hedge, Ian slithered through, cautiously travelling diagonally to avoid his path being picked up either by those in the building or the sniper in the tree. His aim was to get between the tree and the south-east corner of the perimeter fence; guessing that the sniper, now out of targets, would give up his position and join the main force by the shortest route.

A few minutes had passed since Ian had left her, and Morohashi, crouched perfectly still, watched the tree almost unblinkingly. A movement amongst the branches, then two legs dangled from the lowest branch and a man dropped down to the ground to begin a low run across the field in the direction where she guessed Ian had reached. Her heart was in her mouth and she almost shouted a warning, stifling the cry with her fist as she had taken in breath. Slowly she rose, cautiously watching the man's loping run through the corn, his eyes apparently fixed upon the building and site rather than the field itself. Suddenly two rapid shots rang out and the man dropped like a stone to the ground, without even a cry. She waited, hardly daring to breathe, wondering whether Ian had hit the man and killed him, or whether the man had just gone to ground, to remain a deadly threat.

As if to emphasise the danger, the lockdown alarm inside the building started, triggered by the pretty Patsy Smith, who, barely conscious, had made it her final act. In doing so, she had put in motion two security measures; the first being to lock all external doors, immediately they came to the closed position, whilst simultaneously transmitting a signal, similar to that of a distress beacon, on the police band, informing Plymouth Central and the Devon police headquarters at Exeter that Yealmstoke Head was under 'Status Red' alert, meaning that they were under attack from an enemy.

Ian had not quite reached the spot he was aiming for when he heard the harsh rustle of his quarry coming through the corn to cross his track some way in front of him. Drawing his knees up under him he waited for a few seconds before raising his head and arms with gun held firm in both hands, to find that it was pointing exactly at his target. He fired two shots rapidly, both he saw striking his victim. He heard the body hit the ground, as he crouched again for total cover. Quickly now he worked his way towards the sniper, fearful that the man was still alive. The body was in a sparsely seeded patch of corn, and Ian, from the relative safety of denser growth, could make out the man's lifeless stare and empty hands. Still keeping his gun pointed at the target, Ian slithered forward and turned the body over revealing a Beretta M9 in a belt holster. Checking through the satchel the man had over his shoulders, Ian found shells for the sniper rifle, lost in amongst the corn as the man fell, and six spare full clips of ammunition for the Beretta. Removing the satchel Ian retraced his path to find an anxious Morohashi waiting for him at the roadside.

"He's dead," informed Ian. "Here's the pistol he had on him and there is plenty of spare ammunition in there," he continued, handing her the shoulder bag.

Taking the pistol she held it in her open hand, assessing its weight and balance professionally.

"This is American armed forces issue," she said, pointing to a stamp on the pistol butt.

"Yes. Now let's get across the road and through that hedge, then we can make our way down towards the gatehouse; using that for cover we should be able to get across the road and onto the site."

"Then what do we do, charge across the car park like Butch Cassidy and the Sundance Kid shooting in all directions hoping to arrive the other side alive?" Morohashi asked frowning angrily at him. "Didn't you hear Campbell's instructions to wait for backup?"

"Yes I did Butch, but you see I think I know a way for the backup to actually get inside the building without Murata's bunch knowing."

She glared at him. "Huh, Butch," she said, and then punched him on the arm. "Say you are sorry."

"I'm sorry Umeko-san, you are not in the least butch. Now can we get on with it?"

"Just to the gatehouse," she replied.

It was several minutes before they reached the fence protecting the gatehouse part of the perimeter. Ian pulled from his pocket a multi-bladed Leatherman he had brought from his van. Using the screwdriver blade, he opened the bottom loop of a chain link strand and unhooked it from the lower straining wire, then started to unthread the strand for the first three feet. Pushing apart the fence either side he said, "Through you go, make for the door near the corner. If it is unlocked we will be able to get into the reception area."

Moments later he was also through the fence and standing alongside her at the door. Carefully he tried the door handle, to find it was unlocked, and putting a finger to his lips, gently opened the door and went into the gatehouse kitchen and rest area.

"What do we do?" he heard a frightened Shirley Withers say. "Can't phone anybody, Averill leavin' 'er phone off the 'ook, means my line is blocked. All I can 'ear is the alarm an' lot of shoutin' an' screamin' goin' on." Neither woman seemed to be aware of the two dead soldiers lying on the ground just outside.

As Ian approached the doorway to the reception area he saw Withers get to her feet and look out of the window towards the main building. "'Ere, look at that lazy bleedin' Dave sat over there. Some bloody guard 'e is. Knock on the winda an' wake the idle sod up."

"You'll have a job," said Ian, now standing in the doorway. "He and his mate are both dead."

"Shit, where did you come from? Oh it's you," Withers said, staggering in shock at his sudden appearance and holding onto the back of Audrey's chair for support.

"The site is under attack by terrorists, they came in the mail van you let through. Well done."

"It was Lee drivin' the van, 'ow was I to know that 'e is a terrorist?"

"You couldn't tell Lee from Chairman Mao. Come on, we have got to get you to safety, come this way." Withers went to protest. "Now, before the real shooting starts."

Meekly both women followed Ian out to where Morohashi was waiting. "We have made a gap in the fence that you will be able to crawl through. When you are out cross the road and go through that gap in the hedge, then, keeping out of sight, make your way down to the cliff top and wait there. We will send as many others as we can down to you. It is essential that you stay there, otherwise when this is over we will have to waste time searching for you when there will be better things to do, understand?

"You can't go givin' me orders like that," said Withers.

"Alright then, walk over to the main building and get shot, it's your choice."

“Come on Shirl, do as he says, please, I’m frightened enough as it is,” said Audrey, pulling at Withers’ arm.

Reluctantly they turned away and, with the assistance of Morohashi, both women got through the fence, across the road, and into the opposite field before heading off towards the cliffs.

“I’m going over to the contractor’s offices to see who is on site.”

“What do I do?” Morohashi asked.

“If anyone is lucky enough to make it to here, see them out and down to the cliffs. Keep an eye on the back door, if there are any of the contractor’s men about I’ll get them across to you.”

Leaving by the back door Ian used the cover of brick stacks and machinery to get him as far as Jack Craine’s office undetected; it was empty. The ground across to his old office was very exposed to those looking out of the main building, but he could see through its window that it also had no one in it. Slipping back out of Craine’s office Vaughan used the cover of a car, then a pile of reinforcement rods, to get him to a point where he was out of view of the main building. Peering round the end of the steel rods he carefully studied the partially built extension and was about to make a run towards it when a procession of men crossed a window opening, all with their hands on their heads.

Ian waited until they and their two armed captors had gone out of sight, and then sprinted across the open ground to a point where the external wall was only a few brick courses high. Snatching a quick glance inside, and noting that the room on that corner was empty, Ian stepped over the wall and hurried to the doorway opposite that opened into the spine corridor. Another quick glance revealed two things: the first was that the corridor was empty and the second was that the extension works had not progressed far enough for the breakthrough into the main building to be done. Unless the prisoners were going to be marched along outside, and the main building lockdown security breached, they would have to be held in the extension under guard. He had just processed these thoughts when he heard the sound of someone running down the corridor towards him. Moving across to that side of the doorway the person was approaching, he held his breath and waited.

The little Korean private was confident that he had left no one behind when he and the corporal had cleared that section of the site, therefore he walked without hesitation through the door opening, to be struck hard on the right temple by the butt of Ian's pistol. Ian caught the body before it hit the ground and, removing the private's commando knife, slit his throat, in case the earlier blow had not killed the man.

Two down, he thought, as he disarmed the soldier, noting the US forces' issue carbine rifle.

Guessing that he had a few minutes to work out the next move, he sat trying to remember the detailed layout of the ground floor. There was another large office space to the left of the corridor, with a fire exit door to the outside world. On the right he recalled there being two rooms neither with access out of the building. The hostages must be in one of those for the soldier to use the route he did rather than get out via the fire exit door. Ian stuffed his pistol back in his pocket holster, picked up the carbine, and cautiously crept along the corridor to the first doorway on the right, and listened intently.

"The little bastard's scared," Ian overheard a man saying. "Look at 'im there by the door almost shittin' himself."

"Shut up 'Arry or you'll get the lot of us shot, the little bugger's bloody nervous enough," another voice in the room said.

Ian studied the wall by the door opening and noted that at about chest height a square chase had been cut out of the fly ash blockwork, for the installation of a swipe card unit, reducing the thickness of that portion of wall to about 60 millimetres. Fly ash bock that thin would not stop a bullet, but was the terrorist that close to the doorway? There was only one way to find out, and that was by firing the carbine into the square chasing. Edging along, his back to the opposite wall, Ian looked down at the floor inside the room, searching for a shadow that could reveal the Korean's position; nothing. Slowly he tilted his head to gain a better view into the room itself, and saw the raised arm of a hostage standing over by the window. Then there was a scuffing sound, as the terrorist the other side of the wall adjusted his position, and Ian saw the tip of a carbine barrel appear around the blockwork edge to the opening.

Placing the tip of his carbine's barrel into the box out Ian squeezed the trigger. The sound of the shot was deafening in the confines of the corridor, and was immediately followed by a cry of pain. Ian rushed to the opening to see the Korean partially blinded by the cloud of fly ash particles and with half his left shoulder torn and bleeding. The second shot hit him in the chest, throwing him backwards across the room to the total shock of the men stood watching, terrified by the killing.

"Shut up and don't make any further noise," said Ian, trying to muster as much command into his voice as he could. "I am going to lead you out of here, but you must do exactly as I tell you or you will all be dead."

"What the fuck's goin' on mate?" asked a tall tough-looking man Ian recognised as being one of the bricklaying gang.

"The site's been attacked by terrorists, so shut up and do as I tell you."

"'Ow do we know you're not one of 'em?" asked the steel fixers labourer.

"Because if 'e was you'd be dead by now you daisy. Shut up and let's get out of 'ere before someone comes to find out wot the shootin' was abou' right?" said the bricklayer fiercely.

Shocked by what they had witnessed and the sight of the other dead terrorist the men made their way to the point at which Ian had entered the building, and one by one set off along the route to the gatehouse. The last man to go was an electrician that Ian recognised, who had been caught up with the group when the corporal had cleared the extension's first floor.

"Barry Bailiff isn't it?"

"Yeah, I remember you now. Weren't you here for a short time doing Mr Chater's job?"

"Yes, that's right. Look I don't have time to explain the ins and outs, can you tell me if the two roofs have been opened through?"

"What, you mean, can you get from the extension into the main building's roof?"

"Yes exactly that."

"No, not yet, unless you rip off a few roof tiles," said Bailiff.

"Any tools left up on the first floor?"

"Yeah, all mine for a start."

"Right, thanks Barry, careful how you go along to the cliff top, keep your head well down and when you get there make absolutely sure that everyone stays there and does not wander off. We will need to do a body count at the end of this."

Ian watched Bailiff as he crawled behind the stack of reinforcement and disappeared. Not all the building site workers were as lucky, the rest having been rounded up before the lockdown button had been pushed, and forced to join the office staff, held hostage in the first floor restaurant above the foyer. Ian wondered how the cavalry was going to deal with things when they arrived, it would be unlikely that they would try to storm the building with so many hostages held there. He was about to dash across the open ground to the escape route when the sound of someone running down the west side of the building had him retreating hurriedly into the corridor. To turn left would take him back to the room where the hostages had been, opposite the one with the fire exit door; turning right meant being trapped in a dead end, but a place that had a stack of bags containing wall plaster. A crunch of boot on builder's debris from the fire exit room had Ian moving as quietly as he could to take up a position behind the bags.

A second set of running feet was heard, then the more distinct sound of men moving around appeared to echo loud in the unfinished structure. Ian thought carefully about how he was to deal with two enemies working together. Obviously he would have to remain concealed until both were in the corridor. Laying the carbine on the ground, he flexed his fingers and rotated his shoulders to try and relax and calm himself. What was it he had been taught? Ah yes, slow the breathing rate.

It seemed as if hours were slipping past but it was no more than a minute before a hand holding a pistol followed by the head of a lieutenant with obvious European features appeared around the door opening. Believing the corridor to be clear the lieutenant stepped fully across it and stole a look into the room where the Korean corporal's body lay.

"Sergeant, have a look at this, one of them has been shot."

The sergeant appeared in the corridor and Ian stood up saying, "It's alright Lieutenant I'm a member of the CTC." The officer swiftly raised the pistol, and took aim.

"Put that gun down and come here, slowly."

Ian complied and moved out from behind the plaster bags. "I am reaching into my pocket for my identity badge," said Ian, as he walked forward. "The terrorist gang that have so far shot five of your men, to my knowledge, are from Korea and Japan. They are here to destroy some secret work that has been done on this site. They are very thorough, determined and very well trained, so are very dangerous. They also have a large number of hostages held in the main building, whose lives will mean nothing to them."

By now Ian had reached the sergeant who studied his badge. "He is who he says he is Lieutenant."

The lieutenant breathed a sigh of relief. "Five of my men dead you say?"

"How many does that leave?" asked Ian.

"Just us and one other, we left him to guard the weapons truck whilst we checked on the rest. We know there are eight off duty down at the beach and that the cooks and seven others were in the main building, unarmed, when it all started. We found Staff Sergeant Mantell garrotted alongside the weapons truck, that's what alerted us," the lieutenant replied. "I'm Lieutenant Lyons, by the way."

"Hi, my name is Ian. Were weapons taken from the truck?"

"Did you look Sergeant?"

"Yes sir, a few were gone, probably all that one or two men could handle, together with ammunition."

"Sergeant I want you to go down to the beach and bring your lads back," instructed Ian. "Then I want you to retrieve the two machine guns I saw alongside the sandbag positions at the gate and relocate one protecting the freed group on the cliff edge over there and the other one at the north-east corner using the banking just outside the fence as protection."

"Lieutenant Lyons, you come with me, we are going into the main building through the roof."

Neither man questioned Ian's apparent authority, and after showing the sergeant the safe route out to the gatehouse, he and the lieutenant hurried up to the first floor, collected some tools, and using a ladder, climbed into the roof space. As Barry Bailiff had explained, the connection to the main roof had not been made and a tarpaulin had been used to protect the interior of the extension from the weather. Ian slit the cover and studied the main roof trying to remember where the internal walkway was that gave access to all the air conditioning ducting and lighting.

Taking the nail bar he had picked up from the floor below, Ian stretched across and levered up half a dozen of the roof tiles, placing them down in the gutter. Next he levered up two rows of the exposed tile battens then reached back for the lieutenant to pass him a saw. Cutting away the battens, felt and insulation a hole between the rafters was formed, and both men squeezed through to crouch precariously on ceiling joists.

"Sorry I missed," Ian whispered, "The access walkway is along this way, don't fall through between the joists."

Light from the hole gave just enough illumination for Ian to pick out where the section light switch was and soon they were tiptoeing carefully along the walkway towards the roof access stairway.

"Where are Japanese staff?" demanded someone loudly in a room below them and to the right.

"They are not here today, they left last night to go somewhere else," a frightened man's voice replied.

"You lie, they hiding here!" yelled another man.

Ian and Lyons heard a loud slap and a whimper. "They are not; I keep telling you, they were taken away by coach yesterday afternoon around four o'clock. I was not told where they were going."

"Why you, Site Director, not told such simple thing?" the first voice asked, more quietly. Then there was a pistol shot followed by a long scream. "I will shoot other foot, then hands, then knees, until I get truth."

“I am telling you the truth,” sobbed Lambert. “I can only guess that they were taken to Cheltenham GCHQ, but I was in a meeting when it all happened and I have not been told the details.”

Just then the thrumming of a Chinook helicopter blades could be heard in the distance. Ian looked at Lyons and pointed up. The lieutenant nodded his understanding.

“Why you look up so much in hope?” asked the first voice. “Ah, you hear helicopter and think you will be saved.” Then shouting, he said, “Nothing will save you, nothing, unless we hear truth!”

“Where were they working?” asked the second man.

“Room B10,” replied Lambert instantly, not wanting further torture. “But it will…” A blow that obviously rendered him unconscious cut off his voice.

“He was about to tell us more,” said the first man.

“We search room for computers and hard disks,” replied the second.

Ian and Lyons heard a door open and the first voice shout instructions to someone below in the foyer.

Chapter 16

In the gatehouse Morohashi was curious and angry that Ian had not returned with the sergeant. Pacing backwards and forwards she was considering the benefits and risks of entering the buildings herself, then she heard the rattle of the fencing as the sergeant and his men returned.

"Excuse me miss, but I think it will be better if you stand out the back here while we try and retrieve the machine guns," said the sergeant. "If they see us from the top floor there, they will probably start shooting, and we don't want you hurt now do we?"

Reluctantly Morohashi allowed herself to be guided out to where the group of nervous youngsters stood dressed in just their light camouflage overalls.

"No body armour?" she asked.

"Too risky to get it miss, they would have to cross a lot of open ground, and tents are no defence against bullets, even if they got there." Morohashi nodded. "That's why I'm going to do the deed miss. I wish we had that carbine your colleague was carrying."

"This of any use?" asked Morohashi, offering the M9 to the sergeant.

"No miss, it hasn't the range."

After checking the available cover from both the north-east and south-west corners of the gatehouse, the sergeant chose the lower ground and the greater screening of the car park's low surrounding hedge at the south-west; still, he was forced to lay flat and squirm his way along using his elbows for leverage. By making his way towards the furthest firing position first, it allowed him to get halfway across to the other position before a gap in the hedge exposed him to any watchers in the main building. Now, with the first weapon in his grasp he prepared himself for the sprint, pick-up, and return muttering, "As a basic training sergeant, I shouldn't be doing this."

It was then that they heard the sound of the approaching Chinook and all eyes turned to search the eastern sky.

“’Ow’s ’e doin’? Oy Craig, I said ’ow’s ’e doin’?” asked a muscular aggressive looking private, pointing in the direction of the sergeant.

Craig was about to put his head round the corner of the building when his arm was grabbed and he was pulled back.

Morohashi glared at him. “If you were seen, two things could have happened, either you would have been shot or you would have given away the fact that someone was out there. If you want to look do it from the reception door, all the windows and the door in there are darkened glass, so unless you get too close they will not be able to see you.”

“Oh, right, er thanks,” a surprised Craig replied, flexing his arm to relieve the effects of the surprisingly strong grip that had been placed on it. Before the lad could move the sound of the sergeant sprinting back towards them could be heard, followed almost instantly by the sound of rapid carbine fire and breaking glass. A cry rang out, telling them that the sergeant had been hit, but he was still running, and to everyone’s relief skidded round the corner of the building, blood pumping from a wound just above his right elbow.

As Private Craig Amos took the weapons from him, the sergeant said, “I want two volunteers to sneak their way across to the weapons truck and bring back four belts of ammunition. You’ll find Private Pearce on guard there so announce yourselves first. Then I want four others to go to the far side of that field and flag down that Chinook, it appears that backup has arrived. Pick a level spot for them, don’t make it difficult, understood?”

* * *

“Has anyone heard from DI Carter?” asked Campbell.

“Yes, sir,” replied Jackson. “He got straight into interviewing this, er, Michelle Goodwin, and it appears she gave him information regarding a Mr Naraiman, who owned the power boat she was ordered to rendezvous with. She thought that the landing point for the gang was Slapton Sands by Torcross, sir. Plymouth have wanted to nail this guy with something for years, but they've never had enough to even pay him a visit, apparently."

"What were their concerns?" asked Campbell.

"Drug trafficking mainly, and prostitution, but there have also been hints of arms passing through his hands. I would have thought that there was enough there to knock on the door, but apparently the local Chief Super doesn't."

"Not even close observation?" queried Campbell.

"No, not even that."

"It's a strange name," said Campbell.

"Apparently Afghan, sir."

"And still nobody gave the matter their close attention," responded Campbell, with shocked surprise. "The world's heroine production area, good God, what chance do we have if people can't place simple facts together correctly."

"He runs some very successful legit businesses apparently and supports many good causes, including a drug rehab centre. He's very popular with local angling clubs as well, fishing is apparently one of his passions."

"What's Carter doing now?"

"Last heard was that he and half a dozen of the local force were going to arrest the man."

"I don't want him wasting time doing something that the local force can do just as well. Contact him and tell him he is to meet me at Exeter Airport," said Campbell. "You Inspector, I want to send down to Portsmouth and takeover interrogation there, I will deal with the Yealmstoke situation."

"You'll fly down, sir?" asked Jackson.

"Yes, I'll get Mrs Fitzgerald to arrange for the plane at City. I'll take DC Hutchins with me. You better have some support as well."

"Sir!" a constable called from the far side of the room. "We've just had a report from Exeter that Yealmstoke Head has gone Status Red."

* * *

As Campbell's chartered jet took to the air from London's City Airport, Ian Vaughan was waiting for the Chinook's rotor noise to become loud enough for him to walk out along the roof joists without being heard from below. Some shooting had taken place outside a few minutes earlier, and Ian hoped that Umeko Morohashi was safe and no more army casualties had occurred.

Now with the Chinook sounding as if it were just above the roof, Ian signalled to Lyons that he was going to walk to get above the room where Lambert was being held. Balancing on just one joist, Ian, careful to apply his weight gently, moved away from the walkway until he was level with the sound of raised voices.

After shouting instructions to someone below the man had re-entered the room and was starting to bring Lambert round by slapping his face.

"What else did you want to say about Japanese work area?"

"I don't remember," replied Lambert.

"Where are their computer or the hard drive?"

"The computers will not be of any use to you as the hard drives have been removed."

"Where you keep hard drive?" the second man shouted, following another hard slap.

A gun had obviously been raised threateningly as Lambert cried out. "Don't shoot me again, please. The hard drives should be in a steel cabinet along the end wall."

Ian had reached the joist he could see was nearest to the wall separating the room under him from the one in which Lambert and his interrogators were. Opening a knife from the Leatherman he knelt down on the joists and, reaching down, lightly stabbed a ceiling tile above the interrogators' room, lifting one edge of it gently.

"How is this cabinet secured?" asked the first man.

"A six digit code," answered Lambert, "But I do not remember it and I probably was never told what the code was. You see each code is different and is changed regularly."

"What name of person who know?" demanded the second man.

Ian had now raised the ceiling tile enough to see only Lambert's knees, but both of the man's inquisitors were in full view. The one by the door Ian did not recognise, but the one nearest to him was undoubtedly Tadashi Murata. The harsh bark of the Browning L9 filled the room, and as Ian changed target, he knew the head shot to the man near the door had killed him. Murata's reflexes were still good and Ian's second shot did not kill him but merely wounded the man's right arm. In the split second between the first and second shots, Murata also found time to look up and recognise his attacker, but was unable to raise the wounded arm holding the gun, fast enough to beat the next two bullets that shattered his head.

Lambert's scream could possibly have been heard in London and as his breath ran out he just sat whimpering as the doorknob turned and someone tried to come in. The man had to give a huge shove to push Dho's body clear.

"Hamaura-san!" the man shouted loudly, a moment before another two rapid reports were heard from the Browning leaving him slumped dead against the door. It had been Comrade Seon, the man disguised as a postman.

Ian needed to reposition his knees on the sharp-edged rafters, and as he moved, the ceiling tile slipped from his fingers to fall through the gap down to the floor below where he knew it would give away his position. The shooting had created panic amongst the hostages, whose screams and shouted protests hid the noise that Ian made hurrying back to join Lyons on the walkway.

In the hubbub Ian was also able to direct Lyons to the lift shaft motor room, a concrete structure that offered good protection, which was located beyond a crossroads in the walkway system. "You go to the motor room, if the door is locked shoot it out; they will soon guess where we are anyway," instructed Ian, his mouth close to Lyons' ear to avoid being overheard.

Lyons needed no further bidding and on reaching the motor room and testing the door handle stepped back and fired six bullets into the door around the lock before kicking the door open. Meanwhile Ian had hurried along to the stairway access door, and lifting a nearby walkway floor panel, jammed it under the door handle to delay any attacker.

Suddenly wild firing started from below, lifting and smashing ceiling tiles and walkway panels, silencing the frightened hostages. Then the shooting stopped, Ian thought, for the attackers to assess the effects of their onslaught. He froze, not daring to move and frantically praying that something would distract the gang and allow him to gain the relative safety of the lift motor room.

The chilling silence was then broken by the smashing of glass in the foyer, followed by the crump of a stun grenade, starting off further screams and cries from the hostages. The thudding of boots and shouted orders confirmed the arrival of an Armed Response Team. A second stun grenade lobbed onto the first floor gallery threw ceiling tiles in all directions, causing Ian to cry out as he collapsed dazed by the blast. Only faintly did he hear the shouting of instructions that followed and could only guess that order was being restored. As his brain started to clear, he was vaguely aware of directions being issued to the hostages. Shakily, he got to his feet and was making his way towards the lift motor room when he saw a similarly shaken Lieutenant Lyons, covered in dust, emerge from the room, holding onto the handrails.

As Ian went towards the lieutenant a bright light shone up from the floor below through a large gap in the tiles. "Stand still and put your hands in the air," a very British voice commanded. Ian turned towards the light and raised his hands. "Put the gun down on the floor, slowly," came the second order. Nervously Ian bent and placed the Browning on the walkway, guessing that the torch was clipped to the side of a gun.

A second beam illuminated Lieutenant Lyons, who was also ordered to raise his arms.

"I am Lieutenant Lyons, officer in charge of the detachment guarding this site. Who are you?" replied Lyons, in his best English accent.

"Armed Response Police. Stay where you are."

Minutes passed before the access stairway door was smashed open and two ARP officers started to make their way along the walkway, the leader's gun covering Ian.

"Don't come any further there is a floor panel missing!" warned Ian.

"Step back away from the gun and lay down on the floor with your hands behind your head, now!" shouted the leading officer, carefully negotiating the gap.

Ian complied and, slowly recovering from his dazed state, began to wonder why he had not heard anyone demand that of the remaining terrorists.

"What is your name?"

"Ian Vaughan, CTC. If I am allowed to reach for my badge, I will prove it."

"Slowly does it."

As Ian handed over the badge he heard someone ask who he was. "Ian Vaughan, CTC, so he says," replied the second man in the team, who had reached forward and taken the badge from Ian. "This looks kosher, sir."

"Give them a hand down, they are the ones we were told to look for," said the officer.

On wobbly legs Ian and Lyons descended the stairs and were led from the building where a young tough-looking Inspector stood directing the evacuation of the hostages.

"I'm Inspector Melrose. Can you tell me how many terrorists there were?"

"No," replied Ian. "All I know for sure is that a couple were firing blindly up into the roof space where we were, until you threw in the grenades."

"Just two?"

"I think so. It was hard to tell. There must have been at least one more guarding the hostages."

"That makes three at least, none of whom have been accounted for," said the Inspector. "The staff here told us that three of them had taken some females hostage and had disappeared through the kitchens. I've just heard that they may have got away out across the fields behind, but, just in case. Jacko!" he called, "I want another five men to sweep through the building again, tell them to be very thorough."

Ian looked across the throng walking bewilderedly in groups on the pathway around the car park. Some were crying, a few had sat down with heads in their hands, weeping or just staring blankly at the ground. As he watched he saw Umeko Morohashi making her way hurriedly through the crowd. She was just approaching a tightly knit group of young female staff that appeared to be edging away towards the corner of the building, when suddenly she stopped and went for her gun. A shot rang out and Morohashi was hit and her body thrown backwards into the flowerbed alongside the path. An instant later the group scattered and two men, previously hidden by the girls, raced off towards the cover of a brick stack several yards away. The stutter of two Heckler & Koch MP5s spraying bullets had the freed hostages ducking and cowering in fear. The shots, however, had felled both of the escaping terrorists, only one of whom now showed any signs of movement. Two officers cautiously approached the bodies and on arrival called for the medic to attend.

Before Morohashi's body hit the ground Ian had started to sprint across the flowerbed towards her. "Get a medic here!" he yelled, as he arrived at her side. Crouching down he could see that she had been hit high up near her right shoulder. Turning in the direction of Inspector Melrose, he shouted, "We need a helicopter ambulance here immediately!"

"One is already on its way," Melrose shouted back.

"Who's got a clean shirt on?" Ian asked the people who were now beginning to approach. "I need two, quickly, we must staunch the bleeding."

Gently lifting Morohashi's torso, Ian looked up at the group, and, selecting a middle-aged lady, asked, "Can you give me a hand?"

To his surprise a young girl in the front of the group knelt down and helped to support Morohashi, assisting Ian in removing her light jacket before applying one of the shirts to the gaping exit wound where the bullet had smashed its way out through the shoulder blade.

"Stay with us Umeko-san, stay with us, please don't give up, keep that heart pumping," Ian said quietly into her ear. "Don't give up, don't you ever give up, you hear?" Her eyelids fluttered slightly then she was very still again, her breathing shallow and ragged.

Jackets were being placed for Morohashi to lie back on, and as Ian gently put her down, the girl, ripping open Umeko's blouse, applied the second shirt, and held it firmly in position over the entry wound just below the collarbone.

The sound of more sirens was heard, and realising that he did not know enough to help Umeko anymore asked, "Is there someone with first aid training?" The young girl looked up at him.

"Yes," she said. "Me," and smiled at him, "If they can get her to hospital quickly she stands a chance."

A green-uniformed medic pushed past Ian and immediately started to examine Umeko.

"Look after her for me, there are some things I must do."

Whilst attending to Umeko Ian's brain had been rerunning his first words to Inspector Melrose. Moving through the group crowded around Umeko, he broke into a run and headed towards the two men, surrounded by armed policemen, on the ground near the brick stacks.

"I need to look at both of those guys," Ian said.

"You are, oh yes, you're Mr Vaughan," said a sergeant standing guard over one of the men. "That one is dead sir, this bloke might make it, if he behaves himself. He took two in the legs and one in his left shoulder. You can see where his head hit the kerbstone. Medics not that worried about him."

Ian knelt and turned the dead man onto his back, then moved across and looked at the face of the survivor. "The dead man is called Kimura and that one is Hamaura, both are Japanese and are members of a splinter faction of the Red Brigade," said Ian, getting to his feet. "There is at least one more about here somewhere. One of them is called Iwaki."

An officer kneeling alongside Hamaura was searching the terrorist's pockets. Clips of ammunition, a pad and pencil and a broken comb were taken out and placed in a plastic bag. The officer looked through Hamaura's wallet and removed a photograph of a very beautiful woman.

"That's his elder sister," informed Ian. "She was killed some weeks ago, in America on the 3rd of July."

*   *   *

Knowing that the corporal and another of Dho's men were searching the new extension to the building, Hamaura was not concerned by the shots heard from that direction as he stood alone on guard in the foyer. When the sound of rapid fire from the first floor was heard he had turned hurriedly and then laughed at seeing the sergeant retreating hastily behind the gatehouse, unaware that the man had successfully recovered some powerful weapons.

The subsequent shot from the first floor had Hamaura cautiously moving towards the stairwell, carbine raised. A continuation of the shouted inquisition calmed him again and when Murata-san ordered him to search room B10 he had hurried to comply, inwardly praying to be the man to find the all-important disks. Convinced of their success, and buoyed by the task he had been given, he paid hardly any attention when the four shots were fired, believing them to come from Murata's gun. Comrade Seon's shouted summons though, followed instantly by two further gunshots, had a highly alert Hamaura emerging from room B10, to make his way cautiously back towards the stairwell. Loud screams were coming from the restaurant and he could just hear Iwaki and Kimura shouting over the noise for everyone to be quiet.

The sight of Seon's body against the door had Hamaura nervously sliding his back along the opposite wall, eyes fixed unblinkingly on the doorway. On seeing Lambert he thought the man was either dead or in a faint, but it was the sight of Murata, laying in a pool of blood, that had Hamaura crossing the corridor and charging through the doorway, gun pointed towards the blind corner. When he saw that no one was there he spun round fearing an enemy behind him, to have his gun barrel gripped tightly by Kimura looking fiercely at him with a finger to his lips demanding silence.

It was Kimura who, after a brief study of the room, pointed first to the ceiling tile on the floor and then up towards the ceiling at the instant Lyons shot out the lock to the lift motor room. Without a fixed target the two terrorists could only fire blindly in the hope of inflicting casualties, stopping as their ammunition clips emptied. Then the sound of breaking glass and the blast of the first stun grenade had both men crouching on the floor.

Hamaura, jamming a second magazine into his gun was about to charge down the stairs to fire at this new threat when Kimura grabbed him and dragged him along the corridor to Iwaki's position, guarding the hostages.

The offset of the restaurant doors from the main corridor wall line meant that the effects of the stun grenades had little impact upon those held there, or their captors. It was Iwaki who grabbed the first young woman and, holding a pistol to her head, moved with her into the midst of the hostage group. Kimura had followed suit and with a nod of his head indicated that Hamaura should do the same; by the time the armed response officers had arrived at the top of the stairs the three terrorists had passed through the now truly traumatised group and out through the kitchens still holding the women. Ignoring the service lift, Iwaki had led them down the neighbouring stairway that came out in a corridor, which ran from the rear service entrance through to the spine corridor at Level 'A' close to the foyer.

Signalling to the other two to stay, Iwaki had dragged his hostage along to the rear door, which stood open, having been used when the gang were rounding up the nearby building workers. Carefully looking around, Iwaki, to Hamaura's surprise, had turned back and went instead along to the spine corridor. Iwaki had guessed correctly that the rooms on that level had already been searched and the police redeployed.

"Iwaki-san," he had asked in a loud whisper. "Why not go that way?" pointing towards the rear doors.

"No cover, only open field, they will see us and trail us until we are forced to give up," Iwaki had replied. What he did not say was that he had also seen the army sergeant and some men setting up a machine gun position, which ruled out the prospect of releasing the female hostages, who would hold them back, preventing the use of pure speed to reach the next field's hedge undetected.

Slowly pushing open the door to the corridor, Iwaki had looked in both directions, and finding that all was clear had waved the others past him pointing for them to go to the right. The three, and their terrified hostages, had moved along the corridor away from the foyer, through the first set of fire doors, then going into a front office on their left, where each man found a work station to hide beneath. They didn't have to wait long before those released from the restaurant started to pass by along the pavement surrounding the car park, on their way to the gatehouse area, away from the main building. Behind him in the corridor Hamaura had heard a shout as the searching Response Team, distracted by the open rear door, had, to a man, rushed down the corridor and out searching for their quarry towards the field outside of the fence.

Pushing his hostage in front of him Iwaki had gone to the fire exit door in the office and opened it, keeping hidden behind her. Quickly both Kimura and Hamaura had followed suit. Slipping out of the half open door onto the inner path near to the building, and using the girls as a shield, Iwaki had started to lead them towards the corner of the main building. There, further stacks of materials for the extension would cover their escape towards the cliff top and possible freedom.

The ploy had only worked for a short distance when a woman had spotted them. It was Iwaki who had shot her, then apparently disappeared, leaving his hostage with Kimura and Hamaura. Neither of them had reacted as quickly, or seen Iwaki's subsequent move, and chose to make a run across to the brick stacks, exposing themselves to gunfire as they neared their goal.

Aware he was wounded and now probably alone, Hamaura cautiously opened his eyes to see on the ground beside him a clear plastic bag in which he could just make out his wallet, and his comb broken clean in two. No wonder we have failed, with such bad omens to overcome, he thought, closing his eyes again.

*　　　　*　　　　*

"It was neither of the two we caught here that shot her," the sergeant said, checking the clip from Hamaura's carbine, which had been left near where he fell. "They are both full, there must have been a third one we missed somehow."

“That ties in with what their young hostages said,” confirmed Inspector Melrose.

Ian Vaughan stood restlessly looking around hoping that this, probably last member of the gang was being cornered somewhere in the building by the search teams.

“Has anyone checked the mail van they arrived in?” he asked.

“Yes,” confirmed the Inspector, “one of the first things we did. It’s interesting how they fooled their way past the gate guard. You want to have a look, simple but almost guaranteed to be effective if viewed by the untrained eye. Archer, you and Daniels take Mr Vaughan round and show him how they loaded out that mail van.”

“Right away sir,” replied Constable Archer, keen to be doing something.

It was as he rounded the corner of the building that Ian realised his restlessness was more to do with not knowing how Umeko Morohashi was. He and the medic had been concerned about her condition when the air ambulance had taken her away, but he had declined to fly with her.

“Here it is,” said Daniels. “We’ll open up the side shutter, that’ll give you the full view.”

Ian looked into the van, noting the cleverly stacked mailbags in walls: one against the wire screen behind the driver and the other almost to the top of the rear doors.

“These bags on the ground we think blocked the lower part of the side doorway,” said Archer, giving one an idle kick. “Had it been checked by say Marines, with Afghan or Iraq experience, or better still us, the driver would have been told to take the lot out. That poor sod of a new recruit just didn’t have the training or the backup. I reckon on that gate there should have been four armed men to do that job properly.”

They had just turned away to head back to where Melrose had established his command centre when Daniels, seeing a movement in the building to his right, turned to take a closer look.

“Oh it’s Jacko with his party of seekers. I wonder if he’s caught the golden snitch?”

“Ask him,” said Archer. “Though I doubt if he knows who J.K. Rowlings is, let alone what the game of Quidditch is about.”

Neither man got to ask Jacko anything, for, as he pushed open the door, there was a blinding flash and the force of an explosion hurled all three men across the roadway, to be stopped painfully by the bank on the other side.

Ian's first recollection, immediately following the blast, was that of being surrounded by people all mumbling at him. The medic who had worked on Morohashi was delicately trying to peel Ian's shirt from his chest. "It's mainly glass fragments sir; worse than Daniels and Archer as this guy did not have any body armour or face protection," the medic said to a figure Ian could vaguely see bending over him.

"I don't think we should take him by road, some of these bits could well be in deep so the least movement the better," continued the medic. "This chap and Daniels by air, Archer will be okay by road."

* * *

Iwaki, like Comrade Seon, had been amazed at the ease with which they had gained access to a site, supposedly under armed guard. The lack of any resistance within the building was also something of a surprise, but more understandable bearing in mind the type of work carried out there. Unlike Hamaura, Iwaki's fears for the success of the operation started as soon as he realised that the Japanese computer team were not in the building. Knowing that they would have kept the all-important data, or at least a copy of such with them, he knew that the only sensible thing was for the group to make its escape.

Voicing his thoughts to Comrade Seon received a strong rebuke and a threat to report Iwaki's cowardice to the highest Korean command. This was shortly followed by the ridiculous decision of Murata's to summon Hamaura from guard and lookout duty at the main entrance, to conduct the search of a room, when Murata should have used either Kimura or Seon. A warning from Hamaura before the main entrance doors were breached would have given Iwaki sufficient time to kill and throw a hostage through a restaurant window to the ground. That, he knew, would cause a delay while a new line of attack was considered or probably negotiations started.

It was the first stun grenade that had Iwaki planning his personal exit. If others made it, so much the better, but he was not going to risk his freedom for anyone, not when all was lost. Iwaki knew that it was every man for himself and the smaller the number the better the chance. Strangely, he was disappointed that it was Hamaura who returned to the restaurant rather than Comrade Seon. Hamaura, the hotheaded superstitious fool who, if he made it out, would surely be an encumbrance. The open rear door was, Iwaki instantly recognised, the perfect gift to set those that would soon be chasing them in the wrong direction. The only thing he had not planned for was the arrival of the Japanese woman and her sighting of them, partially concealed behind the women hostages. Distraction was his only way out, and having shot the woman before she could even utter a challenge, he had ducked low and doubled back behind Kimura and Hamaura regaining entry to the building without being seen. Iwaki's years of training in the art of stealth had taught him how to move around a building, successfully avoiding discovery. Several times he could actually smell the breath of those seeking him but they had been unaware of his close proximity. Passing through Level B he had stopped to inspect a heavy canvas bag, discarded alongside a desk, that was strangely familiar to him; opening it he realised that it was the one the corporal was carrying with suction-back explosive packs in it. Iwaki remembered it being left behind when he had ordered the corporal and a private to clear the extension building area. Holding a gun, he could only manage one device, but that would be enough for some revenge and possibly sufficient distraction to cover his escape.

Making his way to the post room side entrance, he had planted the device above the right-hand door closure cylinder, stretching the trigger cord around the closure arm, then across to tie it off on the left-hand closure arm. Using both closure arms along the trigger cord route guaranteed, that the opening of either door would set the charge off. Iwaki had then stood back to admire his work, noting that the daylight streaming into the half-light corridor, would blind all but the most cautious from seeing either the charge unit or cord run. Satisfied with his work, he had tried to return for another charge, but had almost run straight into Jacko's search team. During the next half hour the cat and mouse game continued, until Iwaki had found himself finally forced to retreat into the roof space. There he saw natural light from the hole through which Ian Vaughan had made entry, now a beacon showing him a way out.

It was as he crept along the walkway towards the light that the explosive device was detonated; subsequent shouting made it obvious that there had been victims, and only then had he allowed himself a smile of satisfaction. Still moving slowly with great caution he made his way down through the new extension, observing through window openings the commotion and distraction the blast had caused. Picking his moment with great care he slipped from the building to successfully hide under a sheet of plastic covering a stack of timber, where he would wait until nightfall.

*　　　*　　　*

As Ian woke the following afternoon he was surprised to see Commander Campbell standing just the other side of the ward window talking to a doctor. After a few minutes both men came into the ward.

"I have just been told how lucky your are," said Campbell. "I thought I had made it very clear to both you and Miss Morohashi to stay away from any trouble. Since my arrival I have heard nothing other than the pair of you being in the thick of it."

"We had no choice," replied Ian weakly. "When we arrived we found that terrorist snipers were picking off those raw recruits that had been sent down here. There was one up in the oak tree in the field next door."

"Oh, is that how that body got into the middle of the cornfield? We did wonder. That done, why in God's name did you choose to go into the building when backup was on the way?"

"I went to try and reduce the number of hostages the terrorists were taking by evacuating as many of the building workers as I could, the ones I got…"

"And bloodily executing terrorists at the same time, so I have been graphically informed," interrupted Campbell. "We'd better leave the details for when you are fit again."

"Commander how is Miss Morohashi? It looked pretty serious when they put her in the air ambulance," asked Ian.

"She has undergone a long and difficult operation to try and repair some of the damage done to her shoulder blade. She had a collapsed lung as well. I understand that the operation went well, but they fear she has contracted an infection and in her weakened state that is being viewed as much more serious now," replied Campbell. "Her parents are being flown over to be with her."

"What about Daniels and Archer?"

"They are both okay. Daniels will be off duty for some time, but Archer's wounds were relatively light, considering your proximity to the explosion."

"Has anyone contacted my wife?" Ian asked, inwardly praying that no one had.

"Yes, I was on the phone to her only a few minutes ago. I understand that she will be visiting tomorrow," said Campbell. "As you are still technically married I had to inform her," he added, noting Ian's look of disappointment.

"My daughters are not coming with her?"

"I believe that your mother-in-law, who is staying there, will be looking after them and seeing them to school."

"Oh yes, school, of course," responded Ian, knowing full well that school was just an excuse to keep him from seeing them.

"Does Sarah know that Murata is dead and no longer a danger to us?"

"Yes, but she also knows that Fumiko Hamaura's brother is still alive, and though under constant armed guard, is considered by her to remain a threat."

Ian sighed, acknowledging that for Sarah it would still not be over. "Where are you holding him?"

"His wounds were attended to here yesterday when he was admitted. We are moving him a little later to a secure medical ward inside the hospital where he will remain under armed guard until he is transferred to Belmarsh."

“I suppose Japan will want him back,” said Ian.

“Probably, and I for one will be pleased to hand him over, once he has been tried and sentenced here of course, and on the strict understanding that he is never to be released.”

*   *   *

“You are up and about then?”

Ian turned from looking anxiously through the High Dependency Ward observation window to see Sarah standing nearby, also looking into the ward.

“Yes, it was mainly embedded broken glass, nothing life threatening,” he replied.

“Who is she?” asked Sarah, nodding in the direction of Umeko Morohashi.

“A Miss Morohashi, a member of the Tokyo Special Assault Team, sent over to help Campbell and Jackson.”

“What happened to her?”

“She was shot, but the more serious thing apparently is that the wound became infected.”

“You seem very concerned for her?”

“Yes I am, she is a very nice person and did not deserve this,” replied Ian. “How are you and the girls?”

“We are all loving it in Derbyshire. The girls have settled so well into the school and have so many little friends, it’s as though they have lived there all their lives.”

“I suppose we could all start again in Derbyshire as well as anywhere else,” he replied.

“Oh no Ian, it’s over; we can never have you back in our lives again. I was treated, by the WPC that met me at the station, to a detailed account of your recent killing spree. God alone knows how you managed to get involved in that. Then she reminded me that this terrible man Hamaura is alive and in custody. The girls and I are never going to be around you, or even near you, while there is any chance whatsoever of him getting out,” said Sarah, her voice rising in hostility.

"Excuse me," interrupted the monitoring nurse. "If you are going to have an argument can you please go outside, this is definitely not the place."

"Of course," said Ian. "I'm terribly sorry, we will leave immediately. Come along Sarah, there is a waiting room down the corridor."

The row that followed was long and futile, ending when they were both exhausted, and further apart than ever. As she left, Sarah turned to deliver the parting shot, "I will be staying here until this is settled as per my solicitor's letter."

Back in his room Ian was sat on the edge of the bed looking out at the lights of Plymouth as the Commander entered. "Do you mind if I sit down?" Campbell asked.

"Just throw that newspaper on the floor, or better still I'll stick it in the bin."

"How are you?"

"Physically fine, some of the cuts are a bit sore after the surgeon had finished digging around," replied Ian. "At least my hearing has recovered, I was getting a bit worried that the eardrums had been damaged."

"It apparently is a strange thing, that if you happen to have your mouth open and the sinus tubes and the tubes draining the inner ear are clear, then the pressure is balanced. I would think you were in that fortunate situation at that moment."

A slightly awkward silence followed.

"Portsmouth got sorted very quickly, I hear."

"Yes, we got the defences right there. Intelligence led us to think that it was really the only target, leaving it too late to reinforce Yealmstoke properly," said Campbell, with more than a hint of bitterness and self-blame in his voice. "Chief Inspector Jackson is tidying up things down there with Morohashi's partner, Ariyoshi. We have a Korean general's son as a prisoner together with two others; useful pawns in the game of politics."

"Were Jackson and Ariyoshi there when the attack took place?" Ian asked.

"No they were both at the Yard fortunately. It's bad enough having to send one Japanese officer back unfit for duty."

There was a short silence between them before Ian asked, "Is it just my health you came to see me about?"

"No, I have visited your wife."

"Oh, so you know the current situation concerning our marital future, or rather lack of it," said Ian, dejectedly.

"Regrettably divorce is something all too familiar within the police and security services. We therefore have contacts with some of the best lawyers in the field, may I suggest that we put one in touch with you?"

Ian sat silently for several seconds, contemplating Campbell's offer. "Yes please," he said at last. "I just could not handle it the way things are, it is probably better left to professionals to do the hard horse-trading. They won't have the emotional weaknesses of a relationship to get in the way."

Campbell then moved the conversation to the attack and the details of what led up to it. By the end of the debriefing Ian was almost on the point of collapse.

"Come back when you are ready, but not before," instructed Campbell as he left. "They expect to receive the fit and able at The Manor."

Though released from hospital the next day, it was two weeks before Ian left Devon. To the surprise of Miranda Cox he returned to the bedsit resting, but also making daily visits to the hospital to check on the condition of Umeko. To his great relief, after four worrying days, she started to recover, and on the tenth day he was allowed to talk to her.

Her first words were, "Why did you not come back to the gatehouse with the sergeant?" Her frowning expression surprised him, by its obvious concern.

"Why did you not stay at the gatehouse where you were safe?" he replied, trying to mimic her expression.

"I was coming to look for you, I thought they may have wounded or even killed you. We could hear much shooting."

"That was nowhere near me," Ian lied. "I kept well out of the way."

"I know that is not true. Don't tell me lies. Penny came down to see me earlier and told me all about your exploits."

"So much for the security services. Anyway the important thing is that you are on the mend, and I understand, that your parents have flown over and will travel back with you when you are fit enough."

He visited each day until she was declared fit to travel. As the days passed so their conversation became less centred on the attack and more about their own lives. When the day came for her to leave, both Campbell and Penny Heathcote were at the hospital, with Ian, to see her off.

Later that same day Ian drove his little white van through the imposing gates of The Manor. The afternoon September sun warmed him as he stood patiently waiting whilst the vehicle was searched. "You know where to report sir?" said the smartly suited security man.

"Yes, thank you," he replied, getting back into the van. As he pulled away he felt as nervous as he had done on his wedding day; that had been the start of a new life as well.